A Collaborative Novel

STORIES BY

Charlie Jane Anders

Margaret Atwood

Jennine Capó Crucet

Joseph Cassara

Angie Cruz

Pat Cummings

Sylvia Day

Emma Donoghue

Dave Eggers

Diana Gabaldon

Tess Gerritsen

John Grisham

Maria Hinojosa

Mira Jacob

Erica Jong

CJ Lyons

Celeste Ng

Tommy Orange

Mary Pope Osborne

Douglas Preston

Alice Randall

Ishmael Reed

Roxana Robinson

Nelly Rosario

James Shapiro

Hampton Sides

R. L. Stine

Nafissa Thompson-Spires

Monique Truong

Scott Turow

Luis Alberto Urrea

Rachel Vail

Weike Wang

Caroline Randall Williams

De'Shawn Charles Winslow

Meg Wolitzer

Fourteen Days

A Literary Project of the Authors
Guild of America

Edited by
Margaret Atwood and
Douglas Preston

HARPER LARGE PRINT
An Imprint of HarperCollinsPublishers

FOURTEEN DAYS. Copyright © 2024 by The Authors Guild Foundation. All rights reserved. Printed in the United States of America. No part of this book may be used or reproduced in any manner whatsoever without written permission except in the case of brief quotations embodied in critical articles and reviews. For information, address HarperCollins Publishers, 195 Broadway, New York, NY 10007.

HarperCollins books may be purchased for educational, business, or sales promotional use. For information, please e-mail the Special Markets Department at SPsales@harpercollins.com.

FIRST HARPER LARGE PRINT EDITION

ISBN: 978-0-06-326823-4

Library of Congress Cataloging-in-Publication Data is available upon request.

23 24 25 26 27 LBC 5 4 3 2 1

Contents

A Note from the Authors Guild Foundation

You are holding in your hands a novel that is both singular and extraordinary. The word "novel" comes from the Latin word *novellus*, through the Italian word *novella*, to describe a story that was not the reworking of a familiar tale, myth, or Biblical parable, but something new, fresh, strange, amusing, and surprising.

Fourteen Days meets that definition. It is a collaborative novel that is startling and original—you might even call it a literary event. It is written by thirty-six American and Canadian authors, from all genres, ranging in age from their thirties to mid-eighties, who come from a remarkable variety of cultural, political, social, and religious backgrounds. It is not a serial novel, nor is it a classic frame narrative in the mold of the *Decameron* or *The Canterbury Tales*. It is an epic novellus in the ancient and truest sense of the word.

The authors who wrote the stories in this book remain unbylined. Until you look up the list at the end, you will not know who wrote what. Most of these authors are eminent in their various genres, from romance to thriller, from literary to children's books, from poetry to nonfiction. *Fourteen Days* is, in this way, a celebration of the diversity of North American authors and a thumb in the eye of the literary balkanization of our culture.

The storytellers in *Fourteen Days* are a group of New Yorkers left behind during the Covid-19 pandemic, unable to escape to the countryside as affluent city dwellers mostly did at the beginning of the pandemic, and as the privileged have done for centuries in the face of disaster. Every evening, the neighbors gather on the rooftop of their shabby building on the Lower East Side to bang pots, cheer the Covid responders, argue with one another—and tell stories. As in any good novel, there are conflicts, redemption, and a whole lot of surprises along the way.

Above all, *Fourteen Days* is a celebration of the power of stories. Since long before the invention of writing, we human beings have faced our gravest challenges by telling stories. When we are confronted with war, violence, terror—or a pandemic—we tell stories to sort things out and push back against a frightening and incomprehensible world. Stories tell us where we've been and where we're going. They make sense of the senseless and bring order to disorder. They transmit our values across generations and affirm our ideals. They skewer the powerful, expose the fraudulent, and give voice to the disenfranchised. In many cultures, the storytelling act invokes magical powers to heal spiritual and physical sickness and to transform the profane into the sacred. Evolutionary biologists believe the storytelling thirst is hardwired into our genes: stories are what make us human.

We at the Authors Guild Foundation are pleased to present to you the novellus entitled *Fourteen Days*.

The novel's structure and themes reflect the mission of the Authors Guild Foundation, the charitable and educational arm of the Authors Guild, and *Fourteen Days* is a charitable project, with proceeds going to support the work of the Foundation. The Foundation was established on the belief that a rich, diverse body of free literary expression is essential to our democracy. We foster and empower writers of all backgrounds and stages of their careers by educating authors in the business of writing, providing resources, programs, and tools to American authors, and promoting an understanding of the value of writers and the writing profession. The Foundation is the sole organization of its kind dedicated to empowering all authors, reflecting the venerable spirit of the writers who established it—Toni Morrison, James A. Michener, Saul Bellow, Madeleine L'Engle, and Barbara Tuchman, among others—who all came from a diverse background of genres themselves.

The Authors Guild Foundation is extremely grateful to Margaret Atwood for taking the helm and convincing so many talented writers to join the project. We give enormous thanks to Doug Preston, the former president of the Authors Guild, for coming up with the concept and writing the frame narrative. We extend our enormous gratitude to Suzanne Collins, who made a generous donation to the Guild that funded honorariums for all contributors.

Our tremendous gratitude also goes to Daniel Conaway, Writers House literary agency, and its head, Simon Lipskar, who donated 100 percent of their commissions to the Authors Guild Foundation. Dan provided extraordinary and wise assistance from start to finish. We wish to thank Liz Van Hoose, who served as the project editor in originally compiling the stories, and to Millicent Bennett, our wonderful editor at HarperCollins, who recognized the compelling nature of *Fourteen Days* and has been an invaluable steward of the book, helping tirelessly to shape it and championing it through publication. In addition, thanks to Angela Ledgerwood at Sugar23 Books and the rest of the HarperCollins team for their enthusiastic support of the project, including Jonathan Burnham, Katie O'Callaghan, Maya Baran, Lydia Weaver, Diana Meunier, Elina Cohen, Robin Bilardello, and Liz Velez. We also wish to thank the Authors Guild team who work tirelessly to protect the rights of authors.

Most of all, we wish to thank the thirty-six authors who participated in this collaboration.

They are:

Charlie Jane Anders, Margaret Atwood, Jennine Capó Crucet, Joseph Cassara, Angie Cruz, Pat Cummings, Sylvia Day, Emma Donoghue, Dave Eggers, Diana Gabaldon, Tess Gerritsen, John Grisham, Maria Hinojosa, Mira Jacob, Erica Jong, CJ Lyons, Celeste Ng, Tommy Orange, Mary Pope Osborne, Douglas Preston, Alice Randall, Ishmael Reed, Roxana Robinson, Nelly Rosario, James Shapiro, Hampton Sides, R. L. Stine, Nafissa Thompson-Spires, Monique Truong, Scott Turow, Luis Alberto Urrea, Rachel Vail, Weike Wang, Caroline Randall Williams, De'Shawn Charles Winslow, and Meg Wolitzer.

All proceeds from this literary work will benefit the Authors Guild Foundation. Part of the advance for this book went toward the Guild's and Foundation's combined efforts to support writers during the worst of the pandemic, when publication dates were delayed, bookstores and libraries closed, and authors struggled to launch their new books. A survey conducted by the Guild showed that a staggering 71 percent of Guild members experienced an income decline of as much as 49 percent during the pandemic due to delayed publishing dates; canceled book tours, readings, and lectures; lost writing assignments; and other work. The Guild lobbied Congress to include regulations and legislation that included freelance writers in the Covid relief package, after they had been unaccountably left out of the original legislation.

The Foundation has put additional portions of the advance to work on fighting school and library book bans and calls for library closures. It has signed on to and filed amicus briefs in several litigations challenging the removal and banning of books and the recent laws encouraging or requiring such bans.

Projects supported by the foundation include the Stop Book Bans Toolkit and a Banned Books Club with over seven thousand members on the Fable platform that ensures young people and others around the country can read and discuss books subject to recent bans. With the Authors Guild, the Foundation is an active member of Unite Against Book Bans and works on campaigns with the National Coalition Against Censorship.

The Authors Guild Foundation supports the Authors Guild as it vigorously represents authors' concerns in Washington, educating and drafting and advising Congress on legislation that would help—or harm—authors. Together with the Authors Guild, the Foundation litigates and submits amicus briefs in key court cases to protect authors' rights and ensure the health of the publishing ecosystem and the writing profession, as well as to support freedom of expression.

The members of the Authors Guild include novelists in all genres and categories, nonfiction writers, journalists, historians, poets, and translators. The Guild welcomes traditionally published authors as well as self-published, independent authors. The benefits of a Guild membership include: legal assistance from contract reviews to advising on copyright and media law issues and intervening in legal disputes; a marketing assistance program to ready authors for publication of a new book; prestigious press credentials for freelance journalists; a vibrant online community forum to share information with fellow authors; insurance options and discount programs; website hosting; model agreements; local chapters and programs; opportunities to meet fellow authors; and webinars and seminars on the business of publishing, marketing, self-publishing, taxes, literary estates, and more.

Fourteen Days

[THE FOLLOWING NARRATIVE IS TRANSCRIBED FROM AN UNCLAIMED MANUSCRIPT FOUND IN STORAGE AT THE PROPERTY CLERK DIVISION, NEW YORK CITY POLICE DEPARTMENT, 11 FRONT STREET, BROOKLYN, NY 11201. ARCHIVED ON APRIL 14, 2020, RETRIEVED AND PUBLISHED ON FEBRUARY 6, 2024.]

Day One
March 31, 2020

Call me 1A. I'm the super of a building on Rivington Street on the Lower East Side of New York City. It's a six-floor walk-up with the farcical name of the Fernsby Arms, a decaying crapshack tenement that should have been torn down long ago. It's certainly not keeping up with the glorious yuppification of the neighborhood. As far as I know, nobody famous has ever lived here; there have been no serial killers, subversive graffiti artists, notorious drunken poets, radical feminists, or Broadway song pluggers commuting to Tin Pan Alley. There might have been a murder or two—the building looks it—but nothing that made the *New York Times*. I hardly know the tenants at all. I'm new here—got the job a few weeks ago, around the time the city was shut down by Covid. The apartment came with the job. Its number, 1A, sounded like it was on the first floor. But when I got here—and it was too late to back out—I found it was actually in the basement and as dark as the broom closet of Hades and a cell phone dead zone to match. The basement in this building is the first floor, the second floor is the real first floor, and so on up to six. A con.

The pay in the Fernsby Arms is rotten, but I was desperate, and it kept me from winding up on the street. My father came here from Romania as a teenager, married, and worked like a dog as the super of a building in Queens. And then I was born. When I was eight, my mom left. I tagged along as Dad fixed leaky faucets, changed lightbulbs, and dispensed wisdom. I was pretty adorable as a kid, and he brought me along to increase his tips. (I'm still adorable, thank you very much.) He was one of those supers people liked to confide in. While he was plunging a shit-blocked toilet or setting out roach motels, the tenants liked to pour out their troubles. He'd sympathize, offering benediction and reassurance. He always had an old Romanian saying to comfort them, or some tidbit of ancient wisdom from the Carpathian Mountains—that plus his Romanian accent made him sound wiser than he really was. They loved him. At least some of them did. I loved him, too, because none of this was for show; it's how he really was, a warm, wise, loving, faux-stern kind of dad—his one drawback being that he was too Old World to realize how much his ass was being mowed every day by Life in America. Suffice to say, I did not inherit his kindly, forgiving nature.

Dad wanted a different life for me, far away from having to fix other people's shit. He saved like mad so I could go to college; I got a basketball scholarship to SUNY and planned to be a sportscaster. We argued about that—Dad wanted me to be an engineer ever since I won the First Lego League robotics prize in fifth grade. College didn't work out. I got kicked off the college basketball team when I tested positive for weed. And then I dropped out, leaving my dad $30,000 in debt. It wasn't $30,000 in the beginning; it started out as a small loan to supplement my scholarship, but the vig grew like a tumor. After leaving school, I moved to Vermont for a bit and lived off a lover's generosity, but a bad thing happened, and I moved back in with my dad, waiting tables at Red Lobster in Queens Place Mall. When Dad started going downhill from Alzheimer's, I covered up for him as best I could in the building, fixing stuff in the mornings before going to work. But eventually, a miserable toad in the building reported us to the landlord, and he was forced to retire. (Using my master key, I flushed a bag of my Legos down her toilet as a thank-you.) I had to move him to a home. We had no money, so the state put him in a memory care center in New Rochelle. Evergreen Manor. What a name. Evergreen. The only thing green about it are the walls—vomit-puss-asylum green, you know the color. *Come for the lifestyle. Stay for a lifetime.* The day I moved him in, he threw a plate of fettuccini Alfredo at me. Up until the lockdown, I'd been visiting him when I could, which hasn't been much because of my asthma and the ongoing shit-saster known as My Life.

All these bills started pouring in related to Dad's care and treatment, even though I thought Medicare was supposed to pay. But no, they don't. Just you wait until you're old and sick. You should have seen the two-inch stack I burned in a wastebasket, setting off the fire alarms. That was in January. The building hired a new super—they didn't want me because I'm a woman, even though I know that building better than anyone—and I was given thirty days to move out. I got fired from Red Lobster because I missed too many days taking care of my dad. The stress of no job and looming homelessness brought on another asthma attack, and they raced me to the ER at Presbyterian and stuck me full of tubes. When I got out of the hospital, all my shit had been taken from the apartment—everything, Dad's stuff, too. I still had my phone, and there was an offer in my email for this Fernsby job, with an allegedly furnished apartment, so I jumped on it.

Everything happened so quickly. One day the coronavirus was something going on in Wu-the-hell-knows-where-han, and the next thing you know, we're in a global pandemic right here in the US of A. I had been planning to visit Dad as soon as I'd moved into a new place, but in the meantime I'd been FaceTiming him at Pukegreen Manor almost every day with the help of a nurse's aide. Then all of a sudden, they called out the National Guard to surround New Rochelle, and Dad was at ground zero, blocked off from the rest of the world. Worse, I suddenly couldn't get anyone on the phone up there, not the reception desk or the nurse's cell or Dad's own phone. I called and called. First it just rang, endlessly, or someone took the phone off the hook and it was busy forever, or I got a computer voice asking me to leave a message. In March, the city got shut down because of Covid, and I found myself in the aforesaid basement apartment full of weird junk in a ramshackle building with a bunch of random tenants I didn't know.

I was a little nervous because most people don't expect the super to be a woman, but I'm six feet tall, strong as heck, and capable of anything. My dad always said I was *strălucitor,* which means radiant in Romanian, which would be such a dad thing to say, except it happens to be true. I get a *lot* of attention from men—unwanted, obviously, since I don't swing that way—but they don't worry me. Let's just say I've handled my share of fuckwad men in the past, and they're not going to forget it any time soon, so trust me, I can handle whatever this super job throws at me. I mean, Dracula was my great-grandfather thirteen times removed, or so Dad claims. Not Dracula the dumbass Hollywood vampire, but Vlad Dracula III, king of Walachia, also known as Vlad the Impaler—of Saxons and Ottomans. I can figure out and fix anything. I can divide in my head a five-digit number by a two-digit number, and I once memorized the first forty digits of pi and can still recite them. (What can I say: I like numbers.) I don't expect to be in the Fernsby Arms forever, but for the moment, I can tough it out. It's not like Dad's in a position to be disappointed in me anymore.

When I started this job, the retiring super was already gone. Guess not every building wipes out all the super's stuff when they leave, 'cause the apartment was packed with his junk and, man, the guy was a hoarder. I could hardly move around, so the first thing I did, I went through it all and made two piles—one for eBay and the other for trash. Most of it was crap, but some if it was worth good money, and there were a few items I had hopes might be valuable. Did I mention I need money?

To give you an idea of what I found, here's a random list: six Elvis 45s tied in a dirty ribbon, glass prayer hands, a jar of old subway tokens, a velvet painting of Vesuvius, a plague mask with a big curved beak, an accordion file stuffed with papers, a blue butterfly pinned in a box, a lorgnette with fake diamonds, a wad of old Greek paper money. Most wonderful of all was a pewter urn full of ashes and engraved Wilbur P. Worthington III, RIP. Wilbur was a dog, I assume, though he could have been a pet python or wombat, for all I know. No matter how hard I looked, I couldn't find anything personal about the old super, even his name. So I've come to think of him as Wilbur, too. I picture him as an old man with a harrumphing, what-do-we-have-here manner, unshaven, evaluating a broken windowshade with his wet lips sticking out pensively, making little grunts. *Wilbur P. Worthington III, Superintendent, The Fernsby Arms.*

Eventually, in the closet I found a hoard of something far more to my liking: a rainbow array of half-empty liquor bottles, spirits, and mixers crowding every shelf from top to bottom.

The accordion file intrigued me. Inside were a bunch

of miscellaneous papers. They were not the super's scribblings, for sure—these were documents he'd collected from somewhere. Some were old, typed with a manual typewriter, some printed by computer, and a few handwritten. Most of them seemed to be first-person narratives, incomprehensible, rambling stories with no beginning or end, no plot, and no bylines—random splinters and scraps of lives. Many were missing pages, the narratives beginning and ending in the middle of sentences. There were also some long letters in there, too, and unintelligible legal documents. All this stuff was mine, I supposed, and I was sick when I thought of how this alien trash was all I had in the world, replacing everything I used to own that my dad's building had thrown out.

But among the stuff in the apartment was a fat binder, sitting all by itself on a wooden desk with peeling veneer, a chewed Bic pen resting on top of it. When I say "chewed," I mean half-eaten, my mysterious predecessor having gnawed off at least an inch from the top. The desktop was about the only neatly organized place in the apartment. The handmade book immediately intrigued me. Its title was on the cover, drawn in Gothic script: *The Fernsby Bible*. On the first page, the old super had clipped a note to the new super—that is, me—explaining that he was an amateur psychologist and trenchant observer of human nature, and that these were his research notes, collected on the residents. They were extensive. I paged through it, amazed at the thoroughness and density of the work. And then at the end of the binder, he had added a mass of blank pages, with the heading "Notes and Observations." And then he'd added a small note at the bottom: "(For the Next Superintendent to Fill In.)"

I looked at those blank pages and thought to myself that the old super was crazy to think his successor—or anyone, for that matter—would want to fill them up. Little did I know the magical allure that a half-eaten pen and blank paper would have on me.

I turned back to the super's writings. He was prolific, filling pages and pages of accounts of the tenants in the building, penned in a fanatically neat hand—with sharp comments on their histories, quirks and foibles, what to watch out for, and all-important descriptions of their tipping habits. It was packed with stories and anecdotes, asides and riddles, factoids, flatulences, and quips. He had given everyone a nickname. They were funny and cryptic at the same time. "She is the Lady with the Rings," he wrote of the tenant in 2D. "She will have rings and things and fine array." Or the tenant in 6C: "She is La Cocinera, sous-chef to fallen angels." 5C: "He is Eurovision, a man who refuses to be what he isn't." Or 3A: "He is Wurly, whose tears become notes." A lot of his nicknames and notes were like these—riddles. Wilbur must've been a champion procrastinaut, writing in this book instead of fixing leaky faucets and broken windows in this shithole of a building.

As I read through those bound pages I was transfixed. Aside from the strangeness of it all, they were pure gold to this newbie super. I set out to memorize every tenant, nickname, and apartment number. It's my essential reading. Ridiculous as it is, I'd be lost without *The Fernsby Bible*. The building's a shambles, and he apologized about that, explaining that the absentee landlord didn't respond to requests, won't pay for anything, won't even answer the damn phone— the bastard is totally AWOL. "You'll be frustrated and miserable," he wrote, "until you realize: You're on your own."

On the back cover of the bible, he scotch-taped a key with a note: "Check it out."

I thought it was a master key to the apartments, but I tested it and found out it wasn't. It was a strangely shaped key that didn't even fit into the many locks I tried it on. I became intrigued and, as soon as I could, I started going through the building methodically, testing it in every lock, to no avail. I was about to give up when, at the end of the sixth-floor hall, I found a narrow staircase to the roof. At the top was a padlocked door—and lo and behold, the key slipped right into that padlock! I opened the door, stepped out, and looked around.

I was stunned. The rooftop was damn near paradise, never mind the spiders and pigeon shit, and loose flapping tar paper. It was big, and the panorama was stupendous. The tenements on either side of the Fernsby Arms had recently been torn down by developers, and the building stood alone in a field of rubble—with drop-dead views up and down the Bowery and all the way to the Brooklyn Bridge, the Williamsburg Bridge, and the downtown and midtown skyscrapers. It was evening, and the whole city was tinged with pinkish light, a lone jet contrail crossing overhead in a streak of brilliant orange. I yanked my phone out of my pocket—five bars. As I looked around, I thought, *What the hell?* I could finally call Dad from up here, hopefully reach him at last, if it was just a reception problem keeping me from getting through at Upchuck Manor. It was certainly illegal to be up on the roof, but the landlord sure wasn't going to be coming into the Covid-ridden city to check on his properties. With the lockdown now stretching almost two weeks, this rooftop was the only place a body could get fresh air and sun that felt halfway safe anymore. One day the developers would put up hipster glass towers, burying the Fernsby Arms in permanent shadow. Till then, though, why shouldn't it be mine? Obviously, good old Wilbur P. Worthington III had felt the same way, and he wasn't even here for lockdown.

As I scoped the place out, I immediately noted a big lumpy thing sitting out in the open, covered with a plastic tarp. I yanked it off, revealing an old mouse-chewed fainting couch in soiled red velvet—the old super's hangout, for sure. As I eased down on it to test its comfort, I thought, *God bless Wilbur P. Worthington the Third!*

I began to come to the roof every evening, at sunset, with a thermos of margaritas or some other exotic cocktail I'd scrounged up from my rainbow room of liquor, and I stretched out on my couch and watched the sun set over Lower Manhattan while I dialed Dad's number over and over again. I still couldn't reach him, but at least I got a good buzz on while trying.

My solitary paradise, such as it was, didn't last long. A couple of days ago, in this last week in March, as Covid was setting the city on fire, one of the tenants cut the lock off the door and put a plastic patio chair up there, with a tea table and a potted geranium. I was seriously cheezed. Good old Wilbur had kept a collection of locks along with his other junk, so I picked up a monstrous, case-hardened, chrome-and-steel padlock, heavy enough to split the skull of a moose, and clapped it on the door. It was guaranteed not to be cut or three times your money back. But I guess they wanted their freedom as much as I did, because someone took a crowbar to the lock and hasp and wrenched them off, cracking the door in the process. There was no locking it after that. Try buying a new door during Covid.

I'm pretty sure I know who did it. When I stepped out onto the roof after finding the busted door, there was the culprit, curled up in a "cave chair"—one of those seat things shaped like an egg covered in faux-fur that you crawl into—vaping and reading a book. It must have been hell schlepping that chair all the way up to the roof. I recognized her as the young tenant in 5B, the one Wilbur called Hello Kitty in his bible because she wore sweaters and hoodies with that cartoon character on it. She gave me a cool look, as if challenging me to accuse her of busting the door. I didn't say anything. What was I gonna say? Besides, I had to respect her a little for that. She reminded me of myself. And it's not like we had to talk to each other—she seemed as keen to ignore me as I was in ignoring her. So I kept my distance.

After that, though, other tenants began discovering

the rooftop, a few at a time. They dragged their ugliest chairs up the narrow stairs and parked themselves at sunset, everyone staying "socially distanced," the new phrase du jour. I did try to stop them. I posted a sign saying that it was illegal (technically true!), that nobody was supposed to be up there, that someone could trip and fall off the low parapets. But at this point, we'd been under lockdown for what already felt like a lifetime, and people would not be barred from fresh air and a view. I can't blame them. The building is dark, cold, and drafty; the hallways have weird smells; and there are cracked and broken windows everywhere. Besides, the rooftop feels big enough still—everyone is careful not to touch, talk loudly, or even blow their noses, and we're all keeping six feet apart. Too bad you can't find any hand sanitizer in this damn city, or I'd park a jeroboam of it at the door. As it is, I bleach the doorknobs once a day. And I'm not worried for myself—I'm only thirty, young enough that they say the virus won't come for me, except for my asthma.

Still, I missed my private domain.

Meanwhile, Covid was hitting the city hard. On March 9, the mayor announced that there were sixteen cases in the city; by March 13, as I mentioned, the National Guard was surrounding New Rochelle; and on March 20, New York was shut down, just in time for everyone to binge-watch *Tiger King*. A week later, infections surpassed twenty-seven thousand, with hundreds dying every day and cases soaring. I pored over the statistics and then, fatefully, I guess, began recording them in the blank pages in the back of Wilbur's book, his so-called *Fernsby Bible*.

Naturally, anyone who could had already left New York. The wealthy and professional classes fled the city like rats from a sinking ship, skittering and squeaking out to the Hamptons, Connecticut, the Berkshires, Cape Cod, Maine—anywhere but New Covid City. We were the left-behinds. As the super, it's my job—or so I assume—to make sure Covid doesn't get in here and kill the tenants at the Fernsby Arms. (Except the rent-controlled ones—ha ha, no need to bleach their doorknobs, I'm sure the landlord would have told me.) I circulated a notice laying out the rules: no outside people allowed in the building, everybody six feet apart in common areas, no congregating in stairways. And so on and so forth. Just like Dad would have done. No guidance yet from the powers that be about masks, since there aren't enough for the healthcare workers, anyway. We are pretty much stuck in the building for the duration—locked down.

So every evening, the tenants who had discovered the roof came up and hung out. There were six of us

at first. I looked them all up in *The Fernsby Bible*.
There was Vinegar from 2B, Eurovision from 5C, the
Lady with the Rings from 2D, the Therapist from 6D,
Florida from 3C, and Hello Kitty from 5B. A couple
of days ago, New Yorkers started doing this thing of
cheering the doctors and other frontline workers at
seven o'clock, around sunset. It felt good to do something, and to break up the routine. So people got in
the habit of gathering on the roof right before seven,
and when the time rolled around, we all clapped and
cheered from our rooftop along with the rest of the
city, and we banged on pots and whistled. That was
the start of the evening. I brought up a cracked lantern
I found in Wilbur's junk, which held a candle. Others
carried up lanterns and candle holders with hurricane
shields—enough to create a small lighted area. Eurovision had an antique brass kerosene lantern with a deco-
rated glass shade.

In the beginning, no one talked, and that was just
fine with me. Having seen the way my dad got treated
by the folks he'd lived with and helped for years, I
didn't *want* to get to know them. I wouldn't even be
here with them except it had been *my* space first. A
super who thinks she can make friends in her building
is asking for trouble. Even in a merde shed like this,
everyone considers themselves above the super. So my

motto is, Keep your distance. And they clearly didn't want to know me, either. Good.

Since I was new, everyone up there was a stranger. They spent their time flicking at their phones, pounding down beers or glasses of wine, reading books, smoking weed, or messing with a laptop. Hello Kitty sat herself downwind in that chair and vaped almost nonstop. I once caught a whiff of her vape smoke, and it was some sickly sweet watermelon smell. She sucked on that thing literally nonstop, like breathing. A wonder she wasn't dead. With the stories coming out of Italy of folks on ventilators, even if it's mostly old people, I wanted to smack that shit out of her hand. But we're all entitled to our vices, I guess, and besides, who's going to listen to the super? Eurovision brought up one of those miniature Bose Bluetooth speakers, where it sat next to his chair playing soft Europop. Nobody in our building ever seemed to go out, as far as I could tell, even for groceries or toilet paper. We were in full lockdown mode.

Meanwhile, because we were so close to Presbyterian Downtown Hospital, the ambulances howled up and down the Bowery, their sirens getting louder as they approached and then sinking into a dying wail as they went by. All these unmarked refrigerated trucks started showing up. We soon learned they were carrying the dead bodies of Covid victims, and they rumbled through the streets like the plague carts of old, day and night, stopping all too frequently to pick up shrouded cargo.

Tuesday, March 31—today—was a sort of milestone for me, because it was the day I started writing things down in this book. I was originally planning to just record numbers and statistics, but it got away from me and grew into a bigger project. Today's numbers were a kind of milestone: the *New York Times* reported that the city had surpassed a thousand Covid deaths. There were 43,139 cases in the city, and 75,795 in the state. In the five boroughs, Queens and Brooklyn were being trashed the most by Covid, with 13,869 and 11,160 cases, respectively; the Bronx had 7,814, Manhattan 6,539, and Staten Island 2,354. Recording the numbers seemed to domesticate them, make them less scary.

It rained in the afternoon. I got up on the rooftop as usual, about fifteen minutes before sunset. The evening light cast long shadows down the rain-slicked Bowery. In between the sirens, the city was empty and silent. It was strange and oddly peaceful. There were no cars, no horns, no pedestrians surging home along the sidewalks, no drone of planes overhead. The air was washed and clean, full of dark beauty and magical portent. Without the fumes from cars, it smelled fresh, reminding me of my short happy life in Vermont, before . . . well, anyway. The usual tenants gathered on the rooftop as the streets slipped into dusk. When seven o'clock came around, and we heard the first whoops and bangs from the surrounding buildings, we heaved ourselves out of our chairs and did the usual whistling, clapping, cheering thing—all except the tenant in 2B. She just sat there trying to get her phone to work. Wilbur had warned me about her: she was the regal type who called to get a lightbulb changed, but at least she tipped like royalty. "She is pure native New York vinegar," he wrote, and added one of his riddles: "The best wine doth make the sharpest vinegar." Whatever that means. I figured she was in her fifties—dressed in all black, with a black T-shirt and faded black skinny jeans. The dribbles and splatters of paint on her well-worn Doc Martens were the only color on her. She was, I figured, an artist.

The woman in 3C, given the name of Florida in the book, called out Vinegar. "Aren't you going to join us?" I immediately sensed from her tone that there was history between them. Florida—the old super had not explained the origin of the name, maybe that was just how she was known—was a large, big-breasted woman who managed to convey a restless energy, age about fifty, with perfect salon hair and a sequined shirt covered with a shimmering golden shawl. The bible described her as a gossip, with the quip: "Gossip is chatter about the human race by lovers of the same."

Vinegar returned Florida's look with a frosty one of her own. "No."

"What you mean, no?"

"I'm tired of shouting ineffectually at the universe, thank you."

"We're cheering the frontline workers—the people out there risking their lives."

"Well, aren't you the high and holy one," said Vinegar. "How's yelling going to help them?"

Florida stared at Vinegar. "There's no logic to it. Esto es una mierda, and we're trying to show support."

"So you think banging on a pot is going to make a difference?"

Florida pulled the golden shawl closer around her shoulders, compressed her lips in judgment, and eased herself back in the chair.

"When this is all over," said the Lady with the Rings after a moment, "it'll be like 9/11. Nobody will talk about it. It will be like someone who committed suicide—you never talk about them."

"People don't talk about 9/11," said the Therapist, "because New York got a dose of PTSD from it. I still have 9/11 patients working through PTSD. Twenty years later."

"What do you mean, people don't talk about 9/11?"

Hello Kitty said. "They won't *stop* talking about it. You'd think half of New York City was down there running for their lives, choking on the smoke and dust. It'll be the same with this. *Let me tell you all about how I survived the Great Pandemic of Two Thousand and Twenty.* People won't shut up about it."

"My, my," said Vinegar. "Were you even alive when 9/11 happened?"

Hello Kitty sucked on her vape and ignored her.

"Think about all the PTSD this pandemic's going to trigger," said Eurovision. "Oh God, we're going to be in analysis forever." He gave a little laugh and turned to the Therapist. "What a windfall for you!"

She responded with a stony look.

"Everyone has PTSD these days," Eurovision went on. "I've got PTSD from the cancellation of Eurovision 2020. It's the first one I've missed since 2005." He clutched his chest and made a face.

"What's Eurovision?" Florida asked.

"The Eurovision Song Contest, darling. Singers from all over the world are chosen to compete with an original song, one singer or group per country. A winner is voted on. Six hundred million watch it on TV. It's the World Cup of music. It was supposed to be in Rotterdam this year, but last week they canceled it.

I had my plane tickets, hotel, everything. So now"—he fanned himself in an exaggerated manner—"help me, Doc, I have PTSD."

"PTSD is not a joking matter," said the Therapist. "And neither was 9/11."

"Nine/eleven is still with us," a woman in her thirties added. I recognized her from the book as Merenguero's Daughter, 3B. "It's fresh. It touched all of us, including my family. Even back in Santo Domingo."

"You lost someone in 9/11?" the Lady with the Rings asked, a challenge in her tone.

"In a weird way, yes."

"How so?"

She took a deep breath. "Mi papá was this big merenguero, which, if you don't know, means he played merengue for a living. He used to spend a lot of his time at *El Show del Mediodía* or *The Midday Show*. If there's one show in the Dominican Republic that everyone watches, it's that show. In fact, it's still on TV today."

As she started talking, I knew she was about to launch into a story, and I had an idea. Since my early twenties, I've been in the habit of recording the stuff people are saying around me, especially the shit from guys who come on to me in a bar. I'd just casually leave my phone on the bar or table or in my pocket; or at other times on the subway, I'd pretend to be messing with my phone all the while recording what some jackass was saying. You wouldn't believe what I've collected over the years, many glorious hours of idiocy and obnoxiousness recorded for posterity. Makes me wish I could monetize it on YouTube or something. And it's not just the bad, actually. I've captured other things, too—tales of woe, funny stories, kindnesses, confessions, dreams, nightmares, reminiscences, even crimes. The things strangers will tell you late at night on the E train . . . *I once was so desperate, I smoked dog shit to get high . . . I spied on my grandparents having sex, and you wouldn't believe what they were doing . . . I won a hundred-dollar bet by skinning, cooking, and eating my brother's gerbil.*

My dad collected people by charm. I collected them by stealth.

Anyway, so I started recording. My couch was situated too far away from Merenguero's Daughter, though, so I got up and, with a show of eagerness to listen, I dragged the damn red sofa through the six-foot spaces between everyone's chairs, giving them all a big dumb grin and muttering something about not wanting to miss a single word. I made myself comfortable and slipped my phone out of my pocket, pretended to check something on it, oriented it, and hit Record. Then I casually placed it on the couch, pointing at Merenguero's Daughter, and settled back with my feet up, margarita in hand.

What will I do with the recording? I didn't know right in that moment when I hit Record, but later, back in my apartment, I saw Wilbur's fat book sitting on the desk with all those blank pages he'd left for me. *Okay, I thought, let's fill them up. It'll give me something to do while stuck in this bullshit pandemic for the next few weeks.*

But hush: Merenguero's Daughter was talking.

"Back in the day, it would feature the hottest, up-and-coming merengue bands. And by the way, some of the songs from back then had some pretty insane titles and lyrics. That's my trigger warning 'cause this is some racist shit here."

She paused and looked around the rooftop a little nervously, as if unsure of what she was about to say, but also to gauge who was listening.

"There was a song that actually asked this question: 'Qué será lo que quiere el negro?' What is it that the Black man wants? That song was a huge popular sensation in the 1980s, and it was often played on *El Show del Mediodía*, which I would watch as a little kid. I wasn't allowed to go to the studio because my dad didn't want me there, and he was working, so he couldn't watch me. Remember, he was a single father.

He had to have control over me, and he didn't want me going to anything like that.

"Dad was friendly with some of the dancers on the show and met a woman there. I don't know what happened between them. They just said they were 'muy amigos y muy queridos.' I don't know, I didn't ask. But they remained friends over the years. She was always kind to me. Not like a long-lost mother figure, nothing like that, but she did teach me what to do when my blood came the summer I was eleven. I can't even imagine what my father would have done. She disappeared from our lives when I was still a kid, but I always had good memories of her.

"I happened to run into her not too long ago, a few weeks before this shutdown. It was the craziest thing. I was at my favorite salon, getting my hair pulled, you know, how they do. The joke that everyone tells us, that even in heaven, Dominican hair stylists are still doing the curl around the brush pull with one hand, while they're using the other to put who knows how many degrees of direct heat onto your hair to make it as straight as possible.

"Yeah. I used to do that to my hair every week, but then I realized that shit was whack for my hair and my head so I stopped.

"Anyway, I see her at the salon and ask how she's

been. At first, she doesn't look happy to see me, to see anyone she knows. But then she begins this crazy story, which sounds incredible, but it's true. The woman's story began on September 11. Everybody was like, 'Oh man, do we have to go back to September 11?' It's a lot, right? But maybe there is something in it that can teach us about the moment we find ourselves in, sitting up here on the rooftop. I call this story 'The Double Tragedy.'

"Let me just say that when a story catches everybody's attention in the salon, all the blow dryers stop. People can still get their hair put in curlers. They can still get color painted in. They can still get their hair cut. But if somebody has the floor and is telling a story that captures everybody's attention, ain't no blow drying going on. You can be sure of that.

"By the way, I have to mention, Eva was seventy years old and looked like she was fifty. She had gotten her natural gray hair blown out, but there was enough black showing through that you could tell that at one point her hair used to be phenomenally black. Now she was a distinguished kind of gray. She was also, let's just say, a little enhanced in a few areas. And she carried it well. She made those tetas and that pa'trás look good on a seventy-year-old. Maybe that's the way JLo is gonna look. We can only imagine. The point is, she looked hot and she was seventy years old.

"When she was in her fifties, after she had stopped hanging out at *El Show del Mediodía* and we had lost touch, she explained how she fell in love with a younger man. She did that crazy thing—she left her husband, with whom she had never been able to have a child. And she fell in love with this Dominican dude who, strangely enough, played in merengue bands. He was the percussionist, so he played a little of everything—claves, bongos, maraca, triángulo, cascabel, and yes, a percussive instrument from Peru made of dried goat nails. But he played jazzy, woke merengue, like old-school Juan Luis Guerra (before he became born again), Victor Victor, Maridalia Hernandez, and Chichi Peralta.

"Eva said she was hit with that crazy, crazy impulse to finally start listening to her heart and not give a flying fuck. She didn't care anymore about the thing that keeps many people in Latin America and on la isla from doing the things they want to do, which is essentially, 'El qué dirán?' 'What will the neighbors say?' Eva was like, 'Fuck it. I don't care. I'm in love with this dude. He plays in a band. And I'm leaving my husband.'

"Probably because they fell so deeply and madly and wildly in love, she got pregnant. It sounds unbelievable. You know, but like Eva said to the entire salon without a shred of self-consciousness, the sex was amazing.

They were having sex all the time. With her husband, they just weren't fucking, that's all I can say. They just weren't, they had stopped. But this guy was, I guess, around thirty and in his prime. Oh my God. How she talked about the sex! Well, it was so good that she ended up getting pregnant. That's all I can say."

"The hotter the sex, the faster the pregnancy," interrupted Florida, 3C. Well, the bible had warned me she was a gossip.

"That's scientifically bogus," said Vinegar sharply, with a dismissive gesture. "An old wives' tale, disproven years ago."

"And where did you go to medical school?"

After a polite pause, Merenguero's Daughter ignored them and went on.

"Sometimes it's all about sex. Sometimes it's about sex and passion. And the combination of those two things led to the miracle here. She was fifty years old, pregnant with the child of her thirty-year-old lover, now husband. Of course, she was considered scandalous. But by that time, she had already broken with 'el qué dirán.' Like, completely.

"And so had he. Her new husband had come from a very humble background in Santo Domingo, a neighborhood known as Villa Mella. The fact that he had made it as a musician and could provide for himself doing that was huge. He was happy. And had fallen in love with this incredible woman. They were totally nontraditional, but they made it work. They decided early on to never ever bring the war and words from outside into their marriage.

"All of us in the salon were just glued to Eva's story. Yo! People ordered the salon helper to go get a round of café con leche because this story was just beginning and already it was so good.

"Then Eva gets back to September 11. On that day Eva happened to be down on Wall Street for an appointment, and she saw it. She saw the plane fly right above her head and crash into the first tower. She was going to an appointment in that tower. And she happened to be one of those unlucky thousand or so people, one of the unluckiest people—or maybe one of the luckiest, depending on how you see it—who happened to be right there when it happened. She stumbled and tripped in shock, badly twisting her ankle, but the adrenaline kicked in and she started running with her busted-up ankle. All she could think about was getting home to her husband and her two-year-old son.

"That's all she wanted to do. Get the hell out of there, jump on a subway train, and go back to Washington Heights to be with her family. Yes, here she was, the age of most grandmothers. But she was a middle-aged woman who was desperate to see her toddler son and hold him in her arms again. Smell him. Eva was able to get on the subway, but she made it by a hair. It would have been a matter of less than an hour before the entire subway system was shut down in New York City. She made it home, walked in the door, and there he was, her gorgeous husband with the clear hazel eyes and the tight curls that looked like waves in an angry ocean. His hair was dark brown, but the tips were lighter and played with the cinnamon color of his skin.

"His name was Aleximas (a name created from Alexis and Tomas, very Dominican but don't judge, yo), and he started crying when he saw her. The tears were rolling down his cheeks, like a baby's. Because this unconventional couple loved each other so much, it didn't matter that he was a grown man shedding tears. That was the kind of security that Aleximas felt with his wife, twenty years his senior. She made him feel safe. Life had been really rough for him, growing up in Villa Mella. Yeah, that was the truth. His home growing up in the DR had a dirt floor. I mean, I think that's enough said, right?

"By now everyone was sipping their cafecito. Eva continued and talked about how deeply shattered she was by what she had witnessed on September 11. So much so that she couldn't sleep.

"The doctor told her she had sprained her ankle and torn a muscle, so she had to stay at home with her leg up for several weeks. She was going stir-crazy. She was completely dependent on her husband for everything. He was going out to buy groceries. He was doing everything for her and for the family. He didn't mind shopping, or even buying her tampons. She said it was just part of their unconventional love. He was a strong, centered Dominican man who was lucky enough to find a woman who said, 'I don't give a fuck what anybody says about me and what I do.' Soy una de muchas mujeres as!

"Eva didn't know how to handle these new emotions. You have to remember, back in 2001, people had never really heard about PTSD. The Iraq War hadn't started. PTSD, what was this thing? She didn't realize it, but she had it. She said she couldn't get out of the depression. She'd be at home watching television, thinking about how she couldn't move her leg because she had twisted it running away in horror from the most terrible thing she had ever seen. Every time she saw images from that day on TV—it was the only story on the news anymore, and they replayed it over and over—it was like she was back there standing on the street again, and she'd start shaking and crying.

"Aleximas was actually getting worried because her nightmares were keeping the whole family up. The little baby was picking up on his mother's anxiety, and the baby wasn't sleeping either now. Just like the plane had crashed into that tower, it crashed into their home, upending their lives.

"They couldn't get out of the cycle of trauma. To-gether, finally, they made the difficult decision—which they knew, in the long run, was the best decision—to leave New York and go back to the Dominican Repub-lic, back to Santo Domingo. Even though they had essentially made it in America, enough to be able to live their dream life in New York City, in a three-bedroom railroad apartment with big windows, a living room, and a separate dining room."

"Impossible," muttered Florida. There were mur-murs of surprise from our little circle of listeners—I couldn't tell if it was shock at the apartment or at Florida's interruption. But she was just warming up. "How did they afford an apartment like that? These days that's more than three, four thousand a month! Even back then—no! And if it was rent-stabilized, they'd be crazy to leave *that* behind."

"Seriously," said Eurovision. "That's amazing. These days I can barely afford this dump."

"Let her tell the story," said Vinegar sharply.

"Yes." Merenguero's Daughter was nodding. "A separate dining room on 172nd Street overlooking Fort

Washington Avenue. Yeah. They were going to leave all that behind because the terror had come to their home and she couldn't stop having nightmares.

"The plan they decided on together was that her husband and son would travel back to Santo Domingo first while she stayed behind to tie up loose ends at her work. Also, she needed the space to grieve and heal on her own, to work through her emotions without scaring her baby. She would be on her way within a month or two, at the max. And that was it. They were going to relocate to Santo Domingo and start their lives over again. They knew enough people there, things would work out.

"She looked at the flight schedules, and the soonest they could book a flight for Aleximas and their son turned out to be November 11. She was like, 'Oh, there's no way that I am letting my family travel on any eleventh of any month ever again. The eleventh está quema'o. It's cursed.' No flight was to be booked on that date ever again. Never. So she bought the tickets for November 12, and she took her husband and their baby boy to the airport and said goodbye at JFK.

"She was a nervous wreck, but she knew that she would be able to work out her terror now that they were gone. Maybe she would scream into a pillow three or four times a day—something she couldn't do with her two-year-old around. And can you imagine if her husband saw her do that? He would really think she'd lost it, but she *had* lost it. She was traumatized. The only thing that was stopping her from going crazy was the love and responsibility she felt for her husband and son.

"So Eva said she dropped them off at JFK and drove back to Washington Heights. She put in a CD of her husband's music, because that's what people used to do back then, and it instantly put her in a better mood. The sadness at their airport goodbye gave way to relief that she would soon have a new life away from the tragedy. She smiled and laughed and danced in her driver's seat and even got a little bit excited and wet just thinking about her husband and how she already missed him. Imagine. A grown woman feeling hot like a teenager. Ay!

"She was so blissfully unaware, lost in the first moment of happiness she'd felt in months, that she didn't hear the news. When she got back to Washington Heights, she limped into her apartment and saw that the light was blinking on the answering machine (remember, this was 2001). She hit Play and heard the voice of her husband's sister say, 'Where is he? Where is he? How could this have happened? Why did you put them on that flight?' Eva ran to turn on the TV, and that's when she learned that Flight 587 had crashed in Far Rockaway, Queens, ninety seconds after takeoff.

"Flight 587 was so well known in the Dominican Republic that there was even a merengue named after it. And yes, her husband had performed it. They used to play the merengue 'El Vuelo Cinco Ochenta y Siete' on the plane, that's how popular it was. The flight always took off early in the morning so that by the time you arrived in Santo Domingo, you could have your first almost-freezing cold beer waiting for you, sitting in ice. When beer is served that way it's called 'dressed like a bride' because the bottle is covered in ice. It looks like it's wearing a white dress.

"Her husband should have been drinking his beer vestida de novia, but instead, he and their little boy were dead. They had died instantly on Flight 587, on November 12, 2001. They had simply wanted to avoid flying on November 11. Everybody in the salon was completely silent by now, except for one woman who was sobbing."

Merenguero's Daughter looked around the rooftop at all of us. We had been shocked into silence, too. Even Vinegar. I reached for my phone, thinking she was done with the story. I wished I could call my dad more than anything right then.

"Eva just said, 'Yeah, that was my life. I lived

through a double tragedy.'" Merenguero's Daughter was shaking her head as she talked. "I wiped my nose on my shirt and asked, 'How did you deal with it?'

"'I didn't,' Eva said. 'Well, you're the first people that I've told about it. It happened twenty years ago, and I don't talk about it. I buried whatever I could of my husband and my son. I locked up my apartment here in New York. And I moved to the Dominican Republic. No one knows who I am there or what I've lived through. I won't tell you anything more about me because I don't want you to ever find me.' When Eva said this, she looked in my direction, and I nodded back to let her know that I wasn't gonna reveal her.

"She looked at the women gathered around us in the beauty salon as if in defiance: 'I don't care what you think. A mí no me importa el qué dirán. I don't care what anybody thinks about my life or my choices or what I do to deal with my double tragedies. Y así fue, y así es la vida,' Eva added and then turned to her hair stylist. 'Termina mi peinado, por favor.' Finish my blowout.

"When the stylist was finished, this seventy-year-old woman left her stylist a twenty-five-dollar tip and walked out.

"I don't know. What's the lesson?"

On the roof, no one spoke. Merenguero's Daughter paused, as if waiting for an answer, then shrugged again.

"Denial. Basically, denial worked for her. She compartmentalized to a point where she just told herself, I'm not even going to think about it anymore. Later on I found out Eva does indeed have a whole new life in the Dominican Republic. She did not remarry, but she has multiple suitors who call on her and treat her like a queen. Which basically means she's getting some as often as she wants.

"So what do we do? You know, for some of us, we're living through multiple tragedies: people losing family members, their jobs, their homes, their careers, and in some cases, their entire family. A lot of people are in denial. But they're the ones who keep making us sick, and I'm sick of them. Here's what I think—a little bit of denial goes a long way, but a lot of denial goes too far. Y colorín colorado, este cuento se ha acabado."

Merenguero's Daughter turned to Eurovision. "Dude," she said, "put on some merengue now. I gotta dance this double tragedy away. Put on 'Ojalà Que Llueva Café.' I want it to rain coffee."

"Who, me?" Eurovision asked, taken by surprise.

"You're the one with the speakers."

"Of course, of course." Eurovision quickly straightened himself up and rose, fiddling with his phone.

"How, um, do you spell that song title? Spanish is not one of my languages."

She spelled it out. He tapped away and then stood up. "Ladies and gentlemen, may I present Juan Luis Guerra live, singing 'Ojalà Que Llueva Café!'"

I'd never heard it before. The music was soft and longing, not the pulsating beat I'd expected. When it was over, a hush had fallen.

"That didn't sound like merengue to me," said Vinegar.

"That's because it really isn't," said Florida. "That's bachata."

"Bachata *is* a kind of merengue," said Merenguero's Daughter, flaring up.

"Just saying."

"Can you translate for us?" asked Eurovision.

"Ay hombre," said Merenguero's Daughter, "it's a Dominican harvest song. A prayer. It's about hoping the harvest will be good and that the farmers won't suffer. But it's more than that. It's about a simple life and dreams and love of the land—really, it's about who we are." She closed her eyes and hummed the tune and then picked it up, translating into English, swaying slightly.

"I want it to rain coffee in the fields / Let there be a downpour of cassava and tea . . ."

When she was finished, Merenguero's Daughter opened her eyes.

After a moment, Hello Kitty said, "That's crazy, dying on the twelfth because they didn't want to fly on the eleventh. It's like they were cursed."

"Cursed?" said the Lady with the Rings. "They didn't do anything wrong. Tragedy like that is random and indiscriminate."

"Being cursed is all in the mind," said the Therapist. "Claiming you're cursed or unlucky or victimized is how some people deal with tragedy, like this pandemic. I see it in my therapy. People even curse themselves— out of shame or guilt."

"And your job is to uncurse them?" said Eurovision.

"You might put it that way."

"I need some of that uncursing," he said.

"My poh poh—my grandmother, on my mother's side—she was an expert in curses," said the Therapist. "She knew all about them. She had a unique system for handling them."

"Like how?"

"Well, my mom is ABC and so am I, but Ah Poh was born in this tiny little village in Guangdong. I've never been there, but she showed me a picture once—a little gray stone house in the middle of nowhere, just rice paddies all around. My gung gung used to catch fish in the river for dinner. They came over just before the war to San Francisco and settled in the Sunset District, and they never went back. I don't even know if that little house is still standing, or if it got destroyed in the Revolution, or what—a lot of stuff was.

"Anyway, just after I was born, my gung gung died and my poh poh moved in with our family, and she took care of me and my sisters while our parents were at work. She used to let us play with the jade bracelet on her wrist; she'd worn it since she was a little girl, and it was still tiny, but her wrist had grown and it wouldn't come off anymore. My mom had one just like it; it used to get all soapy when she washed the dishes and covered in potting soil when she worked in the garden. Ah Poh gave one to each of us girls when we were little, tried to get us to wear them, too, but I couldn't stand the feeling of it around my wrist. Like handcuffs. I think Mina and Courtney still have theirs; I don't know what happened to mine.

"Ah Poh was tiny, like five feet tall at most, and every year she got a little shorter. She wore these quilted floral vests, and she had that hunch old Chinese ladies get—you've seen them, if you've ever set foot in Chinatown. Quasimodo, my sisters and I used to call her, until Mom heard us one day and smacked the shit out of us. It's osteoporosis, that's what I learned later, due to childhood lack of calcium. Tiny fractures in the spine that break and reheal over and over, like a cup that's been mended with too much glue. At least, that's what they told us in premed.

"But don't get me wrong—Ah Poh looked like a sweet little old lady, but she was fierce. One time on Grant, this guy tried to grab her bag. She wouldn't let go. She yanked it back so hard he lost his balance. Then she gave him a royal cussing-out so loud he just lay there, like he'd been fire-hosed. When she finished, all the shopkeepers were frozen in their doorways, spectating, and the guy scrambled up and took off. I remember I was just standing there, holding the pink plastic bag with the fish and the bunch of bok choy we'd bought for dinner, and Ah Poh turned to me and said, 'Okay, come on, neui neui, let's go home.' Like nothing had even happened.

"Well, after my sisters and I went off to college, we were grown up, we were busy, we were dating and working, and we didn't call home as often. Ah Poh started doing the typical grandmother thing: nagging at us about being single, how we'd better hurry up and find somebody. 'Aren't you lonely,' she'd say over the phone, 'without a family, how do you have a purpose in life.' I suggested this was projection on her part—with all of us gone, she had a lot of time on her hands.

"'Nuh-uh,' she said, 'don't you try that psychology on me, neui neui. That doesn't apply to Chinese people. That's only for *gweilo*.'

"I had switched from premed to psychology by then, and she was the only one who wasn't giving me a hard time about it. My parents, of course, didn't consider psychology medicine—they wanted me to be a real MD doctor. In fact, I think they're still holding out hope. It's a stereotype, but it exists for a reason, you know? What it is, is that they went through so much to get here. They think about Ah Poh growing up in the middle of that rice field, and all those years of scrimping to pay tuition, and we're just going to throw all that away and follow our dreams and become poets or postmodern interpretive dancers or whatever? We're their investment on their down payment of suffering, and they are for damn sure going to get their returns.

"Anyway—Ah Poh kept giving me a hard time about not having anyone.

"'What happened to that Alex?' she said. 'I thought that was going so well.'

"Alex had recently left me for my friend—now my ex-friend—and on top of that he still owed me nine hundred dollars that I'd lent him, which I was pretty sure I wasn't going to get back. When I told Ah Poh that, she made a clicking noise with her teeth.

"'Okay,' she said, 'I tell you what, neui neui. I'm going to curse him.'

"Ah Poh had plenty of superstitions, we're a superstitious people—though maybe everyone is. Don't turn the fish over on the platter or your boat will overturn. Don't put your purse on the ground or you'll become poor. Don't give scissors and knives as presents or you'll cut the friendship in two. Don't say the number four. As kids, we couldn't turn around without stubbing our toes on another thing that would bring us bad luck. But cursing is not any ancient Chinese practice I'd ever heard of.

"'What do you mean, curse,' I said.

"Apparently, she'd learned it from her friend Marcie, who she met playing bingo at the neighborhood church on Tuesday mornings.

"'I thought you thought bingo was boring,' I said.

"'I do,' she said, 'but it turns out, so does Marcie. So I taught her mah-jongg, and now we play that every week instead. And we go to the casino on Thursdays. Senior discount day.'

"'Wait, what do you play at the casino?' I asked.

"'Slots,' she said—a little surprised, like it was so obvious. 'Sometimes some blackjack, too.'

"Marcie had a ritual: whenever someone wronged her, she'd write their full names on a slip of paper, roll it up, and freeze it into an ice cube. And then leave it there in the freezer. Forever.

"'It works,' my poh poh insisted. 'This contractor overcharged Marcie for repairing the roof, so she wrote his name and froze it. Two weeks later, he got sued by the city for letting his license lapse. You tell me that Alex's full name. I've got a piece of paper right here.'

"I didn't feel I had anything to lose, and anyway arguing with Ah Poh was usually a losing battle, so I recited Alex's full name—first middle last, right down to the III—and she wrote it on a piece of paper and told me she'd pop it into the ice cube tray as soon as we hung up.

"And wouldn't you know it, a month later I heard through the grapevine that my ex-friend cheated on Alex with his sister—and now they were a serious thing, and a week or so after that I saw pictures of her three-carat engagement ring on Facebook.

"After that, my sisters and I started calling Ah Poh whenever we had grievances we couldn't right through regular, non-curse means. When Mina got understudy in her show, Ah Poh froze the actress who got the lead, and just a few days later she broke her foot and Mina stepped in. When Courtney's boss at the firm made a pass at her, Ah Poh wrote down his name, and later that year he got caught falsifying evidence and was disbarred. And when the neighbor across the street from my parents hung up his 'Trump' sign, with 'Send Them Back' hand-scrawled across the top, she wrote his name down, too. My mom said last she heard, he got shingles and had to stay inside for months. We'd call Ah Poh with an update each time we heard another justified misfortune. 'Guess what,' we'd say, and inject the next little hit of schadenfreude.

"She took it seriously. She kept those ice-cube curses in there, in a gallon Ziploc bag at the back of the freezer behind the ice cream and turkey leftovers. One time, when I was still living in the Bay Area, she called me.

"'Power's out,' she said.

"'Ah Poh, are you okay?' I asked. 'You need help?'

"She made that clucking noise again. 'I'm fine,' she said, 'I'm not afraid of the dark. But listen, neui neui, your mom's not home, and I need you to do something.'

"What she wanted was for me to come by with a cooler full of ice.

"'Ah Poh, I just got home,' I said. I was living in Oakland then, and I didn't want to cross the bridge for the third, and then fourth, time that day.

"'Aiyah,' she said. 'All these things I do for you all these years, and you won't do this one little thing for me?'

"When I arrived forty-five minutes later, lugging the big red-and-white Coleman cooler I used on camping trips, she met me on the steps with the bag full of curses in hand.

"'Good girl,' she said. She swiveled the cooler open and nestled the bag down into the ice and shut it again, her jade bracelet clink-clinking against the lid. 'There,' she said. 'That should hold it until the power comes back on.'

"It did, and in the morning, when I called to check on her, the first thing she told me was that the cubes were back in the freezer. Not a single one had melted.

"She died last fall, at the ripe old age of ninety-six, shorter and fiercer than ever, still going to the casino with Marcie in her big old visor hat right up to the end. I'm glad, in a lot of ways, that she went before all this started. Believe me, she'd have a lot to say about Covid and all of it. Pity the poor soul who might have said any of that 'China virus' bullshit in her hearing.

"Anyway. I went home in February, right before everything shut down, to help my mom sort through Ah Poh's things. The last night I was there, when everyone was asleep, I went to the freezer. The curses were all still in there, little frosty cubes with the slips of paper cloudy white inside. I wanted to know the full scope of our anger. To see them all laid out in front of me, all the people who'd done us wrong over the years. Who had my poh poh written down for herself? Who were the ones who'd done her wrong?

"I spread the ice cubes out on the table and watched them melt, slowly. The kitchen was cold, and it took a long time. But finally, there they were: little rolls of paper, finally freed, soggy in the growing puddle. I started to unwrap them.

"And would you believe it? They were blank. Every one of them. Just blank slips of paper rolled up and frozen in ice. I still don't know what to make of it. 'Psycho-ology,' Ah Poh would have said."

The Therapist lapsed into silence, and if it weren't for another siren cutting the air, you could've heard a pin drop on the rooftop of the Fernsby Arms.

"Whoa," murmured Hello Kitty.

"Maybe it was a kind of therapy," said Vinegar. "She wasn't out to curse others, but to gratify herself."

"Or," said the Lady with the Rings, "it was because her curses were too terrible to be written down in words. She spoke them into the paper."

The Therapist didn't offer an explanation herself. The group fell silent. It had gotten late. Night had dropped. The midtown skyscrapers, with their lights strangely off, were like great dark vertical whales in a sea. Church bells began to toll in the distance, echoing through the empty streets. Eight o'clock. No one seemed to be sure what to do next, and eventually, subdued by the stories, people began gathering up their things to go down to their apartments. I casually picked up my phone and hit the stop button as I slipped it into my pocket. The stories had reminded me of my dad, locked down and all alone in the nursing home, cut off from the world and human contact, and I felt a wave of nausea.

Back in my room, I sat for a long time at the super's peeling desk, with his massive tome in front of me, thinking about everything. I wasn't the slightest bit tired. The stories I'd heard tonight were still ringing in my brain. I picked up the chewed Bic and opened the book, or rather bible, to the "Notes and Observations" blank pages. Then I took out my phone and began to replay the stories that had been told, along with all the chatter and talk in between, stopping and starting and laboriously writing everything down in longhand, adding my own commentary and connective material.

It took me a couple hours. When I was done, I leaned back in the creaky chair and stared up at the stained, popcorn-foam ceiling of my apartment. I had a feeling I was one of those people the Therapist talked about, who curse themselves. My life seemed to be a long string of self-cursing. But putting the evening down on paper was like a purging of sorts. You always feel so much better after a really good vomitus.

That's when I heard soft footsteps in the empty apartment above me: 2A. I knew it was empty because the super's bible told the story of what happened to the previous tenant. He had gone crazy in there, and when they finally broke the door down to take him to the hospital, they found thousands of dollars in twenties crammed and folded into every nook and cranny. When the cops asked the crazy guy what it was about, he said it was to keep out the roaches and evil spirits.

Tomorrow, I'd better check the apartment for squatters.

Day Two
April 1

When I got up on the roof this evening, it seemed word was getting around the building, and quite a few more tenants were up there—to cheer, bang pots, or enjoy the sunset. One tenant was quite literally taking the air, pushing one of those inflatable pool couches with the cup holes across the rooftop into position. I was still memorizing all these people's apartment numbers, names, and specifics. Normally I don't care much for people, but after last night, I had started to feel a twinge of curiosity about them all. I brought Wilbur's bible with me and flipped through it, trying to identify each person around me, while keeping it as unobtrusive as possible. But nobody was paying me any attention—most of the people up there had journals or laptops with them. When not paging through the bible, I kept it on the couch next to me, covered with a blanket. Today everyone brought up refreshments, too—a bottle of wine, six-pack, thermos, cookies, crackers, cheese. They seemed almost giddy with the rebellion of it, as if by screwing the landlord's rules, they could also screw the pandemic.

The statistics today were ugly. New York State now has 83,712 cases of Covid and 1,941 deaths. The *Times* announced that New York is now the epicenter of the Covid-19 crisis in the United States. Meanwhile, the rest of the country is going about its business like nothing is happening. People are saying it's a blue-state disease, even a New York disease—nothing for *them* to be concerned about. I don't know why they think this won't come for them, too. Cuomo's out there on TV every night, talking his head off, unlike old Cheeto in Chief up in the White House, who keeps insisting it's just going to go away, poof, like magic.

Eurovision arrived, all dappered up with a bow tie and plaid jacket, skinny pants, and monk-strap brogues. It was a chilly evening, but I was well fortified with a discreet thermos, this time filled with a cocktail called an Alabazam, which I had concocted from rummaging through Wilbur's collection—cognac, triple sec, bitters, and Rose's lime juice. God knows, I needed that drink. I had already spent hours that day up on the roof trying to get through to Vomitgreen Manor, and then hours more calling various agencies and health departments. I couldn't get anybody who had any kind of answers for me. I keep hearing rumors of massive outbreaks at the nursing homes, but Cuomo isn't releasing stats. If they even have any. I was desperate to anesthetize my panic, despite how much my dad would hate all this drinking. Not that he'll ever know.

When seven o'clock arrived, we banged and shouted and whistled. All except Vinegar, who just kept on reading a book of poetry. While the sound rose to a crescendo, I had a sudden vision of the Wickersham brothers—I can still hear the name in my dad's voice, reading to me when I was a kid—those Wickershams up in the sky, their hairy monkey faces squinting down at us as we tried to make enough noise to prove we existed. To avoid being boiled alive in beezle-nut oil.

After the noise died down, we went back to ignoring one another. Eurovision had his music on, softly. Hello Kitty tapped at her phone. Vinegar read. I drank.

"Excuse me," said the tenant in 4D, shutting the hardcover book she had been reading and turning to Eurovision. "Would it be possible for those of us who come up to the roof for peace and quiet to be accommodated? Don't you have earbuds?"

She worked, according to *The Fernsby Bible,* as a

librarian at the Whitney. Married to a doctor. I had already had an interaction with her. The bible advised that she was the building's biggest tipper—never less than twenty bucks a visit. I was so desperate for money that I did something terrible. She called me into her apartment to fix a plugged bathroom sink, and I scored a twenty. I then came back when she wasn't there and took a rubber washer out of the kitchen faucet. That earned me another twenty. I knew my dad would be appalled, but without those two twenties, I literally would not have been able to buy food or snag that last case of toilet paper on Instacart.

"I'm sorry," said Eurovision, "I was playing the music for everyone's enjoyment."

"Thank you, but to be frank, I'm not enjoying it."

"Okay," he said. "Fine." He dug his hand in his pocket for earbuds.

"What *I'm* not enjoying," announced Vinegar suddenly, "is that we're all hiding in our bubbles up here. We're all crouching on our little islands with our backs turned to one another. It's not like we're on the subway, and we can all get off and go back to our lives. We're trapped here together for God knows how much longer. Maybe we should be getting to know each other."

"I'd *really* prefer silence," said Whitney, starting to sound exasperated.

"If you want silence, there's plenty of it in your apartment," said Vinegar. "Or out there—" she gestured to the empty streets. "Lots of silence there."

At that, Whitney opened her book and pretended to read, her face flushed. But she didn't leave.

A new visitor to the roof spoke up, the tenant I figured was the one identified in the bible as Monsieur Ramboz in 6A. I wasn't positive, though, because I had no idea what the name meant, since he was not French and in no way like Rambo, being a shabby, lean, frail old man with white hair, who, according to the bible, was a card-carrying communist. "I agree, and I think we *should* be talking to each other," he said in a reedy voice. "The world's changed. It's not going to return to how it was for at least a few months. And here we are fiddling with our phones like Nero while Rome burned."

"I had no idea Nero had a smartphone," said Florida.

"Aren't you the funny one," said Vinegar.

"If I might say something?" said the Lady with the Rings, rattling her hand. "As a gallery owner I've been listening to people talk most of my life—you wouldn't believe the kind of hogwash you hear in an art gallery— and I'm *done*. I, too, would appreciate some peace and quiet on the rooftop."

"Art gallery?" said Vinegar.

"Yes." The Lady with the Rings squared her shoulders. "I've exhibited work by some of the most prominent Black conceptual artists in the country—including Alex Chimère."

She said the name as if we'd all be terribly impressed, but I'd never heard of Alex Chimère and, looking at the blank faces around me, no one else had, either.

"I'm sorry you have to lower yourself to mix with us common people on the roof," said Vinegar.

The Lady with the Rings adjusted the Hermés silk scarf swaddled around her neck, her fingers moving irritably, rings clicking. "You live up to your nickname, that's all I'll say."

Vinegar gathered herself up, and I wondered what was going to happen. She wasn't someone, it seemed to me, to let a comment like that slide. She cleared her throat, looking slowly around the roof, making eye contact with each of us in turn.

"I know what you all call me behind my back— Vinegar. Miss Thing in 4C started it, along with some rumors about my family that I will address shortly. But I want to say at the outset that it's not what people call you that matters but what you answer to. I've been called outside my name since I landed on this planet in a hospital room. My mother says as a newborn I looked like a muskrat, 'just shriveled and wrinkled and a bit mischievous, as if you'd been here before.' My aunt holds her hands up in feigned apology and says, 'You looked more like a bulldog, but you grew into your face. You're pretty now. You've been pretty since you were at least ten, once you got the braces.'

"I attended an arts school here, where, after we read and performed *Huck Finn*, some of the kids used to call me Nigger Jen. Jennifer is my given name, rhymes a bit with Jim, a bit with vinegar, so 4C thinks she's cute, like those kids at my school did. But listen, listen, the same process they use to make wine is the one they use to make vinegar. Beauty, class, sass, art—it's all subjective. If I come off as 'salty,' it's because I know how low people can go. And just like vinegar is the same as wine, you can think of salt as a stinging irritant, or you can think of it as seasoning, which many of you could use. Anyhow, the sassy, salty, sapphire Black woman is a tired, played-out stereotype, and 4C should know it. Everyone should know it, especially now, with the swell of the protests, with the activism to show Black lives not only matter but are rich and full and beautiful.

"My son, Robert, Robbie, named after my grandfather, who was a judge, the first Black one in Rockland County, has never stopped marching with the protesters, even after the governor banned assemblies. I worry for him every day—maybe that's why my face looks scrunched up; worry has a way of aging you, even if Black don't crack. I'm proud of him, despite my fears that he'll catch the virus or worse. Police violence has touched my family far more than this Covid everyone is so worried about. Yes, I empathize with all the people who are losing loved ones and employment, even with 3C, whose fool son is always knocking on her door, first bumming her last crumbs off of her and then her settlement money, and I despise this fool president for his inaction, his sociopathic white supremacist, malignant narcissism. But I worry about my boy and his life and how people see him just as much. It's as if I'm always waiting for the call or the knock on my door or the viral video that alerts me of his death by the hands of the state around his neck. I wonder if 3C—though she owes me fifty-seven dollars and seventeen cents, now three months overdue, even though I know she received her settlement money ages ago—relates as Latinx. Does she worry why her son's stopped knocking?

"My daughter, Carlotta, is pregnant, which is why she never joins us up here. We've been extra careful, which is her nature. A germaphobe since middle school, when all those little overpoweringly scented hand-sanitizer keychains from Bath and Body Works became popular, she has a touch of OCD. Only eats from plastic utensils and paper plates, none of our silverware, uses her shirt or a paper towel to touch any doorknobs, doing everything she can to ruin the environment with her pathological wastefulness. When I was married, we sent her to a therapist for a while, but Carlotta asked to stop after a month or so because 'She only ever wants to talk about you, Mother, and she wants me to do homework assignments like licking a toilet seat and seeing that I can live through it.' I didn't blame her for wanting to quit, and no therapist would suggest that kind of exposure therapy now, spreading Covid and who knows what to their clients. She's six months along now, barely showing on her thin frame. That's how all of us carry in my family, skinny with just a little soccer ball, like those fake pregnancies on TV, until month eight, when we pop. I get the feeling that Carlotta is especially happy, not just because of the baby coming—though how and where she'll deliver Baby Girl under these conditions is another constant stressor for me—but because she has an excuse to wear gloves and masks, even around the house, and to anoint her whole body with hand sanitizer. That girl, sweet but ditzy, would probably drink iodine or rubbing alcohol if she could.

"Which brings me back to Miss Thing in 4C, who I know started the rumor that Carlotta got pregnant in a

McDonald's bathroom by some rogue called Benjamin I've seen standing around but never met. He wears his hair in shiny, natural curls and has what silly people call 'good hair.' He claims to be Dominican, but he just looks Black to me and probably sells drugs. (I say that not because he's Dominican and looks Black—let's be real clear about that—but because he's always outside near some stoop or alleyway.) But back to 4C. Carlotta would never use a public bathroom, especially not in a McDonald's, maybe a Starbucks out of desperation, and she'd certainly never have unprotected sex in one. They say you can't ever really know what your kids are up to, but I know my baby, and the father is her boyfriend of six years, an equally sweet, driven man named—get this—Carl.

"Carl and Carlotta, a coincidence they think is so cute, so fateful, have been together since she was eighteen. They wanted to marry then, but I told her to wait until she finished her studies at CUNY. I didn't want her to end up young and divorced like me, with one or even two babies. She dropped out in her second year to try to emulate my career in art, painting surrealist, absurdist pieces. But let's face it: Some of her work is good, but she'll never be able to support a family with it the way I have with mine and alimony checks. My work is the kind of art you have to look at from just the right angle, kind of like me. Unfortunately, Carlotta needs formal training and perhaps a bit more of my genetics and less of her father's. I can only teach her so much.

"On the bright side, Carl has a good job as an essential worker, an EMT. We never get to see him anymore, and when he talks to Carlotta on the phone, he tells her the gravest stories, stories I don't want to repeat because, unlike Miss Thing, I stay out of other people's business.

"4C would do well to practice the same ethics. Before this lockdown, I'd seen all kinds of people coming in and out of her apartment at all hours of the day, despite the crackdown on visitors. She claims they're essential workers, doing things around her apartment that the super won't do—"

Here I felt eyes on me. I hadn't even gotten a call from that woman. I was opening my mouth to protest when I understood what she was implying.

"—and I suppose that's an accurate description. These so-called plumbers and painters never arrive with tools or supplies in their hands, and they leave empty-handed far after business hours, if you know what I mean, without a mark or a stain on them, unless you count hickies.

"If anyone is salty, then, it's she, because the postman never rings twice for her; none of these men make a second appearance at her apartment. I've heard from a reliable source in the building that she envies my artistic career and my upstanding children. Maybe she's barren. I don't know what she does for a living, unless it's sex work, and there's no shame in that industry, but 4C spreads rumors like social diseases, STDs. She's got a disease of the mouth herself, flapping those overlined lips of hers. I'd pity her if she weren't so messy."

Vinegar paused a moment, then raised her voice as if the absent 4C could hear her through the asphalt of the roof.

"Maybe I do pity you, 4C, in spite of it all. You could be beautiful, even with that giant mole (which you might consider plucking occasionally), if it weren't for your personality, just as I know I'm a fine wine with a complex cork. Anyone or anything can be—except the president—even this ugly, tumultuous time, which has brought us together, if you look at it from the right angle. So, hello, everyone. My name is Jennifer, and that is the only name I answer to."

At the end of this startling monologue, Vinegar—I simply couldn't think of her as a "Jennifer" yet, much as I knew I should try—looked around once more as if summoning a challenge. No surprise her grandfather was a judge. I could just imagine him thundering the law from the bench, wielding his gavel—a person not to be trifled with.

Florida, to my surprise, hadn't interrupted even when Vinegar mentioned her son or claimed she owed her money. She just sat there, hands folded, shawl drawn tight, her face even tighter with disdain. I noticed Vinegar's eyes drift over my shoulder and turned to see a mural, freshly painted on the tarred wall of the hut where the staircase emerged onto the roof. It was so eye-catching I couldn't believe I hadn't noticed it before when I was making my phone calls. Vinegar must have painted it earlier in the day. The work consisted of portraits of three joyful Black children, with a lot of color and vigor in the brushstrokes. I'm no art critic, but I got the sense that it was good. Really good. Other people had noticed it now, too, and a few got up to take a closer look. Even the Lady with the Rings. I noticed Vinegar's "signature"—her initials over a bottle of Heinz vinegar. Clearly, she didn't mind the nickname *that* much.

"Those are my babies when they were young," Vinegar said. "I figure there's lots of space on the wall for everyone else, if you all want. I can put paints and brushes and spray cans in a box just inside the door, if I can trust you not to trash my supplies. Anyone can write a message or paint a picture or whatever." She looked around. "This building's beyond hope, but, at least while we're stuck here, we can make it our own."

Whitney had been studiously ignoring us this whole time, but she put down her book, got up, and came over to look more closely at the mural. I was startled at this sudden interest.

Whitney turned to Vinegar. "You know, I believe I've seen your work. Wasn't it in a gallery on Avenue C last year? I can't remember the name."

"Yes, it was," said Vinegar with immense satisfaction, folding her hands in her lap. "Galería Loisaida. 'Ghost Portraits.' I sold five pieces from that show." She paused. "How did you see it?"

"I work at the Whitney," Whitney said. "Museum librarian. I have a great interest in contemporary art. I used to work in appraisals."

"Oh, I love the Whitney," said Vinegar.

"It seems to me," said the Lady with the Rings, "that the landlord should give you a rebate on your rent—for building improvements."

Florida said stiffly, "Or fine her for vandalism."

"Thank you, Jennifer, for adding a little color to our lives," said Eurovision quickly, heading off a looming altercation. "I can't understand how the landlord gets away with this wreck of a building."

He glanced at me as he said this, which made me want to clobber him. I was starting to get the feeling I was not popular among the tenants. Well, as my father would curse when he was really angry at one of his tenants, "Îmi voi agăța lenjeria să se usuce pe crucea mamei lui— I'll hang my underwear to dry on his mother's cross."

"Why the title? 'Ghost Portraits'?" Whitney asked.

"They're people I knew who died. I imagined what their ghosts would look like and painted their portraits. I have this idea that haunts are just the memories, wishes, desires, and sorrows of a dead person, all knotted and tangled up, left behind after the purified soul departs. So that's what I tried to capture."

"Like old Abe, the man who died in 4C?" said the Lady with the Rings. "You should paint his ghost. I wouldn't be surprised if he's still hanging around."

Merenguero's Daughter gave a shudder. "This talk about ghosts is making me chilly." She pulled her jacket tighter.

"I met a ghost once," said Whitney.

"For real?" Eurovision asked.

"Absolutely for real. It was in May of 1990. I was at a library conference in San Antonio, staying at the Menger Hotel, a rather charming old place built in the late 1800s. It's also located across the street from the Alamo, which now stands in a little botanical park, full of trees and shrubs, each with a little metal label bearing its name.

"A friend had driven up from Houston to see me, and he suggested that we go walk through the Alamo, he being a botanist and therefore interested in the plants. He also thought I might find the building interesting. He said he'd been there several times as a child and had found it 'evocative.' So we strolled through the garden, looking at plants, and then went inside.

"The present memorial is the single main church building, which is essentially no more than a gutted masonry shell. There's nothing at all in the church proper: a stone floor and stone walls, bearing the marks of thousands of bullets; the stone looks chewed. There are a couple of smaller semi-open rooms at the front of the church, where the baptismal font and a small shrine used to be, originally separated from the main room by stone pillars and partial walls.

"Around the edges of the main room are a few museum display cases, holding such artifacts of the defenders as the Daughters of Texas have managed to scrape together—rather a pitiful collection, including spoons, buttons, and (scraping the bottom of the barrel, if you ask me) a diploma certifying that one of the defenders had graduated from law school (this, like a number of other artifacts, wasn't present in the Alamo at the time of the battle, but was obtained later from the family of the man to whom it belonged).

"The walls are lined with perfectly horrible oil paintings, showing various of the defenders in assorted 'heroic' poses. I suspect them all of having been executed by the Daughters of Texas in a special arts-and-crafts class held for the purpose, though I admit that I might be maligning the D of T by this supposition. At any rate, as museums go, this one doesn't.

"It is quiet, owing to the presence of the woman waving the 'Silence, Please! This Is a Shrine!' sign in the middle of the room, but is not otherwise either spooky or reverent in atmosphere. It's just a big, empty room. My friend and I cruised slowly around the room, making sotto voce remarks about the paintings and looking at the artifacts.

"And then I walked into a ghost. He was near the front of the main room, about ten feet in from the wall, near the smaller room on the left (as you enter the church). I was very surprised by the encounter, since I hadn't expected to meet a ghost, and if I had, he wasn't what I would have expected.

"I saw nothing, experienced no chill or oppression or malaise. The air was slightly warmer where I stood, but not so much as to be really noticeable. The only really distinct feeling was one of . . . communication. Very distinct communication. I knew he was there—and he certainly knew I was.

"Have you ever met the eyes of a stranger and known at once this is someone you'd like? I had a strong urge to continue standing there, communicating (as it were, since there were no words exchanged then) with this man. Because it was—distinctly, strongly—a man.

"I rather naturally assumed that I was imagining this and turned to find my friend, to reestablish a sense of reality. He was about six feet away. Within a couple of feet of walking toward him, I lost contact with the ghost, couldn't feel him anymore. It was like leaving someone at a bus stop.

"Without speaking to my friend, I returned to the spot where I had encountered the ghost. There he was. Again, he was quite conscious of me, too. 'Oh, there you are!' Except we didn't yet exchange these words, or any words.

"I tried the experiment two or three more times—stepping away and coming back—with similar results. If I moved away, I couldn't feel him; if I moved back, I could. By this time, my friend was growing understandably curious. He came over and whispered, meaning to be funny, 'Is this what a librarian does?' Since he evidently didn't sense the ghost—he was standing approximately where I had been—I didn't say anything about it. I merely smiled and went on outside with him, where we continued our botanical investigations.

"The whole occurrence struck me as so very odd, while at the same time feeling utterly normal, that I went back to the Alamo alone on each of the next two days. Same thing; he was there, in the same spot, and he knew me. Each time, I would just stand there, engaged in what I can only call mental communication. As soon as I left the spot—it was an area maybe two-to-three-feet square—I couldn't sense him anymore.

"I did wonder who he was, of course. There are brass plates at intervals around the walls of the church, listing the vital statistics of all the Alamo defenders, and I'd strolled along looking at these, trying to see if any of them rang a bell, so to speak. None did.

"Now, I did mention the occurrence to a few of the librarians at the conference, all of whom were very interested. I don't think any of them went to the Alamo themselves—if they did, they didn't tell me—but more than one of them suggested that perhaps the ghost wanted me to tell his story, my being an archivist and all. I said dubiously that I didn't think that's what he wanted, but the next—and last—time I went to the Alamo, I did ask him, in so many words.

"I stood there and thought—consciously, in words: 'What do you want? I can't really do anything for you. All I can give you is the knowledge that I know you're there; I care that you lived and I care that you died here.'

"And he said—not out loud, but I heard the words distinctly inside my head—he said, 'That's enough.'

"It was enough; that's all he wanted. It was the only time he spoke. My visit to the Alamo was complete. This time, I took a slightly different path out to bypass a group of tourists in my way. Instead of leaving in a straight line to the door, I circled around the pillar dividing the main church from one of the smaller rooms. There was a small brass plate in the angle of the wall there, not visible from the main sanctuary.

"The plate said that the smaller room had been used as a powder magazine during the defense of the fort. During the last hours of the siege, when it became apparent that the fort would fall, one of the defenders had made an effort to blow up the magazine, in order to destroy the fort and take as many of the attackers as possible with it. However, the man had been shot and killed just outside the smaller room, before he could succeed in his mission—more or less on the spot where I met the ghost.

"So I don't know for sure: He didn't tell me his name, and I gained no clear idea of his appearance—

just a general impression that he was fairly tall, since he spoke down to me, somehow. But for what it's worth, the man who was killed trying to blow up the powder magazine was named Robert Evans. He was described as being 'black-haired, blue-eyed, nearly six feet tall, and always merry.' That last bit sounds like the man I met, all right, but there's no telling. This description appears in a book titled *Alamo Defenders*, which I bought in the museum bookshop as a final parting gesture. I had never heard of Robert Evans or the powder magazine before." She paused for a moment. "And that's the whole story."

"Huh. Is that a true story?" Eurovision asked, suspiciously. "I mean, everyone who tells a ghost story starts by saying it's true, but I want to know if it's *really* true."

"It's honest-to-God true," said Whitney.

"Do you think he knew he was dead?" Vinegar asked. "Maybe he became a ghost because he didn't know."

Whitney said, "Exactly what I thought. He got shot, taken down so fast that he never had the chance to experience his own death. Then his body was gone in the explosion, so there was no burial and maybe not even a funeral. He got stuck there in that spot, dazed and wondering what was going on, cut off from life but unable to find his way to the next world. People say that ghosts stick around because they have unfinished business on earth, but I think a lot of them may be like him, confused about their status, so to speak."

"I think it runs even deeper than that," said the Lady with the Rings. "People are so frightened of death, or so attached to life, that sometimes when it happens, they can't accept that they've died. They're in denial. Especially if it's sudden and there's no funeral."

"So you think ghosts attend their own funerals?" asked Eurovision, with a strained laugh.

"I would certainly attend my own funeral," said Vinegar. "Just to see who didn't show."

"Maybe it's important to see your body going into the ground," said the Lady with the Rings, "or otherwise you won't believe it."

Florida frowned. "I wonder how many Mexican ghosts are lingering there, too. They were just trying to reclaim their stolen land. Why put energy into mourning the men like Robert Evans?"

"I'm sure you're right," said Whitney, "but how harshly should we judge the dead?"

"Harshly," said Hello Kitty. "Line 'em up against the wall and shoot 'em."

Vinegar frowned. "We have a right to judge the dead."

"Don't you think there's some worth in just having lived?" said the Lady with the Rings. "We're all going to be judged in the end, but at least we had the dignity of having existed."

I couldn't take much more of this kind of conversation. I had been trying so hard to stop worrying about my dad, whose dignity and even existence was being denied by the silence of Snotgreen Manor. That's how it felt, anyway.

A chorus of sirens made it impossible to speak for a few moments. There must have been half a dozen ambulances tearing up the Bowery. I wondered what mass infection had occurred—maybe they were coming from some other nursing home packed with the dying.

By the time the noise of the sirens died away, the talk of the dead seemed to have drawn a curtain over the evening. Church bells intruded on the silence, and I figured they must be from St. Patrick's Old Cathedral on Mulberry Street. We all sensed that the conversation, and our gathering, was done, and with some unconscious signal we all began packing up to go downstairs.

I was glad for the stories, though—no point pretending otherwise. It was good to have a break from the fear. Though, as I picked up my phone and turned off the recorder, I had a shivery thought of the many new ghosts freshly haunting this pandemic city—and the many more to come. I hope this whole thing will be over soon.

Back here in my little broom closet, I immediately got to work transcribing the evening's stories and adding my own commentary. It took me half the night, but even then I was still wide awake—for some reason I'd lately almost completely lost the desire to sleep. I lay down on my bed anyway and was awake for a long time. Sure enough, those footsteps started up again, as slow and measured as the tolling of the bells. And then I heard the distant music of a Wurlitzer piano coming from somewhere in the building, playing a slow, dreamy rendition of an old jazz tune, and it made me feel lonelier than ever.

Day Three
April 2

Once again, after mopping the halls and covering a couple of broken stairwell windows with cardboard and duct tape, I spent the rest of the day trying to get through to my dad at Pucegreen Manor. I thought about trying to brave a train ride up there, but with the National Guard surrounding the area, I realized I'd never get through. And taking Metro North would be like hitching a ride on the epidemic express. My only consolation was that my dad most likely didn't know what was going on. He'd been forgetting who I was most of the time, so he wasn't going to miss me, anyway. I just hoped the virus hadn't made its way inside the nursing home. All I wanted was to see him, to know he was okay. It kills me that Instagram and Twitter are full of posts of sweet-cheeked little grandkids drawing pictures outside of nursing homes, dogs, and teary-eyed adults pressing up against spotted hands on the other side of the glass barrier. Maybe that's how it is if you can afford some expensive private nursing home, but certainly not up at Shitgreen Manor.

I looked up the numbers so I could record today's daily statistics. I don't know why I find this calming when the numbers themselves are anything but—I guess they delimit the catastrophe in my mind. Today, April 2, New York State hit 92,381 cases. That's more than the number of infections that all of China reported in total. One thousand five hundred sixty-two dead in the city as of Thursday evening. CBS news announced that there were more 911 calls received today than on September 11, 2001.

Think about that for a moment. All those ambulances. A city full of 9/11s.

The rooftop had started to become a refuge for people in the building, I could tell. But when I arrived this evening, I saw there was going to be trouble. The tenant in 4C, whom Vinegar had trashed the night before, was up there, dressed to the nines and looking sleek and ready to do battle. She was skinny and gym-rat fit, with ripped arms; long, heavy, swinging blond hair; a discreet mole on her chin—in short, a goddess.

Not my type but my interest was piqued, much as I'd never mingle with the tenants. Perched on vertiginous pigeon's-blood patent-leather Louboutin pumps. Where the hell did she get money for that, living in this dump?

Vinegar had called her Miss Thing, but it didn't take me long to find her in the super's bible. *Pumps*, of course. Apparently she was an Instagram Influencer, specializing in pictures of her pedicures. Two hundred thousand followers.

Pumps remained standing, facing the door, all flexed up like a prizefighter waiting for the bell, as we straggled onto the roof in our usual disorganized way, settling in our socially distant seats with our drinks and snacks. As soon as Vinegar appeared, Pumps rounded on her.

"You been shit-talking me," Pumps said, her suburban Jersey Sopranos accent slicing the air, utterly at odds with her gloriously curated appearance.

Vinegar calmly continued her walk to her seat, unruffled, while Pumps followed her. Vinegar was carrying a wine sleeve in one hand with a small, folding side table under her arm. While Pumps stood over her, glaring, Vinegar set up a little round table, pulled a glass and a corkscrew from her backpack, cut off the foil, uncorked it, gave the cork a sniff, poured herself a taste, swirled it around, tasted it again, while everyone else surreptitiously watched the unfolding drama. Eventually, Vinegar nodded with satisfaction and poured herself the wine.

Only then did she look up at her antagonist, looming over her, arms akimbo. Leaning back in her chair, putting more social distance between them, Vinegar said, calmly, "You've been talking smack about me for as long as I can remember. I just returned the favor." From her backpack she retrieved an alcohol-soaked chamois cloth—the chemical smell only heightened the tension in the air—and a second wineglass, then proceeded to clean the glass with the precision of a painter wiping down canvas. She then filled the second glass with wine and proffered it to Pumps, who took an alarmed step backward.

"Now take yourself and your coronavirus breath somewhere else," Vinegar said, "and let me enjoy the evening in conversation with friends." She turned to Eurovision. "Isn't that right?"

"Um," he said nervously. He had on a fresh paisley bow tie with a plaid jacket and striped shirt and skinny green pants with yellow ducks on them. Clearly our rooftop was going to stand in for Eurovision 2020. "Now, miss, ah, I'm sorry I don't know your name, but you're welcome to join us in conversation."

"I'd rather spend the evening in Satan's ass cuddled up with scorpions than listen to you douche bags *in conversation.*" Pumps whirled about and left, letting the rooftop door bang loudly behind her.

"Whew," said Florida, fanning herself, even though it was a cool evening. "My mother always said, 'Those who bark hang with the dogs, you know what I mean?' That woman's trouble."

Vinegar said, "She pays for those damn shoes by slutting all over Instagram. That's what I heard."

"The world sure has changed," said Florida, "where a moron like that, with a ring light and nice feet, makes a couple thousand dollars a week posting photos of her toes. I remember when a café con leche cost one dollar and the gourmet deli was called a bodega. I've seen a lot of things, and have I ever said anything? You better believe I haven't.

"Not like those blanquitos, who keep calling 311 on us. You like a song on the radio and raise the volume a little bit, and the next thing you hear is the siren out your window and a cop ringing your doorbell, asking you to turn it down. As if a good song ever bothered anybody. It's noise to them only because they're not listening. Music gives us an escape, colors the shit of life, and let me tell you, we need this fucking music, because life has not always been so good to us. Especially now! You know what I mean?"

Florida sounded like she had a story to tell. I was starting to really enjoy this. I poured myself the drink of the night—a Rusty Nail—and eased myself back on the couch, phone charged and recording.

"I've always played it straight, and worked hard and paid my bills, thinking that when I got old, I could retire back home or just retire and collect my checks, but how do they say, you plan and God laughs, and oh my God, we all lost our jobs and the only ones who got spared were the rich, and I was fifty-five years old when the factory moved away. The bosses said they couldn't afford us anymore.

"Do you know how much I made after working nineteen years in that doll factory? Eleven dollars an hour. If I didn't do all that overtime, every Saturday and holiday, I couldn't have made the rent, and the lights, and the gas and the cable and the phone and the food. But bosses said they paid us too much. And I got paid more than the new people, so imagine that. All of us, out of work, with no one to turn to. Even my kid, who went to the fancy college and worked with one of the big banks, lost his job, and he was worse off than me because he never saved a dime. He bought everything with his credit card, thinking he would be making the big money forever. Ha! There is no forever or security for the poor. There is only hard work, and you always need luck. I told him this, but did he listen?

"Anyways, it broke my heart seeing him jobless and desperate, because I'm used to living with very little, but my son likes the designer shoes and has two kids in private school and a wife who likes to get her nails and hair done every week. So of course he comes to me asking me for help, thinking I had some savings. I had thirteen hundred dollars at the time, more than he had in the bank, which is crazy because he was *working* for a bank. But that wasn't even half his rent. I gave it to him, but not all of it, because even if the unemployment checks would cover most of my bills, I kept two hundred dollars for an emergency.

"At the time, even if the world was falling apart, I was optimistic. Remember when Obama got elected, with his *sí se puede* song? Oh, God, I was drunk on hope and the dream he was selling. And c'mon, he's just so fine. So fine! Like those first few weeks when he became president I would wake up feeling all nice inside after he would visit me in my sleep. In the dream we would be in a room in some beautiful house and our eyes would catch and he would give me that look, like—'I see you, Florida Camacho.' And if he wasn't married to Michelle, I know he would've asked me out to dance. Because oh, I love to dance. And the way Obama moves, it's clear he can dance. Yes we can, papi! Yes we can, in my kitchen, in my living room, in my bedroom.

"Oh, don't you all miss it? The dancing, the getting up close to someone, the music so loud you can't hear your mind, and the vibrations of the speakers inside your heart, and your feet digging into the floor, getting to the root of things. And with the right person, someone who can hold you just the right way when you're dancing, their hand pressing on the small of your back, and for that moment in time, one feels like everything is gonna be all right.

"But we're stuck now. God ain't playing no games. We can't even shake someone's hand. Six feet apart. So sad. And if you cough because something is stuck in your throat, everyone's ready to throw a rock at you. Even my own son, who I've been there for, no matter what trouble he gets into, won't visit me. Not even to wave outside my window. He knows I don't see anyone else. Not a soul, because I have the asthma, and the last time I had pneumonia I almost died. He knows I'm careful and that he's safe visiting me. But no, he says he's trying to save me from getting sick, acting like he ever cared about me. But he's lying. And you know what all this solitude has made me realize, that I've been lying to myself. When the shit hits the fan, we're alone. And people will kill each other for that last roll of toilet paper.

"Remember that year we had snowstorm after snowstorm and the sidewalks were like a skating rink? And most supers laid out the salt the night before so we could get around and not kill ourselves trying to get to the bus stop. But the lazy super out by the corner on Clinton Street let the ice get real thick. A real hazard. And I one day, rushing—didn't think a tragedy would ever happen to me—stepped right on the ice, slid on that sidewalk, crashed into the building, and my foot got stuck on that iron fence, broke my knee and cracked my hip.

"You better believe I called that lawyer who advertises on the buses. No case too big or too small, they said. And just like the lawyer says on his commercial, the money did come in. And back then you better believe my son came to visit me in the hospital a bunch of times, always wanting to talk to the lawyer directly, supposedly in my best interest, but I told the lawyer that he could not be trusted. Because it's true. This is the thing about being old—you stop lying to yourself. Or maybe *I* just stopped lying to myself. When my son lost his job, he drank and played the numbers because he always thought he was lucky. But he ain't lucky. I kept telling him that everything he has ever had was from working hard, at school and at work. But he was always looking for the shortcut to being rich. So when the money came, of course he came around a lot. And I gave him a good part of it. But then I told him it was finished, to see if he would stop by just to say hello. Hoping that because he loves his mother and he knows how happy it would make me, that maybe he would bring my granddaughters to visit. But he never did.

"My son thinks I have nothing to give him anymore. He thinks I have no more money to lend and frankly, even my meals, I know they're not as good anymore because I can't smell. Before you start looking at me like I have something, yes, I saw that *Times* article last week, too, but trust me, I don't. I haven't been able to smell for ages, before this novel coronavirus showed up. And because of that, I can't taste the food I make.

"And so I think, this curse, this plague that has fallen on everyone in the world—yes, people are dying, and we have to be careful, but don't you think it's rather convenient, too, the way the plague now is being used by the young people. They go around like they don't care. Maybe they just want us old folks to die so they can inherit whatever we have left. Maybe they're relieved of not having to visit us? Like, do you think that there can be love when there is need and greed? Like, was I just someone my son needed? It all makes me very sad. Like, will I end up like the old man on the fourth floor?

"Were any of you around back then? I can't remember. The red-headed man who lived above me, who smelled like skunk and never shaved. He was always pounding on something, so hard my light fixtures shook. He drove me crazy with all his racket. And sometimes it was as if he was sawing the heating pole in half. What a torture. And I would pound my broomstick against the ceiling for him to stop. And I complained to the super, the old super. I even wrote him a note and begged him to quiet it down. And then it did stop. And how lovely it was. I had forgotten how beautiful the silence was. I loved the quiet so much I didn't even want to turn the radio on. Or the TV. Or open a window. For a short period it was as if my ears were full of water and all I heard was the quiet hum of my thoughts. Even my chatty mind quieted down. I was so happy to be in the quiet. And when the sirens in the distance blared or someone yelled at someone outside, I was jolted from what felt like a dream.

"But then we could all smell it. That smell of decay, and oh, the poor old man who made a racket, who barely said 'thank you' when you held open the lobby door for him, had died. He had been dead for days and days. And I felt horrible at first because I had been so happy those days with the quiet, and all along, he was dead. And you know what? With him went my sense of smell. Gone. Forever. Just like that.

"But then the noise came back. Because the landlord wanted to gut renovate the apartment to triple the rent, and what a nightmare. And this girl, with the shoes and the Instagram, she has money because all alone she pays that triple rent. But don't say you heard that from me. Like I said, I like to mind my own business. All I know is that something is going on with her and the exterminator.

"So you know how the exterminator used to come by on the third Saturday every month? Anyone with eyes knows he's handsome. But he's so respectful, always with 'sí señora, permiso, señora.' And I always offer him water, coffee, because who knows how long his workdays are. And he always says no and quickly sprays the bathroom, then the kitchen. And he does all the apartments, always in order, on each floor. I hear him on my floor going to 3A, then 3B, then me, 3C, and so on down the hall. Then he goes upstairs. And when he is upstairs, I can hear his footsteps so clearly because he has those heavy worker boots, with the hard rubber. And they are big feet, a nice thing for a man to have. And he steps hard. And the floors, as you know, thin like paper. So I know when he's spraying the bathroom, then the kitchen, which requires him to walk down our long hallway. But then the footsteps stop. At first I didn't notice, but then I paid attention. And every third Saturday of the month when he visited, it was the same. I timed the minutes he was in my place and counted the apartments in the building and added up how much time it will take him to finish all the apartments, give or take a few, being that some people aren't home. And you know what? There is always a mysterious amount of time unaccounted for. And you know where he spends it? With the lady who lives above me.

"So of course the next time he comes to my apartment, I try to get to know more about him. Is he married? Does he have children? And he hurries along, his big muscles bulging from under his T-shirt. His wild long hair in a ponytail, thick and dark and shiny like those men on the cover of romance novels. He pretends as if I'm not asking him anything at all, rushing to get upstairs. And always, when he gets to the fourth floor, I hear the door close behind him. I hear the footsteps on my ceiling, stomping down the long hallway, and then not a peep.

"You see, my heating pole runs up through my ceiling into her apartment. And all of you should know that if you talk near it, I can hear what you're saying as if you're in my own kitchen. So be careful what you say. So of course it's not like it's my business, but the not knowing was keeping me up at night, so I pressed my ear to the heating pole to see if I could hear them. Sometimes the volume of the music goes up and then down, sometimes I hear her laugh. And then about thirty minutes later he leaves, his heavy steps down the hallway shaking my ceiling.

"Honestly, who could blame her. Who doesn't miss affection? I mean, the last hug I received was from my son. Maybe he only visited when he wanted things, but when he visited, his mouth was full of honey—and his hugs, he really knows how to hold a person. And I'd dress up for him just so he'd tell me how good I looked. God, I do miss him.

"All I have to do is tell him I have money in the bank and before you know it he would forget everything he had said about keeping me safe during this plague, and he would come over to my apartment, sit in my kitchen, eat my cooking, and give me all the hugs I want. I know this to be true."

The thought of Florida missing her son like that really choked me up. Oh, man. When was the last time I got to hug my dad? Really not since I had that asthma attack last month. Why the hell wouldn't anyone answer the phone at old Pukegreen Manor? What if I just showed up and demanded entry? They'd have to let me through. Or I could just sneak through someone's backyard maybe. As soon as I can get out of this place.

I was yanked back into the rooftop chatter by Ramboz's cracked voice. "The last super found that old tenant's decomposing corpse," he informed us all, with relish. "Or so I heard. Been there for days. Horrible purple color, with all the fluid running out."

It was true, I'd seen the notes in Wilbur's book. I wondered what else the tenants might reveal about my predecessor. I leaned a bit closer to the action, all the time trying to look as if I didn't care at all.

Hello Kitty unfurled herself from the cave chair, her fingers clenching her glittery vape. "He had a name, you know." She threw a look at Florida.

Florida returned the look, uncowed.

The Lady with the Rings jumped in, her voice soothing: "I'm sure he was a lovely man if you didn't have to live below him."

Hello Kitty ignored her. "His name was Bern*stein.* Not 'steen' but 'stine.' He used to tell me, 'Steen is mean, but stine is fine.' You all didn't really know him at all, none of you." She dropped her hand from her necklace, flicking her fingers open as if we were gnats. "You're all so clueless. Mr. Bernstein would be pissed at you, talking about him as a noisy, smelly old man. You know why he was so loud? Because he was almost deaf. And if he was here now, he'd tell you the story of the absolute worst way to die, even worse than what happened to him in the end. You want to hear it?" It felt like she was daring us to tell her no.

When no one did, Hello Kitty settled back into her seat. "There have been other pandemics, diseases worse than Covid. Mr. Bernstein should know—one almost killed him."

"You know that it's a lie that the coronavirus is just like the flu, right?" Eurovision looked uneasy about ceding control of the conversation to this unpredictable young woman. "Haven't you heard all those stories from the hospitals where they're running out of ventilators? People choking? It's a pretty terrible way to die."

"Sure," said Hello Kitty, "but there's something much worse." She edged her chair back so that there was more room between her and everyone else, clearly enjoying the attention. She raised her vape and took a quick hit. "A fate worse than death."

"**Abe was** only eight. It was the summer of 1952, and he and his twin brother, Jacob, were staying with their aunt in Canton, Ohio. They had a blast, visiting the Hall of Fame, fishing and swimming in the lake their aunt's house was on, going out on the boat with their uncle. Everything was great. Right up until the morning when Jacob got out of his bed up in the attic, where they both slept, and fell down the steps.

"He didn't break anything, but he couldn't move his legs, so they rushed him to the children's hospital in Akron and called Abe and Jacob's parents to drive back early from their week in Atlantic City. All Abe remembered was the whispering. Constant whispers hushing whenever the grown-ups noticed he was near. The way they hugged each other but never him. And he knew; he just knew. They were afraid of him. Afraid he had the plague, same as Jacob. The polio.

"Then Jacob died. Abe wasn't allowed to attend the funeral services, not allowed to come downstairs as relatives poured in from Pittsburgh and Cincinnati and Erie and Buffalo and places he'd never heard of, like Altoona.

"All that time, he lay upstairs in the attic, wondering: Would he be the next to die? All alone, locked away with his twin's empty bed and nothing to do but read and worry and try to add his voice to the mourners' below as they recited the kaddish, the prayer for the dead, hoping that God heard.

"But God didn't hear. Two days after Jacob died, Abe couldn't get out of bed. They wouldn't let his mother come with him in the ambulance, the steel doors slamming shut against her screams and tears. Then they jabbed him with a needle, and he fell asleep wondering if he'd ever wake up again.

"Wake up he did. Only to find himself trapped. Locked inside a nightmare.

"He couldn't move. His body had been swallowed whole by a huge machine that clanked and whooshed and stole his breath when he was trying to breathe in and forced his lungs to fill up with air exactly when he wanted to breathe out. He panicked, tried to scream, only to find that he had no voice."

"Oh, very Harlan Ellison," Eurovision interrupted. I'd had my eyes locked on Hello Kitty's face, so even I was startled a bit by this.

"Excuse me?" Vinegar snapped.

"You know," said Eurovision, warming to his subject. "'I Have No Mouth, and I Must Scream.' Classic story—the human race is destroyed by this computer AI, except the computer keeps a few humans alive just to torture and play with them like lab rats—"

"Sounds perfectly horrid," Vinegar said. "Let the girl continue."

Hello Kitty met my gaze, watching me watch them—she was no fool.

"So poor Abe. Just a little kid, alone and scared, and he can't tell anyone how he feels. Even swallowing makes him choke, so they shove a tube down his nose. The iron lung keeps tugging and pulling at his body, and it's worse than any medieval torture device. But the worst thing is how all alone he is. And he can't help but wonder if this is also how Jacob died: alone, unable to scream, unable to do anything except stare at the metal monster that is holding him prisoner, making weird noises like it's eating him alive. Maybe the ambulance guys kidnapped him, maybe this wasn't the hospital at all, but some evil mad scientist's laboratory like in the comics?

"Maybe he'd never see his mom and dad again. Maybe he was going to die here, just like Jacob.

"But he didn't die. Instead, he fought. He learned how to relax and work with the machine. How to ignore the itching he was desperate to ask someone to scratch, the pain of the feeding tube rubbing against the back of his throat, the burn of his eyes so dry because the only things he could move were his eyelids, and that took so much effort that they'd often slide open whenever he fell asleep.

"He couldn't speak, couldn't communicate except to blink furiously, hoping someone, a nurse, his parents during the short times they were allowed to visit, the man who worked on the machine—anyone who came close—would notice. He tried to let them know that he wasn't gone, that he was still alive, held hostage inside his own body.

"Then he heard the doctors urging his parents to let go, that his case was too far gone, that they were keeping his body alive, but Abraham, the child they knew, his mind was probably already damaged beyond hope. Inside he was screaming, but the only thing his parents noticed was a tear after the doctor shone the light in his eyes. His mother wiped it away without even looking at him. He was afraid they were going to give up on him, that he'd die there, maybe even be buried alive—his worst nightmare.

"But after already losing one child, how could they not fight for their last child? And so, Abe's parents insisted that the doctors keep doing everything possible. Their love was what finally saved him—that and a mirror.

"More precisely, a crooked mirror.

"Imagine a little boy, fighting for his life, trapped inside the prison of his own body, unable to even tell anyone he was still alive. Imagine the hours, the minutes . . . the seconds. Every itch tormented him, every stray breeze burned his skin raw. He counted every breath the machine squeezed out of him, counted the rivets and screws and bolts on the machine, counted his own heartbeat echoing through his brain. He played imaginary games with his dead brother, tried to remember the scoring plays of every baseball game he'd ever seen or heard on the radio. He even prayed, this terrified, lonely, bored little boy, who was slowly going insane.

"But then one day—he'd lost count of how many days he'd been held prisoner by the machine and his body—one day, after the janitor left, in a hurry because he had tickets to the Indians hosting the Pirates, a voice called to Abe from the wilderness. A little girl's voice: 'Well, hello. I couldn't see you very well until now. But Mr. Alvarez knocked my mirror when he was cleaning it and now instead of what's behind me, I can see you, isn't that nice? You're Abe, right? I heard your mother call you that. I wish my parents came to see me, but they have to work and take care of my brothers and sisters.'

"Abe had heard the nurses and the girl talking, of course. And he sensed that she wasn't very far away—after all, they were sharing an iron lung, how far away could she be? But his own mirror reflected only the blank wall behind him, and since he couldn't turn his head, he couldn't see her. Until now, her presence had been one more irritation, less annoying than the itch on his nose that he couldn't tell anyone to scratch for him, more annoying than the fly buzzing up near the over-head light. At his age, girls were, well, girls. He didn't understand them; they seemed to talk all the time but not about anything important or interesting; and they couldn't play ball—or wouldn't play ball—so what good were they, anyway? At least that was the consen-sus he and Jacob and all their friends had reached by the ripe old age of eight.

"But now, a girl, this girl, saw him. She prattled on and on—something about her brothers and sisters and missing her friends at school, and woven in there was a story about a squirrel that she had left food for on her windowsill one morning and how suddenly she was responsible for an entire family of squirrels and she hoped someone back home was remembering to feed them all—and Abe felt as if a lifeline had been thrown to him.

"And then she said, 'I know you can hear me. Blink once for yes and two for no. That way, we can sort of talk. I'm so bored. And it's kinda scary being here, all alone. Could you do that? Talk to me?' Abe was elated. He'd tried blinking to his mom and his dad and the nurses, even Mr. Alvarez, but it took a lot of work, and no one noticed—especially not after the doctors told them it was only some kind of reflex. But the girl, she'd noticed. She could be his voice. Maybe. If she wasn't dumb like most of the other girls he knew. So, slowly, determined, he focused all his power on his eyelids and carefully closed them. Long enough for the machine to breathe out and then in. Then he opened them.

"The girl cheered. 'Yes, that was a yes!' She began peppering him with questions: Did the tube they fed him through hurt? *Yes.* Could he still taste the food, because it was yellow like cake batter, but it smelled funny, did it taste like cake? *No.* How long had he been here, because he was here when they brought her in two days ago? Abe wasn't sure, so he stared straight ahead, keeping his eyes open as wide as he could until they watered. 'Oh, you don't know?' she translated, and suddenly they had expanded their vocabulary.

"And so it went. By the time the nurses made their rounds that night, the girl was fluent in Abe-blinks, and, despite being exhausted, he performed for them. The next day, they showed the doctor and more nurses, and then Abe's parents, who cried with delight before immediately bowing their heads in prayer. Slowly, but surely, Abe improved, regaining control of his muscles until they could remove the feeding tube, and his voice, at first just a whisper, became stronger. He still couldn't turn his head, but he asked a nurse to turn it for him and finally, days later, he got his first look at the girl.

"She wasn't much to look at—like him, her body was swallowed whole by the iron lung. She had curly hair that the nurses kept brushed and pulled back in a red ribbon. Her eyes were brown like his, and she had a bunch of freckles, and her two front teeth overlapped the slightest bit. But to Abe, she was the most beautiful thing in the world. He only wished Jacob was here to see that maybe girls weren't so bad after all. Her name was Clarissa, and he decided then and there that he was going to marry her one day. She told him she was getting better. They were moving her to another hospital where they could work on her muscles."

Hello Kitty leaned back in her chair as if waiting for applause. We waited for her to continue, but she just gave us all that unreadable smirk that irritated the hell out of me.

The Therapist spoke. "So? Did they see each other again? Did he find her? Did Abe marry Clarissa?"

"They were just kids," Vinegar scoffed. "How could he have found her?"

Florida said, "I think Abe did have a wife who died young."

"Was her name Clarissa?" someone asked.

"I forget her name."

"What I think we all want to know," said Eurovision, turning to Hello Kitty, "is what happened."

"What do *you* think?" Hello Kitty's hand unconsciously caressed her vape. If we'd been playing poker, I'd say that was her tell—but what did it mean? A full house or a bluff? "Maybe I don't know what happened."

"Obviously you do," said the Lady with the Rings. "If Abe told you the story this far, he would've finished it. Either Clarissa died, or he never knew what happened to her, or he later met up with her and maybe married her. One of those has to be the truth."

Another smirk; Hello Kitty was enjoying the attention. "What is truth," she said, "and what is fiction?"

"God, you're such a drama queen," Eurovision said. "*Did he marry Clarissa?*"

"Fine. After Clarissa saved Abe's life—or, at the very least, his sanity—he never forgot her. Once he finally improved enough to go home, he asked his mother to help him write thank-you cards to the nurses who'd taken care of him. And inside them he placed notes he'd written himself, asking for Clarissa's last name and address so he could write her. For a long, long time he didn't hear anything, but then one day, a letter came. Addressed to Abe. Of course, the nurses couldn't give out Clarissa's private information, most of them hadn't even thought twice about Abe's scrawled note, but one had reached out to Clarissa's parents and passed Abe's request on.

"It had taken a long time—it wasn't like today, when people compose marriage proposals in one hundred forty-four characters and in less time than it takes to watch a TikTok. But Clarissa wrote back. Then Abe replied, and slowly, over the years, they somehow kept going. She was two years younger than him, so he had to wait for her—and spent his first two years at college worried that she'd graduate high school, marry the guy who'd taken her to prom, and Abe would never hear from her again.

"And he didn't. Not that entire summer after she graduated, not even a thank-you card or phone call after he'd sent her a graduation gift—a lovely antique compact he'd found at a secondhand store. He thought he'd lost her forever.

"But then, as he's moving into his apartment to start his junior year, a flash of light hits his eyes, so bright he almost drops the lamp he's carrying. He blinks and turns and it's Clarissa, standing across the street where the sun hits her compact mirror just at the right angle for her to send its rays his way. Blinking, like their old code.

"They were together over forty years until she died, and he couldn't stand living in their house without her, not without the girl who'd saved him from a fate worse than death. So he moved in here."

"And that," she said, with a cool glance at Eurovision, "is what happened."

I looked around at the group, wondering if they were all thinking the same thing I was. But I was surprised to see Vinegar surreptitiously whisking away a tear. Even Eurovision seemed at a loss.

"No wonder he would have seemed so angry all the time," said the Therapist. "Poor guy." She seemed about to say something more, but just then the bells of St. Patrick's Old Cathedral began tolling. Eight o'clock. For the first time, I noticed how clunky they were, and out of tune. One must have been cracked, because it gave out a dead sound on the final stroke. Those bells seemed to have become an unspoken signal for the end of our evenings, because everyone began to shift themselves out of their chairs and start a round of six-foot-distant goodnights.

I was just going to let it drop. What business was it of mine if the kid wanted to lie? But her smirks had gotten to me. She knew I knew. But I wouldn't call her out publicly. I wandered over toward Hello Kitty, hovering near her casually as she tucked away her AirPods. She looked up at me, defiance in her eyes.

"You've never been inside 4C, have you?" I said in a low voice.

"Says who?"

"I know about the old man who died in there." I hoped I wouldn't have to explain how—I was pretty sure these people would not be thrilled to hear about Wilbur's bible.

Hello Kitty held my gaze, her face carefully revealing nothing. I should have kept quiet, but I continued.

"His wife's name was Roxanne, not Clarissa. He met her when he was in the navy. Nothing you just said about his life matches what I know about him, except that he was old and deaf."

Her face broke into a small, cynical smile, not even doing me the honor of looking guilty.

"You made that story up," I finished.

After a pause, still with that hard glint of a smile in her eyes, Hello Kitty said, "So what?"

I couldn't think of an immediate response to that. But Eurovision, who'd been putting his speaker into his knapsack, had overheard and stepped over, always ready to be the center of the action.

"My dear girl, it really isn't kosher to tell a false story about someone who lived in the building. Did you even know him at all?"

"Fine. I never met him, okay?" Hello Kitty let her

voice rise above the rest of the chatter on the rooftop. "But did any of *you* ever bother getting to know him? If it weren't for Miss Know-It-All here, none of you would have had any idea. Who are you to judge what's true or not, anyway? No one should die alone, abandoned and forgotten. And now everyone will remember him. Abe Bernstein."

Hello Kitty climbed out of her chair, turned on her heel, and stalked downstairs, leaving the cave chair and the rest of us in the eerie silence of the city that was never supposed to sleep. Eyes shifted from the door, back to me and Eurovision, frozen in place. I wondered if I had done the right thing. Everyone had wanted to believe her story. Despite the plague, the threat that surrounded us, we all liked to believe the lie that our lives might someday have a happy ending—even if the truth is we all end up like the old man in 4C: purple and draining fluids.

I reluctantly returned to Hades and sat at the old desk, half drunk, and began replaying the evening on my phone, scribbling it down in *The Fernsby Bible*. As midnight neared, the footsteps came again. Tonight they were very soft, like someone tiptoeing in socks, and, strangely, seemed to be going only in one direction. The gentle footfalls would come, barely audible, one after the other in agonizing slowness, like children up to no good. It would take a good minute or two for them to cross the room, right to left. I strained to hear them go back the other way, but they didn't. Maybe I was imagining it. But then the footfalls would come again, right to left. I also heard once or twice a gentle splashing noise. *Christ,* I thought, *there's a leak up there.*

Tomorrow, I'll check it out.

Day Four
April 3

The mayor gave a press conference today and rec-ommended mask-wearing for everyone, and as a result the news was full of a debate about masks, whether they help, whether they should be required, and especially whether there were enough to go around, and if not, shouldn't we be saving the masks for the doctors and nurses. As we arrived in the evening, I saw that some of the tenants had followed the advice and improvised various ragtag masks—scarves, skiing gaiters, bandannas.

This evening, I arrived extra early. My plan was to be first on the roof so that I could make a checklist of all the tenants and match them with their names, apartment numbers, and descriptions in the bible. As they arrived, I could check them off—as a sort of roll call. I wanted to finally and completely get them all straight in my mind, especially the audience members who hadn't said anything yet and were just sitting at the fringes of the gathering, doing their own thing. I'd also drawn a diagram of the building, showing each apartment, that I pasted onto a blank page in the bible.

The first to arrive, besides me, was Eurovision, and it went on from there.

Here's the list:

Eurovision, 5C

Monsieur Ramboz, 6A

Vinegar, 2B

Hello Kitty, 5B

Merenguero's Daughter, 3B

Tango, 6B. This mysterious woman has been sitting in a wicker chair at the far end of the rooftop, a well-put-together blonde of about forty, trim and poised, wearing glasses and a black silk mask. She's been completely silent, but I could see she was keenly observing all of us. "She is

Tango, who dances inside the lives of others," according to Wilbur's bible.

Whitney, 4D

Amnesia, 5E. "She is Amnesia, who carries the universal desire for oblivion." Wilbur's notes also say that her hobby is distressing secondhand clothes, but that she writes comic books and also was a writer for the famous computer game *Amnesia*. I was really curious about her, but she, too, shows no interest in our gathering and hangs out in the dark outer edges of the rooftop.

The Therapist, 6D

The Lady with the Rings, 2D

Blackbeard, 3E. "He is Blackbeard, come to open the purple testament of bleeding war" is what the bible says about this bearded bear, who sits by himself in a dark corner, reading a tattered paperback and drinking bourbon straight from a bottle.

La Reina, 4E. She intrigued me more than most of the silent tenants. She's as tall as me, maybe even taller. Her movements are deliberate, poised, like her whole body is conscious of its location in space. Her brown curls spill down her shoulders. The bible gave her this aphorism: "You may her throne depose, but she is still queen of her griefs."

Lala, 4A. This tenant is instantly recognizable: "She is Lala, with eyes like black infinities." Lala's a small, pretty woman of about forty-five, with dazzling white teeth, long wavy hair, and eyes like huge wobbly drops of black ink. Her hands and fingers are in almost constant motion, like two birds fluttering around her as she talks.

Prospero, 2E. A professor at NYU, "rapt in secret studies." He doesn't look much like an academic, dressed in a warm-up jacket and striped athletic pants, as if he'd just come from the gym. He sports one of those carefully curated quarter-inch beards, to match an aquiline nose and high cheekbones. He's been listening to the group but so far has said nothing.

Wurly, 3A. He sits on a piano bench that he lugs up and down every night. I figure he must be the guy who plays the Wurlitzer with the sound turned low. Shaved glossy head, big beard, deep brown eyes, quiet way of speaking. He gives off the feeling of the sort of man you can trust. "He is Wurly, whose tears become notes."

The Poet, 4B. "He is the Poet, who writes graffiti on the soul" is what the bible says. He's a lanky man, about forty, restless face with a wise-ass look on it, a sort of mocking half smile at the world.

La Cocinera, 6C. "Sous-chef to fallen angels." I can't tell quite what this description means, but she's another strikingly tall woman, long dark hair, who spends her time on the roof hunched over and messing with her phone.

Pardi and Pardner, 6E. Mother and daughter. "The Midnight Special shines its light on them" is the bible's comment. I have seen the mother but no sign of the daughter. Perhaps she's hiding away from Covid, like Vinegar's pregnant daughter.

Darrow, 3D. Super tall, maybe six feet six, in a suit, white starched shirt, cuff links, and silk tie with the knot drawn tight. I figure with that getup, he must be in Zoom meetings all day, or maybe he's just the kind of person who likes to dress up. Wilbur's bible says, "His secrets become cicatrices."

So that's who was on the roof tonight, and it was quite a large group, although less than half had spoken up. I suppose I was among the silent observers.

We were beginning to fall into a rhythm on the roof. People would start gathering about fifteen minutes before seven; we'd mostly be in place by seven sharp to join in the evening cheer; and then an hour later, the bells of Old St. Pat's would nudge the evening to a close.

A leaden sky had covered the city that day, filling the streets with a dreary twilight. In the morning I mopped the hallways, as I'm supposed to do every day, and it pissed me off that people who seem so connected on the rooftop just pass me by with only a nod. I do think some of them don't like me, or maybe are a little suspicious. The building is hopeless—broken windows, cockroaches, and lousy, burn-your-lungs-up heat at random times of day, but with this coronavirus I can't get people in to fix anything, or even order parts. My store of lightbulbs is running out, and I'm down to the last roll of duct tape. Without anything else useful to do, and still unable to reach my dad, I spent the afternoon going through the super's accordion file of random manuscripts. It was a catalog of strange and pointless stuff, but sort of fascinating nonetheless. It gave me the suspicion he went through recycling and trash and pulled out things. I have to admit, when I was working for my dad, I sometimes did the same thing. I once found some cash in the recycling. No discarded money yet here at Fernsby. When I first got here, while inspecting one of the abandoned apartments upstairs— the tenant, I think, went to the Hamptons—I did find a hilarious letter balled up on the floor. I smoothed it out and added it to the accordion files—feeling a little guilty at having taken it, but, honestly, who's ever going to know?

Tonight, our flickering rooftop candles could hardly beat back the darkness. And the wind! A sudden gust blew some wet leaves across the roof, dancing and flipping them over and over. It also snuffed out some candles. The sirens seemed almost continuous. As people relit their candles, I recorded the day's brutal statistics. Today was another day where 911 calls exceeded 9/11. The system is overwhelmed. The number of cases in the world topped one million. The stories coming out of Italy are terrifying, with doctors triaging patients choking to death. Apparently, the Italians have decided to let people over eighty die because they're running out of ventilators. They say we're three weeks away from the same situation. Cuomo ordered the National Guard to seize ventilators and PPE from hospitals and clinics in low-Covid areas upstate to redistribute them to hospitals here in the city. And I read a horrific prediction from the CDC: that in the United States alone, as many as fifty thousand people might die before the pandemic is over. Just imagine: *fifty thousand* dead. New York State has already recorded a total 102,863 cases with almost three thousand deaths. It's Friday, but at this point the days of the week are smearing into sameness. I've been calling my dad nonstop, with no results. I'm exhausted and sick with anger.

This evening there were more tenants on the roof, everyone fussing to keep the six-foot—or more—distance in a random collection of kitchen chairs, stools, milk crates, a bucket, even a beanbag. Not to mention Wurly's piano bench. A lot of the chairs were just left up there, to be rained on, I guess. Eurovision, on the other hand, had gone in the opposite direction and replaced his lawn chair with an antique chair of carved mahogany with gilded accents and a plush velvet seat, covered with clear plastic like in a grandmother's living room in Queens. He placed this quasi-throne in the center of the rooftop, forcing the rest of us to socially distance around the periphery. Vinegar parked her director's chair nearest to him, but not too close.

She was wearing as a mask a crude piece of cloth with shoestrings, which muffled her voice. Her eyes looked worried, and I wondered how things were going with Carlotta, the daughter.

After everyone had arrived and set themselves up, Vinegar looked us over. "I assume we've all had time to appreciate the new *artwork*?"

We all looked over at the communal mural. Someone had spray-painted a poop emoji next to the Heinz vinegar bottle.

"I think we can all guess who the anonymous da Vinci is," said Vinegar, her eyebrow cocked.

"That's disgusting," said Eurovision. "It shouldn't be too hard to cover." He stood and took a step toward the box of art supplies.

"Now you leave it alone," interrupted the Lady with the Rings. "Everyone's got to be free to express themselves up here, or else what's the point? Yes, even Miss Thing," she added, with a pointed look at Vinegar. "What we should do is *add* to the mural, not censor it."

At that moment, the distant cacophony of the seven o'clock cheering emerged from the city in all directions and grew rapidly, like an approaching train. We joined in.

After the noise died down, Eurovision remained standing. He cleared his throat and looked around and clasped his hands together, like someone who'd just emerged on a stage. I could tell from the little curl in his lips that a wicked idea was brewing.

"As I lay in bed last night," he began in a public voice, "I was thinking about the stories that we've heard over the past few nights. And then I thought that maybe we should *all* be telling stories."

He paused and looked around again, even to those sitting in the outer darkness. An uncomfortable silence fell. Nobody replied. *No way is this idea going to fly*, I thought.

"It seems to me," he went on, "that the price of admission to our rooftop refuge will be to tell a story. Each. One. Of. Us." He scanned the group with teacherly expectation.

"Who appointed you Den Mother?" said the Lady with the Rings.

This was seconded with an explosion of disapproving noises, shaking of heads, and the ostentatious insertion of earbuds.

"It's just an idea, for heaven's sake!" he said. "We've all got stories. Love, life, death, a reminiscence, a ghost story—anything!"

"I think," said the Therapist firmly, "that storytelling is a beautiful idea. A *very* beautiful idea."

Monsieur Ramboz cried out, "I do, too! A most excellent idea!"

"*Thank you*," said Eurovision, as if this decided things. "And, to show that I'm a fair person, I'll begin with my own story. A true story. It's a sort of funny story—or maybe not so funny. About an adoption."

He gave a dramatic pause to be sure enough of us were paying attention, took a deep breath, and began.

"So this couple I know, Nate and Jeremy, they were trying to adopt this baby. I say 'trying' because there was nothing easy about the process. They'd been burned before, a couple of years back—they'd had a toddler placed with them for six months, foster-to-adopt, you know? The two of them were totally gaga over that boy by the end of the first week. So was Jeremy's mom, she lived only three subway stops away and had always wanted to be a grandma. In spite of all the warnings about 'protect your heart,' she was all in from day one.

"What the social workers hadn't been clear about was that this couple's chances of getting to keep this particular boy were minimal. The family situation was so complicated: the mom's mother was making a claim, and the dad wasn't entirely out of the picture, plus it wasn't a 'cultural match' . . . And afterward, what pissed my friends off wasn't so much that they'd had to give him back—that broke their hearts, but whatever, they'd signed up for this—it was that they got the sense the social workers had misled them just to get them to agree to a short-term placement.

"Anyway, once they'd had enough time to get over it, Jeremy persuaded Nate to sign up again. Jeremy's mom was such a cheerleader, totally encouraging—in fact, bordering on a nag, but you know, with the best of intentions.

"Turned out, they weren't as over it as they'd thought because they got flashbacks just looking at the website of the Bureau of Permanency Services—does it have to have such an Orwellian name, really?

"So they decided to try going private. They registered with an agency, filled in this super-detailed profile, and waited for a birth mom to pick their file from the heap. A whole year went by, not a peep. They realized they'd probably overestimated the gay-friendliness of the average unhappily pregnant New Yorker. Nate was trying to forget all about it, move on with his plans for his business, trips abroad, that kind of thing. But really, it's a ticking bomb, once you've filled in an application like that, begging for a kid: Who could possibly put it out of their mind?

"Then one day they got the call. A teenager had pulled out their file and slapped it on the top of her heap because, as she said, she had a thing for the gays.

"It all went so well, right through the pregnancy. All of us were excited for them and ultra-supportive. Nate and Jeremy told these great stories about how well they were bonding with the girl, what fun meals out they had with her, how she said she felt so at home in their apartment. They covered all her expenses—maternity clothes, cabs to appointments, got her counseling and an attorney. Of course they wanted to stay in contact after and let her be part of their family, as much or as little as she wanted. Frankly, they felt so freakin' grateful that she was going to give them her baby.

"Now they knew from the last time that everything could always fall through at the last minute, so when she didn't call them or the agency, around her due date, they tried to stay calm. Even when two weeks had passed, they weren't letting themselves lose their minds.

"Finally, they got the call. The social worker said that Mom—weird how they call her that, isn't it, as if it's their own mom they're talking about—that Mom had given birth one afternoon after school, super-fast in the bathroom at home before the ambulance could arrive, and that both she and the baby girl were doing fine.

"Jeremy burst into tears when he heard it was a girl, even though he'd have been just as_excited the other way—it just made it all so real.

"Next thing, the social worker startled them by saying the birth had actually happened last week, and Mom hadn't called anyone—not the agency, not her attorney—because she'd thought maybe she'd like to try raising this kid herself after all.

"My friends just froze when they heard that. But of course they understood and sympathized. How would anybody, least of all a teenager, know in advance how they'd feel after something like giving birth?

"But the social worker was happy to report—well, happy for them, Nate and Jeremy—that Mom had now changed her mind after what she said was the shittiest week of her life. The agency was offering her ongoing support, of course, but no, she said she was sure at this point, she wanted Jeremy and Nate to take the baby, like right away. She'd already signed the surrender, that's what they call the agreement to give up your parental rights.

"Apparently, when Jeremy's mom heard, she screamed.

"Well, I'll skip over the next forty-five days. That's how long it takes for the birth mother's consent to become irrevocable, in New York State; unless the mother signs the papers in front of a judge and with her attorney right there, she has a full month and a half to change her mind. Which seems only fair, because postpartum sounds like such a crazy time to be making any hard decisions.

"So by that point, Nate and Jeremy were blissed out but also totally strung out—not on drugs!—I mean, just exhausted from waking up every couple hours. Because even though they were meant to be taking turns, when a baby lets rip in an apartment, it's not as if one of you can manage to stay asleep. By the six-week mark, little Sophie (they'd named her for Jeremy's grandmother) had gained four pounds, she could follow you with her eyes, lift her head off the rug during tummy time, and she was producing these smiles that the baby book said were probably gas but, nah, they looked like real smiles to me. (We'd all met her at various brunches by now.)

"In the final week, Jeremy's mom Facebooked me to say she was organizing a party for midnight on the forty-fifth day—like, to mark the exact moment that Sophie was definitely, absolutely, legally going to be theirs forever. I was a bit surprised Jeremy was letting her handle it, because he's known for his party planning, but I figured he just had too much on his plate.

"So midnight on that Tuesday, about forty of us were standing in the street outside their building, with balloons, streamers, flowers, champagne, the works. Jeremy's mom buzzed their apartment, which is on the third floor.

"No answer.

"'Maybe they're getting the baby up,' somebody said. 'Diaper and a cute outfit and all.'

"So we all stood around chatting and joking some more.

"But I could tell Jeremy's mom was getting antsy. She kept pressing the buzzer.

"'Could they be out?' I asked.

"'Who goes out with their new baby at midnight, especially when they're having a party?' That was a woman I barely knew, in a tone I thought was more scornful than was called for.

"A friend of Nate's from the gym said he'd often push his daughter around the neighborhood in her stroller when she just couldn't settle, and it was easy enough to lose track of the time.

"We stared up and down the block.

"I had my phone out, but Jeremy's mom spotted me. 'No! I'll call him,' she said.

"'Jeremy?' she said into the phone. 'Damn, it's gone to voicemail. Jeremy, this is Mom, pick up!'

"Nothing.

"Next, someone tried Nate's phone, while someone else pushed the door buzzer a couple more times.

"No answer.

"It was as if the three of them had all been kidnapped by some psycho stalker. Maybe massacred!

"I tried to rein in my imagination.

"Was that a baby crying on a balcony above? At about third-floor level? I put back my head.

"'Nate?' I shouted. 'Jeremy? Yoohoo!'

"A long pause.

"Then the faces loomed over the railing. Jeremy had the baby on his chest in one of those carriers. The two guys looked down at us in—well, at the time I thought horror, but now maybe I'd say rage.

"Jeremy's mom put her hands in the air and shrieked, 'Surprise!'

"It was only then that the rest of us realized what she'd—what we'd all—done.

"To their credit, Nate and Jeremy did let us all come up to the apartment. And once they'd told the story from their point of view—their blind panic when they'd heard the buzzer at the stroke of midnight, how they were convinced it was the birth mom come to take Sophie back, how they knew they couldn't stop her legally or even ethically, but they just couldn't bear to open the door, how their phones had kept manically playing 'Staying Alive' and the Minions ringtones over and over, how Sophie had wept but not as hard as Nate, how they'd run out on the balcony to get away from the buzzer and their phones, how it had actually occurred to Jeremy (he was embarrassed to admit this) that it might end with the three of them leaping, Thelma-and-Louise-style, over the railing . . . Well, after all that, and Jeremy's mom's endless apologies for her thoughtlessness, they did open the champagne. Sophie spat up right across the glass coffee table, and it was, shall we say, a party to remember."

Eurovision stopped and looked around, beaming. It dawned on us that he was waiting for applause. So we clapped—it was a very good story, after all—and his whole face glowed with the pleasure of it.

"Thank you," he said. "Thank you."

I almost expected a bow. It was clear that having an audience was something he lived for, a lifeline that had been taken away by Covid. God, so much was being taken away by Covid.

"Now," he said, "who's next?"

"I'm not much of a storyteller," said a tall man near the edge of the circle. "But I've got a story about a baby, too." This was apartment 3D; the nattily dressed attorney Darrow, I assume after Clarence Darrow.

"Wonderful!" Eurovision clapped his hands together, so pleased with his idea.

I made sure my phone was adjusted and recording. Darrow began, his gentle southern accent drifting over the roof.

"I grew up on a cotton farm in Arkansas," he said.

"We were poor but the kind of poor where you don't know you're poor because everyone else is just as down and out as you are.

"The week before my brother was born, a heavy snowfall covered the farmlands of eastern Arkansas, giving us a white Christmas, our first ever.

"The snow-swept fields and roads promised to make the season even more magical; on the negative side, my mother was expecting her fourth child. As a sheltered six-year-old, I knew nothing about human reproduction and such matters were never discussed. But I remember thinking that a fourth child was completely unnecessary. There was hardly enough to go around to begin with.

"In those days, pregnant women went to great lengths to conceal what was becoming more and more obvious, but soon even I realized that things were getting serious. My sister was a nosy brat and, being a girl, knew far more than me and my clueless little brother. As we counted the days to Christmas, she gravely informed us that our mother might give birth around the same time we were expecting Santa Claus. This caused some concern. I'd memorized the Sears & Roebuck Christmas catalog and was not interested in managing expectations.

"Sure enough, upon leaving church on Christmas Eve, we were startled when Mom groaned painfully in the front seat and grabbed Dad's arm. Then she let go, and she seemed fine. Then she groaned again, though she tried her best to hide her discomfort.

"'She's in labor,' my sister whispered to me in the back seat.

"'What's that?' I asked. I'd been watching the skies for reindeer.

"She rolled her eyes and said, 'You're so stupid.'

"The cotton crop that fall had been another disappointment, and though we didn't know it, our parents were planning to leave the farm and move on to another life. Times were tough. A lot of bills were past due. There wasn't a spare dollar anywhere, but, somehow, they always managed to provide a wonderful Christmas.

"As soon as we got home, Dad cleverly informed us that a neighbor down the road had just spotted Santa. Enough said. We sprinted to our bedrooms, pulled on our pajamas, and turned out the lights. It was only eight o'clock.

"Within minutes, it seemed, Dad was back, turning on the lights and announcing that Santa had just left.

"Who cared if we had not actually had the chance to fall asleep? We raced to the den where the tree was glowing and surrounded by the toys we'd longed for.

"We had barely touched the spread that Santa had left behind when Dad announced that Mom was ready to go to the hospital and have a baby. She was lying on the sofa, trying gamely to enjoy the moment with us. Though she was obviously in distress, I wasn't that concerned. I had a shiny new Daisy BB gun, a set of Lincoln Logs, and an electric train, and I was preoccupied. When I didn't move fast enough, my father gave me a rather firm pat on the rear and told us there was no time to change clothes—just get in the car, pajamas and all.

"Dad gunned the engine, and the car began sliding. Mom barked at him; he barked back. Through the rear window I could see the little white farmhouse with its front window lined with sparkling Christmas lights that Dad had forgotten to turn off. Santa had just left. Our toys were inside. It seemed so unfair.

"My father was a reckless driver on a good day, but the thought of his wife giving birth in the front seat while his three children watched from the rear was more than he could handle. He was driving too fast on a frozen road, and after the car slid for the third or fourth time my mother snapped, 'I'm not having this baby in a ditch.'

"The hospital was thirty minutes away, and my grandparents lived on a farm halfway in between. Back in those days, folks had telephones, but they tried not to use them, especially if long distance was involved. Visits to relatives and friends were never cleared with an advance call. No sir. You just showed up whenever you wanted. The surprise was part of the ritual.

"My grandparents were certainly surprised when we came sliding down their driveway at nine o'clock at night, the horn honking frantically. By the time they staggered to the front porch in their pajamas, my father had us out of the car and scrambling to meet them. The hand-off took only seconds.

"My grandparents, Mark and Mabel, were salt-of-the-earth farm folks who lived off the land and, much more importantly, lived by the Holy Scripture—every literal word of it, and only in the version according to King James. My grandmother made hot chocolate while my grandfather built a roaring fire, the only source of heat in their old farmhouse. Huddled under a quilt and warmed by the fire, we listened as he read the story of Baby Jesus from his worn and beloved Bible.

"When we awoke the next morning, we were told

that our mother had given birth to a little boy shortly after midnight. Thus, he was indeed a Christmas baby. We really didn't care. We were just relieved that she was okay, and we wanted to get home to check out the rest of our toys.

"The following morning, during breakfast, we heard a car horn. My grandmother looked out the kitchen window and exclaimed, 'He's here.' We raced for the front door, across the porch, and down to the car where our mother sat, beaming, proudly holding her latest. She named him Mark.

"We loaded up and hurried home, where the Christmas lights were still on, where Santa's gifts were still scattered throughout the den. We immediately picked up where we'd left off before being so terribly interrupted.

"With snow on the ground, our father had little to do but hang around the house and play with us. He knew he would never plant another cotton crop, and I've often wondered if this was a relief or a fear. But, of course, we were sheltered from such conversations. Six weeks later, we abruptly left the farm, never, mercifully, to return. He found a good job with a construction company, one that moved us every summer to another small southern town.

"The following season, we waited with great anticipation for the arrival of the Sears & Roebuck Christmas catalog. Within hours, we made our lists of wishes, lists that invariably began much too long and were slowly whittled down by our parents. When Santa made a surprise visit to my second-grade classroom, I told him, in all seriousness, that I wanted this and I wanted that, but what I really did not want was another brother for Christmas."

As Darrow finished speaking, Eurovision leapt up and led the acclaim, clapping, nodding, and beaming. "Who said you couldn't tell a story? Good, good!" He looked around, and I could see he was searching for another victim among the reluctant ones at the back of the audience, all of whom were suddenly pretending a great interest in their phones.

"Come on, folks! Who's next?" His eye wandered across the nervous group before coming to rest on me. "I reckon our super has some interesting stories to tell about this place."

I was shocked and temporarily paralyzed by panic. I shook my head. "I've only been here for a few weeks."

He looked at me askance. "But in your previous building?"

"I worked at Red Lobster. Nothing happens at Red Lobster."

Again that sideways look. "Well, we'll get back to you, then. I think we're all a little curious about you."

"Curious? Why?" His penetrating look made me nervous, almost like he suspected me of something. I could see a certain level of distrust, or at least wariness, in the faces of the others. I worked so hard to be invisible, it was a shock to think they had opinions about me.

"Well," said Eurovision. "You have to admit you're not exactly what we're all, uh, used to in a super."

"Oh. Right. Because I'm not a man?"

"No, no, no. It's just— Well, a little bit. Yes."

I had to laugh at the look on his face. I was tempted to leave him squirming, but instead, to get the focus off of me, I said, "I'll tell a story, I promise. Just give me time." I wondered if there was something in Wilbur's stash of stories I could pretend was my own. The last thing I was ever going to do was tell these strangers *my own* secrets.

"Fair enough."

"No freeloaders!" Vinegar said. "Everyone who listens, tells."

"I have a story," said Amnesia. She was wearing an array of distressed clothing, with acid stains and paint and ragged knife cuts, like she'd just been hauled out of the rubble of a collapsed building. Back in Vermont, my girlfriend and I had played the *Amnesia* computer game. It's about someone who wakes up in a desert and can't remember anything about her previous existence and is pursued by ghouls and demons and curses. It had been pretty cool, at least until the theme hit a bit too close to home.

"Thank you," said Vinegar decisively, settling back to listen.

"All my life," Amnesia began, "I've had this dream about a woman. It's not a nightmare, not exactly, but it's unsettling because it's always the exact same. I'm in a yard. It's summer. In front of me is a huge dark house with white shutters, curtains drawn over every window except one. That's where she is, the woman, standing darkly in the white frame and looking right at me. She has a scar on her cheek and a little gold cross at her neck, and I know that doesn't sound scary, but the thing is, she never smiles. Like, most people, they see you, they smile, right? But she just stares at me with this hollow face, and that's usually when I wake up.

"I told my mom about it once when I was a kid, and she got super intense about it. *How old was the woman? How big was the scar? What was she wearing? What kind of house? What state was it in?*—like we were trying to find someone who'd been kidnapped. I remember because she was digging her nails into my arm even though we were at the Waffle House and it was after church and everyone could see. And my dad said, 'Let it go, Kath.' Firm, like he would actually do something if she didn't.

"You know how in relationships, one person takes up more space? That's them. Like, if my mom's the sun, my dad is Mercury or something—small and way too close to her to be anything but uncomfortable. Sanjay and I used to joke that the only reason they were together at all is because she got pregnant with me and then him, but now I think we just turned the truth into a joke so we could say it out loud. My parents don't have any stories about how they met, or what their first dates were like, or anything. You ask them, and they just say, 'Oh, we met at TCU,' like the rest is inevitable, like a man who'd left everyone he knew in Tamil Nadu to study was of course going to end up married in Lubbock.

"Anyway, I never brought up the woman from the dream again. It made my mom too upset, and the truth is, I did that all on my own. I didn't know why. You've seen those commercial moms who cry at ballet performances and put Band-Aids on skinned knees and such? My mom tried all that with me, but it was like she just couldn't. She'd grit her teeth when she hugged me, or wince when I laughed, or leave the room if I started crying. She was different with Sanjay—she'd get all 'soft cow eyes' around him, hug him for no reason at all. She even said once to Mrs. Hewson, when she didn't know I was in the next room, that she knew she wasn't supposed to have favorites, but Sanjay was just easier for her, he didn't need her as much. Mrs. Hewson laughed and said that's just because she and I were too alike—people said this all the time, us with the pale hair and potato chins, Sanjay and my dad dark and birdy—but my mom said, '*She and I are nothing alike*,' and Mrs. Hewson didn't say a thing after that.

"Sanjay was seven the Easter Mom fell apart. I was twelve. We whispered about it for years afterward, like it was a favorite movie we weren't supposed to have seen. How it was extra nuts because Mom was always her most perfect self at First Baptist, always smoothing something into place, and squaring the programs, and treating everyone like they were in her living room just because she was one of the Greeters. The night before, she'd laid out two yellow dresses and two navy suits so we looked like some terrible dollhouse family come to life: light/dark/light/dark, sitting in the second-to-last pew, where she could keep an eye on the door.

"We were miserable that morning. That part I remember, too—how she'd yelled at us the whole way in the car about embarrassing her in front of everyone even though we hadn't gotten there yet, how she frowned in the rearview mirror and asked twice if I'd remembered to wear deodorant. Sometimes it felt like the only thing to do was hope for something bigger than you would come along, take her eyes off you. So when Pastor Mitchell boomed, 'He is risen! He is risen!,' the relief I felt was real. His voice filled us up, throat to waist, and for a minute it felt like the whole ceiling might crack into one of those goldeny heaven murals.

"That's when Mom stood up. Fast, like maybe she, maybe she'd forgotten something, her fists balled by her sides. But then she started walking slowly in the wrong direction. One step and then another and then another, right down the center aisle. And no one knew what to do because this was Kathleen Blair Varghese, the one who was always putting everyone else in line, so what was she doing inching toward the podium like she'd been called to it? Even Pastor Mitchell looked confused, waiting until she'd stopped right in front of him to say, 'You okay, Kathleen?'

"She said something. We couldn't hear her. Then she said it again. 'My mother is dead.'

"Little murmurs curled up from the pews and then my dad stood up, too, even though he usually tried to get through church without anyone noticing him. It wasn't that people were mean on purpose, just they

were always saying little things like, 'Well, here in Lubbock, we celebrate Christmas with the Carol of Lights,'
like he wouldn't know after fifteen years. Anyway, he
walked quick and reached for my mom's arm, and when
she turned and looked at him, everyone gasped. She
was panting like a dog. Her whole face was red and wet.

"'She's gone, Arvin,' she said. 'She's gone and she's
never coming back.'

"'Grandma Cindy?' Sanjay whispered, eyes big because we spent every Saturday afternoon with Grandma
Cindy, smoking candy cigarettes on the lawn while she
smoked real ones.

"'No,' I said, because Mom and Dad were coming
back down the aisle with all those eyes on them, and
then on me, and then on Sanjay, and what was I supposed to say anyway? What did I know back then? Dad
opened the door to the vestibule and gave us a look,
and we slid out and followed them. And then we were
all standing outside. Just like that, the four of us in the
sun with the noise of sprinklers and the smell of water
on hot cement.

"'Is Grandma okay?' Sanjay said. I looked at Dad
and Dad looked at Mom and Mom's mouth stretched
into a dark hall before she slammed a hand over it.

"'Is she?' Sanjay said again, his voice kicking high,
and my dad took out his phone. It rang a few times,

and then Grandma Cindy was yelling through the convertible wind that she'd have to call back when she'd pulled over. Dad hung up. We all looked at Mom. Mom looked like an outline of herself.

"In the car on the way home, Dad held her hand whenever he wasn't shifting, which was the second strangest thing we'd seen all day. She went to bed once we got there and stayed in it all night. Grandma Cindy came to see her, and afterward she and my dad talked in the driveway for three cigarettes, but we couldn't hear them without opening a window. I thought maybe they were talking about having her sent to Sunrise Canyon because that's what happened to Laura Gibson's mom after she lost the baby, but the next morning when I got up, Mom was at breakfast same as always, making toaster waffles, and checking under our nails, and walking us to the bus five minutes early. The following Sunday at church, she slammed away the looks of concern so hard that everyone got a little disoriented, like maybe they'd just imagined the whole thing. I probably would have thought the same if Sanjay hadn't seen it, too, if it hadn't become the thing we whispered about as kids and then laughed about as adults because, honestly, what was more Kathleen than our mother interrupting Easter sermon to say Grandma Cindy was dead and everyone being too scared of her to ever bring it up again?

"We held Mom's funeral at First Baptist last year. None of the rest of us had gone for years, what with Dad's hip and Sanjay's living in Austin and me being out here, but it didn't matter—the ladies from her Wednesday prayer group who'd been taking turns driving her to chemo pulled everything together. All we had to do was walk in and collect the condolences. Pastor Mitchell's replacement gave her eulogy, forgetting to mention how Mom organized the Sunday school picnic, and was the first candle lit in the living Christmas Tree, but when we sang 'Abide with Me'—her favorite—I felt her approval all around us. Afterward, a few people came by the house with frozen dishes, and then it was just over, a whole life folded neat like a tablecloth, ready to be put away.

"But we couldn't, right? We couldn't. You live your whole life with someone that big, and it doesn't matter if you're the one she forgot to love, or didn't know how to love, or loved too much, you still feel her everywhere. I didn't miss her yet, not like I do now, but I could tell Dad and Sanjay did, so I poured us Jameson in the nice tumblers, and then we were sitting around the kitchen table, trading all the batshit stuff she ever did. Remember the time she ironed our sweatpants? Remember when she called the neighbor's dog *a walking bowel movement*? Remember when she made the guy paint the whole porch again because that squirrel ran across the corner and she said the new paint wouldn't dry the same color? Remember when she told all of First Baptist Grandma Cindy died? We were laughing the way you laugh about a thing when you're trying to forgive it for scaring you.

"'In the middle of the Easter sermon! And no one said a thing!' Sanjay said.

"'Nothing to see here, folks.' I made usher hands. 'Just a grown woman announcing the death of her mother who is . . . not dead!'

"'Grandma Cindy'—Dad started, but we were laughing too hard to hear him; he waited until we calmed down to say—'wasn't her mother.'

"He said it like that, like he was telling us any other thing about Grandma Cindy. *Grandma Cindy liked her younger men. Grandma Cindy and the damn lottery. Grandma Cindy only went to Costco on samples day.*

"'What?' I said.

"'Her birth mother lived in Oklahoma City,' Dad said.

"Sanjay and I looked at each other. Sanjay said, 'Dad, are you fucking with us right now?'

"Dad pointed at me with his chin. 'You met her once, when you were just a few months old. Barbara. Barb. She said call her Barb. She drove all the way here and got lunch with us at La Quinta and then went home that night.'

"'To Oklahoma City?' I said, like that was the weird part.

"'She was married and had more children by then. She was scared, I think, that they might find out, that the husband might find out. She showed us their pictures. The girls looked like your mother.' Dad looked at me. 'Like you.'

"You know how sometimes someone will tell you a thing, and all these little levers and dials just start clicking in you because you got back a part you didn't even know was missing? My dad said '*like you*,' and my whole body started vibrating. Sanjay looked sick.

"'That was the woman that died?' he said.

"My dad nodded. 'She had it, too. The ovarian cancer.'

"'But how did Mom—'

"'I don't know.'

"'Had she been in touch with her?'

"'No.'

"'Then how did you guys know what day she—'

"'We didn't right away. We read it in the obituary later.'

"'But you guys never *talked* about it?'

"'What was there to talk about?'

"'Was Barb . . . was she . . .' I didn't even know what I wanted to ask, really. 'Nice?'

"You wouldn't think it would hurt, that question, but somehow it did. My dad was quiet a long time before saying, 'She was young.'

"Then he starts rattling off all these numbers. Barb was fifteen when she had my mom. Barb saw her for only two hours before Grandma Cindy came to the home to pick her up. Mom was twenty-three when she started looking for her. It took them a year to find her and another three months to negotiate where and how they'd meet. And I'm quiet, thinking about how Mom must have started looking for her own mom a few months before she got pregnant with me, and heard from her about the time I was born. Sanjay was straight angry though. He starts in on Dad about how he can't believe they never told us, that he can't believe this is the way we're finding out, and then my dad starts yelling, too.

"'It didn't matter!' Dad said. 'This woman comes and eats one lunch and holds the baby and cries to your mother about all the time she lost and how she will be back soon, but she never comes back! She never calls and she never writes and she moves and never tells your mother where, so what's to tell?' His face was hot and panicky and bunched up like a kid's, and that's when I knew for sure that he really did love her.

"'What home?' I said.

Dad looked confused.

"'Grandma Cindy came and got her from a home. What home?'

"And that's when he started to tell me the rest, but I already knew, you know? I knew even before he said 'Florence Crittenton House for Women' and 'Little Rock, Arkansas,' before I googled it and blew up the small picture on my phone until I was looking right into that white-framed window in a dark house. It was empty in the picture, but I knew."

I didn't even want to look at Amnesia at the end of this story. I just stared at my drink. Goose bumps. It made me think of my own mother, whom I've hated ever since she abandoned us. My most vivid memory of her isn't even a memory of *her*; it's a memory of Dad sobbing and telling me she'd gone back to Romania. That was the first and last time I ever saw him cry. (Except in February, when I visited him right after I first dropped him off. Dad thought I was his mama and began crying and begging me to take him home, that this was not a good school, that he missed Zbura, his pet starling. But that doesn't count toward his lifetime crying total because he has dementia.) I don't cry either—not crying runs in the family. I haven't cried since I was ten and broke my arm roller blading down Poyer Street. Not that there's anything wrong with crying, if that's your thing. It's just not for me. Dracula didn't cry either.

"That's a ghost story," said Darrow.

Amnesia shook her head. "No. It's a story about connections. We're under the illusion that we're separate beings, but underneath, we're metaphysically connected."

"That's too deep for me," said Vinegar. "I don't *want* to be connected to most people—just my children, Charlotte and Robbie, and only then sometimes."

"I think it's a story about the stoicism of women," said the Lady with the Rings, turning toward Amnesia, but Eurovision broke in.

"*Please.* Let's not overanalyze one another's stories," he said. "This isn't a lit class. So—who's next?"

"As long as we're on the subject of stoicism and death," said Lala, sweeping us with her huge black eyes, "I have a story." She leaned forward, hands clasped and then opening, eager, even desperate to tell it. She adjusted her seat—a tall stool that she perched on like a nervous bird—propped her hands on her knees, and in a small but intense voice began to speak while looking at the surface of the roof, as if she were speaking to herself instead of the group.

"It happened a few years ago, before I moved to New York.

"I was still working that Friday night, though getting ready to shut things down, since it was after three a.m. When the phone rang, I looked at the caller ID and saw my father-in-law's number come up. My father-in-law is eighty, my mother-in-law eighty-four, and both in fairly feeble health, so I was already mentally preparing to go out to meet the emergency when I picked up the phone.

"It was my father-in-law, Max himself, though; he said that my stepmother's sister had just called him, being unable to reach me (in the stress of the moment, they must have been calling an old phone number)—my dad was at Good Samaritan Trauma Center, and that was all Max knew.

"I woke my husband—scaring him out of a sound sleep—and got dressed, thinking as I did so that I must take a warm sweatshirt, because hospital waiting rooms are always cold, and no telling how long I might be there. I promised to call home as soon as I found out anything, promised not to drive too fast, repelled the efforts of the dog, who wanted to go with me—I didn't know how long he might be left in the car alone—and left.

"I was driving carefully, all right, but in that state of nervous agitation attendant on being pulled out of the solitude of the night to face unknown anxieties. I was praying, of course, in the unformed fashion one does in the face of such things. And then, some distance down the highway, that stopped.

"The praying stopped, the agitation stopped, the anxiety disappeared. It was 3:26 by the dashboard clock, which is always two minutes slow. I never saw the death certificate, but I don't need to.

"Everything was simply . . . still.

"I was still driving; a car passed by me now and then. The lights went by, I took note of the road signs, but my heartbeat and my breathing had gone back to that state of quiet solitude from which I'd come. I tried to form a prayer, but the words wouldn't come. Not that I couldn't think of them, but that there was no need; whatever I would have asked had already been answered.

"Everything was just . . . peaceful.

"I sometimes feel my mother near me, sometimes summoned, sometimes not. She isn't always there when I call, but always comes again, sometime. I reached for her, in the middle of the stillness, and felt her there, but it wasn't she who answered me.

"I daresay I haven't thought of my grandmother Inez

once in ten years, if that. She was very old when I was born, died when I was eleven (I remember only because she died on my birthday). We saw her once a year, pro forma: a tiny old lady who smelled funny and spoke no English. We learned a few Spanish phrases, which we repeated to her like Latin prayers in church; understood, but with little sense of communication.

"She came into my mind then, though. White-haired, but with her face quite young—and with what appeared to be her own teeth, rather than her dentures, I noticed.

"'*Somos duras*,' she said to me, and then, 'Somos.'

"'Dura' is a word that means hard. Depending on the usage, it means everything from difficult or painful (things are hard) to tough and resilient—strong. 'Somos' means 'we are.'

"'Okay,' I said.

"I reached the hospital and parked in the visitors' lot. There was no need for hurry, and I didn't want to take space that might be needed near the Emergency entrance. It was a gentle night, very balmy. I passed a woman sitting on a bench outside the Outpatient Surgery Department, smoking. I smiled at her and nodded as I passed.

"I walked up the long ramp to the Emergency Trauma Center; it's on the second floor. Two of my stepmother's sisters were standing outside, crouched over their cellular phones like Secret Service agents. I touched one on the shoulder and she turned; her face crumpled up with grief and she embraced me, squeezing hard and thumping my back.

"'It's okay,' I said, after a little of this. 'I'm all right.'

"'*I'm* not!' she said, and clung to me, sobbing, as we went in.

"'Somos duras,' said my grandmother again.

"I saw his feet first. They're just like mine; short and wide, remarkably small in proportion to his body. I don't have sparse black hairs on my toes, and he had a chronic nail condition that made his toenails thick and yellow. The same round heel, though, and short, high arch; the broad, short toes that point up just a little, when the foot is at rest—ugly feet, but happy feet.

"There were several people around him; he was lying on a gurney, half covered by a flannel sheet. My stepmother was there, holding his hand; I took no notice of the others. I needed to see his face.

"He looked as he always did when asleep; he had a habit of falling asleep watching television. In the years after my mother died, before he married again, I would always get up at midnight when I was in the house with him, to wake him and tell him to go to bed. I think he was afraid to go to bed alone.

"His ears were faintly purple. My son has his ears; a smooth clamshell with a fleshy lobe. There was a deep crease across each lobe; I'd read somewhere that that's an indication of a predisposition to heart disease.

"I had thought I would be seized by grief at the sight of him, and was surprised to feel instead the most peculiar sense of . . . completion. He was a happy man, for the most part, but not in any way a peaceful one; he had jagged edges that crossed his personality like fissures through a glacier. Always restless, always moving. A vicious and accomplished hater, a bearer of implacable grudges. Now that was finished. Not gone, exactly, but *finished.* Now he had a peace that he had always missed; he was complete.

"'Somos,' said my grandmother, very softly, and I knew what she meant.

"My stepmother embraced me, and I her.

"'What happened?' I said. She said she'd gone to bed at midnight; Dad followed her a little later. She woke about a quarter to three, because his breathing had changed; he was snoring very heavily. She poked him to roll over, and it changed again, to 'horrible noises.' She turned on the light, saw his face, and knew something was wrong; ran to the front bedroom to get her sister and brother-in-law, who were visiting from California.

"They ran back and did CPR while my stepmother called 911. They live only a few blocks from a major hospital, so the paramedics arrived in two minutes. They worked on him there, and on the way to the ER, managed to (she said) restart 'part of his heart muscle' but could not revive him.

"The unknown man at my father's head came to shake hands with my stepmother, explaining that my father had been 'nice and warm' when he arrived; everything was all right. The priest, come to give the last anointing; there is a popular supposition that if the body is at least warm, the soul is still close enough to benefit.

"He was still warm; everyone had a hand on his body: bare shoulder, hand, or the huge round mound of his stomach—he was always overweight, but carried it all there. I laid a hand on him, too, for a minute. Then looked up and realized that I was looking at my uncle Albert, who lives in Albuquerque; my father's last surviving brother, also my godfather. I hadn't noticed him at first, because he looks like my father—all the brothers had a strong facial resemblance. It seemed completely unremarkable to see my father lying down and standing up, simultaneously.

"Under the rather surreal circumstances, it first seemed quite natural for Albert to be there. Ours is a very large family, and all through my youth, whenever someone died, all the relatives would gather, going from Albuquerque to California or back the other way; they'd all stay briefly at our house, as Flagstaff is midway. Then it dawned on me that my father had been dead for less than half an hour; I knew it takes at least an hour to fly from Albuquerque.

"'What are you doing here?' I blurted, thinking a bit too late that I hoped this sounded only astonished, and not ungracious.

"He was solemn, but not outwardly upset. He's the last of the brothers, and in his seventies; he's seen a lot of death.

"'I was here,' he said, with a little shrug. He'd come, by coincidence—or not—for a New Year's visit. He and Dad stayed up all evening, talking and laughing, then went to bed at twelve thirty.

"My stepmother's sisters—three of them, by then— came and went, bringing Kleenex, cups of water. The hospital attendant came now and then, a quiet, compassionate young woman, bearing forms to be signed, questions to be answered.

"Which mortuary? Burial or cremation? And—she apologized, saying by law she had to ask us—would we consider organ donation?

"'Yes,' I said firmly, hands on my father's stomach.

I felt strongly about it; I could feel my stepmother hesitate. She is the kindest and gentlest of people—no one else could have stayed married to my father—but consequently she can be bullied. I would have done it, if I had to, but she said yes.

"'But are they usable?' I asked, glancing down at him. 'He's sixty-seven.'

"'I don't know,' the young woman said, frowning uncertainly. 'I'll check.' She did. The corneas, she said; they could use the eyes and corneas.

"The sisters touched him constantly, exclaiming every so often, 'He's still warm here!' and clutching whichever part it was (my father's often-expressed opinion to my stepmother—frequently given in their hearing—was, 'Your sisters are very good people, *but*').

"I stood aside a little. They asked if I wanted to be alone with him for a little while, and I said no. It wasn't necessary. It wasn't necessary to touch the body again; I had no feeling that this was my father. I knew exactly where he was; he was with me, with his wives, with his brother, with his mother. Somos. We are.

"I was not upset at all, though I wept now and then in sheer emotional reaction. After a time, it became clear that there was nothing more to do—and yet it seemed impossible to leave. Albert said quietly that he would go back to the house and rest. More of my stepmother's family came—she has a huge family, too, all very loyal and supportive.

"I looked very carefully. What of his features remained in me and my children, those I could still see. But what was unique, that I must remember now, because I would never see again? My hands are his, as well as the feet; my sister has his eyes. The swell of broad shoulders I've seen in my son since his birth; my youngest daughter shares the shape of his calves.

"At last the young woman came back and said softly but firmly that she would need to take him now, 'to finish taking care of him.' I touched one foot, said, 'Goodbye, Dad,' and walked out without looking back.

"Out in the waiting room, we met the young man from the organ-donor program and went with him to fill out the necessary forms. I have had few experiences more surreal than sitting in a consultation room at five in the morning, answering questions as to whether my father had ever accepted money or drugs for sex, or had sex with another man.

"The answers (no, by the way—or at least not so far as *I* know) all proving satisfactory, we left at last. I prevented any of the sisters from coming with me, with some difficulty, and headed home across the dark city. It seemed important to get home before the night ended, maybe because I thought it might seem more real by daylight.

"So now there are rips and rawnesses, surges of grief that catch at throat and belly. All the difficulties and distractions of dealing with sudden death.

"And yet I remember, and reach to touch that great stillness, like a smooth stone in my pocket.

"Somos.

"I was . . . astonished."

Merenguero's Daughter was watching the storyteller, nodding, clearly moved, murmuring something about la familia. I could tell none of us on the rooftop wanted to break the spell Lala had just cast. Into the silence intruded a faraway siren, of course, as always, with its whisper of distant pain. I thought of how, all through the city, right now, people were being ripped from their loved ones. Fathers and uncles and sisters-in-law were dying all around us, on ventilators or worse. The way she described her father—his ugly, happy feet—God, it made me ache for my dad.

"What a story" came a woman's voice from across the roof. "Thank you for sharing it. It's such a reminder of what we're losing, keeping people away from their loved ones as they die. The loss of those last touches, the hands on the warm body. It's heartbreaking."

She was right. From where I was sitting I couldn't see who it was, but she spoke for all of us. This damn coronavirus wasn't just stripping away our ability to be together in life but also to be together at the moment of death, to say our goodbyes. A terrible thought passed through my mind before I could stamp it out: a wish that my father had died before this pandemic hit at all.

No. I would find a way to see him again.

Eurovision had turned to the new speaker, his eager-emcee smile looking a bit frozen at this point in the evening. "Welcome," he said, a little too cheerfully. "I'm not sure we've met. Which, uh, apartment are you in?"

"2C."

I was a little surprised. My bible listed 2C as empty. I hadn't recorded her arrival on the roof that evening, either—she must've slipped past me, or joined us late. Her ponytail, lack of makeup, collared shirt, and preppy LL Bean plaid skirt looked out of place, especially here on the hipster Lower East Side. Plus, she was wearing a mask—an actual surgical mask. Where the hell did she get her hands on one of those?

"I just got here," she said, a little nervously. "I'm from Maine."

"Maine?" Eurovision asked, as if she had just declared her arrival from Outer Mongolia. "And you moved to *New York City* during a *pandemic?* Are you crazy?"

"Maybe I am," Maine said with a little laugh. "I'm a visiting ER doc, right around the corner. At Presbyterian Downtown. I was surprised to land this apartment so close, actually. I volunteer through a program of medical workers coming to New York to assist with the Covid-19 crisis."

"Oh," said Eurovision, "sorry, I didn't mean to— Thank you. Really. *Thank you!*" He said this—in complete sincerity—while also moving his chair back bit by bit, trying to look nonchalant. It's not like I could blame him. Looking around, I could see others pretending to adjust their chairs, giving delicate little coughs as an excuse to cover their mouths, all the time quietly backing away. Taking stock of their distance from her. I don't think the mask was making anyone feel any better. I realized I, too, was leaning back a bit harder against my red sofa.

"You're one of the people we're cheering for every night!" said the Lady with the Rings, with an edge of extra enthusiasm, as if to cover the rising tension.

"All except Vinegar," said Florida acidly.

"That's *Jennifer*, and I am thankful. Of course I am. Very thankful. I just don't think banging on pots and hollering is a decent way to thank anyone." She glared at Florida and then turned to smile at Maine.

Maine nodded, unperturbed by our nervousness. "My story is also about the end of life." She paused. "Perhaps it isn't appropriate? Given how much we're surrounded by death these days."

"It's not like we can keep ourselves from dying by not talking about it," said Vinegar, patting her knees decisively, "no more than we can get rich by not paying our bills. They come due when they come due." She raised her chin and looked around at the rest of us. "So you go ahead and tell your story, because nothing's off-limits on this rooftop." Was it my imagination, or had these past few days of storytelling softened even Vinegar a bit?

Maine gathered herself up, speaking louder than the others had, perhaps to make up for the muffling of that surgical mask.

"This, too, is a true story. I hesitate to share it, because I am a person of science, trained to believe only in what can be tested and confirmed using rigorous scientific methods, and this story is about what cannot be proved. Some of you won't believe me, and why should you? I am new to your building, just the temporary tenant in 2C, and since I never leave my apartment without a mask, you've never even seen my face. While you hide safely inside this building, I step out every day to meet the enemy. And when I return after my shift in the hospital, I'm sure you worry that perhaps I've brought the enemy home on my clothes, on my hands, in the air I exhale. I know this is why you avoid me; it's because you're afraid, and no wonder. With every ambulance that screams by, you're reminded that death is right outside the doorstep. You can feel it, smell it, circling closer and closer.

"Just as Sister Mary Francis once could.

"She was a nurse in the Catholic hospital where I worked thirty years ago. She belonged to the Franciscan order, what I think of as the 'friendly' nuns, and Mary Francis was certainly that: round-cheeked, smiling, a dark-eyed little dumpling of a woman who wore clunky orthopedic shoes beneath her white nun's habit. At forty-something, she had the serene face of a woman who's at peace with the choices she's made in life. She was one of a dozen Franciscan nuns who worked as nurses in the hospital, and initially, I didn't pay any particular attention to Mary Francis.

"Then I discovered her secret gift.

"I first encountered it during morning rounds, when we medical interns accompanied the senior physician as he visited patients on the ward. As we approached one of the rooms, I saw Sister Mary Francis standing outside the door with her head bowed. Quickly, almost furtively, she made the sign of the cross and then she walked away.

"'Uh-oh,' one of the other interns whispered. 'That's a bad sign.'

"'Why is it a bad sign?' I asked.

"'Because Sister Mary Francis always knows.'

"'Knows what?'

"'When someone's about to die.'

"It's not particularly difficult to ascertain that someone's about to die. It certainly doesn't require any supernatural talent. Any doctor can read the signs, whether it's a deepening coma or a stuttering heart rhythm, and I assumed that Mary Francis could simply recognize the same clues a physician would. But when we stepped into that room, we did not see a patient on her deathbed; instead, we saw a woman who looked very much alive, even chipper. She was scheduled for a coronary catheterization, and she expected to go home that afternoon.

"But the patient did not go home. A few hours later, during her catheterization, she suffered a cardiac arrest and died on the table.

"That's when I began to pay attention to Sister Mary Francis and her furtive little blessings. You had to be alert to catch her doing it because she did not make a big show of it. She'd simply pause to dip her head, sketch a cross in the air, and then she'd move on. A few days might go by, sometimes even a week, but whenever I saw Mary Francis perform that silent little ritual outside a patient's room, death inevitably paid a visit.

"I know you are all thinking exactly what I thought: that Sister Mary Francis was one of those homicidal nurses you read about in true crime stories, an angel of death who slips into a patient's room at night and smothers him with a pillow or injects him with a fatal dose of insulin. It's only natural to assume there must be a logical explanation, because the alternative is . . . well, there is no alternative. Not if you believe in science.

"So I kept my eagle eye on that nun. I noted which patients she singled out for her ominous blessing, and how and when those patients expired. There had to be a pattern, I thought, something that would reveal how she managed to ensure their deaths.

"Except there was no pattern. While some of those patients died during her shifts in the hospital, others died in the operating room where she did not work, or on days when she was not even in the building. Unless she'd found some way to commit murder by proxy, Sister Mary Francis could not have killed them.

"The mystery began to drive me crazy. I had to know how she did it.

"One afternoon, while she and I were sitting at the nurses' station, writing in charts, I finally found the nerve to ask her. Clearly she'd been asked that question before, because she did not even look up from her paperwork when she answered.

"'Death has an odor.'

"'What does it smell like?' I asked.

"'I can't really describe it.' She was silent a moment, thinking. 'It smells like the earth. Like wet leaves.'

"'Then it's not a bad smell?'

"'I wouldn't call it bad. It just is.'

"'And that's how you know someone's going to die? You smell it?'

"She shrugged, as if that ability were completely normal. To her it must have seemed so, because she'd been born with it. Whenever the door to the afterlife creaked open, she could catch the scent of what was approaching. She felt it was her duty to prepare the departing soul for its journey from this world to the next, and so she blessed them.

"I am not a superstitious person. I'll say it again: I believe in science, so how could I accept this mumbo jumbo? Yet my medical colleagues in that hospital believed that Sister Mary Francis really did have the gift, that she really could peer through the veil between life and death. Perhaps they'd worked for too many years in that creaky old building, which was generally acknowledged to be haunted. In such an institution, where ghosts are considered part of the ambience, it wasn't hard to believe that a Franciscan nun could smell death's approach.

"If there was a logical explanation, I could not find it. Yet I continued to be skeptical. I kept waiting for her to show her hand, to make a mistake.

"And one day I believed she did.

"I saw Mary Francis pause outside the door of a newly admitted patient. She was not the man's assigned nurse, and she had no reason to know who was even inside the room, but something made her stop. She bowed her head, made the sign of the cross, and walked on.

"A week went by and the man was still alive. Not just alive—he seemed to be in fine fettle. He'd had a minor heart attack, but his cardiac function and rhythm remained perfectly normal. On the day he was cleared to leave, I saw him walking in the hallway, smiling as he said goodbye to the staff. Sister Mary Francis has finally made a mistake, I thought. This man is definitely going home alive.

"Then 'Code Blue! Code Blue!' blared over the hospital speaker system. I sprinted down the hall to join the scrum of doctors and nurses trying to resuscitate a man who'd just collapsed. The same man who had smiled at me only moments before.

"Sister Mary Francis had been right. She had indeed caught the scent of death on him.

"It's been thirty years since I worked in St. Francis. The place no longer exists. Buildings, like people, have finite life spans, and that old hospital, ghosts and all, was demolished to make way for condominiums. I still think about Sister Mary Francis, especially these days. When I pass people on the street, I wonder which ones will show up in my emergency room with a cough and a fever, which ones I will have to intubate. Which ones will not make it, no matter how hard I work to save their lives. With so many desperately ill patients now pouring into my hospital, I sorely need a Mary Francis at my side. Someone who can tell me which lives I should fight to save, and which ones are already lost.

"If she is still alive, she would be in her seventies now. I like to imagine her enjoying her last days in a cozy home with her sister nuns. A place with good food and kindly attendants and a garden where roses bloom. In such a place, death would not necessarily be an unwelcome visitor. And when her end comes, as it's bound to, she will surely catch its scent. She'll know that this time, the door has opened for her.

"And she will smile as she walks through it."

There was a long, silvery silence. For once, the city was quiet, free of the ubiquitous sirens, even the distant ones.

"Oh my," said Eurovision. His emcee affectations had temporarily abandoned him.

The Therapist said, "I can't imagine what it's like in that ER right now."

"You have no idea," said Maine quietly. "I've been a doctor for twenty-five years, and I've never seen suffering like this. They suffocate to death. The ICU is like a roomful of people being waterboarded, except all you can hear is the sighing of the ventilators. But you can feel the silent, end-of-life terror."

Please, God, protect my father from that in New Rochelle. "When *will* it be over?" I asked. "Another month? Two?"

She looked at me, an infinite weariness in her eyes, and simply shook her head for a long time, her ponytail swinging, as if shaking would somehow derail the future.

Old St. Pat's began tolling out the hour.

"Ah, the bells," said Eurovision. "What would you all say to calling it a night, and meeting back up here tomorrow evening? That'll give time for others to prepare your own stories. And maybe a few more will join us."

Subdued, people began gathering up their stuff to go down to their separate apartments. I casually picked up my phone and hit the Stop button as I slipped it into my pocket. Back in Hades, I spent half the night transcribing the stories, surprised that I was almost beginning to like some of these tenants—despite my best intentions. Then I had an idea: maybe I could get the ER doc to find out what was going on in my father's nursing home. They couldn't just blow her off like they were doing to me.

When all this was over and I could see my dad again, I thought, I'd read him my account of our rooftop gatherings. It would at least get him off the TV, which, last time I was there, had echoed down the halls of Pussgreen Manor like the jabbering voices of the damned.

Day Five
April 4

The seven o'clock rooftop cheering was especially enthusiastic this evening. It sounded like the whole Lower East Side had erupted, not just with the usual banging and whistles, but with cheering and firecrackers and bottle rockets shooting into the night, like a Fourth of July celebration. The day, of course, had been nothing to cheer about: 113,704 people in New York State have tested positive for Covid-19, the death toll rising to 3,565, with 4,126 patients struggling for their lives in the ICU. Cuomo warned the peak number of cases could come in four to eight days. "It's like a fire spreading," he said. New York had ordered and paid for 17,000 ventilators, he said, but the order fell through and the state is screwed. The mayor said that the city alone would need another 15,000 ventilators, 45,000 medical professionals, and 85,000 more hospital beds just to get through the next two months. These numbers are wild, crazy, insane. Thank God no one in our building seemed to be going anywhere. Maybe we'll be able to keep old Fernsby safe until it's over and we can all emerge from our little cocoons. Cuomo talks a lot about "flattening the curve," but what's really being flattened is the city itself. It's hard to imagine what would be happening without the lockdown. Would it be like a dystopian movie out there, everyone dying in the streets? Or did it even make a difference? Were we even helping, being locked down in our building all this time? Is this what everyone else was doing? It didn't seem like anyone was out on the streets besides police and medics.

As we were assembling, I motioned to Maine and asked her if she might help me contact my dad. She looked so sad when I told her about the nursing home and shared my fears about what might be going on up there.

"I'm on a temporary leave from the ER," she said. "I'll do my best to call around and see what I can find out—give me his name and the number and the name of the home."

I ripped a page from my notebook, wrote it all down,

and tossed it over at her—but it missed her and fluttered to the rooftop in between us. Crazy six-foot distancing. She picked it up and gave me a thumbs-up and smile that crinkled her eyes and filled me with hope.

"Well, well," said Vinegar after we assembled, "have you all noticed the new art?"

Someone had painted an ice-cream cone below the poop emoji. Near it, someone had brushed some lines of calligraphy.

"What's this? Japanese?" the Lady with the Rings asked.

"What does it say?" A few people were curious.

Finally, the tenant in 4B—the Poet, according to Wilbur's bible—cleared his throat rather conspicuously. "It's a Japanese death poem, written by Minamoto-no-Shitag in the tenth century, translated by myself."

"What does it say?"

"I'll read it in Japanese, and then translate to English." He paused and spoke slowly in Japanese.

Yononaka o
nani ni tatoemu
aki no ta o
honoka ni terasu
yoi no inazuma

After a pause, he switched into English.

This world—to what may I liken it?
To autumn fields darkening at dusk,
dimly lit by lightning flashes.

Maybe the Poet wrote that down after hearing all the stories about death last night—the ghosts, the father in the hospital, the nun who could smell death. I was having a hard time sleeping, and I had to say, looking around, that most everyone was looking sunken and haggard, as if they, too, had been marinating in the death all around us.

Finally, Darrow broke the mood: "On a more earthy subject—who transformed the pile of shit into a Mister Softee?"

We laughed in relief.

"That was me," said Eurovision proudly.

"Clever," said Vinegar. "Thank you."

"Let's begin then, shall we?" Eurovision grinned. "I hope to see more art and fine literature on our Covid wall—there's lots more space. Thank you! Now: Who has a story? Don't be shy."

"Let's have a story about love and beauty," said the Lady with the Rings. "There've been too many stories about death."

Vinegar cast a glance at the Lady with the Rings, suspicion crinkling her face. "Love and beauty?"

"Something uplifting."

"Stories about love," said Florida, "are uplifting only if they're phony. Real ones are always heartbreaking."

"Not true," said the Lady with the Rings. "The world is full of simple love stories that don't end badly."

"They're the ones you don't hear about," said Vinegar, "because people like *her*"—she looked at Florida—"would rather hear about disaster, misfortune, and heartbreak."

Florida pursed her lips and said nothing. Eurovision was about to speak when Wurly's voice interrupted.

"I can tell you a story about love that's uplifting and real," he said, leaning forward on his piano bench. "I grew up around many strong, fascinating Black women in North Carolina. One of them, a great lady by the name of Bertha Sawyer, passed away when I was ten years old."

"Oh, I hope it involves music?" asked Eurovision, brightening.

"Everything involves music." Wurly released a deep chuckle. "Like a lot of us musicians, I got my start in church, messing around with the organ. We walked by Bertha's house on the way to church, so I always associate her with the awakenings of my music. Sometimes when I'm playing a slow riff with massive augmented seven-nine-thirteenth chords, I'll think of Bertha sitting on her porch. I don't know why—maybe because, like those chords, she was also big and complicated and dissonant. She's there, in the background of my music, along with so many other people in my past."

"I think of weird things and long-gone people when I'm singing sometimes," said Eurovision, "when I'm lost in it."

"And when your singing voice is coming through my wall late at night," said Vinegar icily, "I also feel lost. In a different kind of way."

"I'm sure I'm sorry," Eurovision shot back.

"So am I."

Wurly bowed his head, passed a giant hand over it before looking up again, and began.

"Bertha had been a part of my family long before I was even born. She was the longtime girlfriend of my great-uncle Leo. It was many years later when I came to understand that she wasn't his wife. Bertha's presence at most of our family gatherings, and the photos, suggest that she was more than just welcomed. The intimacy with which she and some of my family members are positioned show that she was respected, like a matriarch. In practice, she was.

"I have three very vivid memories of Bertha—each showing a different side of her. But all three memories remind me of her strength, her love for others, and how much people loved her.

"My mother was once a member of the usher board at Antioch Missionary Baptist Church in South Mills. Many generations of my family had been raised up in that church, as was I. The usher board almost always held their monthly meetings early on Saturday afternoons, and I often went along with my mother. I went for the organ. The usher board meetings were the only time I got to experiment with the church's organ without having to share it with other children; they wanted to play with the organ (as they would a toy).

"I wanted to *play* the organ.

"One Saturday, on our way to the church, Ma and I saw Bertha sitting on the porch of the house Ma and her siblings had been raised in. Bertha lived there, off and on, with my great-uncle. And whenever they had a couple's spat, she'd go to her old bus, which was parked behind the house. Bertha spent a lot of time sitting on that porch, waving at passersby and entertaining neighbors who'd come over for conversation or to share a drink.

"Ma and I stopped to talk to Bertha that day, and when it was time to head to the church, I asked Ma if I could stay with Bertha instead. I can't remember why I would pass up an hour on the organ, but Bertha didn't seem to mind my company. (If she did, she pretended not to.) So Ma agreed as long as I promised to behave for Bertha. Bertha said she'd pop my tail if I didn't behave, which, in those days, and in my community, was completely acceptable. In fact, it was expected.

"The best part of my time with Bertha that day was getting to see the inside of her bus. All the seats had been removed, and there was a twin bed and a love-seat. There were rugs on the floor. The windows were covered with heavy blankets, and there was a kerosene heater in the center of the bus. Where the driver's seat would have been stood a small table covered with an abundance of canned foods, cookies, crackers, and the like. Among those cans were sardines—something I'd never eaten. I asked Bertha what they tasted like, and she explained that sardines were similar to tuna.

"Bertha made me a sardine sandwich. I watched as she spread mustard on both slices of white bread. As soon as I took my first bite I knew it was too fishy. I didn't want to finish the sandwich, but I'd been taught not to waste food—especially not at other people's houses.

"Bertha must have been able to tell I suffered from every bite. She laughed. And with her raspy voice—I don't think she was a smoker—she said something like, 'I knew damn well you won't gon' like sardines. Brang it here.' And she finished the sandwich for me with no complaints. I could be wrong, but I believe Bertha liked that I was going to tough it out. She rescued me from sardines and mustard.

"The second vivid memory I have of Bertha is from about a year or two after the sardine-and-mustard incident. Bertha and my great-uncle Leo were both under the influence of whatever 'spirit' they'd been imbibing all day. They were half fighting. As soon as Ma and I arrived on the scene, Ma had to jump out of the car and pull the two of them apart. They were trading hits and curses. Leo and Bertha were roughly the same size—both drunk out of their minds. I'm not sure who had the greatest advantage over whom.

"Sadly, domestic disputes between men and women weren't entirely foreign to me by that age, but I wasn't accustomed to those disputes being out in public. As long as I live, I'll never forget that Bertha didn't shed nary a tear during that fight. My great-uncle did, though. Ma told him to go inside the house and get himself together, which meant 'go inside and pass out.' And Bertha was instructed to get in the back seat of Ma's car. As drunk as Bertha was, she was concerned with diverting my attention. She began asking me about school, my 'lessons,' and so forth. But she did not cry. Of that, I am certain. One doesn't forget that kind of strength and resolve.

"Even with her T-shirt stretched and torn, her hair sticking every which way on top of her head, Bertha wanted things to appear to be normal to me—the child.

"The third striking memory I have of Bertha is incredibly special. It was June of 1989, shortly after my tenth birthday. Bertha was in an intensive care unit, and Ma and I went to visit her. Children weren't permitted in those rooms, so I sat in the lobby for a short while, flipping through magazines. Eventually, Ma came and hurriedly pulled me past the nurses' station and into Bertha's room. My great-uncle was there, as were a couple other people I knew from the community. They were watching TV and talking amongst themselves.

"Bertha was awake and buried deep under sheets and blankets, with only her head poking out. Her hair had been brushed into a loose bun that sat at the top of her head. Perhaps my mother had done that for her before sneaking me into the room.

"By that age, I had a better understanding of death. I'd gone with my mother to visit other people in hospitals, and not long after, I would end up either attending their funerals with her, or watching her leave to attend their funerals. I was attuned and pessimistic enough, even at that age, to gather that I might never see Bertha out and about again.

"Bertha lifted one of her arms from under the covers, and she motioned for me to approach her. My answers to whatever questions she asked were 'Yes, ma'am' and 'No, ma'am.' She held my hand for a few minutes, and it was awkward. Bertha once again seemed to be making sure that everyone around her was okay, even when she was the one in pain.

"Bertha died two or three days later.

"My mother had gone to the funeral home to see Bertha, and she told me that they'd made her up to look very nice. I attended Bertha's funeral, which was right after our regular Sunday service. Bertha drew a big crowd. There were more people at her funeral than there were at the eleven thirty worship service. In fact, there were so many people in attendance, Ma and the other ushers had to search the church closet for extra folding chairs.

"In the coffin, Bertha looked like she belonged in a soap opera. She had been transformed, but she was recognizable. Her hair had been curled tight. And there was makeup. I could no longer see where years of drinking had damaged her lips.

"She was not a schoolteacher; she was not an avid reader; she wasn't even a mother. But I believe she had the capacity to be all three.

"Ma was right. Bertha looked beautiful. Bertha *was* beautiful. To me, my family, and many others in South Mills, North Carolina, Bertha Sawyer was a star."

Merenguero's Daughter sighed in satisfaction as Wurly stopped speaking. "I heard you playing last night," she said. "What was the name of that song? It was so beautiful."

"Let me remember," said Wurly. "I was messing around with a Jimmy Rowles tune. 'The Peacocks.'"

Merenguero's Daughter turned to Eurovision. "Hey, Music Man, you got that on your system?"

"I've got everything." Eurovision smiled at her, tapped on his phone, and in a moment, big dreamy piano chords came drifting over the rooftop, below a weeping sax line. "Wayne Shorter and Herbie Hancock."

The sound of the sax floated out over the city.

"There are those pain-filled augmented thirteenth chords I'm talking about," said Wurly, nodding.

The song came to an end. In that moment, a rich, earthy scent of something damp drifted across the rooftop: Rain was coming.

Wurly said, "Jazzmeia Horn did a fantastic version of that." He hummed and began to sing, "'Hold the memory forever . . . A mirage is all it's ever been.'"

"As long as we're on stories about love and pain," a voice from the darker end of the rooftop said, "I'll tell one. About being a child well loved, even by flawed people. Because flawed people are the most reckless and generous in their love. There's music in my story, too."

She stepped into the light: it was Pardi, the beautiful, fierce-eyed mother who lived in 6E with her daughter. Her voice was extraordinary—low and powerful.

"How can we resist?" said Eurovision. "We're all ears."

Settling into an empty chair, she began.

"I was my father's only adored child. He had other children, boys, by women other than my mother—raised well but at a distance. He raised me his 'motherless little brown baby with sparkling eyes' by his side and called me Pardner.

"In the early sixties, a Texas week didn't pass without Daddy announcing I was his 'pardner in crime' as we sat in the dining room of our house that overlooked Galveston Bay. It was a rare day that passed without Daddy pronouncing me his 'best dance pardner' as we shimmied around our front parlor in house shoes, mine larger and larger sizes of fuzzy and bright orange-pink, his size-twelve silk-smooth oxblood-red Moroccan leather. When Leadbelly sang 'man,' we yelled 'pardner!'

"Daddy's enunciation of 'partner' as 'pardner' was a legacy pronunciation. The word, as honored title bestowed on beloved child, had been handed down from Daddy's daddy to Daddy, who gifted the word—and all the rest of the words in the only poem my father or his father knew by heart, 'Lil Brown Baby' by Paul Laurence Dunbar—to me as a most treasured heirloom.

"When it was time for me to go to school, though, Bell Britton stopped calling me Pardner in public and started calling me Pardi, because he thought that sounded more appropriately feminine.

"Daddy had unique ideas about what was appropriately feminine and masculine. They boiled down to: He thought women should do more shooting and men should do more cooking and everybody needed to do a little of both—but not with everybody.

"He didn't believe, for example, in interracial marriages. This subject came up as frequently as the name Jack Johnson, which is to say, not infrequently, in our Black and masculine Galveston.

"Daddy lavished me with superlatives, and his friends did, too. His old friends from South Texas and West Texas and his army buddies would heap me with extravagant and colorful praise that said more about the poetry in their souls and their love of brown babies than my virtue.

"Daddy's army buddies typically visited for at least a week. They loved to take their time walking the brown sand of the beaches near Galveston. These visits were a tonic for Daddy.

"The buddies might come any time of year, but most often it was Juneteenth, June 19, the day when all of Black Texas celebrated both the end of slavery and the pleasure of getting good news at long last.

"Daddy's best army buddy friend was a man named Lafayette, who would come down for a week at Juneteenth, then come back for another week at Thanksgiving. I loved it when Lafayette came to town. He always brought Daddy and me the best new albums; and me, a pretty purse no one else in Galveston had.

"Daddy liked to tell me what he had told me so many times before, that once upon a time, a long time ago, before I was born, Lafayette had saved his life and his sanity in a Korean town called No Gun Ri.

"Juneteenth was important in our house, and celebrating it big was the main way my father was like the other daddies in Galveston.

"In almost every other way, my father was an anomaly in my hometown. He had attended college, Prairie View, where he met my mother, but when he got out, he was drafted and shipped off to Korea before they could tie the knot. When Daddy got back from Korea, he married Mama, but he didn't become a reverend as has been planned, or attend Yale Divinity School, where he had been accepted. He started working in gas stations, and my mother started crying.

"When Mama wasn't crying, she was pleading. But Daddy said the only thing he wanted to do in a church after he came back from Korea was sing in the choir and barbecue at the summer church socials.

"This was the period when Daddy slipped away from crying-Mama and made my half brothers who lived in Houston, who I never really got to know because their mothers wanted nothing more to do with Daddy. This was when he lived not in a two-story house overlooking the bay but in an old clapboard cottage walking distance to the sea wall with two tall palms in the yard.

"That was the house Daddy came back to with infant me in his arms but no Mama holding his hand. Mama died in the hospital shortly after my birth.

"I suspect Daddy thought it was a judgment on him. I know this: Daddy didn't hold the fact Mama died against me. He had promised Mama on her deathbed that he would be my mama and daddy, and he did everything he could imagine to keep that promise, starting with keeping me close and ending with not taking another wife.

"Daddy understood Mama's death as an invitation to do something new with his life, something that wasn't the church or the gas station.

"He hoped it might be something to do with the sea. He grew up riding and shooting and fishing but also sailing and swimming, and I grew up that way, too.

"Daddy loved water more than earth. Daddy was so proud of his adopted hometown, Galveston. Pride was an act of liberation for Daddy. It was never selfish—it was always communal. He was prouder of Galveston than he was proud of me, and that's saying something.

"He loved to say, and ardently believed, though it is not an established fact, that the first Africans to step foot on the land we call Galveston were pirates. He was proud of the fourteen old Black churches in Galveston, and he was proud of the fact Galveston had a high school for Black students before Birmingham, Alabama; before Houston, before Dallas, before Fort Worth. And there was a Black library, too. He claimed Jack Johnson for Galveston, and he would talk about the real Charlie Brown, who was so much more than the Charlie Brown in the funny papers, the Black man who arrived in West Columbia, Texas, in 1865, so poor he didn't own himself—arrived enslaved, but before the century was out, owned land on the Brazos River, and made a fortune selling cedarwood while audaciously claiming, 'Lumber on the root was better than beef on the hoof.'

"When Daddy hit what he called his 'first big lick,' he bought us a house on the water and had a table made out of cedar and commissioned portraits of Charlie Brown and his wife, Isabelle, that he hung in our parlor. He didn't hang Mama's portrait because that would have made us cry.

"He was proud of Norris Wright Cuney, who was the first Grand Master of the Prince Hall Masons in Texas and the reason Daddy became a Mason. Cuney had founded a stevedore company that trained, equipped, and employed five hundred Black men when the Lily-Whites, the Republican powers that be, didn't want any Black, skilled dockworkers, didn't even want Blacks in the Republican Party.

"Daddy was proud of the fact that his mother's father had had a bank account at the very first Black-owned bank in Texas—Fraternal Bank and Trust—founded by William Madison McDonald.

"Daddy was proud of his pop-pop, his mama's daddy, a man he described as having the same profession as Jesus's stepfather, Joseph. Pop-Pop was a carpenter and a Mason, and Daddy's mother remembered walking between her father and mother through the streets of Fort Worth to Fraternal Bank and Trust to open their account the year the bank opened in 1906.

"Daddy's family were strongly influenced by William Madison McDonald, and part of that influence was manifest in the discipline with which they voted a straight Republican ticket—because the Republicans were the party of Lincoln and the party of McDonald. And the party of Cuney.

"Cuney died in 1898. McDonald died in 1950. Daddy's family broke with the Republicans before that. In 1948, Hobart Taylor Sr., who had gone off to Atlanta to make money selling insurance, was back in Texas making more money, building up a cab company while working for civil rights and generally riling up things in Houston in ways that would be good for Black people. So in 1948, Hobart got Daddy's daddy to vote for LBJ for the senate, and we Brittons have been Democrats ever since.

"It was because of Hobart and Charlie Brown and Cuney all being so entrepreneurial, and Pop-Pop always putting their lives in my daddy's face, that Daddy decided, upon return from Korea, that he would pump gas until he figured out how to make a fortune.

"He had some strange idea that the act of acquiring might cure the pain that plagued him after his stint in Southeast Asia. He wanted to make money for him and for me, but even more, he wanted to make money to give away. He had witnessed firsthand in three different countries—America, Korea, and Mexico—how poverty could explode a soul true as a bomb.

"As he had no interest whatsoever in driving a cab or owning a fleet of them, or opening a funeral parlor, or hauling goods like Britt Johnson or Matey Stewart, he didn't know how to start getting rich without working too hard. He pumped a lot of gas and pain and wiped a lot of dust and bugs off a lot of windows before it occurred to him what he should be doing. Or rather, it occurred to one of his friends, and the idea caught fire until it was burning up Daddy's ears.

"I was there, in a stroller nibbling on a soft roll, when it happened. I've seen the Polaroid, so I know it's true. It was a Juneteenth. Bronze men were gathered in the lawn by that cottage with the two palm trees, eating ribs, when Lafayette said, 'Man, you really should bottle this; it's better than Scatter's.'

"Then one of the other buddies—a fellow from Cleveland, Ohio, who had played football at Alabama State and always wore an Alabama State Magic City Classic sweatshirt to remind folks of his heroic gridiron exploits—started in on talking about how Texas barbecue was 'all right,' was 'good,' was 'mighty fine,' but classic Cleveland barbecue was 'the alpha and omega.'

"In Daddy's world, calling something the alpha and omega was giving it a 'Sweet Jesus, best of the best' anointing that could not be challenged—without doing serious injury to either the one who had bestowed the anointing or the one who challenged it. The only ways forward were: to agree, to rip away all of the other fellow's authority, or to have him rip away all of yours.

"The crowd was not divided. Everyone, including Daddy, was eager to agree. Soon all present were swept away on a wave of accord into a sea of Ohio 'cue nostalgia.

"But just because you've silenced a man doesn't mean you've converted him. I heard that a lot around my house growing up. Daddy stayed up all night, cooking, dry rubbing, simmering, fire tending, and slab turning with his sacred long-tined fork nobody could touch but Daddy. Next afternoon, a new Galveston barbecue was served.

"Mr. Magic City Classic was prepared to enjoy his meat, as Daddy had properly genuflected to Ohio 'cue. He was prepared to enjoy his meat, but he was not prepared for what he tasted. He shook his head like his jaw was heavy. The first words out of his mouth after the bite: 'You giving me the mumps!' Then he gnawed on the rib bone in his fingers until it was clean as something sacred. By then, they all realized he meant the meat was so good he was going to get fat in the face.

"Intrigued, Lafayette reached for a bone off Daddy's grill. Lafayette took a big chomp, then cocked his head toward Daddy as he chewed, swallowed, finally pronouncing, 'You are about to be a very rich man. You need an investor?'

"Daddy liked to say that our money came from a lost Black pirate hoard that he'd found through careful research at the library. And some people insisted on wanting to believe that Daddy did something nefarious. But his ribs were just that good. I was soon a sop sauce princess.

"It didn't take long before Daddy could take pride in knowing anything money could buy in Galveston could be mine. It did not trouble him that there were things in the world beyond Galveston we couldn't afford. We weren't ambling far from Galveston County.

"We had a house on the bay, friends, and food, and finally Daddy was paying rent when rent was overdue for folks we didn't know, and water bills, and gambling debts, and sometimes even the occasional pusherman.

"He bought so much rice and beans and grits, we never had to pay to have his shirts or my dresses ironed, or our yard swept clean. There was always somebody wanting to do something sweet to thank Daddy. And he always let them do it.

"Daddy lived the difference between charity and

helping the other fellow out. All our Galveston called me Pardi, and each year, more and more of our Galveston started calling Daddy Pardner because I called Daddy Pardner. The way the town pronounced 'Pardner,' there was an inflection I didn't put in it. That difference rang loud enough in Lafayette's ears that he called it up out loud at Thanksgiving dinner in 1967.

"I was eight, Lucky Eight, as Daddy and Lafayette put it. We were going around the table saying what we were grateful for, and I had said I was grateful for my 'Soul Man' Sam and Dave single, and Lafayette looked at me and said he was grateful for the fact that 'you put your foot in this sweet potato pie, Pardi!' Then he took a big swig of brown liquor from a heavy crystal old-fashioned glass, pointed a mahogany finger at my daddy, and said what he was almost as grateful for as the pie was what all 'the most cursed bronze citizens of Galveston are thankful for, that you, sweet son, pardoned them for their sins, like you sho' 'nuff pardon me for mine!'

"Daddy shot back, 'I will till . . . I won't,' and Lafayette smiled at the lie. I got goose bumps. Daddy didn't lie. Or maybe he did. He certainly changed the subject.

"On Daddy's turn he said he was grateful for me. I said I was grateful for barbecue sauce—because I knew it would make Daddy laugh.

"Daddy sold all kinds of sauce. Mainly, Daddy sold the recipe and variations on the recipe to a conglomerate while negotiating a royalty. Daddy knew all about oil and gas royalties, and Daddy believed oil and gas were not fundamentally different from sauce. Soon he was in a position that meant he didn't have to lift a finger.

"Only he kept lifting fingers, and I assisted him as he continued manufacturing and shipping under a private label, a gourmet, more expensive version of his sop sauce, while making big profit on the everyday jars, while claiming not to be working.

"That perplexed me. Daddy didn't lie. I called him out on it like he taught me to call out lies. I thought maybe Daddy was testing me to see if I would call him out. 'But you do work, Pardner. I see you. Shipping. Selling. Hiring. Overseeing.' Daddy tapped me on the nose gently. 'Find something you love to do, Pardi, and you will never work a day in your life.'

"The year Armstrong walked on the moon, 1969, we were having the big Juneteenth barbecue. There was red drink. There was all kinds of meat, not just spare ribs, but chicken, pulled pork, and beef brisket. I had made, with the help of church ladies from our old neighborhood, little fig pastries for all my friends, hand pies, and fingerprint cookies. The boys in the neighborhood were wild about my hand pies. The girls seemed to prefer the fingerprint cookies.

"I was giving the neighbor boy who I was sweet on the prettiest, brownest of my hand pies because he had the sweetest, prettiest brown eyes, when Daddy said, 'If you ever bring home a white boy, I promise I will shoot you both. The only question will be if I shoot you or him first.'

"Given that I didn't know any white boys and wasn't intrigued with the ones I saw on television, and given that I had just gifted Lamont Hill my prettiest hand pie, and earlier that day he had given me a flower, and given that Daddy was smiling when he made that strange promise, I wasn't afraid. I was *informed*. I would never bring home a white boy. It would kill Daddy to kill me. And I would never kill Daddy. That's what I knew.

"Between Juneteenth and my tenth birthday, in the summer of 1969, Apollo 11 launched into space, circled the moon, and sent back pictures to earth, which flashed across the television in our parlor. Daddy was off and on glued to the television and agitated from lift-off to splashdown. I was not interested. My nose poked in a book, I was moving with Gandalf and the Hobbits through Middle-earth. But Daddy insisted I look up from my book to see Neil Armstrong walk on the lunar surface. Shortly after that, I climbed the stairs to my bedroom, climbed into my canopy bed, and read myself to sleep, expecting to see Daddy in the morning.

"That was not to be. Shortly after midnight, there was a glow in the dark clock on my night table. Daddy shook me awake, pulled me out of bed, grabbed his rifle, and walked us out on the pier.

"As we settled into a familiar sitting position with our butts on the pier and our feet dangling in air just above the water, tranquility returned as my father seized the occasion of the moon walk not to celebrate Armstrong but to remind me that it was a Russian who had first orbited earth.

"This observation calmed Bell Britton. Realizing that he hadn't yet told me all about Alexander Pushkin, he dived into the story, telling me about how Pushkin's grandfather—or great-grandfather, Daddy wasn't sure which—had been a Negro slave owned by Peter the Great. That the first Pushkin had been born a slave and raised to the Russian nobility, and how Pushkin, 'a brilliant Black man like Cuney and Brown and Taylor,' said my daddy, was 'a man who wrote with a pen that he dipped in an inkwell that looked like cotton bales supported by dark-blue-black enslaved Africans, a Black Russian might have been more than Cuney, Brown, and Taylor.' Daddy admitted it hurt him to say this about his Galveston heroes, but that it had to be said, 'because Pushkin had added more words to the Russian language than Shakespeare added to English.'

"He told me all of this in words like oil gushing out of a derrick. His words were pressured and precious and swift, and I was rich because they were splashing on me. I felt good on the pier smiling at my daddy with my eyes and my mouth as he smiled back at me and talked like gushing oil. We were good on the pier. Daddy walked us back to the house and I slept good, knowing he was good again, finally, like before the Apollo 11 launch.

"But in the morning, just like that, over our breakfast of tortillas and scrambled eggs and bacon, I knew Neil Armstrong walking on the moon had taken something significant from my father.

"That year my birthday, July 29, fell on the full moon. We had a barbecue in the yard, and every brown, Black, and beige child in Galveston and La Marque was invited, and all the whip-smart brown girls from Houston and Fort Worth—they came, too, because their mamas wanted to dance with my daddy and their daddies wanted to eat my daddy's barbecue and drink up some of his free-to-them liquor. When my party guests had left, Daddy and I walked down the pier, gazing up at the sky.

"Daddy declared that bright full moon a gift from God

just for me. Then Daddy said, 'White men have the moon, white men have the Supreme Court, they have the Senate, they have the Congress. You are more than the moon, the Supreme Court, the Senate, and the Congress. They have all that, but I have you, so I have more.'

"When I was grown and told Jericho my double-digit birthday story, he asked what seemed a foolish question: 'Did he take his gun out to the pier when he told you that?' 'Of course not. He took his rifle.' Daddy always took his rifle out to the pier when there was something to celebrate. Double digits was something to celebrate. He answered with silence. (We moved on. I was really good at moving on and so was he. It was a thing we liked about each other and found lacking in most other people.)

"My double-digit birthday was celebrated for almost a month and included a trip to Mexico City; then birthday time was over and school got started good—they were jumping me from fourth to sixth grade. Everything was true good; then Jimi Hendrix died. A month after that, Janis Joplin died. You wouldn't think that would make a difference in our little house on the bay, but it did.

"In the immediate aftermath of Jimi Hendrix's death, Daddy told me that 'snow' was a word that could mean heroin or cocaine. By the time Janis Joplin died—a loss mourned in our house because Janis Joplin and Stevie Nicks were the only two white women singers my father appreciated—I came to understand that Daddy's buddy Lafayette was a heroin dealer.

"Lafayette arrived for Thanksgiving dreaming of a supper of smoked turkey and turnip greens and sweet potato pie, not the feast of choice, sharp words that can only be prepared by an angry and indulged child. When Lafayette left the Saturday morning after Thanksgiving, I didn't hug him bye. Daddy did.

"My father had compassion for Lafayette. When we drank our coffee at the kitchen table that Saturday morning, a table still set with a plate and cup and cutlery for Lafayette, who was already gone, Daddy explained that to understand why he loved Lafayette, you would have had to know Lafayette as Daddy first knew him when he arrived in Korea; know how he was before he witnessed the bodies of slaughtered civilians fermenting in the sun, little children's bodies getting eaten up with heat, insects, and feral animals; how, before being taken prisoner, he had tried to save any child he came across, North or South Korean; how he ran straight into gunfire to pull a little girl out of the line of fire; how more than once he refused to fire on civilians when ordered; and how when Lafayette came back from the war, all he could say was, 'One two three jump! One two three jump!' When I didn't understand what he was saying, Daddy pivoted to a simple sermon.

"'Forgive those who trespass against you as you wish to be forgiven.' Then he reminded me of all the sweet afternoons we had spent together, with Lafayette and Daddy telling what Daddy now explained were not 'war stories' but 'love-in-the-middle-of-war stories,' as they took turns dancing around the living room with me to T-Bone Walker and Billie Holiday and Big Mabel, to Big Mama Thornton and Aretha Franklin, to Sam and Dave and Jackie Wilson.

"Lafayette brought the Billie and the two Bigs, and Aretha. I would miss that; I was prepared to miss that. I was a hard little girl when I had to be.

"The next Juneteenth, Lafayette didn't come to Galveston, and he didn't come the next Thanksgiving. Mr. Magic City Classic and a growing circle of others would still come, but not Lafayette. Sometimes Daddy would visit Lafayette in Detroit. When I would hear Big Mabel or Big Mama, I would miss him. But then I would see some skinny, skanky brown person on the news or on a television show who was 'hooked on heroin,' and I would get mad at him again.

"I first learned of Lafayette's death by reading it in the *Michigan Chronicle*. Daddy had known about it for days, but it wasn't a thing he had wanted to tell me.

Daddy loved Lafayette. And he didn't want to speak ill of the dead—but he never did lie to me—so when fifteen-year-old Pardi Britton asked Daddy, asked Bell Britton, how a man like Lafayette come to be killed in broad daylight by a young woman with 'no previous record,' Daddy told me a simple sad story.

"The girl, she was sixteen or seventeen, too young for Lafayette, according to Daddy, to be messing with 'any kind of way.' She had a brother who was addicted to smack and owed Lafayette a small amount of money— Daddy thought it was something strange like sixty-seven dollars, the remainder of a larger bill. The girl had paid Lafayette some of what the brother owed but not all, and Lafayette was pressuring the girl to pay the rest of what was owed—if not with money, with sex. The girl needed time to raise more money, or the courage to caress Lafayette. Lafayette gave her the time because one of his boys got shot and was laid up in the hospital and he had other related urgent matters to attend to, as it appeared somebody was making a move on his throne. This last fear was part of the reason he was trying to distract himself with this girl he shouldn't have been messing with.

"So he gives the girl a week, to get up the cash or give up the love. Two days later, he has gone to visit his fallen comrade in the hospital. The convalescent is recovering, Lafayette's leadership no longer being challenged. A wary truce has been brokered. Lafayette is walking down the hospital steps flanked by stalwart and loyal men, each with a gun in their heavy coat pockets, ready to die for him. It was shaping up to be an all-is-right-with-my-world kind of day for Lafayette.

"There's a gun in her hand, and the girl shoots Lafayette dead. On the front steps of the hospital, in front of his bodyguards. Those bodyguards assumed that girl was no threat. Lafayette assumed that girl was pleasure without danger. They had underestimated her, and she used it to her advantage."

A gasp went around the rooftop at this. I suppose none of us was expecting it any more than Lafayette himself must have been.

Pardi smiled. "That story was Daddy's fifteenth birthday present to me.

"Daddy had forgiven Lafayette a lot of things, but he was the father of a teenage daughter, and he would not forgive a man for forcing himself on a child—or even for wanting her. Daddy said that girl didn't even kill Lafayette; to do what that man did, Lafayette had to be already gone."

The story had cast a spell over us all. When Pardi didn't continue, after this final line, I could feel us all kind of shaking ourselves back into the present.

"You call that a love story?" Eurovision said, eventually.

"Hey, there's plenty of love in there," said Merenguero's Daughter. "Sounds to me like it's a love-in-the-middle-of-war story, like Pardi said. I guess you could also say it's a hate story. And an everything-in-between story. Real life is so mixed up."

"You said there was music," Wurly said.

"That's coming," said Pardi, "in the rest of the story."

"Well, let's hear it!" said the Lady with the Rings.

"Nah. I'm tired tonight. I'm sure there will be a time to tell a story about music—and lies." She winked.

"You want a story about lies?"

It was the tenant in 4E, La Reina, who hadn't said much yet.

"Well, of course. I adore lies," said Eurovision. "As Oscar Wilde said, 'Lying is the telling of beautiful untrue things—the proper aim of Art.'"

La Reina laughed. "I'd say this is less a story about beautiful untrue things than it is about ugly true things."

"That sounds like fun!" said Eurovision.

My former husband used to force me to come along on these ridiculous bro-centered vacations with him and his friends, always around the Fourth of July. Every summer we'd take a week and explore some city within driving distance, but mostly these trips centered around him and his boys drinking and retelling every story from high school, with us wives also drinking and pretending to listen. Sort of like what we're doing up here, but with more history between us and without the raging pandemic. I'm guessing it won't happen this summer unless everything is back to normal by then, though that's assuming the boys are taking Covid and this quarantine seriously—and for a few of them, my former husband included, that's a big assumption—but I wouldn't know, considering I've been free of that obligation for three years now, thank God, ever since the summer we all went up to Maine.

"We were at the Second Annual Lobster Roll World Championship, the first stop of that year's reunion trip, up in Portland, and we had each paid a hundred bucks to serve as judges, which meant sampling ten lobster rolls apiece. It sounds like fun if you don't think about it too much. In the parking lot, after we'd paid another ten bucks to park, my then-husband turned to me after cutting the engine and said, 'I have a feeling Laura's not gonna be here,' then rushing out of his seat and slamming the car door before I could ask what the hell he meant.

"Laura was Marco's wife, and they'd been married the longest of all of us couples. They'd been together basically since their first week of college, is how she told the story. She was from New England—New Hampshire or something—whereas the boys all had gone to high school together in Miami. She was the one who got me calling them that: the boys. For the four years I knew her, since becoming one of the wives myself, whenever we were down in Miami for the holidays or together on these summer trips, there always came a moment when Laura sat back in her chair after too much Scotch and stared at the group of them—playing dominoes, all of them smoking the cigars my husband brought but that I'd paid for—and she'd say, her eyes a little closed so that the scene looked sufficiently blurry, 'Look at our boys, Mari—don't you just love seeing them together like this?' I usually gulped down whatever was left in my glass and mumbled 'mmm-hmm' around an ice cube. All our boys were Cuban like me, and Laura was a white Americana, so I could see why, having not grown up around boys like them, she could feel nostalgic for something she'd never had to protect herself against.

"Through the windshield—I was still sitting in the car, preparing myself for the ways the boys amplified each other—I saw my husband slap Marco's back. Marco looked tanner than ever, thinner than I'd ever seen him, wearing the kinds of clothes—as if about to board a yacht—that Laura had always tried but never succeeded in getting this Miami boy to wear. The other boys closed in, and the five of them took turns lifting each other off the ground while the other wives—who I should say were also Americanas, who I didn't know so well, because unlike them I grew up in the same city as our boys, in Miami, and the other wives were all from places that seemed calmer, like central Pennsylvania and Connecticut, places the boys eventually moved to with these wives, leaving their mothers behind for *me* to hear from, when they'd call to ask if I've heard from their sons—stood back, kissing each other on the cheek. I got out to join them after seeing that it was true: Laura wasn't there.

"Right then, a woman hopped out of the passenger side of Marco's Land Rover and stood vaguely by his side. Honestly, the thing I remember most about her—another Americana, Marco had a type—were her legs, which looked super long and skinny and completely bruise free in these tiny shorts with frayed edges—shorts that gave away that she was way younger than the rest of us. He introduced her to the group as a colleague at his law firm and said nothing else, not even her name.

"The other wives took a look at this new woman and

didn't even flinch. I could see them quickly processing the implications and deciding their best strategy was to just go with it, to believe Marco that she was just someone from work, and that it would be stupid to waste the ticket, because their husbands seemed to believe him. What choice did we have, their quick faces seemed to signal to me, their arms slinging a little tighter against their husbands: Didn't we all see this coming? Weren't we all relieved it was Laura and not us?

"This new woman had a ticket in her hand—it had my name on it because they all did, all ten of them. It had been my job to buy the tickets, the easiest of the jobs we'd divided among the couples, the job assigned to me because I'd proven over the years I couldn't be trusted to pick hotels or rental cars or anything else that gave you the option to go cheap. I can't help how I was raised. What I *could* help was asking Marco why this woman—who finally told us herself, as we entered the venue, that her name was Ashley, the name lost on half of us as someone in a volunteer shirt affixed our 'Judge' wristbands to our left wrists—was holding the ticket I'd bought for Laura. I'd learned to hold my tongue since becoming my husband's wife.

"The ten competitors in the Second Annual Lobster Roll World Championship ringed the warehouse walls, banners behind them tacked up to rustic-looking wood panels. I have no idea how it was narrowed down to just ten, as every place for miles on the drive up there advertised having a lobster roll. Only five of the competitors were local; the other five—from places like Atlanta, Venice Beach, and Paris—seemed immediately out of place, their branding too slick, clearly outsourced. At the front of the venue there was, inexplicably, a bluegrass band.

"'So wait, bluegrass is a Maine thing?' I said, just to say something. No one had said a word since getting our wristbands. I laughed when no one responded and said, 'Just kidding, I know it's not.'

"I subtly steered us to the booth for the team from Paris—two brothers who claimed they'd fallen in love with lobster rolls as kids while on a family trip to Maine. They were rumored to have the best lobster roll there by a long shot, and I was all but certain they wouldn't win: While buying the tickets, I'd read that the year before—at the First Annual Lobster Roll Championship—the winner had been a roll from Boise, a place called Salty's, and though Salty's owner was born and raised in Maine, the folks who still called the state home were eager to bring the title back. I let my husband think he was leading us toward the Frenchmen.

"My hope was that the show the Parisians seemed to

be putting on—they'd hired a documentary film crew and were making liberal use of lime zest, for the love of God—would be enough to distract us from Ashley's unexplained presence for long enough for us to regroup, though for some reason I was the only one with a kind of frantic question on my face about who she was, what she was doing there. Why did none of the boys seem as confused or as unnerved by her presence as I was? Why had none of them asked outright what on earth Marco was thinking, foisting this girl on us? Where the hell was Laura?

"I was trying to pull my husband far enough aside to find a way to ask him at least some of these questions. But once we were up close to the booth and trapped there by the growing crowd, Ashley squeezed in next to me, as if someone had given her a heads-up that the other wives followed my lead. This was wrong: It's the boys who did that (but only to a point) because I reminded them of their mothers. Because they knew their mothers would call me at the end of the week and ask, *So how was the trip to Maine?* The other wives never thought of me this way, as any kind of leader. They thought that by having gotten their boy to move away in the first place from the city that made us, they'd already won. They weren't wrong.

"'So Marco tells me you're from Miami as well?'

"*As well? Really? What else did Marco deem essential for you to know?* I said in my head. Out loud, I just said yes.

"She nodded heavily a couple times, waiting for more from me. She had blue eyes, lashes shellacked with mascara, eyelids black with faint glitter. Her hair was blond, with even blonder streaks, fried in a way that aged her. I noticed now that her top was a button-down shirt—a man's or just meant to look like a man's—and I looked down at her cutoff shorts, the pocket liners like upside down sails visible against her thin thighs. This was a lawyer? What else did Marco expect us to believe? Had he even told her where he was taking her?

"'Cool, cool,' she said, nodding and nodding and nodding.

"And then, watching her nod, I felt something I'd never felt around the other wives: power. More and more of it with every second I refused the polite conversation Ashley was trying to start. I looked toward the other wives and their boys. Each couple was loosely holding hands and facing away from each other, away from me and Ashley, chins tilted up at the other stalls. I could almost hear Ashley's mind scrambling for her next question.

"She seemed to not need to blink. She was wearing

so much bronzer that I wondered if she was trying to mock or match me and my coloring.

"'So how did you find out about this event?' she finally churned out.

"The boys had been joking about coming to this since the summer before, after hearing about what a disaster the First Annual Lobster Roll World Championship—then an outdoor event—was; how some crazy storm had materialized out of nowhere, destroyed all the booths amid Zeus-esque flashes of lightning, and then rolled away over the ocean just as quickly. One of the boys had sent around a link to a YouTube video of a Maine-based lobster roll vendor who hadn't even made it to the final ten complaining about the whole event in general and, more specifically, about how a lobster roll made in Idaho won the whole rain-drenched show—the intent of the sharing being to laugh at how his agitation played against his thick Maine accent. And then, in the way the boys have always had, the video became a thing they quoted, sampled, remixed—until it was fully integrated into their bro repertoire, the same phrases flying across my in-laws' domino table months later when we were all down in Miami for the holidays. Early spring comes along, all of them suffering a New England winter only slightly worse than our New York one, and my husband finds a web page advertising the second annual event—*these fuckers are going to try this again!*—and before he could morph the news into the next iteration of the months-old joke over their group chat, I said, 'What if we actually went? What if we drive up this summer, and then we all meet up there?'

"I just looked at Ashley, waited until I saw her blink, then said, 'The internet.'

"She nodded some more, gave another round of, 'Oh, that's so cool.' Smiled with these pageant-ready teeth. I'd never in my life had another woman want me to like her so much. The feeling was usually the other way around; that's how I knew what it was.

"Which meant, if I was going to play this right, that it was time to turn my attention to a man.

"My husband was on his toes, his phone in his hand, trying to snap a perfect photo that captured the entirety of the line leading to the Parisians' booth. I knew better than to ask for his attention then, so I turned toward Willy—we'd grown up calling him Guille, short for Guillermo, but he was Willy to his wife and, therefore, to us now—and tried to think up the most insidery question I could manage.

"'Has your brother found a new job yet?' I said, though I already knew the answer, thanks to my weekly call with his mother.

"Ashley surprised me with a hand on my shoulder and said, 'Oh yeah, your brother, Lazaro—Laz, right? He got let go from Best Buy, what, a month ago now?'

"Her, showing off those straight teeth through all of this.

"Willy looked at me like it was somehow my fault that she knew about Laz, that he even existed. My husband was still pretending to be very committed to taking the perfect photo of the line, and I got so angry so fast that I barely stopped myself from reaching for his cap's brim to knock it off his head, who cared what trouble it caused. I took Willy's cocked look to mean what it had back when we were kids—he was not going to answer, and *I* was supposed to say something mean. Like: What, did Marco brief you on all of us, that what you lawyers do? Or perhaps: I'm sorry but why the fuck is my friend's name even in your mouth? Or more simply: Excuse me, but was anyone even talking to you?

"Willy took a step back, ready for any of these. Every single one of these boys: They were always ready to let women do their dirty work, to cover up their own garbage. He'd sensed what I'd sensed about the power shifting, thinking it was my job—because I was the only wife from back home—to say something right then, to signal who did or didn't belong, but Willy was reading the shift all wrong. I wondered if he'd already known that Laura wouldn't be there, if he already knew all about whatever went down between her and Marco, and what it meant.

"'Your teeth are really white,' I said.

"She showed us even more of them, patted down the side of her hair though there was no need, and said, 'Oh, yeah, thank you,' as if my description were a for-real compliment.

"She relaxed and squinted at me. She was pretty in the way Miami Cuban boys predictably found alluring precisely because it was so foreign to their home turf: fair-skinned and straight-haired and thin-limbed in ways not physiologically possible for women like me. They even found it sexy until the novelty wore off, when they realized they recognized this body type—the absence of hips and breasts—from their own boyhoods. But her being new to them, along with the way her shorts showed off what the magazines call *thig space*, was enough to melt Willy into niceness once he'd mistaken my response as me deciding we were all on the same team. Ashley wandered next to my husband in line, phone in her hands and over her head, everyone suddenly interchangeable in a way that made me want to leave. She lowered her arms and showed him her screen, and he laughed at something she said.

"Here's what I mean about the power: No one ended up saying anything that day about Ashley's sudden arrival, and even though I watched her and Marco through every bite of those ten mini lobster rolls, I never once caught them holding hands. Marco was, if anything, kind of ignoring her. Kind of ignoring everyone. It made Ashley keep trying. She spent the afternoon floating from wife to wife, as if she were hosting the Lobster Roll Championship herself, making sure we all had enough water and enough napkins, holding out little plastic tubs of melted butter to us for dipping our last bites of bread, forcing that intimacy. She apologized for how loud that bluegrass band was playing, like she'd been the one to hire them. She asked us our thoughts about who we'd vote for after eating the roll from each booth, running us through the various categories—best presentation, best taste, mayo versus no mayo—as if it actually mattered what people who'd paid to be judges thought, as if the whole event were anything other than an expensive way to pass an afternoon. Her trying so hard like that distracted me that whole trip from remembering to ask my husband how he'd known Laura wouldn't be there. When was it that he'd talked to Marco about them splitting up. Why he'd decided to keep that conversation—a bunch of conversations, it turned out—a secret from me.

"I'd remember wanting to ask all this only after he'd fallen asleep, or after he'd pretended to have fallen asleep, or when we were with everyone else. And I was seeing how I wasn't really myself anymore, how I was now instinctively afraid to shake him awake and insist we talk, afraid to speak up in any way that threatened to potentially embarrass him. I started to wonder when that fear had started, how long it had taken me to even understand that hesitancy around him as fear. How he'd managed to keep me from seeing it for as long as he had.

"I ended up leaving him before the next summer (and whatever trip came with it) rolled around, but not before another set of Miami holidays, where Ashley was apparently in town with Marco but not trapped around my former in-laws' domino table like the rest of us. And somehow Marco didn't seem pissed about it, and he told anyone who asked where she was to shut the fuck up, that it wasn't their business. And from the way my husband cut his glance at me through the cloud of cigar smoke, I knew better than to press, even with a joke: We'd had one of our bigger blowouts before any of them had shown up that night, and so I'd spent the hour leading up to them arriving cleaning up the aftermath of that in time for everything to look fine. That night, I didn't feel like sitting around them anyway, and that was one of the first nights I let it show. I smoked my cigar away from the other wives, letting it ash all over his parents' patio, and I planned out how I could get my husband to stay down there with his parents for a while, find some excuse that would make him feel needed back home so I could have our place up here to myself for a little while, figure out my next steps. Marco made some joke he makes every year, and I watched smoke tumble heavy and thick from my husband's open mouth, a ready volcano. I wondered how Laura was spending her Christmas.

"Last I heard, my former husband is still down there, living in Miami with his parents. The kind of Cubans they are, I'm sure they're happy to have him there for the pandemic. He's a strong guy, and that might end up being useful for them. I could see him knocking someone out to get his parents toilet paper, no question. He doesn't know I live here now, that I moved out of our apartment as soon as the divorce went through. I want him to think I still live in our old place. It's safer for everyone that way.

"Can I tell you about those lobster rolls, though? Those French guys were robbed. The lime zest was—well, shit—chef's kiss, people. Taste-wise, presentation-wise, obviously no mayo needed because what was there to try and hide: The locals didn't even come close. But in the end, I was right. One of the locals—I forget which one out of the five, because let's be real, they were all interchangeable—won the title, brought it back to the great state of Maine like I figured they would. Ask me if I even care what loving that French team's roll says about me. It was the most delicious thing I'd eaten in a long, long time."

The tolling of Old St. Pat's, with the dead stroke at the end, sounded just as La Reina finished her story. With the taste of those imagined French lobster rolls still sitting sweetly on our tongues, we bid each other goodnight—and I returned here to my peeling desk and the soft footfalls above.

Day Six
April 5

D eath is like the distant sound of thunder at a
picnic,'" quoted Eurovision when he arrived
on the rooftop with his thermos, blanket thrown over
his arm, pausing to read a new graffito on the mural
wall. "Nice."

I watched him take a seat in his dramatic, plastic-
coated chair and arrange around him his own little
picnic things: a shaker, the highball glass with two
olives on a spear, a silver plate of cheese and crackers,
an old dented saucepot with spoon for making noise.
He draped the blanket over the arm of the chair, ready
to ward off the chill after sunset. He shook up and drib-
bled the martini liquid into the highball, to the point
where it just slopped over the side. And then, with ex-

treme care, he raised the glass and, with pursed lips, sipped off the excess before putting it down on his side table. I found something comforting in this precise, busy arrangement of little things around him, creating a home inside his six-foot radius.

"How dearly I wish we could clink glasses as in former days," he said, "but consider this a salut to all of us storytellers and listeners!" He raised his glass, and those of us already gathered did the same.

More people arrived. Tonight there were quite a few I didn't recognize from my previous roll call, people whose apartments I hadn't been in yet or seen in the halls. Word of our little story hour was getting around, I guess. People arranged their chairs in semicircles as far from each other as possible. These people were desperate to get out of their stuffy apartments, to find some human company where they could—if they dared. I realized I hadn't left the building myself in more than two weeks. I wondered if anyone else had.

Tonight my thermos was filled with Singapore Slings, put together from ingredients scrounged from the rainbow closet. I wanted to have something sweet and tropical, a drink that tasted like travel to faraway places, alligator luggage with ocean-liner stickers, and old hotels with verandahs and ceiling fans and waiters in white gloves. Ha! Who did I think I was?

Vinegar took her place near Eurovision with her wine sleeve, glass, and side table; Hello Kitty in her cave chair; the Lady with the Rings with her cheetah scarf; Whitney in her ugly Bauhaus chair; Wurly on that piano bench he hauled up every night; Florida with her golden shawl; and so on.

"Greetings, everyone," began Eurovision, standing up and giving his bow tie a few tugs. He checked his watch. "Thirty seconds till showtime."

At seven we clapped and hooted our hardest, and for the first time, I heard, cranked up from somewhere down below, Sinatra belting out "New York, New York." The clamor died away as it did every evening, in a sad sort of withdrawing sound, like a wave retreating on the beach.

After my super's chores, I had written down the summary of the day's statistics: 122,031 people in New York State were now positive for Covid-19, up from 113,704 on Saturday—bringing the total number of cases in the tristate to 161,431, with 4,159 deaths, up from 3,565 on Saturday. I put the book, as usual, next to me, and casually covered it with the blanket.

"That's a mangled quotation from W. H. Auden," mused Ramboz, his attention drawn to the mural. "It should be, 'Thoughts on his own death, like the distant roll of thunder at a picnic.'"

"Distant?" said Maine. "Not anymore. The storm's right on top of us."

"Yes, and pounding the crap out of us," said Darrow.

"We are the riders in the storm," said Eurovision, ostentatiously sipping his martini. "Or, more to the point, collateral damage in a war."

"At least we're surviving," said the Lady with the Rings. "So far."

"It feels to me it's only a matter of time before the pestilence comes for us," said Florida. "Gets in the building, infects the air, and then we're all being taken to Presbyterian Downtown in those screaming ambulances. I never want to go back *there* again."

"Let's at least acknowledge," said Maine, "that we're doing a pretty good job in this building of quarantining—nobody comes in or out. Not even me at the moment."

I tried to catch her eye, wondering if Maine had had a chance to make the calls she promised. She didn't look my way, though, so I figured I'd find her at the end of the evening; I didn't want the others to know my business.

"It'll be over soon enough," said Eurovision, continuing the conversation with false cheeriness. "We just got to hang in there. We're making progress against the virus."

Ramboz said, "You think so? Progress? You call it progress? That's a damnable word. Progress is really just the fiction every generation tells itself to justify the current fashion in ignorance, fear, and prejudice."

"It's even worse than that," said Vinegar, "we're going *backward*. Look at the MAGA racists, crawling out like cockroaches in the dark, now that the Orange Fool turned off the lights in America."

"In every age," said Ramboz, "the stupid and ignorant outnumber the enlightened and educated a hundred to one. And they invented a perfect economic system to nurture it, called capitalism."

I thought it was sort of ridiculous and galling that the man was a communist. He didn't have a clue about what communism was really like. My dad had hated Communists with a passion, and he filled my ear growing up with stories of their brutality.

"Come on, it's not quite as awful as all that," said Eurovision. "Some things are getting better. I'd hate to go back to the fifties. Think how they treated people like me back then."

"You mean like how other people are still being treated today," said Vinegar.

"I do think we've come a ways," said Darrow, "since the times when sodomites were burned at the stake and Blacks were enslaved."

Ramboz shook his head vigorously, back and forth, his white hair like a floppy halo. "No, no, no. We're just as ignorant now as when we were naked apes in the forest, eating snakes and grasshoppers. And we'll be just as brutish and stupid when we're living in a city of crystal towers on Alpha Centauri. Same old nasty, contemptible species."

"Ah yes, we have a true cynic in our midst," said Eurovision, irritation creeping into his voice. "Now, shall we move on?"

The Lady with the Rings said, "I'm sorry some people are so sunken in fear they can't appreciate the beauty in humanity."

Ramboz continued shaking his head. "He is a man nourished by his regrets" was what the bible had to say about Ramboz. I was starting to understand why.

"Enough chatter!" Eurovision snapped, annoyed. "Who has a story?"

"That's where I was going—I've come with a story," Ramboz continued, unperturbed. "A story about Vietnam. About my radical awakening. About why I became a journalist."

"Radical awakening?" said the Poet, misgiving in his voice.

I could see a few others rolling their eyes.

"Well, have at it," said Eurovision.

———

"I was eleven when my mother saw a flyer that the Wellesley News was looking for paper boys. She started saying that it was high time for me to become a useful member of society instead of running wild. She kept nagging me, relentlessly, until I finally went down after school to the Wellesley News office. It was a shedlike building behind an auto-body shop. I knocked and heard a gruff sound—a loud voice and a heavy Boston accent—that seemed to be an invitation to come in. A big fat guy, parked in a swivel chair, sat behind a metal desk. He was dressed in a T-shirt that was too small, which exposed the lower part of a hairy belly. He had wicked BO.

"'Yeah?'

"'I heard you're looking for paper boys,' I said.

"'Where do you live?' He gestured at a giant map of Wellesley that covered the entire back wall of the shed, showing every street and house.

"'Ten Vane Street.'

"'Don't tell me, for chrissakes, show me on the map.'

"I showed him.

"'You got a bike?'

"'Yes, sir.'

"'Fill out this form. You start Monday.'

"'Um, how much do I get paid?'

"'Fifty cents a day, six days a week. Day off Sunday. Bring your slips down here on Saturday between noon and two for your three bucks. We drop a bundle of papers on your doorstep at five thirty and you gotta finish by six thirty. Shut 'em in the screen door or leave 'em on the stoop, don't toss 'em on the lawn. Got it? *No tossing.*'

"'Yes, sir. No tossing.'

"He looked through a greasy three-ring binder and consulted the map of Wellesley, flipping pages and mumbling to himself, pressing a grimy finger here and there, jotting down a list, and checking it against the map. 'Okay, you gonna deliver fifteen *Globes* and one *New York Times*. One *Globe* is for your own house. Here are the addresses. Have your mama drive you around to figure out the best route.'

"'Yes, sir.'

"'And here's how you fold 'em.'

"The fat man picked up a greasy demonstration newspaper and showed me how the paper was to be folded. 'Like this.'

"Then he reached under the table and pulled out a white canvas bag with "The Boston Globe" printed on it in Old English lettering. He thumped it down on the table. 'Your bag.'

"I took it, thrilled.

"As I was turning to go, he said, 'I don't want to hear any complaints. You toss the paper on the lawn, they complain. It gets wet, they complain. Late, they complain. When they complain, you get a pink slip. Three pink slips, you're fired. Got it?'

"I carried the bag out of the office, slung it over my shoulder, and headed home. It looked sharp. This was not some dumb paper like the *Wellesley Townsman*. This was the *Boston Globe*.

"I called up my friend Chip to brag. I still remember the sting of his reaction: 'You're going to be sorry. You're gonna get rained on, snowed on, chased by everybody's dogs.' He shook his head at my folly. 'You know, those dogs are just itching to sink their teeth into your ass.'

"I was up early Monday, in the dark. Oh man, the feeling of that first day. The papers arrived at first light with a thump on the front stoop, the delivery-man burning rubber as he drove off. I broke open the bundle, the smell of paper and ink rising from the interior, still warm from the printing press. I folded each paper in the special way and nestled them carefully in the bag. I looped the strap over my shoulder, went to the shed, rolled out my bike—which I had already spent the previous day oiling and adjusting and pumping up—and took off as a pale light broke over the elms.

"It was a fresh morning, and I got through with my route in forty minutes. Nobody was up in the house yet. Out of curiosity I glanced at our own paper and a headline caught my eye:

SEN. MURPHY ESCAPES BOMBING BY MINUTES

"The article began: 'There was blood all over, blood dripping on the walls, dripping all the way to the street . . .'

"The article garishly described a terrorist bombing in a place called Vietnam. A US senator had just missed being blown up. Sure, I'd heard of Vietnam and knew there was some kind of war going on, but to my eleven-year-old brain it had been vague and distant. In Wellesley, in late 1967, the war was background noise, something happening far away, fought by other people. Certainly nobody we knew had gone over there. But this blood dripping on the walls was not vague and distant at all. I read the article with sick fascination.

"And then I turned to the sports section. The Red Sox were in first place."

Ramboz's voice had become tremulous with emotion at the distant memory.

"It was the beginning of the season of the 'Impossible

Dream.' The Red Sox seemed to be on their way to capturing the American League pennant for the first time since 1946. You can't imagine how important that was to an eleven-year-old boy.

"Now that I was the esteemed *Boston Globe* delivery boy in our neighborhood, I began to take a proprietary interest in the news. Every morning, after I finished my route, I looked through the paper to read about the Vietnam War and the Red Sox. Every Saturday, I bicycled down to Wellesley News and gave the fat man my six slips, and he handed me three dollars, which I put in the tin safe behind a secret panel in my room. I didn't know what the hell I would do with the money, since my parents bought me anything I wanted. I just wanted money: lots of it. I was being raised a good little capitalist.

"But Chip was right. The dogs sure chased me. Every morning, about midway through my route, a vicious terrier came flying off a porch and took off after my bike. The owner, an old lady, stood on the porch scolding her dog in a feeble voice and calling out insincere apologies, while the nasty little cur raced alongside me, leaping and snapping at the bag. Sometimes he latched on and hung by his teeth, swinging like a pendulum while I pedaled furiously and tried to swat him off.

"Every day, the paper chronicled the thrill of the Red Sox moving gloriously, game by game, toward the Impossible Dream, and every day it reported on the bizarre, violent, and senseless war in Vietnam. There were lists of Americans killed, stories about saturation bombings, attacks and counterattacks, hills taken, hills lost, protesters in the streets. This was all mixed in with news of Yaz hitting another homer and Lonborg pitching a no-hitter. And then there were the pictures—bombs dropping, villages napalmed and burning, terrified boys on stretchers with blood soaking through their bandages, soldiers huddled in jungle holes in mud up to their thighs, politicians hollering and stabbing the air with their fingers. The *Globe*, like many newspapers at the time—some of you must remember, don't you?—was beginning to cover the war with graphic and unforgiving precision.

"Never, not once, in any story I read, could I find an explanation of what the war was about. Even my parents seemed confused in trying to explain it to me, talking about dominoes and other crazy nonsense. Had we been attacked? Was there a reason for fighting? Who were the Vietcong and why were we killing them? Where *was* Vietnam? Up to now, the war could have been on another planet, but suddenly here it was, in my living room every morning, death rising from the warm inky pages of the *Boston Globe*. The war headlines rolled in, week after week, along with the Impossible Dream stories. The two have been commingled in my mind ever since. The Red Sox was a story that made sense, an American hero journey. It had a beginning, middle, and end. It had a clear moral arc and arose from an orderly universe. As a kid, I understood that kind of story. But Vietnam was the opposite, different from anything I'd ever been told. Just the murderous and futile movement of troops across a sinister geography. The Red Sox story darkened in the end, when they lost the World Series, but at least I *understood* that kind of loss, as much as I hated it. In Vietnam, were we losing or winning? There was no way to know.

"In late October came the headline that finally staggered me:

PRIEST, 2 OTHERS POUR OWN BLOOD ON DRAFT FILES

"It was published on the front page with a photograph of a Catholic priest, Father Philip Berrigan, pouring a stream of blood from a plastic bottle into an open filing cabinet, looking as composed as Julia Child on television pouring milk into a bowl of flour to make a cake. The article explained:

"'Before and after the men poured the blood from small plastic bottles, they handed out a prepared statement saying they were doing so to protest "the pitiful waste of American and Vietnamese blood ten thousand miles away. We shed our blood willingly in what we hope is a sacrificial and constructive act."'

"I could hardly believe it. His own blood! How did he get it out of his veins without dying? And a priest, no less! I was shaken to the core. Was it possible the grown-ups in charge didn't know what the hell they were doing? Teenagers not much older than me were getting blown up, for no reason that anyone could say, in an unknown jungle halfway around the world.

"And as the months rolled on, the war and chaos got worse. The protests grew in ferocity and the country came undone. January of 1968 brought the Tet Offensive; in March, the My Lai Massacre; in April, the assassination of MLK; in May, two thousand American boys killed in the war's bloodiest month; in June, the assassination of Bobby Kennedy; in August, the police riots in Chicago at the Democratic Convention. I was horrified and confused, but my friends all seemed oblivious and went about their business like nothing was happening. I started to feel separate, even alienated.

"The year 1968 was my coming of age. It defined my generation. When you're a kid, life feels like the beginning of an Impossible Dream, new and wonderful and full of promise—but then you grow up and you realize it's all shit. We had awoken from childhood to find ourselves in a boat piloted by madmen and scoundrels, tossed on dark seas, adrift and bewildered, without a chart."

Ramboz stopped and tugged a kerchief out of a pocket and mopped his brow and face, then wiped his mouth. "Nothing has changed. Look at the world today. Look at our leadership. 'It is going away,'" he croaked in an imitation of the president's voice. "'It will be a great victory.'"

"Um, thank you for the story," said Eurovision. "I'm a Yankees fan, I'm sorry to say. But still—thank you for that reminder of how senseless and complicated the world can be." Eurovision, the eternal optimist, was shaken by the story, I could see, and covering it up with a book-club style comment.

Ramboz shot up his bushy eyebrows. "Yankees fan? How sorry I am for you."

Eurovision was offering up a smile, but the conversation was interrupted by a booming voice that I hadn't heard before. "Yeah, I hear what you're saying about the horrors of war, but you were living in a nice suburban town delivering newspapers. Some of us were actually *living* it."

"Who is that?" asked Eurovision, peering out beyond the candlelight. "We can't see you."

A big guy appeared in the space between the Lady with the Rings and Darrow, grasping too-small a chair. Blackbeard in 3E. He placed it backward and sat down precariously, as others shifted slightly to maintain a safe distance. "How's that? Can you see and hear me now?"

We could, almost too well. His tone was sarcastic. He wasn't young, maybe forty, short black beard, shaved head, face so deeply creased it looked like it had been carved out of wood.

Blackbeard went on. "I've got a story about war and sex—the two most mindless, destructive things that human beings do." He paused, and, when no one objected, he began.

"It can be Trump and Stormy Daniels, or Jeff Bezos with his dick pics, but I'll tell you, sex is the sworn enemy of common sense, it just is. My dad once said to me, 'Some men will jump off a cliff if they think they're gonna land on the right person.' I'll give you a for instance.

"I was sent to Iraq in 2004. Twenty years old and

ready to be schooled, and I learned a few lessons, I'll tell you. It was still the Wild West over there. They all hated us, the Iraqis, some more than others, but there was no telling who the enemy was, whether it was some young stud without a shave or a grandma in a burka.

"In a place like that, there was a lot you didn't want to talk about, like how there really were no friendlies, or who'd gotten a hand and foot blown off the day before, or the way no one in DC actually knew WTF was happening there. So when we were together, the single dudes talked a lot about sex, how bad they wanted to get it, and how to do that, same as soldiers always. Not everybody wanted to hear it. The married guys and the religious guys, a lot of them just tried to shut it out, and more power to them, and some of the brass made it clear that we should keep it to ourselves when there were female troops around. But the single guys, they'd moan to each other, and scheme, and plan. The kind of war that was, where you never knew where the front was, where an IED could blow up in the middle of a post, seemed to sharpen the appetites of some guys, since even going to sleep on the wrong day could be hazardous duty.

"We had a second lieutenant come in to lead our platoon. He was not a bad sort, compared to the run of jerks you sometimes find in the army, but he had too much shine on him to be likable. He was straight out of West Point, and he didn't know anything but the book. He was cycling through, so they could say he'd seen some combat, before they would send him to the Green Zone, where he could be some full-bird colonel's chief of staff for the rest of the war.

"About a month in, he started coming around the enlisted men's quarters. He had something on his mind, and finally, he came out with, Where does a man go around here to get his needs met? I didn't answer him, no one did, but the second time he asked, a guy, Mallory, a farm boy from Idaho who was actually pretty funny, Mallory pointed toward a goat farm that was right at the edge of the base. The lieutenant looked at Mallory like he'd slipped a cog and Mallory kept nodding, and the lieutenant just walked off, pissed.

"So another week or so passed, and one night we're sitting around, playing cards, I think, and the lieutenant came in the tent and he was mad as anything, looking for Mallory. The lieutenant had a big kind of evil-looking knot on his head with a little blood trickling out, and Mallory says, 'What happened, Lieutenant?' and the lieutenant says, 'I got kicked by a fucking goat, that's what happened, I'm lucky I'm not dead.'

"There was nothing we could do, every man in the room, we just busted out laughing so hard, guys were rolling off their seats. Finally, one joker, he pipes up while he has his back turned, 'Was that before you fucked her or afterward, sir?'

"I mean, that was the best laugh in weeks, even the lieutenant was smiling. Mallory was just stammering, and a corporal named Jonas, he could see this wasn't going to end up anyplace good, and finally, he put his arm around the lieutenant's shoulder and he said, 'Not the livestock, sir. You go up to the farmer's hut to see if one of his four daughters is around who wants to make some extra money.'

"'Well, Jesus,' the lieutenant said. 'You could have explained that, Mallory.'

"'Yes, sir,' said Mallory.

"So it's only a few days later, it's the middle of the night, and somebody says a medevac chopper is coming in, and when it lands a couple guys run out with a stretcher, and I could see in the light it's the damn lieutenant. He'd gone and knocked on the farmer's door. Words were exchanged, neither spoke the other's language, but the farmer got the point and he went for a weapon and told the lieutenant to beat it. And the lieutenant, he's young and stupid, I don't know who he talked to, but word was out that the guy was horny enough to believe anything, and somebody convinced him he'd just had bad luck, usually one of the daughters comes to the door. So the lieutenant went back and got his poor West Point–ass gutshot. When the chopper took off, none of us had any idea whether he was going to pull through.

"Well, then the CO got involved, 'cause he can't have an Iraqi farmer shooting a US officer. One of the NCOs decided this had gone far enough and went up and told the old man the whole story. It turns out the lieutenant's uncle is a three-star in the Pentagon, and nobody was going to pass a story up the chain that this young looey got killed looking for love in all the wrong places.

"So it was told that al-Qaeda in Iraq had set a decoy trap at our perimeter and the lieutenant had been shot by the damn terrorists while he was leading a patrol. The poor farmer was hip enough to run before Army Intelligence got hold of him, but God only knows when it was he saw his farm again or his family, or even his goats. Jonas was busted back to private, and nobody knew where the hell they sent Mallory.

"The lieutenant, who was up at Ramstaad for a couple of months, came out of it with a Purple Heart and a colostomy bag and some other medal. He got sent back Stateside, and they called him a big goddamned hero. He's probably a freakin' general by now. I don't know. It was a year before the enlisted guys told that story, and only when there were no officers around, and it was always with a moral: These are people here, same as anywhere. You tell me where it is, Baghdad or Paris, Arkansas or Beverly-freaking-Hills, where you can show up at a man's door and offer him $20 to screw his daughter and think you're not going to get your ass blown off."

"That's not a story," said Eurovision, eyes watering with laughter, "that's an urban legend. Kicked by a goat! Oh God, I love it."

"Iraq messed me up pretty good," said Blackbeard, "and I wasn't even wounded. Just being there, not knowing who the enemy was, not knowing which pile of trash had a bomb, hated by everyone. You drive beyond the wire in these monster MRAPS, and all the little kids of the village are lined up along the road, throwing rocks at you. Kids traumatized by the war that was supposed to save them. We were supposed to save them. When you see that, it messes with your mind."

"War is where brutality meets farce," said Vinegar, in a clipped voice. "It screws up everyone back home, too—kids, wives, grandparents, friends—everyone."

I got a feeling she had her own personal reasons for hating war.

"Not knowing where the deadly enemy is—that sounds pretty familiar right now," mused the Therapist. "This uncertainty, the swirl of constant danger is all around us, even if the virus isn't carrying guns. It's going to result in so much lasting trauma."

Eurovision barked out an uncomfortable laugh. "Good for business, I guess, eh?"

The Therapist cut him a dirty look, and he coughed awkwardly by way of apology.

"Seriously, though. That reminds me of a story about trauma," he said. "I heard it a long time ago but could never get it out of my head. It actually seems quite relevant today. May I?"

"Haven't we had enough trauma and war?" Florida said. "How about a nice story for a change, an uplifting story?"

"Oh, *please*," said Vinegar, turning on her. "A *nice* story? There's no such thing. To hell with *nice*. Real life is mostly trauma and shock—so yeah, let's hear a mean ugly story right now."

There was a silence as everyone waited for Florida to explode. It was like someone had lit the fuse of a bomb, and we were all watching it burn down into the casing.

Florida turned slowly toward Vinegar, her face compressed, her body still with anger. "So you don't like nice stories? You think what we need is more violence, hatred, and racism?" She began gathering up her things with great deliberation. "Fine. I'll let you folks up here bring more misery into the world with your stories. I'm done. Thank you all, but I'm *done* with this rooftop confab-whatever."

After a shocked instant, Eurovision spoke. "Wait. Hold on. You can't leave us."

"Why not?"

"Maybe a couple of stories have gone a little too far," he said. "But that's just—we can do better. What we need is to show more respect to each other." He looked around, his face in a panic. For all his emcee-ing act, it was clear he actually cared about the little community we'd built on the roof. He turned to Vinegar. "Jennifer. That was a bit harsh, what you said, don't you think? Let's not spoil the good thing we've got going."

Here was the Boy Scout leader all over again. Vinegar at first said nothing, hands tightly folded. But then after a moment, she said, quickly: "No offense intended."

"Good," said Eurovision. "There you have it. An apology."

Florida continued to pack up her things.

"We're castaways," said the Lady with the Rings. "We're a bunch of strangers washed up from the wrecked world. And now we're stuck with each other on a deserted island, whether we like it or not. 'Forgive everyone everything,' my momma used to say. Stay with us, please."

But Florida was unmoved. A moment later, clutching all her stuff, she disappeared through the broken door.

After a troubled silence, Eurovision began a story, his voice loud and strained.

"When I first started graduate school, I befriended a young straight couple who had just adopted a pet rabbit. When I say they were young, I mean that they were fresh out of college. Harvard, to be exact. The story goes: She was a staff writer for *The Crimson* and had been assigned the task of reviewing an undergraduate production of a Shakespeare play that he was starring in. She watched the play and took notes, but ultimately hated it. In her review, she panned his performance, calling it overwrought and saccharine. This hurt him. One afternoon, he marched into *The Crimson* office, where he found her sitting and drinking a cup of tea, and defended his interpretation of the role. She was unmoved, telling him to get over it, it was only a review for a silly little play, there were more important things to worry about. He asked her out to dinner, but she said no. He was persistent, which I imagine she found annoying, but she eventually agreed, if only to shut him up. Three years later, they found themselves standing outside of a government building in Iowa City, trying to find two strangers who would agree to be witnesses to their marriage. That task seems simple enough, but apparently, Iowans take the act of witnessing very seriously. They couldn't find two people willing to do it, so they drove three hours to Illinois, a state that, for whatever reason, requires no witnesses.

"But the point of this story is not about witnesses or persistence or marriage or young love. It is about trauma, but we aren't quite there yet. Recall the pet rabbit that I mentioned earlier. You see, my friend and her new husband loved animals. They already had a cat. The cat and the rabbit lived in harmony together, so they decided that they would get another rabbit. What could go wrong, they thought. Or perhaps it never crossed their minds.

"And this is where the story runs awry: When she came home with the newest rabbit and placed him in the cage he would share with the other, she set out a bowl of fresh carrots and lettuce. Instead of eating the food, the rabbits attacked each other. They shrieked all through the afternoon, then throughout the night, clawing at each other. My friend came out for drinks a few nights later, after an evening seminar, and told us that she was at her wits' end. She and her husband could no longer sleep because they were afraid the bunnies were going to kill each other, and they didn't know what to do.

"None of us knew what to tell her. One person suggested she cut her losses and give the newest rabbit up for adoption. Another person suggested keeping them both, but in different cages. Maybe, another suggested, they needed separate bowls for their food and water? No, someone said, what you need to do is bring them out to a field and let them run free. They are rabbits, after all. We were all, as you can see, pulling for straws.

"A week passed. When we got drinks after seminar, as had become our ritual, she told us that she had scoured the internet and found a woman thirty miles away who was a rabbit-behavior therapist. She charged two hundred dollars, due in advance, and her website, my friend claimed, had several customer testimonials. Perhaps it is the New Yorker in me that has trained myself to distrust anyone and everyone promising miracle cures, but I was shocked that two Harvard-educated English majors—people who have surely read their Chaucer—were about to be swindled by some charlatan bunny whisperer. I felt enraged on her behalf, though I didn't say anything because I generally believe that, when it comes to how a grown adult chooses to spend their money, it is best to keep all opinions to oneself. If my friend and her husband wanted to spend two hundred dollars for a rabbit therapist, who was I to tell them not to?

"The following week, we eagerly awaited the next update in the bunny saga. I will tell you what the bunny whisperer told her: First, buy a cardboard box and puncture small holes into the side, large enough so the rabbits can breathe but small enough that they cannot escape; next, place a towel in the box, in case the rabbits piss on themselves; then, you will place the rabbits in the box, close it shut, turn it over gently a couple of times, and place the box in the back seat of your car; finally, drive around your neighborhood in circles for approximately one hour, or until you get bored, occasionally stopping to gently roll the box onto a new side. When you get home, open the box and you will find your rabbits calm, with a renewed sense of love for each other.

"The theory, my friend told us, was that the rabbits would bond over this shared experience of trauma and would live the rest of their lives together in peace.

"We asked, 'Did it work?'

"'Yes,' my friend said. They were officially bonded.

"The nuances of bonding rabbits through a shared experience of trauma is something I thought I'd never have to think about again. In fact, if I'm being completely honest, I nearly forgot about that incident until a year later, when a completely different friend called me from Chicago, where he lives with his husband and their pet rabbit.

"'We got another rabbit,' he said. 'And Liam is not having it.'

("Liam is their first rabbit, because my friend is the type of person who gives human names to pet animals.)

"'Oh no,' I said. 'And let me guess: they want to kill each other.'

"My friend was exasperated. He wanted to know how I knew. 'Liam has never been like this. It's unbelievable,' he said. 'This is not what I signed up for.'

"'Listen,' I said. I told him that I knew exactly what he needed to do. It would sound crazy, but all he needed was a box, a towel (which seemed optional, in the grand scheme of things), and a car.

"'We don't have a car,' he said. 'We live in Chicago. We bike everywhere.'

"I told him the car was integral to the success of the plan, so he would have to ask a friend or rent one for the day.

"I could hear the reluctance in his sigh.

"'Trust me,' I said. 'It's an exercise in bonding. You're going to traumatize the rabbits.'

"'*Traumatize* them?'

"'Just trust me on this,' I said. And then I gave him the full details, as if I were the certified bunny behavior therapist extraordinaire.

"A few days later, a text message arrived: THANK YOU!!! My friend and his husband had enacted the plan with the precision of a diamond laser. And it worked, because of course it did. They were elated. The bunnies, they said, were darlings now, only occasionally causing a ruckus by gnawing on the potted house plants, which they now needed to move onto countertops. But that comes, they reminded me, with the territory.

"'I've been thinking about trauma,' my friend told me on the phone.

"'Human trauma or bunny trauma?' I asked.

"'No,' he said, 'just your garden-variety trauma. The shared kind.'

"'Heavy,' I said.

"'Did you know that people who've experienced a shared trauma, like surviving a fire or a plane crash, or even something smaller like being trapped in a falling elevator—they will come together every so often, like maybe each year, for reunions to, like, commemorate it?'

I did not know this.

"'Well,' he said, 'it's true.'

"I believed him, and this is the final twist that makes this story come together. You see, in order to understand my friend and his interest in trauma, you need to know the story of how we met and why he left.

"We had met in Barcelona six years earlier. We were both American ex-pats working as English teachers after college. Those years were aimless and freeing: beach parties, rooftop parties, house parties, you name it. He was quite the ladies' man, and I think he had slept with all, or most, of the American women in our English teacher cohort. Six months into our friendship, he told me he was questioning his sexuality and asked if I would take him to a gay bar. Of course I said yes, and I brought him to one of the larger gay *discotecas*, where he took some molly in the bathroom, but that is a completely different story for another day. A few months later, I heard from someone else that my friend had left Barcelona without saying goodbye. He had deactivated his social media accounts, and I felt sad that I had lost a friend and wondered if I would ever hear from him again.

"A couple years later, when I had moved back to the States for grad school, he reached out to tell me that he was now living in Chicago and was living with the man who is now his husband. I was very happy for him but, of course, was curious to know why he had left Barcelona without a word. The story was a sad one, he said, but after a few tries, I finally convinced him to tell me what had happened in those final months in Barcelona.

"He had moved into a new apartment that he shared with the landlord, who also owned a small shop on the ground floor. The man had a young lover who was not his wife. As the landlord told it, his absent wife had fallen into a life of prostitution and drugs, and the man did not want to share that kind of life.

"One night, my friend needed to ask the landlord a question. He approached the man's bedroom door, which was slightly ajar, and knocked. When the door swung open my friend saw the lover in the room, in a compromising situation with the man. The lover was crying, and my friend became convinced that the man was harming her. Distraught that this was going on in the same apartment where he lived, he told me he felt—no, he knew—that he needed to do something, but had no idea what. At a loss for a solution, he emailed an old psychology professor of his, someone who has dedicated her life to researching the effects of trauma on the human psyche.

"The professor responded with empathy and compassion but told him that the reality of the situation was like deciding between two very bad options. She told him that there were only two things that could happen: Either the young woman continues living with the landlord, or she goes out on her own without shelter or security. If she went out on her own with no resources to support herself, it would be likely she would be trafficked, endure more grievous abuse, and eventually turn to a life of sex work and drugs. If she continued living with the abusive landlord, she could possibly sock away enough money, over time, to find a way out.

"'There was nothing I could do,' my friend told me. He believed that his professor was right. Between two options, the lover would probably have had a better chance at escape if they stayed with their tormentor who sheltered them.

"I could tell that this devastated him. I'd had no idea of the horror that my friend was grappling with at the time.

"But even as she forced on him this unpleasant truth, the professor had extended a lifeline, inviting him back to Chicago to work for her as a research assistant. She needed to do fieldwork, interviewing women in Mount Greenwood about their experience with domestic abuse in the trappings of affluence. He left Barcelona quickly, without looking back. And while he was in Mount Greenwood, he met the man who would later become his husband.

"Perhaps this is an odd sort of silver lining to take away from this tale: that out of trauma comes the potential for connection. Perhaps things had just lined up right for him, that he was able to move to Chicago and meet the man of his dreams. Sometimes I wonder if he thinks about that young person in Barcelona. I know that I do. I wonder if she is okay. I did not share in their trauma, nor did I witness it, but when my friend told me his story, I felt its weight shared between us. There are no annual events for us to commemorate our sadness, the way that the world, in spite of its beauties and small wonders, reveals to us the ways in which people can hurt other people. It is a sad truth to learn, and one that we carry with us everywhere. We are not bunnies, trapped in a box with a blanket, driving around in circles, and yet there are certain ineffable things that bond us in our experience of life in this world.

"My question is: If bunnies can bond over a shared experience of a box, why can't we?"

As Eurovision's question hung in the air, sirens sliced up from the Bowery, a trio of ambulances heading for Presbyterian Downtown. They were exceptionally loud, deafening even, punctuated by blaring horns. We paused and waited while the noise, echoing and distorted among the canyons, diminished and was replaced by the bells of Old St. Pat's.

Without another word, we broke up for the evening.

I spent several hours transcribing everything that happened this evening, and then turned off the lights and lay down in bed. Tonight, there was only silence from above. That disturbed me as much as the footsteps, and waiting for them to come was even more insomnia-inducing. As I lay there, I was seized with a feeling of paranoia that maybe whoever had been walking around up there had died.

After a while, as my paranoid thoughts piled up, I couldn't stand it any longer. I got out of bed all in a sweat and went upstairs and let myself into the apartment, just to make sure there wasn't a body rotting on the floor. But the place was empty and undisturbed: same broken window, cheap furniture, and dusty floor. I went back to bed, more than ever convinced there were ghosts coming and going up there, diligently at work on some otherworldly business. Turning over our rabbit box.

Day Seven
April 6

There was a new line of graffiti on the mural wall, written in a neat, small hand:

The graves stood tenantless, and the sheeted dead
Did squeak and gibber in the Roman streets

Shakespeare. I knew it must be, but from what play I had no idea. I'd loved the Shakespeare class I took in college, even though I almost flunked it because of all the personal shit that was going on that semester before I dropped out.

I took my usual place and tried not to make eye contact with Eurovision. I could tell he was itching to ask me to speak and probably getting irritated at my standoffishness, but I sure as hell had no intention of getting up in front of everyone. I had, though, tucked away that balled-up letter into the bible, ready to be pulled out in case I was cornered. Mostly I just hoped they'd continue ignoring me. The Singapore Slings the night before had given me a hangover, so I dialed it back and made sangria with a bottle of cheap wine. I had noticed there was a lot of serious drinking happening on the rooftop. If this thing goes on much longer, we're all going to be alcoholics.

The news broke today about all the refrigerator trucks parked in Queens overflowing with dead bodies, and a tent hospital being set up in Central Park. The more we all avoided talking about the pandemic, the more palpable the fear grew under the surface. People were still showing up, and everyone was pretty religious about the six-foot distance and absolutely no touching, but still: I hoped we weren't dooming one another to invisible death up here, telling stories every night.

Adding to the tension, I had now run out of lightbulbs. I sure as hell wasn't going out shopping, and I couldn't raise the landlord and his management lackeys on the phone. Maybe they were all up at Shitgreen Manor with Dad. I guess the lights in the building would just have to burn out, one by one. It felt fitting, in a way. The sense of antagonism I got from the tenants probably had something to do with the state of the tenement, and I wanted to smack them upside the head and yell that it wasn't my fault. Although, to their credit, nobody had said anything overt. Under normal circumstances, a bunch of New Yorkers cooped up together in a building like this would already be in full revolt.

As the rest of the folks gathered, I busied myself with my usual number therapy. Today infections hit 130,689 in the state, with 4,758 deaths. Cuomo claims the pandemic is peaking. (Everyone is swooning over Cuomo and, yeah, maybe he's better than the guy in the White House, but I think he's just a really good talker who eats up being on television. He's a faker, like his brother.) Deaths in the US topped 10,000, with 347,000 cases. The numbers are getting unthinkable. The *Times* reported that a Malayan tiger named Nadia in the Bronx Zoo got sick with Covid. Meanwhile, China, for the first time since the pandemic began, reported no new deaths—or so they claimed.

The lies are getting thicker.

I thought the news would eventually scare people away from the roof, but more people than ever showed up tonight.

Eurovision arrived with his usual fanfare, bustling about, greeting everyone with *ciao ciao*, waving his hand this way and that, all energy, before taking his seat on the throne. He's a bit of a showman, but I've started to like him and his Pollyanna attitude. With Vinegar nearby in her director's chair, they kind of looked like a king and queen of old, seated at the head of some medieval banquet hall. But the big surprise was that Florida was back, all dressed up and dignified, seated as far from Vinegar as possible. Her face was so tight she looked like a grenade about to go off—not that I'd mind. Anything to add a little excitement to Life in the Time of Covid.

We went through the usual seven o'clock cheer, and then Eurovision began the evening by pointing to the graffiti. "I see we have someone up here with a literary bent. That's a line from *Julius Caesar*, if I remember my high school English class, correct?"

"Um, no," said the tenant in 2E—the NYU professor, Prospero. "It's from *Hamlet*. I thought it appropriate for the present circumstances."

"But the *Roman* streets?" asked Eurovision. "Hamlet takes place in Denmark."

I couldn't be sure, but I thought that might have been a bit of pride sneaking into his voice, pleasure at upstaging an academic.

"Indeed," intoned the professor, "but the line is from Horatio, who's recalling what happened just before Julius Caesar was assassinated. He's comparing that to the recent sighting of ghosts and evil portents in Denmark. He's suggesting something awful is about to happen." He added, "Quite apposite for our situation today."

"Ah," said Eurovision. "Thank you, Professor."

I kept my smile to myself.

"It brings to mind," said Ramboz, "how Shakespeare wrote *King Lear* during the great plague of London. I have no doubt the horrors of the Black Death were responsible for that play's spectacular cruelty and nastiness." He shuddered.

At this, Prospero turned and fixed Ramboz with a look of exasperation. "Not that canard again! That meme has been showing up everywhere. But it's 'fake news,' as they say. Couldn't be more wrong. Shakespeare wrote *King Lear* in the plague-free summer and autumn of 1605. At the time, eighteen perfectly calm months had passed since the end of the terrible pandemic of 1603—which, by the way, had taken the life of every seventh Londoner."

Under this blast of scholarship, Ramboz froze with a sort of daffy smile on his face and nodded sagely as if his sentiment had just been confirmed.

"The not-so-subtle message," Prospero said, "is that if the Bard managed to write a masterpiece during a pandemic, you had best have something to show for yourself before this quarantine is over—and it had better be more impressive than baking sourdough bread!" He gave a lecture-hall chuckle. "But there *is* a true story about Shakespeare and the plague, very much more interesting. And one that has a lesson for today."

"Let's hear it," Ramboz said, studiously making his way back into the imposing professor's good graces.

"My story dates back to the early summer of 1592, when Shakespeare was a struggling freelancer in his late twenties. He had been living and working as an actor and playwright in London for three years or so, having left his wife, Anne, and their three young children behind in Stratford-upon-Avon.

"We don't know much about Shakespeare's life at this time—where he was renting, with whom he was sleeping—but we do have a glimpse of how his career was coming along. In 1592, the cantankerous Robert Greene warned his fellow playwrights about an 'upstart crow, beautified with our feathers, that with his "tiger's heart wrapped in a player's hide" supposes he is as well able to bombast out a blank verse as the best of you, and . . . is in his own conceit the only Shake-scene in the country.' The resentful Greene paints a vivid portrait of an up-and-coming Shakespeare, a player turned playwright who owed his recent success to what he was learning—or in Greene's view, stealing—from the leading dramatists of the day.

"A freelance actor's life—which is how Shakespeare had started out in theater—wasn't easy. The half dozen or so shareholders who made up each Elizabethan playing company, and pooled expenses and profits, would employ up to a dozen 'hired men' to flesh out their ranks, mostly doubling bit parts, depending on the casting demands of the play they were staging that day. Adolescent boys, typically apprentices (the unpaid interns of their day), played the women's roles. The pay-per-day for a freelance actor, only a shilling, wasn't much. But in a good year a dependable hired man could earn as much as twelve to fourteen pounds—more than a day laborer, less than a schoolmaster.

"Since a different play was staged every day, with twenty or so new plays a year in repertory with as many old favorites, actors lucky enough to be employed for the day were expected to meet that morning to rehearse the day's play, then, after a break for a meal, perform it in the afternoon. It was a precarious life, made worse by periodic closures due to plague or a government crackdown when a scandalous play caused outrage. One of the sadder surviving letters from the time comes from the accomplished actor Richard Jones, who begs for a loan so he could join a touring company heading to the Continent, 'for here I get nothing, sometimes I have a shilling a day, and sometimes nothing, so that I live in great poverty.'

"Twelve pounds a year was enough to cover Shakespeare's rent and meals. But he had many other mouths to feed, and not only his wife and three children back in Stratford-upon-Avon. His aging father had fallen so far into debt that he couldn't leave the family home on Henley Street for fear of arrest. So the eldest-born Shakespeare likely had to support his father and mother as well as his three younger siblings. To do that, he needed to make more money. And that meant taking on a second and no less precarious freelance career, as a playwright. When his fellow hired men relaxed after a long day of acting, Shakespeare went off to write plays.

"Playing companies were willing to pay dramatists a modest six pounds for a play, which they then owned all rights to, including any profits from publishing it. There were many guilds in Elizabethan England, but none looking out for rights of authors. It was almost impossible for freelance playwrights to support themselves on what they might earn from a few plays a year, and almost no writer at the time did, or did for long. It proved to be more economical writing collaboratively, though split between two or more writers that six pounds didn't come to much.

"In less than four years, from roughly 1589 to 1592, Shakespeare managed to write, coauthor, or contribute a few scenes to *Arden of Faversham, The First Part of the Contention of the Two Famous Houses of York and Lancaster, The True Tragedy of Richard Duke of York, The Taming of the Shrew, The Comedy of Errors, Henry VI, Edward III, The Two Gentlemen of Verona,* and *Titus Andronicus.* We don't know the order in which they were written, and perhaps one or two were drafted a little earlier or later. His pay from all this writing came to a little more than he was earning as an actor, perhaps fifteen pounds a year.

"But there weren't enough hours in the day for Shakespeare to earn more than this. The only way to get ahead was to become a shareholder, dividing the playhouse profits with the theater owner, joining the ranks of those exploiting freelance actors and playwrights. But first he had to be invited to join a company, and there's no evidence that by 1592 any company had extended to him such an invitation. Even if one had, becoming a sharer in what was a joint-stock company required a capital investment of thirty pounds or more, money that Shakespeare likely didn't have. And as good a writer as he was becoming, his path was still blocked by more celebrated playwrights who had produced box-office hits and whose new plays were keenly sought after: Greene, Christopher Marlowe, George Peele, Thomas Lodge, Thomas Kyd, John Lyly, and Thomas Watson.

"Still, he was doing pretty well, about as well as an overworked freelancer holding down two full-time jobs could. But that came to an abrupt end in the summer of 1592, when plague suddenly arrived in a London that had not seen an outbreak this viral since the Black Death of 1348. The authorities at first closed the playhouses until September, then until December, when colder weather usually killed off the plague. But the outbreak persisted. Though the theaters reopened briefly when weekly plague deaths dropped below thirty, they were closed again in February 1593, as dozens, then hundreds, of Londoners died every week. By August of that year, Londoners were struggling to bury eighteen hundred plague victims a week.

"That month, the owner of the shuttered Rose Theatre, Philip Henslowe, wrote to his son-in-law, the star tragedian Edward Alleyn, that the actor 'Robert Browne's wife in Shoreditch and all her children and household be dead, and her doors shut up.' Browne himself had been away, touring on the Continent, when his family was wiped out. Their home would have been sealed, along with everyone quarantined inside who was still alive, for four weeks; the words 'Lord Have Mercy' would have been painted in red on the front door. When hearing this news, Shakespeare may have been relieved that he had not brought his family with him to the infectious city. The summer of 1593 must have felt like the end of the world—and certainly, the end of the theater world.

"The challenges facing the young Shakespeare at this moment were daunting. He couldn't write plays on spec at such a volatile time, as they were written with particular playing companies, and sometimes star actors, in mind. And who would pay for them? Companies that left town to tour in the safer provinces didn't need new plays; they just staged the same old favorites in every town that allowed them to perform. And he couldn't earn a penny from acting unless he toured himself (and the rates for hired men who went on the road were notoriously low). Had Shakespeare toured, he would have cut himself off from opportunities to collaborate as well as from the books on which he depended for his plays' source material. Yet remaining in an infected London put his life in peril. The thought must have occurred to him, as plague numbers ebbed and flowed, and those teasing reopenings of the playhouses turned into renewed closings, that it was time to get out, leave the contagious city, and find a better way to use his talents.

"He could have given up the writing life and gone back to Warwickshire, finding work as a schoolteacher or perhaps employment in his father's trade, making gloves. He decided instead to stick it out in London, writing a couple of wildly popular long poems—*Venus and Adonis* and *The Rape of Lucrece*—dedicating them to the Earl of Southampton, who by convention would have rewarded him with a gift of a few pounds for each. Both poems sold exceptionally well, going through multiple editions—but it was his publishers and not Shakespeare who cashed in on their success. While the poems brought him praise and attention, he earned little more than a pittance from their publication. Had the plague that began in 1592 and lasted the better part of two years stretched on much longer, it's hard to imagine a future for Shakespeare in the theater, or as a self-supporting writer.

"The month that Shakespeare turned thirty—April 1594—the number of weekly plague deaths finally dropped below thirty and London's playhouses reopened. By then, more than twelve thousand Londoners—of the 150,000 or so who had been alive when the outbreak struck—had died of plague. Leading London companies in which Shakespeare likely acted as a hired man or for whom he had written—the Queen's Men, Sussex's Men, and Pembroke's Men—were broken by the long closure. By the time that playing resumed, Marlowe was dead as well as Greene. Watson had been one of the first to die, most likely of plague, one of nearly two hundred Londoners who suffered and died from pestilence in the last week of September 1592. Peele had given over writing plays, as had Lodge and Lyly. Kyd was dying. Most of them were still in their thirties.

"That left Shakespeare—and no other dramatist of note. Surviving actors regrouped. One newly formed company was the Chamberlain's Men, which boasted the best tragedian (Richard Burbage) and the funniest comedian (Will Kemp) in the land. By the summer of 1594, they had added another shareholder to their ranks: the actor and playwright William Shakespeare (who, along with Burbage and Kemp, is recorded as receiving payment for a court performance later that year). It's hard to see how Shakespeare could have afforded the front money to join the company. Perhaps the fee was waived, or he offered playscripts in lieu of payment. The Chamberlain's Men did well to secure the services of the best surviving playwright, one who could act as well.

"Shakespeare would never have to peddle a play again. Inviting a freelance writer to become a full partner was unprecedented in 1594, and rare ever since, but turned out to be a lucrative decision for the Chamberlain's Men. Job security turned out to be a pretty good thing for the promising young playwright. Within a year of becoming a sharer, Shakespeare had finished two of his most popular plays, *Romeo and Juliet* and *A Midsummer Night's Dream*. In the plague-free decade that followed, he continued to write two or three plays a year, all of them far better than what he had previously produced as a freelancer. In 1598 he was invited to become part owner of the Globe Theatre.

"Had a maddened, flea-ridden, rat-carrying *Yersinia pestis* fled down one muddy lane in Southwark rather than another in 1592, Shakespeare's name might be relegated to a footnote, and we might be celebrating Thomas Watson as England's greatest playwright, or perhaps venerating another, now nameless, upstart. Some find their health and livelihood and families destroyed by a pandemic; others are luckier. Why this alternative story of Shakespeare and plague has not become a Covid-19 meme, I'll leave to others to explain."

"**How much** of human history," said the Lady with the Rings, "has been decided by maddened, flea-ridden rats?"

"And how many young writers are dying of Covid right now," said the Poet, "before they can gift the world their genius? It's our very own 'Elegy Written in a Country Churchyard' moment."

I had no idea what he was talking about.

"Covid is killing mostly older people," said Maine. And then, looking around at the shocked faces of the "mostly older" people on the rooftop, she added hastily, "Of course, the death of an older person is no less troubling than that of a younger."

"Of course it is," said the Lady with the Rings. "I'm sixty-five. If I die, that's sad. If"—she made a thumb gesture at Hello Kitty—"dies, that's a tragedy. Especially if she keeps up with the cancer cartridges."

Hello Kitty took a long drag from her vape and issued a stream toward the Lady with the Rings.

"We don't know where Covid is headed," Maine said. "Viruses mutate. That's why everyone should be wearing a mask up here." She glanced around. There were still quite a few who hadn't covered up.

"Masks interfere with eating, drinking, and talking," said Eurovision defensively. "Not to mention breathing."

He was one of the holdouts. So was I. Where was I supposed to find a mask? Go out there and get Covid trying to fight someone in a Duane Reade to buy the last one? That would be funny. Besides, can you imagine trying to have a conversation with your face covered?

At that, a woman sitting in a wicker chair near the mural reached down next to her chair and held up a wadded mass of fabric. She hadn't spoken yet, and I'd been wondering who she was. I guessed this must be Tango in 6B. She stood up and shook it out, and I saw it was a chef's apron, homemade and badly sewn, of fabric imprinted with dopey chicken heads.

"What in the world is that?" asked Prospero.

"It's an apron—and maybe an idea for this group." Tango smiled.

"God love it," said Eurovision. "That would win the ugly-apron contest, hands down."

"Thank you. I made it in home economics class, half a century ago. It never even had a chance. The minute I sat down to sew it, the minute my hands touched the ugly, polyester-blend fabric, the minute I started spending what would turn into eighteen hours trying to thread that fucking needle, all was lost. I kept putting the end of the thread into my mouth in order to keep it really, really thin, but somehow every time I did that, the eye of the needle grew mysteriously even thinner. And it soon became clear to me that this experiment in thinness and ugliness was only going to end in tears. And that the true victim would be this sad little apron."

She held it up for us all to see. Behind the surreal floating hen heads, there was the image of a teeny henhouse in the back, all out of perspective.

"This was the 1970s, in a town on Long Island that you've never heard of. Boys and girls had their boyish or girlish interests, and that was that. I did not like the classic interests of girls, nor did I like the classic interests of boys. This apron-in-progress meant nothing to me.

"But the experience wasn't all bad. There was a girl who sat across from me in home economics class—let's call her Jennifer Esposito—and she was very cool. She came into class every day smelling as if a cloud of marijuana had descended over our town like nuclear fallout. Once, when we were supposed to be sewing our aprons, Jennifer said to me, 'Hey, have you heard this new song, "American Pie"?'

"In fact, I had, because I had an older sister who had bought the record. Together at our table in home ec, Jennifer Esposito and I parsed the lyrics to Don McLean's "American Pie" as if we were two poetry scholars going over *The Divine Comedy*, Canto XI.

"'. . . And a voice that came from you and me . . .'

I recited aloud, using my very best poetry voice. Then we both sat there in silence, thinking about the words. I said to her, 'I think that speaks to the inclusiveness of art. Which comes from all of us.'

"The boys, meanwhile, took shop class across the hall. I had no shop envy whatsoever. The sounds that came out of the shop room were so loud, it sounded like the Daytona Five Hundred in there. To this day, I feel unaccountably proud of myself when I use even the most basic tool-related vocabulary. I said to my husband recently, 'That handle on the drawer is loose. I think we need to use a Phillips head screwdriver.'

"I love that phrase, 'Phillips head.' Who is this Phillip? And how did he get to name the head of a screwdriver? It's like when you get a star or a comet named after you, but much more pedestrian. I'll tell you one thing: There will never be a sewing needle head named after me. And no thread. My one apron is all I've got to show for my time in home ec, back in another era. I did not go on to become one of those women who love to sew or knit, and who do it for comfort or relief, or for the craft challenge of it all.

"The idea of walking into a craft store makes me ill. If you were to say to me right now, 'Here's twenty dollars. I need you to go pick up a bolt of fabric . . .' (And, as with screwdriver heads getting named Phillip, why does fabric get to be a bolt?) '. . . with little corn cobs all over it, so go on off to a fabric store and pick this stuff up,' I would obediently go off and do it. But the minute I enter a fabric store I become overcome by the smell of the wool and glue and fabric. The smell of sewing. The smell of *crafts*. And it all somehow makes me feel sad.

"My apron had a smell when it was still just a bolt. When it was still just a billowing piece of fabric, not transformed into anything yet. The way once, when I was thirteen and in home ec class, sitting across from Jennifer Esposito, I had not turned into anything yet, either. I was neither home ec nor shop. I was neither good nor bad. I did not know what I was. We all start off as an empty bolt of fabric, and it's our job to turn ourselves into something meaningful, or useful, or beautiful, or original. It took me a very long time to do that. I never came to love this apron, but I've held on to it all these decades. I kept it because, in an odd way, I like to be reminded of myself when I was still unformed.

"And sometimes I see myself in that classroom, which is all tiled floor and cinderblock walls and fluorescent lights shining down on the top of the head of this hopeful girl who doesn't yet know where she fits in the world. Because how can she know yet? How can anyone know? In front of me, my apron is spread out like (sort of) a patient etherized upon a table. And it's covered with the heads of hens and their corresponding henhouses. I've kept it all this time, but I've never once worn it. Not when I 'cooked' Stouffer's French Bread pizzas for my gaggle of friends in high school, and not later on, when I was no longer a teenager but instead a grown woman, a mother who made entire meals, pulling dishes out of the oven, saying 'Careful, careful, it's hot,' as my children swarmed me. I went apronless then, just as I do now. I take my chances."

She held it up again. "I was thinking about that, and this apron, last night, and I dug it out of the back of a drawer. I'll take my chances without an apron, let life fall as it may. But this feels different, this Covid thing. One opens you up to more possibilities, but this disease is just going to take us all down. So here"— without ceremony, she plucked a pair of big scissors from a basket at her feet and began to slice into the fabric, severing chicken heads as she went. "For those of you who know how to sew, take a few swatches back to your apartment and come up tomorrow with masks for everyone." As she spoke, she continued cutting up the apron and stacking swatches on the arm of her chair.

Maine scanned our faces, assessing who needed

extra convincing. "It's a minor inconvenience," she said. "We should all be wearing masks. Trust me as someone who knows."

"Yeah—and see if you can get the hen head centered right on your mouth—for maximum coverage," smirked Hello Kitty.

"For maximum ridiculousness," said the Lady with the Rings. "No thank you. I prefer Hermès." She touched her cheetah scarf.

"If you sacrifice your Hermès to Covid," said Eurovision, "make me a mask too. I will *not* wear a chicken."

"Cut up Hermès? Not on your life."

The busy sound of snipping filled the air.

"Who on the rooftop," said Wurly suddenly, "besides me hates that song?"

"'American Pie'? I thought everyone loved it," La Reina said.

"Four hackneyed chords," Wurly continued, "high-school-level guitar strumming, inane overrhyming lyrics. I mean, what the fuck? That song is supposed to be deep? Listen to some real music, man. Listen to Satchmo, or Billie Holiday, or Coltrane. Or Mahler, for fuck's sake."

"It's a sort of folk music," said Eurovision. "Meant to be simple."

Wurly sucked his teeth. "No. Great folk music is

never simple, and it arises from the soul of the people and their lives and struggles. 'American Pie' was muzak for privileged white hippies."

"Ouch," laughed Eurovision.

I didn't know the song, never heard of the singer, and frankly didn't give a shit.

"All right," Eurovision continued, collecting himself, "instead of trashing Don, who's got another story?"

We lapsed into an awkward silence, while Eurovision's eyes roamed threateningly around the rooftop. I tried to avoid eye contact, pretending to fiddle with my notebook.

"Ahem," he said, and I could feel his stare even though I was looking down. "What about that story you promised?"

I looked up. "Me?"

"Yes, you. Tell us a story. Anything. The Adventure of the Leaky Faucet, maybe!" He laughed at his dumb joke.

For a moment, I wanted to choke him. But it's okay, I had prepared for this. "I don't actually have a story of my own to tell," I said. "But I can read a letter I found." It was a wild letter, and funny—a good way to distract from myself while appearing to play along.

"Found? Where?"

"In the trash."

"You go through our *trash*?"

"I was cleaning out an apartment in the building," I said, flaring up. "I think the tenant left for the Hamptons. It was balled up on the floor."

"One of *those*," said the Lady with the Rings, her voice dripping with disapproval. For a moment I thought she was talking about me, until I realized she meant the New Yorkers who fled the city at the first sign of trouble. "Which apartment?"

I shrugged. "I'd better not say."

Eurovision sighed, more dramatically than necessary. "Well, I was hoping for something *real*—more personal. But okay. Let's hear your letter."

He seemed to be stuck on the idea that there was something suspicious about me, something I was hiding. I wasn't going to give him time to probe any further. I took out the crumpled pages, smoothed them out against my thigh, and began to read.

Dear Cheryl and Steve—

Happy wedding day!

Hope you're celebrating anyway, on what would have been your wedding, except for this awful pandemic. What a disappointment. I hope today is still special for you, despite missing out on your extravagant event at that gorgeous oceanfront property, which I know all about from Facebook and Instagram, even though I wasn't invited. Here's a vase.

My gift to you as you begin your new life together, plus this letter which I paid extra for, because, you're worth it! Maybe Steve will get you some flowers to put in the vase, Cheryl. That would be so romantic! One time he bought me a watermelon. That's not as random as it sounds; it's kind of an inside joke/you-had-to-be-there kind of thing. It was cute and kind of funny, in the way inside jokes are when you've been together for a long time. It was Valentine's Day and, well. A watermelon. Still, I could have reacted with more grace. We were all so much younger then. I'm sure we've all grown up so much in the past eighteen months!

If he gave me a watermelon today, I would probably laugh instead of crying or "making a thing of it."

Especially because I would be like, Steve, why are you giving me a watermelon on the day of your wedding to my ex-best friend? You goon.

I used to call him a goon sometimes, and he would call me a goober. Hopefully he has a better nickname for you, Cheryl! Of course I have a million nicknames for you, some of which go back to second grade (Starburst!) all the way through middle school (were you Snick and I was Snack or the other way around?) and beyond, straight through these past few months when— boy howdy, you don't even want to know those new nicknames! Or maybe you've heard some of them through our mutual "friends." Seven of them were invited to the wedding so I guess you haven't cut off ties with everyone! Which is smart. It's hard to start a new life from scratch.

Though all those engagement pictures of you and Steve are a good effort. I mean, blond hair! That's new! And I know how much you used to mock those girls who posted swimsuit selfies, so your bravery in overcoming any feelings of hypocrisy about posing in so many bikini shots with Steve on the beach is definitely not lost on me.

Or your mom, I'm sure. Is she okay? Oh, "Aunt" Jeanie and "Uncle" Paul. They must be devastated at this latest calamity, having to cancel after throwing the wedding together so quickly after your sudden engagement shocked everybody.

Everybody except the photographer Steve hired to document every second of the proposal. What says intimate and spontaneous better than three dozen posed shots from multiple angles of the exact moment when Steve got down on one knee in his khakis and white shirt that matched your white dress and new beige kitten heels that definitely don't make you look taller than him—the same height, just about. Don't worry, either of you! So cute!

I just hope you are holding up, despite the many disappointments you're suffering. Obviously, there are worse things happening right now than the cancellation of a lavish wedding. Still, a broken leg (like you had in fifth grade—remember when I carried your books from class to class that whole month? Good times) or even a stubbed toe (wow, remember when I stubbed my toe on the weird chair in your kitchen and then, like, ten minutes later we were laughing so hard we were almost choking on the ice cream we were eating straight from the carton you were holding on my toe?) is not as bad as, say, terminal cancer—but here's the truth: In the moment, the fact of other people having terminal cancer doesn't negate the pain of the stubbed toe. (As we, in hindsight callously, tried to explain to your grandmother, may she rest in peace. God we were beasts sometimes.)

So, the fact that your wedding is ruined is still a big deal, you two lovebirds, despite all the death, sickness, and economic collapse surrounding it. I hope you can somehow manage to just forget everybody else's feelings and have a romantic time tonight. It's bad luck to leave a vase empty, of course. If flower shops are all shut down by the nonmetaphorical plague so you can't fill the vase—which I realize was not on your registry but honestly, I just could <u>not</u> get you some of that hideous stuff which I'm sure some saleslady must've bullied you into—maybe you should just fill it with gin and have a party! I left a bottle of Hendrick's, Steve's favorite, in the freezer. It was going to be a present for him, before I found those pictures of you in his underwear drawer, Cheryl.

If it's still there, the gin, I mean, consider it just an extra wedding day gift from me to both of you now! To go with the vase.

Although I heard you're trying not to drink now, Cheryl. Good for you, by the way. One day at a time. Of course, you and I never drink gin anyway, ever since that night when we were twenty-one and had more than our share of it together. Remember that, Cheryl? Barely? Well anyway, some details of that night are obviously never going to be shared with you, Steve!

You don't even have to send me a thank-you note, either of you. I know you both hate writing those! I know you both so well.

Stay safe. Who even knows how this pandemic affects a fetus in the first (or is it the second already?) trimester.

With all my love!
Goober/Snick-and-or-Snack

Uncomfortable chuckles rippled across the roof. I heard a burst of laughter over my shoulder, which sounded like Blackbeard. I was really enjoying this funny and furious woman, whoever she was—but noticed Eurovision trying to catch my eye. He was looking at me suspiciously. "Is that real?"

"I assume so. I don't know," I said. "Like I said, I found it crumpled up on the floor. I figure the letter writer wrote it and then decided against sending it."

"Exactly," said the Lady with the Rings, with a sniff. "You don't *send* a letter like that. She wrote it to get it off her chest and then tossed it. Good for her, I say."

I nodded and glanced at Hello Kitty. Of all the people on the roof, she would be the one who was most likely to have been friends with the letter writer, but it didn't seem like she recognized her.

The sad cracked bells of Old St. Pat's began tolling, saving me from further interrogation at the hands of our meddlesome emcee.

After transcribing the evening's stories, I turned off the light and lay down, anticipating with a dull feeling of anxiety the slow footfalls—would they come or not come? They were back again tonight, a shuffling procession of the damned, along with that mysterious sound of oars in water. But even worse, I now heard what sounded like muffled voices—frightened, confused, and babbling. How many tenants were there in this place, anyway? I covered my head with the pillow, trying to shut it all out. It took a long time to go to sleep.

Day Eight
April 7

When I arrived on the roof that evening, Tango's silly hen masks were sitting in a basket by the door. The Lady with the Rings, on the other hand, was resplendent in a silk mask covered with golden cheetahs—she had sacrificed her Hermès after all. She had left another mask on Eurovision's throne, and he picked it up with glowing eyes.

"In better times, I'd give you a big hug, darling," he said, fitting it on his face, plucking and adjusting it to get it just right. He turned his head. "How does it look?"

"Fabulous, of course."

I was not going to be caught dead in a hen mask. Instead, I'd tied a cowboy bandanna around my face like a desperado. That was more in keeping with how I see myself. There were other masks, too—Hello Kitty with a Hello Kitty mask, of course, Merenguero's Daughter with sequins, Maine with her surgical mask, looking a little worse for wear, and Darrow with a mask made out of a pink power tie. Vinegar had made herself a mask out of black velvet, with the head of a ghost painted on it.

The mural wall sported a new painting: a grotesque devil with a bat's face and peacock's tail writhing in flames; and hovering above it was an angel with blue and pink wings, looking down with an expression of delight on her ethereal face. It was incredibly striking and obviously done by a true artist.

"Wow," said Eurovision. It was hard to tell if it was awe or disdain. He raised his chin toward the mural. "Who's the painter?"

"Me," said Amnesia proudly.

"That's intense."

"I used to write and illustrate comic books for a living, and sometimes weird images just pop into my head. This came to me last night—an angel digging the torture of a devil."

"What an absolutely cruel image," said the Lady with the Rings. "Cruel . . . but perhaps justified."

"But don't you wonder," Amnesia said, sipping her

drink, "what the angels up there are thinking now? Looking down on the pandemic, at all of us hidden away and dying. All the people in the hospitals. Are the angels weeping—or laughing? Is this just one more cycle for them?"

"God only knows," said the Lady with the Rings.

"God does know," said Florida sharply.

"The image popped into my head when I heard about what happened at that Columbia dorm uptown," Amnesia said.

"What happened?" Hello Kitty asked. She sounded surprised that she might have missed a piece of news.

"After they evacuated Columbia, they went through one of the dorms and found dead people in half the rooms."

"That's not true," said Whitney. "I have friends up there. I would have heard."

"Have you been in touch with them?" asked Amnesia.

"Not recently."

"Then how do you know?"

"It would have been in the *Times*."

This elicited a bold laugh from the Lady with the Rings. "Precious, there's a lot that doesn't make the *New York Times*."

"In writing computer games," Amnesia said, "and

comic books, I used to make up crazy scenarios every day, but this reality beats all. Someone up there is eating this up, I swear. The crazy shit they watch us earthlings do."

"Speaking of angels," said a woman on the roof who hadn't spoken before, the tenant in 6C—La Cocinera. She'd been lingering in the background almost since the beginning, but always messing around with her phone after the cheering was over, ignoring everyone. "I saw an angel once."

"What kind of angel?"

"Not like that one at all," she said, pointing at the painting.

"An honest-to-God, real-life, *magical* angel?" Eurovision asked, his voice tinged with irony.

"First of all," La Cocinera said, "this is not magical realism. We are sick of magical realism." She spoke with a soft Mexican accent threading a contralto voice. "That being said, the campesinos of my country know the truth: there is magic all around us. I'm from San Miguel de Allende, but my father's putting me through culinary school here because he thinks it will make me a citizen of the world. I am, or was, training to be a chef at Xochitl, in Brooklyn. I was supposed to go home last month—then Covid hit." She made a wry face. "Have any of you been to San Miguel?"

Florida raised her hand. So did Whitney.

"The rest of you should go," said La Cocinera.

"Before the plague hit, the streets were alive all day and all night. You could walk anywhere at any hour. San Miguel, a magical kingdom surrounded by the fifteenth century. It looks like an artwork, my pueblo. Like a painting. In most parts. But you know, outside of the bubble, outside of the bright walls and galleries and cathedrals, it's ancient land. Chichimeca land. And people there suffer as they always have. So you must understand, for the sake of the story, I am telling that those people come into the *centro* to sell their wares, to show their weaving and carvings. And to go to Mass.

"In the center of the town we have a plaza. A very small Central Park, if you will. Humble. We call it The Garden—El Jardín. It is full of trees. On the western side of the plaza, the cathedral. All around the plaza, colonial buildings now housing shops and candy stores and my favorite ice-cream stand. It was my habit to go there every day and just watch the families and lovers and Indios stroll. Especially as the day of my coming here to New York approached.

"And that day, it was sunny. I was a week away from coming here. Feeling sentimental, as one does. I sat outside in the sun, reading Lorca's poems. So cosmopolitan in my shades, watching two young men celebrating their engagement with a photographer in the lovely cobble streets. Their mothers were there. I blew kisses at them. And the small Indian girls around them were selling wooden burros their families had carved and painted in the Otomi villages downhill. The church bells began to ring, and I glanced that way. And that is when I saw the angel.

"At first, I wasn't sure what I was seeing. San Miguel is not a stranger to street performers. We have a Pancho Villa in full regalia who poses with tourists for a small fee. He even holds his machete in the air, if asked. It is not uncommon to see people wearing ten-foot-tall papier-mâché costumes—giantesses walking down the alleys. Anything is possible. And when I saw her, she might have been some mime, some contortionist.

"How do I describe her? Imagine an old woman. No, older than what you're thinking. Smaller. Yes? Bent. Bent all the way, into a ninety-degree angle. And wrapped in tatters. White hair peeking out from under her scarf. Do you see her? Picture her in your minds?

"Good. I'm glad. Because nobody else seemed to see her. She was stumbling up the street. Did I tell you? I don't think I did. She was balanced on two canes. Short canes, you see. Rough wood, as if she had found two small branches broken off by a storm. She seemed to be a four-legged creature struggling uphill over those ankle-breaking cobblestones. Tourists almost knocked her over. Dogs harried her. Children ran past. A car, then a bus, seemed to be pushing her over. And once, just once, her head rose and her face turned toward the church. Then she looked back at the cobbles and crept on.

"I had never seen her before. But even worse, and this is my confession to you, I might have simply never noticed her. What did she have to do with fine food or artwork or imported clothing in the shops? What did she have to do with the laughter of my friends or the foolishness of my romances?

"As she neared my corner, a terrible thing happened.

"The angel came to the corner of the Jardín, and was turning to make the last, most awful, climb to the church. I saw it all in that instant—how she must have struggled up the hill every day for the church service. It must have taken hours. And nobody saw. Nobody offered her help. What did she ask God for? I asked myself. Who does she pray for? Surely, not herself. And then, it happened. Her left stick caught between two cobbles and jerked out of her hand, and she fell.

"She fell flat on her face. There was a mesh bag, I saw, over her shoulder, and it spilled an orange into the street. People looked. One man stood and stared. But no one went to her.

"She lay as if dead. She was just feet away from two carts that sold fresh fruits, juices, and water. I threw away my ice cream and ran out to her. I realized later that I was ashamed to be doing it. Blushing because I imagined everyone was watching me. Mocking me, perhaps.

"I knelt beside her and took hold of her arm. I could hear her faint voice as I pulled her up. Her flesh was loose on the bone. She smelled like urine and onions. She turned her face up to me. Her eyes were cloudy. 'Daughter,' she said. 'God bless you.'

"I told her to move slowly, be careful, and I helped her stand as far up as her bent back would allow. I myself was bent low to support her weight, and I walked her to a curb and sat her down. 'Bless you, bless you,' she kept repeating. I told her to rest there and rushed to collect her canes and her orange. 'Are you hungry?' I asked. 'Water,' she replied.

"I ran over to the carts and asked if they'd seen what happened. 'Very sad,' one man said. I bought two bottles of water and two tall plastic cups of fruit salad in a rage. After he took my money, he just turned away. I wanted to smite him. I wanted to slap everyone in the Jardín for not seeing the angel fall.

"When I took the water to her, she gulped much of

the first bottle. She put her hands on my face and said, 'God and the spirits will bless you, Daughter. Love to you for caring for the poor. Love to you for caring for the hungry.'

"She made signs over my head as I bent to her, and she sketched a cross on my forehead with her thumb. 'Love for you forever for your mercy.' Everyone now seemed to be watching us. I was overcome. I shoved all my remaining money into her hands.

"I started to weep, and I never weep in public. I had to go to one of the shops across the street and act as though I was looking at the clothes in the window until I collected myself.

"When I turned back, she was struggling up that hill again. Trying to get to the church."

La Cocinera paused, and we all waited.

"So how did you know the old lady was an angel?" Florida asked.

"I'm getting there," said La Cocinera. "I want to show you something." She took her phone out, tapped at the screen a few times, and turned it to face us.

"That's the Jardín at this very moment, and that's the Parroquia in the background. One of my cooks at Xochitl is from a nearby city—Celaya. He reminded me of the twenty-four/seven San Miguel web cam. Here it is, live."

She made to hand the phone to Vinegar, but Vinegar recoiled from the touch. Apologetically, as if just remembering this nightmare of a pandemic, La Cocinera held the phone up for Vinegar to view from a distance. Then stepped to the next person, and the next, and we all took turns staring at a pixelated portrait of this magical place, three thousand miles away, as it appeared right at that very moment. I could see the empty public garden in spring flower, beyond which stood a fantastical Gothic church of pink stone with wedding-cake towers.

"My friend said his mother went there every Wednesday at three in the afternoon to wave hello to him. I couldn't believe it. I had forgotten it in all the excitement of New York. It was like a drug for a homesick girl. As soon as work was over, I hurried here and fired up the laptop. It was after midnight, of course. And San Miguel is in another time zone, but it was night there, too. I didn't care. I just wanted to see.

"And the image opened and there it was. All lit with its colored lights, the facades of the shops along the far side all lit as well. Lovers strolled. I could see they were eating ice cream! I was like some child screaming with happiness!

"Even better when the mariachis began to play.

"Just a moment. Once you see it, you'll want to go

there. It became a thing, you know? As soon as I woke up, I turned it on. I watched the pigeons, so different somehow than our pigeons here. The dogs. And the schoolchildren in their uniforms trudging to school. It was my daily ritual. Even the empty streets were magic. And then, one day . . .

"But all of you already know.

"I was looking. And she came out from under one of the trees. Still painfully slow. Agonizingly slow. She stepped out of the shadows and into the sun. And here is the story. She looked up. She looked up to the camera high above her on its pole. She looked up and she locked eyes with me. Looked right into my eyes. And she smiled. That's not all. I swear to you, I saw her mouth say, 'Daughter.'"

She stopped. Nobody said a word. That moment hung in the air. Finally she continued.

"Then this plague hit. And the streets were empty except for men in white sci-fi suits with hoods and faceplates. They sprayed chemicals from wands. The streets were deserted. I've never seen her again. But I kept looking for her. I looked for her every day. I was sure she was dead. I have tried to be resigned to it—she was only human. Not an angel at all. I know it doesn't make her any less.

"Some days, I have stayed at the screen for hours.

Now that we're locked in, I am here, waiting for her. Calling to the angel."

La Cocinera had finished her circle among us on the roof. "And now." She looked around. "What time is it?"

"Almost seven thirty," Eurovision said.

"Maybe, just *maybe* . . . this time she'll come." She held up her phone again for all to see. People leaned in, staring at the tiny screen, glowing like a brilliant jewel in the dim light. The silence was profound.

We stared at the San Miguel web cam, every one of us hoping for a miracle. My eyes began to water from the strain, but I swear I saw it: the barest movement, the appearance of a bent shadow just entering the tiny frame of the phone from behind some trees—and then the phone blinked out and went dead.

A chorus of dismay rose from the group. La Cocinera pulled back her arm and looked at her phone with a frown. "Damn." She waved her hand. "It's my battery."

I felt acutely disappointed. I had really believed I might see the angel—I'm not sure why.

"You did that on purpose," said Amnesia.

La Cocinera shook her head vehemently. "Mine was a good angel, even though she's old and ugly. Not like your beautiful sadist."

Amnesia laughed. "You never know in my comic books which are the angels and which are the demons. I get a lot of my ideas from Hieronymus Bosch paintings. And fairy tales. If you think about it, computer games are like the new fairy tales."

"Computer games are worse than fairy tales," said Vinegar. "And more violent."

"That's where you're wrong," said Amnesia. "The old fairy tales were just as dark. Cannibalistic witches, girl-eating wolves, vicious stepmothers, poisoned apples, mutilated women. I don't know why, but kids love that dark, violent stuff, as long as good triumphs in the end. I'm always dreaming up weird tales, a lot of which I just can't make into a computer game or comic book because they don't have a happy ending."

"Why don't you tell us one?" Eurovision asked. "One of those that ends badly."

"Sure. Let's see, there's one I wrote a few years ago, but it was rejected by my publisher . . ." Amnesia took a deep breath behind her mask. "Once upon a time, there were two sisters named Frannie and Tara who did a favor for the goddess of truth."

"What kind of favor?" asked Eurovision.

"I don't know. They picked up her dry cleaning, or they found her lost orb, or they saved her from an obfuscation monster. It doesn't matter. The point is, the goddess of truth owed them a boon."

"So Frannie asked for the obvious thing that you would ask the goddess of truth for. She wanted to never be lied to again. Either people would tell her the strict truth, or they would hold their fucking peace. She didn't want people to be forced to tell her the whole truth—just, no more lies. You get sick of it. You know?

"But Tara? She asked for something a little more complicated. She wanted a spell that made it so that any time someone lied to her, it automatically became true. So if you told Tara, 'I'll give you the money to-morrow,' that would be the absolute, unshakable truth. But she was careful to add that this wouldn't apply if someone was exaggerating on purpose, for dramatic effect, or making a joke—only if people were actively trying to deceive her.

"A few years went by, and Frannie and Tara ended up living together, because they were the only ones who they could talk to.

"See, Frannie had gotten tired of hearing the truth all the time. If she'd stopped to think it through before she asked for that particular favor, she'd have known. Right? People were constantly being just a little bit too brutally honest with Frannie. About her looks, her job performance, the sound of her voice, and so on. Not being able to blame these people for their truth telling was the worst part.

"And meanwhile, Tara found out the hard way that not every lie people tell is sugarcoated. 'I never loved you' is just as much a lie as 'You're the only one I love.' Or, 'You don't have what it takes to succeed around here.' Tara might be the most beautiful woman in the world one day, because someone had said so, and then the next she might be hideously unfuckable.

"Sometimes your family are the only people you can get through a truthful conversation with. These girls had lost their parents when Frannie was seventeen and Tara was fifteen, and they weren't close enough to any other relatives for that kind of radical honesty. Tara didn't mind being forced to tell nothing but the truth to Frannie, and meanwhile, Frannie was careful not to tell any excessively cruel lies to Tara.

"I could tell you about how Frannie tried to find a career where her gifts would be valuable—counselor, investment manager, police officer—only to find that all of those jobs required someone who could be lied to successfully. Or how Tara became monumentally wealthy, by meeting up with a bunch of con artists who promised to bring her fantastic sums of money in exchange for a small deposit, but then lost it all when one man told her she would never be good at holding on to money.

"I could even tell you about the time they started a religion. Okay, a cult. They started a cult, and it was great for three days. Until it wasn't. They had to change their phone numbers and burn sage and bring in an exterminator, and it was a whole thing.

"But that stuff is just shoes falling, and we all know how that goes. Shoes fall down: thud thud thud. But also, they protect your feet?

"Frannie and Tara bought a slow cooker secondhand from someone, like in a yard sale or something. The old owner swore it worked perfectly, and luckily they were talking to Tara, so it was a dream. And the two of them became low-key obsessed with slow-cooking things. Everything from fancy sous vide beef to taco soup and weird kale concoctions. Their little house was always full of a starchy, yeasty smell: tomorrow's meal in the works. I swear to god, they would have conversations that lasted an hour about that slow cooker, and all the things they could put in it. It was their whole satisfaction.

"That house, too, was a lot on their minds. They had inherited it from their parents, and they owned it free and clear, so they just had to worry about upkeep and taxes. Tara had to be the one to talk to plumbers and contractors; Frannie was the one who talked to the city. The house was always somewhere between falling down and perfect, depending on whether you looked at the beams or the foundation. To be honest, neither of the sisters really knew much about being homeowners, and that house worried them all the time. They felt like their parents were judging them for their poor upkeep (and the dead can say whatever they want to you, no matter what).

"One day the sisters were sitting in a café, and it was the first time either of them had left the house in ages. (This was before it was normal to never leave the house.)

"'I'm so fucking old. I'm as old as fucking dirt,' said Tara.

"'I'm even older, I'm as old as dirt's grandmother,' said her older sister, Frannie.

"'Excuse me,' said the man at the next table over, addressing them in that manner of cis men in coffee shops speaking freely to unfamiliar women. 'But you're both very young.'

"They stared at him until he shut up and went back to talking to his computer.

"But . . . he had been speaking to both of them at once, so there was no way he'd been lying. And also, Tara and Frannie were fully aware that they were in their twenties (twenty-five and twenty-seven, respectively).

"'Let's just go home and slow-cook something,' Frannie said to Tara.

"'I want to stay and finish my coffee.' Tara gestured at her mug, which was still mostly full and lukewarm. 'I paid for this coffee, I want to drink it here.'

"Frannie said nothing, just brooded. She knew better than to tell her sister something was okay when it wasn't. A few minutes later, she stood up. 'I can't stay here any longer. People are going to want to talk to us, and every time someone tries to tell us about ourselves, I get more tired.'

"'I'm tired of being alone,' Tara said. 'In that house in the middle of nowhere with you, slow-cooking things. It's good, but it's not enough for me.'

"'We could get a dog.' Frannie didn't mean it until she said it, and then she did.

"Another man approached, wearing too much denim and smiling without teeth. 'Beg your pardon,' he said. 'I couldn't help noticing—'

"'No,' Tara said to the man.

"'Just no,' Frannie agreed.

"'I wasn't going to—' he protested. But they waved him away, and he went.

"'We could get a skillet,' Frannie told Tara. 'Or a wok, even. We could fry stuff.'

"'Can I just sit here and finish my coffee?' Tara pleaded.

"The sisters only had one car between the two of them. I should have mentioned that earlier. And it was a long, annoying walk back to their cabin, most of it on the soft shoulder. The car was a ten-year-old fizz-colored Hyundai, without a ton of mileage on it, and the back seat was strewn with CDs even though the CD player refused to disgorge this one Johnny Cash album that Tara had shoved in there a few years ago. It didn't even have any of the songs about murdering someone, it was all ballads and courtship, stentorian declarations of love.

"Frannie could tell Tara was getting ready to leave her. And maybe Frannie could tell her younger sister the right kind of lie, so that Tara would stick around.

"Like: 'You'll never have the guts to go out on your own.'

"Or: 'You'll never be happy living with anyone but me.'

"But either of those projections would be a garbage thing to say to your only blood relative. And you wouldn't want to be stuck living with someone you said such things to. Plus, Frannie also knew that Tara was scared to leave, because anybody could say anything to her, out there in the world. And it really wouldn't take much to scare Tara into staying.

"For the first time ever, Frannie found herself wishing their gifts were reversed. Like if Tara had Frannie's gift, then Frannie could tell her sister, 'I'll be broken-hearted. I understand why you want to make your own way, but I'll be broken in any number of places without you.' And Tara would know it was the simple truth.

"The two sisters visited their parents' graves, in a grassy yard surrounded by walls that were made of nettles as much as stone. They put fresh daisies and crocuses on the plain granite markers, and just sat on the grass without talking.

"As they walked back to the car, Tara said, 'What if I moved to the city for a while?'

"'There'd be less Lyme disease,' Frannie replied. 'And more nonsense.'

"'I'd hear so many falsehoods, I'd be able to surf them, keep on an even keel. Maybe a thousand people's lies would cancel each other out, or I'd learn how to find the right kind of liars. I don't know.'

"Frannie couldn't risk saying half the things on her mind. So all she said was, 'Maybe.'

"'I'd come back here regularly,' Tara said. 'I'd visit

all the time. You could come visit me there, too, if you wanted. I just want to try living surrounded by voices and see what it does to me.'

"'And what if you don't like how it changes you?' Frannie asked.

"'Then I'll come back here, and you can remind me of who I actually am.' Tara smiled and let her sister get behind the wheel. She started playing with the radio.

"'What if I don't want that to be my job?' Frannie was being very careful to phrase everything in the form of questions and hypotheticals, rather than half-truths and untruths.

"'It's not a job, though.' Tara decided to try and eject the Johnny Cash CD, maybe so she could leave her sister with a wider choice of music options once she was gone. 'It's part of being sisters. It's a thing you are, rather than a thing you do.'

"'Yeah, but what if you go to the city and listen to so many falsehoods that come true, and then one day you come home and expect me to help pick up the pieces, and I just can't?' Frannie was feeling waves of grief and nausea and lonesomeness, and she couldn't help thinking about the way Tara had talked about surfing. Frannie could barely doggy-paddle, much less stand upright.

"'It'll be fine.' Tara jabbed at the CD player with

a pair of pliers. 'Really. I can handle myself and I always know the difference, deep down, between the truth and a lie that became true. You know I can handle this.'

"'Stop messing with the CD player,' Frannie snapped. 'I'm trying to—'

"Both sisters focused on the car stereo and Tara's fumbling attempt to rescue Johnny Cash, like the trapped CD was the whole problem between them, and then Frannie looked up at the road too late to see a large, muscular deer plunging out of the woods into their path. The car hit with a raucous crunch, sound of confused applause for a sudden own goal, and suddenly the sisters' seat belts were taut and there were fluffy white shapes inflating in front of them.

"A short time later, the sisters watched the deer saunter away, limping slightly, from the crumpled remains of their car's front bumper and engine housing.

"The two sisters stood there by the side of the road, waiting for the tow truck. Frannie found a packet of rich tea biscuits in the back seat detritus and offered some to Tara. They both munched and watched the smoke dissipate.

"'It's going to be okay,' Tara said, weeping gently.

"'I know it will.' Frannie was all cried out—but she still cried, a little. 'That's what frightens me.'

"**And that,**" said Amnesia, "is the tale of two sisters who got into trouble by trying to banish lies from their world." She laughed.

"That's not where I thought that story was going," mused Eurovision, as much to himself as to anyone else.

Amnesia shrugged amicably. "No matter what, there's no way to give that one a happy ending."

"Lies are the lubricant of life," said the Lady with the Rings. "I, for one, would not wish to live in a world of truth." She looked around. "I lie every day. As I'm sure we all do. In fact, I lived a lie for thirty years—with spectacular happiness. And when it all unraveled . . . I was still happy."

"Tell us about it," said Eurovision, leaning forward eagerly.

"Not yet."

"*I* love a good lie," said Hello Kitty.

Florida snorted and shook her head. "There's no such thing as a good lie."

"I've got some good lies," said a voice from behind me.

Pardi was back. She was leaning against the wall near the doorway, her eyes alight. "I promised you the second half of my story, didn't I? It's got plenty of lies in it."

Eurovision grinned. "Yes, ma'am, you did. Sit down and tell us."

Pardi smiled her mysterious smile and settled herself again in an unused chair at the edge of the circle.
We all shifted to hear her better. Her last story was so
wild, I couldn't imagine what might be coming next.

"**Where was** I? I told you about my daddy and his
story about Lafayette the year I turned fifteen. The
story Daddy told me about Lafayette was not my
only birthday present. He gave me a gold-chain
necklace with a solid-gold moon charm. And he
bought me a subscription to something called *Paris
Match*, which was like a French gossip magazine
with pictures, because he thought it was the most
likely way I was going to really learn some French—
until he got a better idea and hired an old Haitian
lady to come cook and clean for us. He thought
learning French was important in case we ever had
to leave the country.

"It became clearer and clearer that part of what
was motivating Daddy's crazy plan involving French
language lessons was that I was getting older, and he
didn't want to shoot me. He thought we should move
someplace warm, where the people spoke French and
Black folks were in a majority and a lot of good-looking
Black men were well educated and sane. That way it
would be easy for me to find a Black husband, and

Daddy wouldn't have to kill me first or second, before or after the white boy.

"I thought it easier not to pick a white boy.

"Eventually, I landed at the University of Texas, Austin, in the fall of 1977. Eventually, I fell in love with a white boy. And eventually, I told my daddy. He turned on a dime. He said, 'I can't help but love who you love.'

"It was not without a price. Daddy was diminished. That look he had the night Neil Armstrong walked on the moon came back and took up semi-permanent residence on his face. That was enough to take the shine off that first love. It helped that the boy was a boy, and the kind of boy who didn't want his girlfriend playing music in bars. That I shouldn't play music in bars had actually been the one thing Daddy and the boy had agreed on before the boy and I parted ways. But I kept playing music in bars.

"He wasn't my last white boy. For a while, hanging out at the Driskill Hotel, I was surrounded by a particular kind of white boy and white-boy music, while I dated bronze doctors-in-training until their mothers got strange about my daddy making money cooking up barbecue sauce, stranger about my having half brothers in Houston, and strangest about me having no mother at all, meaning, to them, not having a mother who was a Link, or a Girlfriend, or a Circlette, a properly re-spectable bougie Black woman. Those boys wanted me to be ashamed of my guitar-playing, horse-riding, boat-sailing, Black Black Galveston ways. That was not possible.

"I was following in T Bone's footsteps. And proud to be. And maybe in my own way, Jack Johnson's. Back then in Austin, we listened to Jerry Jeff Walker and Townes Van Zandt. It was Guy Clark and Steve Earle, Robert Earle Keen and Lyle Lovett, Rodney Crowell and Larry Willoughby. And what we listened to was Uncle Walt's Band. My playlist was all of that plus Charley Pride, and Ray Charles, and Lil Hardin, and Big Mama Thornton; it was my original T-Bone Walker and this tall and brilliant new man—T Bone Burnett. And I was listening to me. I knew the world needed some Black cowgirl-pirate music, and I was going to write it.

"One night in Austin, it may have been my third or fourth gig ever, I was playing a not-so-tiny club, and only three people turned up.

"Jericho was one of the people. His cheekbones were so high women feared his kiss would cut their face. His legs were long. His frame was lanky. You could see the muscles on his stomach bright as the tattoos on his pale arms. He was proud of having his mama's eyes, not dazzling blue-gray-green eyes but eyes that could see right from wrong. People would talk about his drug addiction, but he only did cocaine so he would have more energy to drink, and he only stayed up all night to drink so he could stay up all night and write. He was fully in love with brown liquor. Besotted. He was thirty-seven years old, and his best work was behind him. Seven albums and hundreds and hundreds, thousands of shows, in clubs across the world, on cruise boats, in radio stations, in record stores, and sung to me in my early morning kitchen. He gushed language just like my daddy, splashing it all over me.

"At that show with no audience except a handsome Black couple and the beautiful white man, Jericho, I was playing what I called my Mother Dixie songs about the South as an abusive mother of Black culture but her mother nonetheless. When I came to the last one, he applauded so long I started shaking my head. He invited me to go out to find a bar that wasn't closing soon. But I noticed the way he slurred his words and grazed his hand on my hips. I said, 'We probably need to find some coffee. Drunk as you are and little as you know me, you are likely to do something inappropriate and I'd have to shoot you.'

"When he laughed, I showed him my pistol. Then he laughed harder and said he knew an all-night diner with very good coffee and he would bring his best manners. We wound up in a booth in a diner that served blue cornmeal pancakes, Hawaiian coffee, and off-the-menu bourbon to regular patrons. Jericho was a regular patron.

"He had made a name for himself as some kind of cross between Kristofferson and Glen Campbell with a lot more grit. When I told him that was nothing but a modern Merle Haggard, he kissed me full on the lips. Then he gave me the best proposition I have ever received, and I would receive, in years to come, propositions from poets laureate of multiple nations and winners of Grammys in multiple genres. I think because a great soul can smell previous great souls tangled in the scent of your curls, Jericho said, 'Let's make a poet tonight.'

("If my father hadn't been my father, I would have taken Jericho up on the proposition that very first night, but my father was my father, so it took a few weeks.)

"He told me I was a Texas cowgirl poet, then he proceeded to tell me all about Black cowgirls and cowboys like I hadn't grown up in Texas. We talked about how the West was Black and brown and Native American, not just white, and how those folks at the Alamo owned slaves and nobody wanted to talk about it, and how the Yellow Rose of Texas was probably a woman of color who helped the Texans win the war, and we wondered why she did that, and I told Jericho what my father had said, and Jericho wondered if Texas might still belong to Mexico today if the Yellow Rose of Texas's Daddy had said the same thing.

"Soon I was living in Nashville, too, though enrolled in the University of Texas. I was his little secret. Back then in country, just like you couldn't be gay, you couldn't have a Black girlfriend. Couldn't didn't mean didn't—it meant couldn't let it be known. So I was just the backup singer, traveling with the band.

"Jericho declared 'keeping up a front' to be Nashville's third greatest performance art, with songwriting being first, and guitar picking being second. Singing, according to Jericho, was a distant fourth. By the time I graduated from Austin and landed in Nashville and got myself a publishing deal and a recording contract, I was prepping to record the Mother Dixie songs and beginning to cultivate Music City's third great art: seeming to be something I wasn't. The record contract required that. I was willing. I had a project I was in love with, and when you are in love, you will do anything.

"Around then, my father died, of natural causes. Bell Britton said that was a triumph—to die Black and in his own bed, with a loving daughter beside him, from a combination of semi-old age and his favorite vices—

and I had to laugh, if I didn't have to agree. After Daddy died happy, I felt like I could marry Jericho.

"We were in some little town, and Jericho walked into a pawnshop and he came out with a big diamond ring and he slipped it on my finger and he said, 'You don't ride in the bus with the band and the girls anymore—you call your record label, let them know the truth, then ride in the Cadillac with me—or you throw my ring into the river.'

"I didn't throw his ring into the river. I hopped in his green Cadillac convertible in Birmingham, and he pointed the wheel toward Jackson, Mississippi. From there we were headed to Shreveport then up to Dallas. It was an easy run. Birmingham to Jackson isn't four hours—unless your car breaks down at a gas station in Meridian, Mississippi.

"I liked gas stations. I had been raised in one. If you grow up in Texas, gasoline smells like new shoes. But not if you're traveling with a white boy and you're brown as a berry. Some drunk old boys in a red pickup truck—there were just three of them, looking back in my mind, I call them Eenie, Meanie, and Minie Moe— all they saw was a white man and a Black girl, and they started in on hassling me.

"We were in the convertible with the top down, parked at the pump, when they rolled up in the pickup. We were close together on the front seat, with the gas nozzle stuck in our tank. Eenie, the biggest one of the three, said, 'Why you want to go do that?' Off stage without a hat, Jericho didn't look like Jericho. And he especially didn't look like himself with a Black woman wearing overalls beside him, instead of a Black girl wearing sequins behind him.

"Jericho gave the country-biker boys—they looked so familiar to him—his big Jericho smile, the smile he had given so many biker boys and farm boys and state trooper boys and grocery clerks just like them from the stage. It was a smile that usually won him a smile back. Then he said something that was a riff on one of the opening lines in one of his biggest songs. 'Howdy, boys, let's turn this thing around.' He knew if he flashed that smile and said those words, they would recognize, they would see he was Jericho. So he flashed the smile and said the words. And snap, it all went strange.

"Suddenly, it wasn't some white man with some Black girl. It was their Jericho, the friend whose voice had been present at every intimate moment in their lives, from the day they buried MiMaw to the night they laid their first girl to the afternoon they punched their best buddy for no reason whatsoever to the day they cashed their first paycheck and to the first time they called in sick on a Monday. Jericho, the voice in their head through all of that, was sitting with a colored gal plastered to his side. Eenie, Meanie, and Minie Moe blinked: Jericho was at their local gas station and Jericho was *loving*, not fucking, a hippy Black chick.

"My man had blown their sunburnt little minds. They didn't like it one bit. I'd like to think it was the hippy thing that got to Jericho's fans. The tallest fellow said, 'I'm going to go home and break all your records.' The fattest one said, 'You spending the money you made off me, off us, off three upstanding white men, risking our lives wrestling oil up out of the sea, on some Black bitch wearing dungarees?'

"'Shut the fuck up!' Jericho said this loud, firm, and smiling. He was a mesmerizing performer. Nobody said anything as Jericho got out of the car and pulled the gas nozzle out of our tank. He took out his wallet. Everyone watched as he tucked a hundred into some crevice on the pump. We were all still watching when he threw three one-hundred-dollar bills, one after another, in the direction of the pickup.

"Now, Eenie, Meanie, and Minie Moe were insulted. Minie Moe said something horrible to me. Why did he want to do that? I screamed-ordered Jericho, 'Get in the car!' But Jericho had already started hard drinking for the day, so neither taking orders nor backing down was a gear available to him. You have to understand, he shot up one summer to six foot two and filled out. He had been short and chubby for all of middle school, the kind of boy who made folks say, 'It's not the size of the dog in the fight, it's the size of the fight in the dog.' There was ginormous fight in Jericho, and now he was six foot tall and his shoulders were broad. He punched one of those boys, Eenie, right in the face, and Minie Moe started whaling on him, and it was looking like they were trying to keep it a fair fight because no one else jumped in. But the bastard Meanie looked over to me. So I started to cry. Jericho peeped that immediately and took a step back toward me. Nobody was paying attention to me except that sadistic bastard, Meanie.

"I knew he was sadistic because my tears got his eyes shining. I bit my lip, and I let him see me bite my lip. My fingers twitched like I was trying to grab the seat of the car for strength. Meanie called out to Jericho, 'Your bitch want me.' At which point, sad sadistic Meanie looked away to see Jericho's reaction, and I took the opportunity to reach for both the guns I kept loaded and tucked into the seat of the car, the guns I had been tapping with my fingers wondering how this event would unfold, and in a flash, I had shot part of blue-eyed Meanie's ear off.

"They were not prepared for that. Jericho was, he

knew me. The moment tears had risen in my eyes, he started backing up to the car. By the time I bit my lip, his hand was reaching for the car door. He knew how I rolled. My daddy taught me to shoot straight, and fast, and first. We lit out of there with me shooting out the tires on that redneck truck using both guns. We only stopped to buy more ammunition. We pulled into Jackson laughing and singing Johnny Cash.

"We played the show in Jackson. We played Shreveport. We played Dallas. We didn't drive the Cadillac, but we played the shows and rode the bus as far as Dallas, then flew back to Nashville first class. We didn't back down. We didn't get scared. I didn't forget my fifteenth birthday present. I had my lucky moon around my neck and Jericho's ring on my finger.

"But when we got back to the house in Nashville, every nice thing Jericho owned reminded him of sad, sadistic, and vicious people. He couldn't see any of the pretty in his house or hardly see me—all he could see was the people who had paid for everything he owned. And he did not love them anymore. I was the only thing left in the house he did love.

"He decided he would stop writing and performing songs and write novels instead and have all new fans who would love us both. He flew up to New York City without me and rented a nondescript apartment under an alias. He stopped playing stadium gigs and big clubs and started only playing places like the Bottom Line, and the Cellar Door, and the Birchmere—and only when I was playing there, too.

"The Mother Dixie album became a small cult phenomenon, but he assured me it was an unrecognized masterpiece and tucked all his Grammys into my side of the bookshelves.

"Then he stopped playing out and we became, for a minute, full-time hang-out-at-the-clubs-as-performance-art people. Before he moved to New York, the only music he had known was country, bluegrass, and a little jazz. When we moved here, we started eating smoked salmon from Russ and Daughters and listening to punk and jazz and glam rock. We bounced from Club 57 and CBGB and the Bitter End, to Gerde's Folk City and the Bottom Line. We were welcomed behind velvet ropes and gritty glares. He had record money and I had sop sauce money, and if in the VIP rooms they thought his records were shit, they thought I was doing something strange enough to be interesting. They didn't know about the Black cowboys and the Black whores of the West, so everything we could tell them was a revelation. And we looked pretty together, like a sculpture—Basquiat called that. The first night he met us, he marveled at the tall and straight, the short and dangerously curved of us, the thrilling wingspan of Jericho's arms that sheltered the immense mass of my curly hair and boobs that hung authentically and improbably high. He predicted we would be widely welcomed and seldom home before dawn. He was right.

"We didn't have one particular club; we roamed the whole East Village like Daddy and me roamed Galveston, but we had a place where we never went: Harlem. Neither of us wanted to risk having what happened to us with his people in Mississippi happening to us in New York with mine.

"One day I awoke at noon, and my ring was missing. I looked for it all afternoon long. I asked Jericho about it. Then I had to go out. I was interviewing guitar players. I was ready to make another studio album. When I came back midevening, he was in a chair, dead. It was like that song 'Whisky Lullaby'; he put a bottle to his mouth and pulled the trigger. He was kind enough not to use one of my guns. I quick figured out he had pawned my ring and bought a gun. He left a note. His handwriting was pretty to the end. It said: 'I put the lease in your name when I took this place. I said it was because your credit was better. That wasn't it. I am tired of the world and of my people. You are ready for the world and for all your people. This is my last will and testament. I leave you a guitar with a lot of songs in it, and the key to a room with a lot of stories in it.'

"He didn't know we were going to have a daughter, Jericho. I call her Pardner. I gave her the guitar on her tenth birthday and the key to the apartment on her twenty-fifth. Jericho was wrong about a lot of things. But there were songs in the guitar and books in the room. He was right about that."

Pardi halted. "That's my love story, hate story, and in-between story." She turned to Wurly. "Enough music in there for you?"

"Oh, yes."

"As love stories go," said Eurovision, "that one didn't have much of a happy ending, either."

"It was happy enough," said Pardi. "Happy enough is better than nothing. And I got a beautiful daughter out of it."

Day Nine
April 8

I blew off my chores early, because the building was getting more and more hopeless, and nobody seemed to notice or appreciate my efforts to keep the hallways clean. I spent the extra hour sorting through the liquor closet and arranging bottles. The old super kept an astonishing collection of liqueurs, aperitifs, digestifs, and bitters in weird bottles of various shapes. I'd already gone through a lot of the usuals, so out of curiosity I started sampling the ones I'd never heard of. Some of them were truly awful, bitter herbal concoctions probably made by monks in remote monasteries. I finally poured myself a thermos of ginger ale mixed with a liqueur called Malört. It was so disgusting that its ability to clear the head was almost like getting electroshock treatment.

By the time I reached the roof, I was already feeling no pain. I was late, and I missed the seven o'clock cheering. I ducked over to my fainting couch and took my seat as unobtrusively as possible, firing up my phone. Eurovision was launching the evening as usual, theatrically clasping and unclasping his hands as he looked about with anticipatory cheerfulness, urging someone to tell a story.

Just then, I noticed a newcomer to the roof, a young, nervous-looking woman, not making eye contact, body language stiff. I was alarmed. How did she get in? I checked the door every day to make sure it was latched. She wasn't in the bible, I was sure of that. I wondered if she, too, was paying any rent, but reminded myself that none of us owed any loyalty to our absent landlord. I took another pull from my drink.

Eurovision noticed her, too. "Greetings," he said, as she took an unoccupied seat, folding her hands in her lap. "How's it going?"

"Good," she said tentatively. "And you?"

"I don't think I've seen you up here before."

"I'm not very familiar with the city," she said. She had a strong accent—English clearly wasn't her first language. I guessed she might be Chinese.

Eurovision gave her a sparkling smile, ignoring the non sequitur. "Well, welcome to the roof. We've been having some fun up here while we're all locked in the building. Do you have a story to tell us?"

"Not really," she stammered. "But maybe you can help me? I have been looking for a friend. But I wonder if it's time to stop."

Eurovision's face clouded in confusion, but before he could say anything, she continued.

"I arrived in the city eight months ago for the start of fall semester. Before, I had only seen pictures of the Statue of Liberty, the Empire State Building, and the shops along Fifth Avenue. I didn't realize how large Central Park was, in the dead center of the is-land, huge and rectangular, with its own forests and lakes, the occasional bird of prey. For an apartment, I'd imagined park views and those of a typical sky-scraper, maybe a place that also sold 'I Love New York' shirts and sesame-seed bagels. Two big win-dows, I'd allowed myself—but my studio turned out to only have one. This window frames a fire escape and has zero parks or skyscrapers in sight. I had read on a travel site that no place in the city should take longer than twenty minutes to get to. The site must have meant by car because, while on Google Maps the southernmost tip, the Battery, looks close, the walk there took three-quarters of an hour. I went to salute the Statue of Liberty, who was stuck on her own island, and to wave at the Charging Bull in the middle of the street."

She had been staring at her hands, but now she looked up at Eurovision and shrugged.

"So this was America. A lonely green woman. A bronze-plated male cow.

"Like many international students from my country, I was here for two years on a student visa, to study data science, after which I would apply for a work visa, and go into finance or corporate analytics, doing behind-the-scenes work.

"At the airport, the departure gate, my parents and I didn't know when we would see each other again, so we spoke not of that and they offered their final pieces of advice.

"Don't overeat, said my mother, a firm grip on my arm. Don't accidently become corpulent and unrecognizable. Don't talk to strange men, and don't worry about us.

"Focus on your studies, said my father, a firmer grip on my other arm. Listen to your teachers and mother; yes, don't talk to strange men.

"There were no teachers anymore in grad school, but professors you could call by first names and sit in bars with, many of them strange men. American irreverence, I had trouble getting used to. American friendliness. 'Hey, how's it going?' To which the only correct response is 'Good, and you?'"

I glanced over at Eurovision, whose smile had frozen at this last bit. I wanted to laugh as the storyteller continued.

"Why prodigal son and not daughter? Because a daughter is never meant to leave. And an expression in my country states that a daughter is a parent's safety blanket, a daughter is like a warm winter duvet.

"On the first day of classes, I knew no one. By the second, another international student had approached me to ask about an assignment, which our professor had skipped over to go on a long tangent about the Second World War. The international student also confused about the assignment was from the same region as me, but not the same province or city and, had neither of us left our homeland to study here, we never would have met. He had a familiar quality about him, which was comforting, and uniformly cut hair. He wore an ugly knit sweater—black with purple nested Vs—and in all my time of knowing him, he didn't change into another sweater, or appear in a second set of clothes. We worked on the assignment together. We both got mediocre marks. The professor liked to scribble in margins. Circuitously, inscrutably, but sometimes just exclamation marks or the words 'No, no, no.'

"There were many restaurants in the area that cooked food typical of our region, and, on weekends, we would choose one of them to have a meal. But compared to dishes that I'd grown up with, a similar one here had more salt, more oil, and the portions were incredible to the point of indecent. My friend and I often ate in silence and kept moving the best pieces of meat off our bowls to that of the other. I thought of my mother, my father, but we didn't talk about our families, since the story about them was probably the same. He asked about my hobbies, in case any of them aligned with his. I didn't play online RPGs, unfortunately, or go on runs along the river hours after dark.

"'Why do you do that?' I asked and reminded him that the city was still dangerous.

"He asked what was so dangerous about a run. He was a fast runner. Worst-case scenario, he could sprint.

"'But say something did happen to you.'

"'Like what?' he asked, defiant of me and my question, which to him was probably girlish. Girls had more to fear than boys. Girls had to fear boys, for one, and their own uterus every month.

"He invited me to run with him, but I wasn't a fast

runner to begin with, and, should he resort to sprint-ing, I would be left behind like bait.

"On Sundays, I called my parents and for an hour they appeared on my computer as fuzzy faces who took turns moving the camera to their side while they spoke. They told me that our cat had died, and I gasped because it had been my cat for fourteen years. My mother said that, since I'd left, the cat waited on my bed every night.

"'I tried to reason with it,' said my mother. 'But of course, I don't speak cat.'

"One night, the cat decided to stop waiting and, by the next morning, had curled up into a ball on the bal-cony and died.

"From old age, my father clarified. Fourteen cat years is equivalent to a human's seventy-two.

"When the holidays arrived, my first Thanksgiving and Christmas in America, I found building decor dis-tracting, the singing and celebrating, the over-the-top trees, and what everyone called being merry. On the actual holidays themselves, the group of us who weren't traveling gathered at someone's apartment, around a borrowed folding table and a fragrant cauldron of food. I usually went with my friend, who had made other friends throughout the semester and become more ex-troverted around company. Whenever we arrived to-gether, there were jokes about us being a couple, about the two of us getting hitched. He would then put his arm around me, but never touch me, never drop his actual arm on my shoulder or waist. I didn't need him to embrace me, and I wasn't attracted to him that way, though I wouldn't have minded the gesture either, since he and I were each other's first friend here.

"Winter break was a month long, and several times during, I had an insatiable craving for hot chocolate but no milk or cocoa powder. So I would bundle myself up in a floor-length down coat and wrap my entire head in a scarf. Seeing myself in the mirror, I'd become as my mother had feared, corpulent and unrecognizable, and the drinking of hot chocolate did not help. On one of these trips to the store, I spotted my friend on the other side of the street. At night, the purple of his sweater was almost glowing, almost neon, and the Vs resembled arrows, pointing me in his direction. He was with someone else, and they were both standing in a building's shadow, bodies very close, smoking, which I didn't know my friend did. He had let his hair grow longer, pinning the small excess back into a tiny, black bun like a warrior from thousands of years ago. The other person was a stranger to me. He was no international student from my country or a face I recognized from our program. I started to walk toward them, but as I was doing so, I changed my mind. I pulled my scarf higher up and quickened my step. I sped past them without turning my head.

"When spring semester started, my friend and I continued to study together and get mediocre grades. He asked if I could look over his résumé. I asked him for some interview tips.

"'You need to practice better eye contact,' he told me, pointing two of his fingers at his eyeballs, then turning those fingers to mine.

"I said I was looking at him.

"He said I was staring at a vanishing point. Some dot behind him at infinity and the convergence of parallel rays.

"This led to a discussion about parallel rays and vanishing points, which then led to an argument about immigrants and assimilation.

"He said we tried to blend in too much and that was our problem.

"I said I didn't think we had a problem, and he said that was another one of our problems, never talking about or admitting to our problems.

"'Well, maybe we don't have any,' I offered. Do all immigrants have to have them? And if not, then why discuss things that don't exist?

"'You mean never talk about anything?'

"'I mean, what's gained from talking about everything? Can't we keep a few things to ourselves?'

"My friend didn't answer and inspected me carefully from across my small breakfast table. I worried he would reveal something about himself that would require something of me in return. But before I could fail this test explicitly, his phone buzzed, and, without reading the text, he stood up and said he had to go.

"'Go?' I asked. 'But you just got here.'

"Which was not entirely true, we'd been arguing for a while. It was hard to argue about assimilation, a process that was inevitable and that required you to erase large parts of yourself. I didn't know if I had been erased yet, or if it had already happened back in my own country, when I first considered coming here.

"He never called to finish the assignment we were working on, and the week before spring break, he stopped meeting me at the university gate before class. I looked for him in the auditorium. I saved him a seat, like my cat. When I really couldn't get ahold of him anymore, my first thought was that something had happened to him on his nightly run. He had fallen into the river or been kidnapped. He had done something to himself or been forced to disappear. Why did I think all those things instead of the obvious? That, while I was actively looking for him, he was actively not looking for me."

The storyteller again folded her hands, signifying she was done. I could see on her face the same loneliness expressed in the story. I shivered. Even having grown up in Queens, I knew instantly what she meant about resisting assimilation, the feeling of not wanting to shape myself for others. It was a feeling I'd had most of my life.

In the silence, a big spider suddenly shot out from a crack in the parapet and skittered across the roof, disappearing under a loose flap of tar paper.

"Ugh," said Eurovision, wiggling his fingers in disgust.

"When can you go home?" Hello Kitty asked the storyteller.

"I'm supposed to finish grad school first, but now everything is remote. I don't know. I can't travel back to China until the pandemic ends."

"That could be a while," said La Cocinera.

The storyteller nodded.

"Well, I'm a lifelong travel addict," said Eurovision. "And I hate being trapped like this. I would die to be at the Grace Hotel in Santorini right now."

"Don't be dramatic," said Florida. "We just have

to survive a few more weeks of this. It'll be over by June."

"I hope so," said La Cocinera. "I'm in the same boat—dying to see my family in San Miguel."

"When this pandemic is over, I'm going to go all over the world and see everything," said Hello Kitty.

Whitney laughed. "Even after the pandemic, no one will ever be able to travel the world the way I could when I was your age."

"What do you mean?"

Whitney smiled. "I'm talking about a time when you could still meet people who'd never seen a west-erner before, you could head off to places where you could disappear and no one back home would ever know what happened."

"No way. Like where? When?" This time I couldn't tell if Hello Kitty's tone was genuine or just more of her usual sarcasm.

"Okay. Every word of the story I'm going to tell you is true. It was during the reign of the last king of Af-ghanistan."

"Afghanistan?"

"Yes. I was there in the summer of 1972. One morn-ing, I was sitting by an outdoor fire on a dry, deserted Afghan plateau bounded by mountain ranges. With me around the fire was a mix of six or seven young Europeans and Americans. We were not Peace Corps volunteers, diplomats on an outing, naturalists, scientists, archaeologists, experienced trekkers, or even hikers. We were just a ragtag group of twentysomethings who'd earned a little money back in our home countries doing nothing impressive. We had all met one another for the first time in Kabul and decided to travel together to this remote spot in central Afghanistan.

"On this particular morning, we were sitting around a small campfire, all of us eating bowls of oatmeal, when a vision appeared: Across the deserted plain, a female horseback rider was heading our way—her straight brown hair floating on the wind, her long red dress billowing to the side.

"Before I go further, let me explain that I personally would never have been in Afghanistan without the domineering companionship of a man from Spain whom I'd met many months before while camping in a cave on the southern side of the island of Crete. I'd first noticed him the day his beat-up old white van had arrived in the seaside village below the cave. He wore fringed suede pants and black leather boots. What caught my eye was the way he walked: with a merry and enthusiastic step. The two of us had known each other only a few days when he asked in his heavy accent, 'Would you like to go on a journey to the East with me?' Considering myself an accomplished student of eastern religions, having read both Hermann Hesse and Alan Watts, I said yes.

"I pooled my money with his (the total came to about seven hundred dollars, which was worth more then than it is today) and transferred my backpack from the cave into his beat-up van. The van only started if one person pushed it while the other one popped the clutch to get the engine going. Since I couldn't drive a stick shift, he was always the driver. I spent a lot of time trying to enlist strangers to help me push.

"From the city of Heraklion, we caught a ferry to Athens. In Athens, the Spaniard hired a carpenter to build a large wooden box. The box makers then helped us strap the box to the top of the van. We then purchased a number of massive bags of oatmeal to go into the box, because the Spaniard said we would never go hungry as long as we could find water and make oatmeal over the camp stove in the van.

"And so, we set off for the East.

"For the next ten months, I pushed the van alongside men from Greece, Turkey, Lebanon, Syria, Iraq, Iran, Afghanistan—and then later Pakistan, Kashmir (where we had eleven flat tires!), India, and Nepal. I have one bad memory of pushing the vehicle: In one of those countries, an elderly man slipped and fell as he was helping me push, and when his friends laughed at him, he started hitting me. But that happened only once.

"As we bumped along and alone over land from city to towns to villages to remote uninhabited spots, looking for places to camp, we played music on the van's cassette player. The Spaniard had a large collection of tapes, but I only remember Neil Young's *After the Gold Rush*. To this day, whenever I hear 'Till the Morning Comes,' 'Tell Me Why,' or 'Cripple Creek Ferry,' I feel the exhilarating call to adventure.

"I should add that the romance of taking a journey to 'the East' with a man from Spain obscured the fact that he and I did not speak the same language. I spoke no Spanish, and his English was very poor. So, for most of our ten-month journey, I had no idea what he was talking about. One thing I thought I understood was that he had once been a doctor and given up medicine to travel, but he insisted I was never to ask anything about that, as the experience of forsaking medicine had been very painful for him. He was only twenty-three years old, which should have made me question his story. But perhaps one could become a doctor sooner in Spain than in the United States, I thought.

"Our adventure to the East had a number of predictable moments of fear and danger. We survived an extortion situation with Turkish border guards, a midnight interrogation by Turkish police, a bumpy drive through the no-man's-land of desert between Syria and Iraq (over tracks in the sand, not even a road!), and soon after we arrived in Afghanistan and were camped by a river beneath a mountain, I caught my first fish by hand and experienced my first earthquake.

"After we ate the fish, the ground started to shake. I crouched into a fetal position. All I could think was that, if I die by this river, crushed by fallen rocks, no one will ever know I was even here. My family will never hear from me again. I was horrified at the thought of doing that to my parents. I wasn't estranged from them. I had sent a number of cheerful postcards, but overseas communication was so sketchy I was pretty sure they never knew exactly where I was.

"But the Spaniard and I survived the earthquake, and then we headed for Kabul, a popular destination for western wayfaring kids in 1972. We parked the van at a campsite in the city and walked to town for food and water. I had a pair of leather boots handmade for five dollars and bought a bright-red-and-black embroidered dress that still hangs in my closet.

"Our two-month stay in Kabul came to a desperate end when a minor traffic altercation between the

Spaniard and an Afghan driver led to a small riot. Local shopkeepers invaded our van, tore out our speakers, and stole all our tapes! Others jumped in to defend us, and in the melee, the Spaniard ran away. I was left searching for anyone who could help me push the van and drive it back to the campsite, where the Spaniard was waiting.

"Afraid of being arrested, we escaped the city that night and traveled north in a caravan with a few others who had been staying at the campground, and that brings us back to where I started this story—with our group sitting on a deserted plain, eating oatmeal, the mysterious horseback rider approaching in a billowing red dress . . .

"As I said earlier, her straight brown hair was floating on the wind as her horse galloped closer and closer. Others in the group were as mesmerized as I was. (I don't remember what they said exactly, but most likely it was something like, 'Dig that.' 'Far out.' 'Who's the chick?')

"As her face finally came into view, though, I do remember exactly what I said:

"'Meredith!'

"The rider in the vision had been one of my college housemates. I thought she was still in Chapel Hill, North Carolina. I had no idea she had also set out on a journey to the East. And she was just as surprised as I was to find me there.

"Meredith jumped off her horse and joined us all for oatmeal.

"Many months later, my parents got a call from the office of their North Carolina congressman, telling them that the American embassy in Nepal had sent word that their daughter was in a hospital in Katmandu, being treated for blood poisoning and malnutrition. Arrangements were made for me to fly home.

"These many years later, the only thing I remember about what my mother said regarding my great adventure was that she'd had a heartbreaking dream during my absence in which I was skipping through a field, tossing flowers. The only admonishment I remember from my southern army colonel father was, 'Darling, you've got to come down from the clouds.'"

"That's all true?" Hello Kitty looked impressed, despite herself.

Whitney nodded.

"What happened to Meredith? Did she stay with you?"

"No. After our brief rendezvous, she went on her way to India. For the last twenty-five years, she's been a photographer in Paris."

"No way. What happened to the Spaniard?"

"I worked night and day to bring him to the States. I married him. Then he went insane and tried to kill me. But that's another story for another time."

"Oh! Do tell!" cried Hello Kitty, full of real enthusiasm now. "I love murder mysteries."

"It's not a murder mystery," said Vinegar, dryly. "She's not dead."

"Attempted murder mysteries, then."

"May I suggest we move on to another story?" said the Lady with the Rings. "I, for one, am not interested in a story about how a Spaniard went insane and tried to kill someone. Doesn't anyone have a story about ordinary life, for a change?"

Hello Kitty said, "I have a story about dog walking."

"Dog walking?" Eurovision snorted.

"That's right. I was a dog-walking pro up until a few weeks ago when the lockdowns started," said Hello Kitty. "Helped me pay my way through NYU."

"How riveting," said Eurovision. "Can't wait to hear all about it."

"Picture it—" Hello Kitty set down her vape, hopped out of her cave chair, and struck a dramatic pose. "I'm in this Upper East Side apartment, in the kitchen. All black and white, cool matte surfaces, you know the kind of kitchen I'm talking about"—she swept her arms around—"And here, of course, is the titanium-faced Sub-Zero, which I'm standing in front of."

Hello Kitty mimed opening the refrigerator door and peering in.

"At first, it wasn't much. A handful of raw almonds, a neglected Granny Smith, a single-serving tub of non-fat yogurt from a shelf lined with them. Items that usually would go unmissed, unnoticed.

"Buster would look up, cock his head to the side, and watch me like a cat.

"Buster smells of his owner, a forty-something lawyer who slathers herself in green tea body milk. I help myself to that, too. Body milk, cream, butter. My hands deserve something rich, especially now with all the washing.

"She probably smells a bit like Buster, too, an off-white Old English sheepdog, whose breath I actually don't mind. That's the hardest thing to get used to with a new client. It all depends on what they eat.

"Buster's food also comes in single servings, larger than the nonfat yogurts, stacked on the shelves right below them. He must have a weight issue, too, as his containers are filled with cubes of cooked carrots and skinless, white meat chicken. There are no labels on these containers, so it's likely that she cooks for him.

She could eat right along with Buster, if she wants. Throw in a bit of chopped celery and parsley, a cup or two of broth, and voila! Chicken soup. I've thought about taking some home to do the same, but *that* she would have noticed.

"Except for our interview at the beginning of January, I've not seen her. She sends me emails and more recently leaves handwritten notes on the counter:

> "*If it snows this afternoon, Buster's boots are in the entryway closet, in a canvas bag, which is also where you'll find his puffy jacket.*'

"The most recent one:

> "*'Going forward, Buster MUST not be allowed to interact with strangers and other dogs. I've a call in to the vet re whether a mask is advisable. My friend in Hong Kong says her dog is wearing one. For Buster's safety, please buy a surgical-grade mask and wear it whenever you're with him, outside or inside the apt.*
>
> "*'Except when you're eating, of course.*'

"Of course, there's a nanny cam in the kitchen. Or, in her case, a dog walker cam.

"Here's what I've learned from years' worth of working for the wealthy and their canines: They like to watch, to witness the work that others do for them and theirs. It makes them feel useful to monitor us.

"I didn't care. I ate anyway. Popped the dry almonds in my mouth as if they were salted caramels. Licked my lips after the bites of sour apple. Rolled my eyes, fluttered my lids with each spoonful of watery yogurt.

"It's not pilfering, if I do it in the open.

"It's not thieving, if I feel no guilt.

"If Buster gets a treat, why shouldn't I?

"You know who thinks that way? A dog walker who needs to find a new way to make her living.

"Buster agrees, but he's, of course, not the tattler.

"First, there was a tart, so dainty that only a single raspberry sat atop of it. That was in February, right before Valentine's Day.

"When Buster and I returned from our usual walk to the Guggenheim, it was waiting on the kitchen counter. A miniature red beehive on a robin's-egg-blue plate. It wasn't there before our walk. Believe me, that I would have noticed.

"I looked around, half expecting to see her. Or a houseguest, the friend from Hong Kong?

"I eyed the tart.

"Buster eyed me. He knew before I did.

"I ate the tart. The berry was cool as it touched the roof of my mouth, so was the fillip of pastry cream underneath it. The crust melted on my tongue. I grabbed the edge of the marble counter to steady myself.

"I looked in the refrigerator, hoping there were more. Nothing but his-and-her nonfat proteins, as usual.

"During the interview, I'd asked her if there were children who might be at home in the afternoons, when my sessions with Buster would be scheduled. She spat out a quick, hard *no*. Then, she volunteered that an Old English sheepdog hadn't been her choice. She lowered her voice as she got to the end of that sentence. Buster belonged to an ex, who had gone to Oslo for a month-long business trip and stayed.

"'You can throw out his clothes, but you can't throw out his dog.'

"She said it to show me that she has a heart. The wealthy fear that they lack one. That's why they own dogs—and have children—and then leave them in the care of others.

"Buster, he's being held hostage, kept in this Upper East Side two-bedroom with a wraparound terrace and a view of Central Park in the hope that, one day, Mr.

Oslo will return, smell the green tea body milk, change his mind, and stay.

"Buster is the vestigial tail of a man, the tail end of love, the tail that once had wagged the dog of a failing relationship.

"That's what she really meant.

"From the start, I'd tried different variations of his name to see which one he would respond to, which one would make him bark out something revealing about his true owner.

"'Buster Keaton, come here Buster Keaton!'

"'Ab Buster, you want a treat?'

"'Who's a good boy? Filibuster, you're a good boy!'

"Buster Poindexter? Buster Scruggs? Buster Douglas?

"I was disappointed—still am—that Buster is just Buster.

"A child would choose that name, not a grown man. Not news to her, I'm sure.

"I hope she never calls him Busted when they're alone.

"For two weeks in a row, those little tarts kept on appearing, increasing by one each time. I ate them all. At first, I'd paced myself, allowing a minute or two before I'd reached for the next. Soon enough, I was wolfing them down, one in each hand. When their numbers passed half a dozen, I no longer used my hands, bowing instead, my face almost touching the marble, the tongue doing all the not-so-heavy lifting, Buster-style."

We all waited for her to continue, but Hello Kitty simply curtsied, climbed back into her chair, and resumed vaping.

"So . . . ?" asked Eurovision finally.

Hello Kitty winked at him, inhaling.

"Not this again," he said.

When it was clear Hello Kitty wasn't going to offer anything more, Vinegar weighed in. "Obviously," she said, "the lady who owned the apartment was testing you. Leaving out those tarts as a kind of challenge for you to steal them. And then watching you steal them on her nanny cam. She did it for her own sick satisfaction."

Hello Kitty didn't respond. I wondered if this story, like her last one, was a lie. But, weird as it was, it felt true.

"You can imagine what happened in Oslo," said the Lady with the Rings, with a salacious cackle. "All those tall blond Nordic girls . . . They don't need any green tea body milk. And all she got was a shaggy dog. No wonder she was mad."

"Who said she was mad?" said Hello Kitty. "On the contrary, she was as cool as a snow cone."

The Lady with the Rings waved her hand. "Trust me, that snow cone was boiling inside. Like some of us here on the roof, trying our best to get along, because, what else?" She cast an ostentatious eye around, lingering, I thought, on Vinegar and Florida, who had both been pretty quiet for the last few nights, after their fight. "The truth is, in normal times, we wouldn't give each other the time of day. We've got almost nothing in common, do we?" She looked around and gave her rings a little rattle for emphasis.

"Nothing."

The bells of Old St. Pat's saved us again, ringing the evening to a close.

Day Ten
April 9

You ain't gonna learn what you don't wanna know
—Jerry Garcia

This was the new graffito that greeted us that night on the rooftop, badly slopped on the upper part of the mural in a careless hand. Vinegar asked who did it, but nobody would own up. As we took our seats, Eurovision said, "Did you know that Jerry Garcia accidentally got his middle finger chopped off with an ax when he was five years old? It was just a stump. But even with four fingers, he was one of the greatest guitarists of his generation."

"Oh yeah," said Darrow. "I saw the Dead in concert

once, and Jerry Garcia gave the audience the finger with that stump of his. It totally cracked the place up."

"Brings to mind Big John Wrencher," said Wurly, "the great blues harpsman. He lost his arm in a car accident and had to relearn the instrument. He figured out how to play with one hand, and it was sooo sweet."

Ramboz said, "Or Paul Wittgenstein, the pianist who had his arm shot off in World War I. He got a bunch of famous composers to write pieces for him to play with the left hand."

"How did we get on amputee musicians?" asked Hello Kitty.

"Ever heard of Elijah Vick, the blues musician?" This was Maine.

"Sure," said Wurly. "Crazy dude, but the real deal. You knew him?"

"Oh yes. Years ago," Maine went on.

"It was one of the strangest medical cases I ever handled. The guy almost lost his arm—and his guitar career. In one of my clinical rotations in medical school I was assigned to the intensive care unit of St. Joseph's Hospital in Memphis—a historic institution, and sadly, the place where, in 1968, Dr. Martin Luther King Jr. was declared dead. Over the decades, I've seen every kind of pain and pathos, every flavor of tragicomedy, come through those ER doors. But I'll never forget Elijah Vick.

"Elijah was forty-five years old when I first met him, a successful concert promoter with a slight paunch, prone to coughing from his years of smoking too much weed, but otherwise in good health. He had a balding thicket of prematurely white hair, and a well-groomed flavor-saver patch on his chin. A tattoo of a Gibson hollow-body guitar graced his left arm.

"As he told it to me, he was born and raised in Memphis, a city he could never imagine leaving. Maybe the thing he loved most about Memphis, besides the music, was the Mississippi River, the way it swirled and glurped along the banks. He lived in a loft apartment right on the bluff, and he would often stare for hours, baffled and mesmerized and thoroughly entertained by the great sprawling river. A mile across the water lay the floodplain of Arkansas, a world of chiggers and ducks and water moccasins that nested in swampy oxbow lakes. On the long sandbars, feral pigs ran among graveyards of driftwood and rotten cypress stumps. In the clearings beyond these wild margins were hundreds and hundreds of square miles of cotton fields, cotton as far as the eye could see—white gold, mined from the world's richest alluvium.

"All his life, Elijah had been told to never, ever go in

the foul stinking water of the Mighty Mississip. It was our national colon, they said, an unsavory sewage ditch that teemed with every category of peril: snags, whirlpools, industrial sludge, burning chemicals, snarled trotlines, coliform bacteria, not to mention a wicked current intent on sweeping away everything in its path.

"The laws of hydraulics didn't seem to apply to this crafty torrent of gravy. Without warning, Elijah had been told, the river would suck you down, swallow you up, smother you in its miasmal embrace. It was basically a conveyor belt of quicksand.

"And then there was the story of the *Sultana*, the worst nautical disaster in American history. The doomed steamship had passed Memphis early on the morning of April 27, 1865, with nearly twenty-five hundred passengers, many of whom were Union troops newly freed from various Confederate prisoner-of-war camps. A few miles upstream, at around two a.m., the *Sultana's* boilers exploded. Hundreds were instantly scalded to death. Passengers jumped into the cold Mississippi, but many of the soldiers were too weak and emaciated to swim—or they simply didn't know how. In the end, seventeen hundred people burned or drowned that night, more souls than went down on the *Titanic*.

"Monsters lived down in the Mississippi murk, too. Elijah, who'd been an avid outdoorsman and an angler since he was a teenager, had become fascinated with a certain gargantuan fish, often hundreds of pounds in weight, that lives in the shoals of the river. This is the alligator gar, *Atractosteus spatula*, a primeval creature with a long snout, evil-looking teeth, and sharp scales so iron-hard that fishermen have to use wire cutters to get to their flesh. Chickasaw warriors used to fashion gator-gar scales into breastplates and battle shields. These bizarre fish were slithering, dragon-like carnivores that grew to beastly sizes and lived ridiculously long lives—in some cases, more than a century. They weren't known to harm humans, but they could be vicious ambush predators, impaling prey with their long spiked teeth. Another weird thing that struck Elijah was that the alligator gar was equipped with gills and also a kind of a lung, so that it could breathe both air and water.

"Elijah once showed me a famous photograph of one of these behemoths that had been taken in 1910. The gar had been caught south of Memphis, in a back channel of the Mississippi, near Tunica; in the photograph, a bemused-looking man sits dwarfed behind the spiny leviathan. The creature was reportedly ten feet long and must have weighed a thousand pounds. Something about this weird life-form, seemingly half fish and half reptile, had intrigued Elijah. It was as though a living dinosaur was swimming right there beside his hometown.

"But over the centuries people had demonized gator gars, had called them nuisance fish, trash fish. Rednecks would hunt them down at night in the glare of spotlights and shoot them in their wallows. Or they'd wrangle the biggest specimens and sell them for many thousands of dollars on the black market—wealthy Tokyo businessmen apparently prize them as aquarium curiosities. Elijah thought the modern world had grievously wronged the hapless alligator gar, just because it was ugly and freakish and strange, a monstrous denizen of a prehistoric world.

"Ever since his divorce from his wife, Florence, Elijah had been obsessed with the idea of swimming across the Mississippi. He'd found that he needed a project, a diversionary adventure to remind him that he was still alive and still able to take a risk once in a while. He had given up on his musical career, and was instead managing and promoting the careers of others. Good music seemed to leak from the city's every pore, but for Elijah, who'd once been a guitar player well known in the studios and bars around town, music had become a vicarious pursuit, one that he'd grown to hate. Little by little, parts of him had died.

"He'd stayed close to Florence, even after they finally

realized they couldn't be happy living together. She found his fixation on the Mississippi strange and disturbing. He stayed up all hours of the night reading Twain. He became a master swimmer. He studied maps from the Army Corps of Engineers. He befriended some old river rats who seemed to know every kink and bend, every fact and legend, of this stretch of the Big Muddy. For him, the Mississippi became mythological, like Scylla and Charybdis, something malevolent but also endlessly alluring.

"What would it be like, he wondered, to jump into that roiling mess? To splosh and drift in it, to feel its fish-redolent muck against his skin? And, most important, to get out into the full swiftness of its main current and cross it, from shore to shore?

"He imagined it would be a cathartic act, that the exertion of crossing it would turn him into a different person. It was like a phase or stage he had to go through. People from Memphis were known as Memphians, and that seemed apt. Shades of amphibian, rubbery beings of the water and mud, life-forms that started out as one thing but morphed into something else. He wasn't sure why he was drawn so powerfully to the river, but he felt swimming across it was just something he needed to do. Facing down his boyhood fears was part of it, but there may have been something larger, more metaphorical, at work. It was as though he believed that the very act of crossing it would take him to another, better place.

"The night before his swim, Elijah camped in his old International Harvester on the Arkansas side of the river, ten miles upstream from Memphis. This was at a place called the Devil's Racecourse, so named (on old maps, and even in Twain's *Life on the Mississippi*) because this stretch was once infamous for its steamboat-wrecking snags.

"As he drifted off to sleep, he could hear coyotes howling in the canebrake. A crescent moon crept into the sky, and the heavy FedEx jets—one, then another, another one still—came roaring overhead in a great lockstep, dropping south toward the sorting complex in Memphis, bearing the packages of the world.

"At daybreak, Elijah sipped a mug of instant coffee, then walked along the water's edge, studying the current, testing the temperature, surveying the far bank with binoculars. He climbed into his wetsuit and zipped it up, then strapped on a waterproof backpack he'd stuffed with shoes and a change of clothes.

"'Here goes nothin!' he muttered, then eased into the water, which was surprisingly cold. He felt his heart pound, his skin tingle, his nerves race. He looked across the channel to the Tennessee bank, clothed in a vegetational haze.

"For the first thirty yards or so, Elijah oozed through slackwater, easygoing. Then he crossed a distinct line of demarcation and hit the main channel, and suddenly he was fired downstream as though shot from a cannon. It would be impossible to fight this current, he realized, even for a second. It was unnerving to be swept along by something so powerful, but after surrendering to it, Elijah felt an intense exhilaration.

"Now the water surface was rippled and agitated, slapping with crosscurrents, surging with boils. He could feel the river pressing in on all sides, grappling with the impertinence of his presence. Out in the channel, he lost all sense of the current's velocity. At times, he thought he wasn't moving at all, but then he looked back at the bank and saw that, on the contrary, he was, as he described it, *hauling ass*—effortlessly sliding down the nation's gullet.

"The river tasted like all rivers do: slightly metallic, alive with nutrients, a faint and not unpleasant hint of algae and fish. He didn't know if dioxin had a flavor, but his taste buds weren't picking up anything funny—no tannic notes of Monsanto, no satiny finish of Dow.

"What was unusual, though, was the grit. Elijah had

never swum in water this clouded with sediment, all that northern dirt flowing south. It was, of course, just that—good, clean dirt—but it worked into his eyes, coated his tongue and nostrils, and crunched in between his clenched molars. He'd read that in the old days, river pilots used to pride themselves on drinking a stout glass of this granular stuff every morning, for good health. Nature's Metamucil!

"Underwater, the sound was like a thousand bowls of Rice Krispies popping at once. This, Elijah concluded, was the sound of untold tons of sediment tumbling on the river bottom, a churning cloud below him.

"He was making good progress now. For him, this was a good, brisk workout, but if there was a feat in swimming across the Mississippi River, it was a feat more psychic than physical, more conceptual than aerobic. Any half-decent swimmer could do it.

"Still, Elijah could hear himself chuckling. He couldn't believe he was out here, doing this most exotic thing, which was also, given his background, the most obvious thing. It was as if he were a guy from Pamplona deciding, perhaps a little late in life, to go ahead and run with those demented bulls. He was swimming . . . across . . . the . . . Mississippi . . . River. And he was feeling strangely at home, as though he was meant to be here, as though it belonged to him and he to it.

"Elijah crawled toward the thickety bank, where stands of willow and cypress were choked in muscadine vine. Then, with his left hand, he touched the Great State of Tennessee. It had taken him nearly an hour to get across, and he'd been swept several miles downstream in the crossing. He looked back toward Arkansas and savored his accomplishment. He was exhausted, coughing up a little river water, but elated.

"A few minutes later, as he was stomping through the shallows and starting to peel off his wetsuit, he caught something out of the corner of his eye—a flash, an eruption of water, a sudden sideways motion. In the confusion, some creature grabbed his arm. It knocked him off balance, and he tumbled into the water. For a moment, he could feel a presence of tremendous mass and weight.

"Then the thing, whatever it was, let go. Elijah saw only a tail and dorsal fin as the being vanished in a blur of olive-colored spines and slimy scales. He would never know for sure, but all his instincts told him what it was: He had stepped on a slumbering alligator gar, and the startled dinosaur had seized his arm.

"When Elijah took off his wetsuit, all he saw was a pattern of deep punctures. The creature had left an engraving upon him in the form of an immaculate wound—a long, clean row of tooth marks. Oddly, there was not a drop of blood, and he felt no pain whatsoever.

"Elijah spent the rest of the day hiking to the nearest town, hitching a ride to Memphis, then driving with Florence back over the bridge to Arkansas to fetch his truck and camping gear. By the time he got home, the wound was starting to fester and sting. The long rows of tooth marks had become ragged and itchy and raw. Elijah figured it would go away. But the next day, he awoke with shooting stabs of pain and menacing red streaks that extended up and down his arm. The bite from the fish had left perfect little portals that, in turn, had introduced a decidedly nasty infection.

"A few hours later, his forearm had swelled hideously, the skin rigid and hot to the touch. Elijah was breathing uneasily. He felt dizzy and feverish, then collapsed on the floor.

"He managed to call Florence. She hurried over and rushed him to St. Joseph's Hospital, where we found he was in septic shock. 'I told you not to swim in that fucking river,' Florence told him, full of rage.

"After a battery of tests, we learned that Elijah had a rare flesh-eating streptococcus infection. Technically known as necrotizing fasciitis, the infection was something out of Stephen King: Ravening armies of microbes were laying waste to the meat of his arm, filling his subcutaneous tissues with exotoxins.

"I took a black Sharpie and drew a line on Elijah's arm. I told him that if the redness advanced beyond this boundary, he was in serious trouble. Over the next hour, the strep marched right past that Sharpie mark and was well on its way to Elijah's hand. Half of his arm had been consumed. It was like the old days in the Civil War, when people brought out picnics and blankets and, from a distance, watched the hourly progress of the battle. Except the battle was all happening right there inside his flesh.

"Now he was vomiting, convulsing, his skin slick with erratic fevers. I told Florence they should be prepared: I might have to cut off his arm. It might be the only way to save him.

"In his delirium, hearing the distant skreak of a medieval bone saw, Elijah found himself asking questions: Is this how it ends? Have I lived a halfway-decent life? If I get out of this, will I live any differently?

"Several times I sliced open his arm to irrigate and debride the tissues, and the stuff that came out was beyond disgusting—curds of black gunk, sour-smelling soups, puddles of pus. We pumped various IV antibiotics into him, but nothing worked. I thought it was a lost cause. Fading in and out of consciousness,

Elijah thought a lot about the uninvited guests that were consuming his sinews and corpuscles. He seemed both repulsed and fascinated by the idea that these superbug strains were just out there, a skin thickness away, loitering in their millions on the surfaces of the world, waiting for a tiny cut or abrasion, some way in, to reach the Food Court of our flesh.

"I told Elijah that we had one more item in our quiver, an astronomically expensive designer antibiotic.

"'This one,' I said, 'is on loan from God.'

"It worked. After a day, the red armies began to recede. In a few weeks, Elijah's arm was more or less back to normal. But that scar will remain with him for the rest of his life, an indelible stamp, left by the razor-sharp teeth of an ancient and misunderstood species of fish. Elijah looks upon his river adventure as time well spent, and told me he viewed the rest of his days as time on loan from God—or at least from God's antibiotics department.

"Elijah Vick soon resumed his guitar playing with a vengeance and became one of the city's most legendary session musicians. He never put a toe into the Mississippi again."

"Whoa, now that's a scary story," said Wurly. "If he'd lost his arm, we'd have lost some great music. I can just see him up onstage: 'Sorry, folks, dinosaur ate my arm.'"

"My dad," said Merenguero's Daughter, "broke his wrist once and kept right on playing, even though it hurt like hell. He said, 'Toco o muero.' I play or I die."

"Now there's a fine piece of wisdom," said Vinegar. "Play or die. Those folks didn't spend the rest of their lives whining about God and fate." She cast a pointed glance at Florida.

I drained my Coke and Cynar on the rocks and poured myself another from the thermos. How the fuck had the conversation gotten stuck on the subject of one-armed men? It was like God was mocking me, looking for ways to punish.

"Whiners carp about whining," Florida said, "'cause they don't like the competition."

At this, Vinegar turned around to give Florida a long stare. "Speaking of competition, when is that fool son of yours going to stop draining your settlement money so you can pay back that fifty-seven dollars and seventeen cents you owe me?"

Eurovision clapped his hands. "Friends, friends! Let's move on! Now who's going to tell the next story?"

The Lady with the Rings said, "What we need now is a story of reconciliation. Something to calm us down and take us away to another world."

"I'm quite calm, thank you," said Vinegar. "It's another body who's agitated."

"Who's got a story that will take us far away from here?" Eurovision asked loudly.

"I've got a story about imagination," said Tango. "I take people out of their lives for a living."

We all turned to her. "I've been imaginative since I was a child," she said. "I look at people and envision their outer—and inner—lives. I invent what they think, what they feel . . . and, especially, what they want. Then I package that in a way for other people to enter those lives. As my late husband used to say, it pays the bills."

"What," said Eurovision, "may I ask, is this unusual profession of yours?"

"I'm a romance novelist."

"Oh my. How interesting. I've never met a romance novelist before."

"Fiction writers have to imagine a lot more than what you see on the outside," said Tango. "We have to expose inner thoughts. For me, it all goes back to the Lady in White."

"We would *adore* hearing about the Lady in White," said Eurovision.

"Obviously, I've ended up in New York, but I didn't start life here. That happened on the other side of the country, in Los Angeles. I was born and lived in Inglewood for a spell, a place my mother remembers fondly for the Spanish-style homes with their red-tile roofs. I don't remember anything about the city at all. My first memories start when we moved to Redondo Beach, onto a street the city decided to call a lane.

"The apartment we moved into was on Carnegie, which lies between Rockefeller and Vanderbilt. There were many apartment complexes on our street, all with flat roofs and siding painted in shades of coffee—espresso and latte, with lots of cappuccino and mocha thrown in for good measure. The cars that lined the curbs were mainly harvest-gold, walnut, or avocado, similar shades to the kitchen appliances.

"I lived with my mother in a bottom-floor unit. Two of my friends, sisters, lived in the complex next door, a shotgun-style building where vehicles tucked into carports on the ground floor, and the apartments sat above. We often played in the long stretch of driveway, chasing balls or playing hide-and-seek between the cars.

"One afternoon we did neither, instead waited for the ice-cream truck with its sun-faded stickers and warbling tune. We sat cross-legged on the sidewalk, counting the sticks left in our packs of candy cigarettes. Mine were chewing gum wrapped in paper tubes. Theirs were sugar with red-painted tips. The sounds of the neighborhood surrounded us: dogs barking, the buzz of conversations, and dueling televisions and radios.

"The sun was high in the sky and unshielded by clouds. Oppressive waves of heat rippled off the asphalt, making the icy-white Corvette that turned onto our street even more astonishing.

"Lean and long, with exaggerated curves over the wheels and a sloping hood, it was the most beautiful car I'd ever seen. Gleaming and bright, the convertible perfectly showcased the stunning woman behind the wheel, her dark hair confined in a thick chignon.

"She, too, wore white, which contrasted beautifully with the rich caramel hue of her skin. Oversized sunglasses protected her eyes from the unrelenting rays of the sun. Her full, wide lips were painted a deep burgundy, and her sleek jawline was shown to advantage by slim shoulders and a graceful neck. Like the car she drove, I'd never seen anyone so striking in real life.

"The Corvette slid into the parking spot reserved for prospective tenants. The three of us watched with disbelief as the woman unfolded from the driver's seat, revealing a figure as curvaceous as the vehicle she drove. Encased in a tight white dress with thin straps tied at her nape, she approached the manager's office on stiletto heels with an unhurried stride.

"'Mr. Hogan,' my friend Tara breathed, her eyes wide.

"We laughed, imagining Mr. Hogan, the manager and super, lifting his head to see that goddess walk in. He was a good man, happily married, and not too tough on us when we played around the parked cars. Still, we couldn't imagine him as anything but flustered when confronted with a woman who looked like that.

"We just didn't get extraordinary on Carnegie Lane very often. Well, ever.

"Tara, Torrie, and I picked ourselves up and headed to examine the Corvette. There was a lingering trace of a rich floral and musk perfume around it, the smell of wealth and beauty and mystery. The interior was immaculate, with no hint of anything that didn't belong to the car.

"We loitered for the twenty minutes or so that she was inside, then straightened to attention when she appeared again. There was a second before she slid her sunglasses back onto the bridge of her nose when we could see the whole of her face. Big, dark eyes heavily fringed with long lashes and rimmed in black liner. When I've described her in later years, people inevitably suggest Sophia Loren or Raquel Welch. I always redirect them back to Nefertiti, a woman we imagine as regal and sublime.

"'Are you moving here?' I asked, hardly daring to believe it. No one like her lived anywhere near the row of streets named after the men who built America.

"'For a little bit,' she said, with a faint smile and low voice.

"A moment later, the Corvette was prowling down Carnegie, and a few days after, it returned, leading a moving truck into the parking lot.

"My friends and I settled in for the show, watching with fascination as burly movers hauled low-slung, curved, and white furniture up the narrow staircase and into her apartment. Every piece was very different from the dark woods and amber florals prevalent in every home I visited. She, too, was dressed casually in white, her pants wide-legged and her raglan top large enough to hang off one shoulder. Her hair was up and restrained with a braided white headband. My mother had a few similar outfits in her closet, a comfortable staple that had never been elevated from laidback to elegant.

"Over the next week, I kept an eye out for the Lady in White and her car. Most times, the Corvette was parked neatly in its stall next to the dusty sedans and trucks. But she remained elusive. Then, one day, I saw through her screen door that her front door was open.

"'Let's go talk to her,' I said.

"Tara shook her head. 'No way.'

"'Why not?' Torrie rolled her shoulders back, ever

the adventurous one. 'Mom's talked to her a few times. Said she's nice.'

"I tried to picture Mrs. Bracken, a generously hearted woman who smoked a lot and drank a lot of iced tea laced with Sweet'n Low, talking to the Lady in White. I decided to go for it and headed toward the stairs.

"It took a bit more courage to knock than I expected, but it was worth it when she appeared down the hallway, her hair twisted in a white-towel turban and a white silk kimono wrapped loosely around her. She was barefaced, which made her look younger but no less impressive.

"'Um, do you want to hang out with us?' I asked.

"Her brows lifted above widened eyes. She took a few long seconds to answer. 'That's really sweet of you to ask, but I'm getting ready for a date.'

"'You're going on a date?' I just couldn't imagine any guy living up to her. I just didn't know anyone who had the quiet command that she did, the unhurried refinement of her movements, the sense that nothing ruffled or surprised her or caught her off guard.

"Her mouth curved. 'Yes. And I'm running a little late, so I have to go. Maybe some other time?'

"'Sure,' I agreed, now more curious about who could possibly be confident enough to ask a woman like her out.

"Torrie, Tara, and I set up shop on the short wall by the street, eager to check out the date and how she looked. We all wrinkled our noses when he showed up and shook our heads. He was just all right. Average. Dark hair, brown blazer, slacks. I remember thinking he didn't appreciate her the way he should, showing up like that. His car wasn't as memorable as hers.

"Disappointed, I called out, 'She's really pretty.'

"He startled, then frowned.

"When she left with him, she looked like a million dollars; her hair finally freed into a thick curtain of loose black curls that fell to her waist.

"I never saw her again. A week later, I learned that she'd moved out the day before, a two-week stay in total. But I've never forgotten her.

"When I started writing, she was often an inspiration. Unsolved mysteries, especially those that linger from childhood, just stick with you. Initially, she was the femme fatale, the other woman, or the ex. Later, she shifted from the antagonist to the heroine, but she'd be an underworld boss's mistress who crossed paths with a hunky law-enforcement guy or a trophy wife having a renaissance after being dumped for someone even younger.

"But over time, I've reevaluated how I think of her. Am I a woman who perpetuates stories in which another woman is agentless in her fate, a person who drifts powerlessly through the whims of men who objectify her? I decided I didn't want to be. Why limit her to the role of arm candy? Why make her extraordinary beauty her primary selling point or something she has to overcome? And her date has gone on to be a hero in my books more than once. That's what writers do—we spin what we see and feel into something fresh and new.

"So, the Lady in White has been a bestselling novelist who works from home, a CIA agent in town for a single mission, and a successful business owner who's expertly built a staff that no longer requires constant oversight. Her date is sometimes her agent or handler or brother. Sometimes, she's between homes and waiting for her loan to close, and others, she's a survivor moving beyond trauma and into the next chapter of her life.

"I will never know her true story, but the tales I invent for her now are crafted with the grace and respect we all deserve. That's the power of imagination."

As she finished, Tango settled back in her chair, raising the mask once again over her mouth. I looked around. Most of us were half-shit-faced by this stage of the evening, and not a soul seemed to know how to follow that story. As soon as the bells of Old St. Pat's began ringing out the eight o'clock hour, everyone began packing up.

But before any of us made it out the door, we noticed a young woman who had suddenly appeared in our midst. This was not someone I'd ever seen before, either in the building or on the rooftop. I was quite sure that if she were in Wilbur's bible, I would have remembered her. She was odd-looking, even for New York. From the way everyone was staring at her, nobody else knew who she was, either. I hadn't noticed her come out the rooftop door—she must have been hiding in the shadows all along. And she was *not* wearing a mask.

She had short, spiky hair, dyed green, with black fake jewels stuck into it. Her bare arms were long and thin, with spindly fingers, and her eyes were round and shiny, and so dark they seemed all pupil. Her skin was pale, almost greenish; her dress, too, was pale green, with a bulb-shaped skirt; the fabric had a rough texture, like a sparse pelt. The effect she created was oddly chilling, but beautiful in its own way.

"Good evening," she said. Her voice was light and dry. "I came to thank you for your stories. They've taught me so much! I never knew about the one-armed pianist, or vengeance, or ghosts, or the smell of death."

We looked at one other. She'd been here among us? All week? Really?

"Oh yes, I do live in this building," she said, as if reading our thoughts. "But I specialize in not being noticed." She folded herself into one of the empty chairs, drawing her knees up under her skirt, and regarded us attentively with her round black eyes. "Many of your tales have been unusual, but I suspect my own may be the most unusual of all."

Eurovision stared at her as if mesmerized. "We were going to close shop for the night, but . . ." He looked to the rest of us, as if for permission. "Of course, we'd like to hear your story."

"Thank you," she said. She sighed a sigh that was almost a whisper, and began.

"By day I work with a bedbug-extermination company. We should all do jobs we're skilled at and that we love—don't you agree?—and I happen to have a special affinity for this vocation. I can spot and capture these disagreeable home invaders with a speed and accuracy that my fellow exterminators marvel at. They say I must have eyes at the back of my head. I haven't yet told them that in fact I do have eyes at the back of my head, more or less: three eyes on each side, as well as the two at the front, making a total of eight.

"Don't be alarmed, I'm not from outer space. You'll understand better in a minute.

"I work without pesticides, which many of my more ecologically minded customers consider a plus. Bedbugs can be such a problem in this city. They can ruin a person's life, I'm told; it's a stigma, so there's no one the sufferers can confide in except me. I'm happy to help—that's how I put it to them. Plus, I'm not against augmenting my diet with a nutritional snack when occasion offers.

"In addition to my official job, I've been attending classes at NYU, or I was before the plague. I myself have a natural immunity to this particular virus—but the majority of my classes were postponed. I'd been dabbling in the humanities, as I wished to investigate the meaning of 'human.' So, philosophy and mythology, primarily.

"In one of my classes, I learned that the ancient Greeks told a story about a girl called Arachne, who was an excellent weaver. She annoyed some god or other, who turned her into a spider. This was supposed to be a terrible punishment, which made me laugh when I heard about it, because I myself used to be a spider. Given the choice between a girl and a spider, who wouldn't opt for the spider? A female spider, needless to say. Girls are always being predated by male humans, but with spiders it's the other way around. We don't eat all the males: that's a stereotypical exaggeration. We eat only the smallest ones, and those lacking in nimbleness.

"A hint of threat keeps a fellow on his toes, don't you think? That's what I suggest on my Tinder profile: a hint of threat. You'd be surprised at the responses I receive.

"I know my story sounds weird, and you probably think I'm crazy, but what I've told you is the simple truth. I'm not sure how or why I was transformed. Most likely it was by a god, as in the Greek story: Gods are capricious. Or it may have been an experiment in genetic engineering that got out of hand. Was I a human being with arachnid materials added, or was it the other way around? But we can't spend too much time fussing about our origins, can we? From my philosophy classes I've learned that humans can fret a lot about things that can never be known, such as the ultimate meaning of life. I personally feel that the ultimate meaning of life is eggs, but I may be very old-fashioned.

"Back to my story. One day I was no longer running around in the foliage. Instead, I was sitting in a train from Cambridge, Massachusetts, to New York City. Luckily, I'd been supplied with underwear, a suitcase to put it in, and a credit card: The gods can be whimsical, but they do have an eye for detail.

"I'd been given a name, as well: It was on the credit card. Gabriella Cambridge. 'Cambridge' makes sense in view of the gene sequencing at MIT; Gabriella may be a reference to the Angel Gabriel, the messenger who, by blowing his horn, will announce the end of the world. Is that the secret of my materialization in this hybrid form? Have I been sent as a messenger? If so, what is the message? Could it be that the world as you have known it is coming to an end? I have no idea, but I expect I'll be told eventually—whether by a god or a scientist remains to be seen.

"Meanwhile, I've been spending these days of lockdown—when I'm not engaged on a bedbug case—researching the history and prehistory of the arachnid part of my heritage. We are very ancient, we spiders; we appear in many traditions. In some, a spider wove the world; in others, we are tricksters, crafty but sometimes rash and stupid, and in this latter mode we wove human beings. We protect you from bad dreams, say some; we make it rain, say others. Always—I do emphasize this—it's bad luck to kill a spider.

"On the practical front, some of us control pests in houses, others are garden specialists. Yes, it's true that a few of us are severely toxic, especially in Australia, but what group of beings wishes to be judged solely by its most alarming members? Are all human beings Caligulas and Countess Báthories? Surely not!

"As you are storytellers, may I humbly point out that many of the terms you use—spinning a yarn, weaving a tale, following a thread—are borrowed from our arachnid culture. 'Text,' of course, comes from 'textile.' We spiders do object to a pejorative human saying, namely, 'Oh, what a tangled web we weave / When first we practice to deceive.' You also speak of 'a web of lies.' Spiders are not lying and deceiving when we weave webs, we are simply eating. Supermarket packaging of meat products: Now that's deceptive! Little children grow up believing that steaks are created in plastic wrap, rather than being sawed from the bodies of dead cows. Spiders are not hypocritical about their ingestion practices. We take no pains to conceal the corpses of the flies we have sucked dry.

"But this talk of eating has made me hungry. I have an appointment in a condo just down the street—another distressing bedbug problem—and I must excuse myself, though I hope to return before this evening has concluded: As I've said, I'm very fast. Would any of you like to accompany me to see how I work? My methods repay study. You, sir? No? How about you?"

She gestured at Darrow, who shook his head with a nervous laugh.

"You need not be mistrustful of me, sir," she said, with a smile that was meant to be reassuring. The points of two black, curved teeth showed at the corners of her mouth. "You are far too large to be appealing to me as a prey object."

"I bet you say that to all the guys," Darrow said, glancing around. Several people giggled, as if to back him up.

She extended her spindly legs from beneath her bulbous skirt. "Excuse me? I do not say it to all of them, as some are a lot smaller than you." She stretched out her arms, flexed her fingers. Was she angry? "Are you accusing me of lying, once again? I never lie."

Darrow tried to shrug it off. "Hey. No offense meant. Just a joke."

"Oh. We spiders and affiliates have difficulties with this key human concept of 'joke.' But I am trying to untangle it. Catch you later!"

One moment, the pale greenish woman was there, solid as you or me, and the next moment her chair was empty. It was dark and misty in the corners of our rooftop, so she may have blended with the shadows. We looked at one another: What had just happened? Was she real? Could she have been someone in an old Halloween costume, crashing our party? Taking advantage of how much we'd all been drinking to dupe us, just for the laughs?

Or—but surely not. Your guess is as good as mine.

She didn't come back, however. That tells us something. Or I think it does.

Day Eleven
April 10

P rank or alcohol-induced hallucination, whatever it was, I'd thought about the strange spider-girl all day. I wondered if it was going to scare away any of our storytellers, but when I arrived on the roof, it looked like most of our usual suspects had come back. I was glad, despite myself.

While no one seemed ready to actually bring up the spider-girl again in the light of day, on the mural someone had painted a picture of two terrified, wide-eyed bunnies in a box with holes in it, in the hands of a big old man with a beard sitting on a cloud.

"I see," said Eurovision, settled into his chair and pouring his martini until it slopped over, "that God Himself has decided to join us tonight."

"Nah. Some old white dude sitting on a cloud, pulling our puppet strings?" said Vinegar, with a snort. "That isn't my God. No, thank you."

"I did a comic in which God appeared as a character," volunteered Amnesia. "I made him purple, with a big nose, mustache, and five-o'clock shadow. Oh, and tentacles."

Hello Kitty said, "God is just some dumb-ass kid and we're his science experiment."

"For which he will get an F," said Darrow. He looked at Amnesia. "I'm kind of curious about you. You wrote comic books?"

"I did, until I was hired to write computer games. That was after I won a Ringo Award for my comic series *Polypore*, when I had my fifteen minutes of fame and riches."

"*Polypore?*" Eurovision asked Amnesia. "What was *that* about?"

"It was a sci-fi horror series about a shelf mushroom that colonizes the human penis. There was a rush of offers, Comic Cons and cosplay sorts of things, and I got hired by Frictional Games for a freelance gig at gargantuan fees. I didn't invent *Amnesia*, but I was involved in writing later versions. It happened so fast—I was a millionaire for a year, until I got sick with HIV, and like a fucking idiot I hadn't bothered to get insurance. I went through all my money down the street right over there—in Presbyterian. My whole life collapsed, and then came Covid and when I got out of the hospital that's how I ended up in this joke of a building. Anyway, during my glory time of fame and riches, I tried my hand at acting."

"I got a gig doing *The Vagina Monologues* at the Westside Theater in New York. I never wanted to be an actor, but I got talked into it by the producer and the writer. It turned out to be a very interesting experience. Writers live alone. Actors are always involved with one another. An actor's day is totally different from a writer's. You wake up late, eat a late breakfast, promise yourself you are going to do something like writing or telephoning but—knowing you have to leave for the theater at five o'clock—nothing else gets done. At five, if you're lucky, you get into a car the show has sent for you, and you go to the theater. There, you put on makeup and whatever clothes you are wearing and talk and gossip with the other actors. This is the best part of the day. This is the part of the day where you figure out auditions; where you get the gossip of the business and you wish it would go on forever. Honestly, doing your makeup, planning the rest of the day is kind of marvelous. And then it's time. There's a knock on the door.

"'Be ready to go on at such-and-such a time.'

"And you fix your makeup yet again and go backstage, getting ready to go on, heart pounding. Always at this moment you're sure you will forget your lines, and yet, when you take your place, everything comes back. The humor, the voice, the craziness of being in front of a darkened audience of invisible faces. It's like living an alternate life, apart from your normal life. And it's even more vivid than your life. You can't eat before the show, and the hunger sort of propels you. When it's over and the lights go up and you actually see the faces of the people who have been listening, you are absolutely ravenous, and all you want to do is go out and eat. I never like to eat when I have to speak in public—somehow, the food weighs me down—but after the show, I feel free and all I want is a glass of wine and food. No matter how dreadful the restaurant, the food tastes better than anything you've ever eaten, and the company is wonderful because the people you've been performing with are totally open. They will tell you anything after the first glass of wine.

"So even though I never wanted to be an actor, I loved the rhythm of an actor's day—the fact that you go home and collapse, totally exhausted, sleeping until eleven o'clock the next morning, totally blissed out. As a writer, you always struggle with self-doubt, but as an actor, the words are not your own, so you inhabit the character with a kind of irreverence and joy. When I did *The Vagina Monologues*, some of my actor and director friends came to hear me and told me I was 'not bad.' Yet I would not trade my difficult life as a writer for the more social life of an actor. I'm glad I know about the rhythm of their lives. Someday I will write a play.

"The most remarkable thing that happened during the show is that, as I was doing my vaginal piece, someone in the audience, a man, dropped dead! Naturally I didn't know this until after the show. I don't blame myself for the death, but maybe the material was too upsetting."

Amnesia stopped, and Hello Kitty began to laugh uproariously. "I love it," she said. "*The Vagina Monologues* killed a man!" She pealed with laughter. "That's priceless. You say you were 'not bad'? I bet you were fucking awesome! A millionaire writer and an actress! How many actors can say they actually *killed* someone in the audience with their talent?"

No one else seemed to think it was funny.

"Did you ever find out how he died?" Darrow asked Amnesia, pointedly ignoring Hello Kitty's outburst.

"They said a heart attack." She looked a little uncomfortable at the direction the conversation about her story had taken. The man's death interested me less than the part about how Amnesia had gotten HIV—of course, I wasn't about to ask any questions that might draw attention to myself. But boy, is that an awful disease. She must have come down in the world pretty hard to end up in the Fernsby Arms.

Hello Kitty was still laughing, though less enthusiastically now that she realized others weren't sharing her mockery.

"I'm sorry, but I don't think that's very funny," Maine said. "You should pay a visit to the ER someday and see what it's like when someone is having a heart attack."

Instead of responding, Hello Kitty just took a huge inhale on her vape and folded her legs back up into the cave chair, looking defiant.

The Lady with the Rings spoke up. "I love what you say about an actor's day. I was never a stage actor, not exactly, but . . . Well, perhaps it's time to tell my story."

I was starting to appreciate how deftly the Lady with the Rings handled tension on the roof.

"Yes!" said Eurovision. "Didn't you say you lived a lie? I'm dying to know what that means."

"Yes, well, first, let me first tell you that I started out

as an artist. And I was good. Well . . . ," the Lady with the Rings paused, nodding at Vinegar, "maybe not as good as you. But, I'd gotten into Pratt. And, back then, it meant something. I really thought . . . well." The Lady with the Rings shook her head almost imperceptibly.

"You see, my brother, my darling, clueless brother Glenn fancied himself a playwright *and* a producer . . . ," she laughed softly. "Not *good* plays, mind you. So he had to produce them. It had always been his dream and, somehow, when one of his actors decided he needed a real job and left him hanging on opening night, Glenn roped me into standing in for him. One night. Just a fluke. Glenn was so . . . desperate, said he had 'a possible backer, some guy with deep pockets and *please* . . .'

"I played 'the Butler,' of all things: just a few lines, just one night." The Lady with the Rings chuckled softly, running her long fingers along the line of her chin as she remembered.

"Picture this: a much-used wig, one scratchy mustache, and a ratty old tuxedo Glenn had scared up from the Goodwill in Red Hook. I had to wrap my chest pretty tightly to hide my . . . um, assets," she grinned.

"Sometime during the second act, it occurred to me that I had never once expected that anyone would

attend, much less underwrite, Glenn's play. He had
sworn that an investor was coming but, trussed up like
I was, I just felt light-headed and annoyed that I'd ever
agreed to help out. The guy operating the lights was so
heavy-handed that I could barely see the audience. But
I could see . . . and smell . . . Glenn's secondhand props,
still damp from the flooded basement where he'd found
them. The actors swanning around me in period dress
looked comically flimsy. Maybe I was just dizzy from
wrapping my breasts too tightly. Plus, the cheap mustache glue had dried up and itched like hell. Still, I could
make out my dear, sweet Glenn, giving me a thumbs-up
from the third row, grinning like he'd just gotten paid.
I realized then that his 'money' guys must've shown up.
So I got in one good scratch to my upper lip by adding
an elaborate mustache twirl and delivered my big line:
'Madame, I believe the constable has arrived.'

"Act three was a hot mess. By the time my character had been cleared of suspicion and the culprit was
revealed to be a nanny named *Agnes* . . . wait for it . . .
Butler, most of the audience had taken advantage of the
dark and slipped away. I was seeing halos around every
light by then and just wanted to get the wrapping off
before I passed out.

"But there were bows to take. Even a second round
of bowing, thanks to Glenn, who led the applause him-

self. Where had he even found an audience for this pun-ridden farce? RH Playhouse had been a produce warehouse, washed out of business by a recent hurricane. The space had only been affordable because my dear brother was desperate enough to slather paint over water stains and have his actors shout lines at each other over the whirring of gigantic fans. It had taken a week to dry out the walls and floors.

"Ever since he had graduated two years earlier, Glenn had been staging his plays at area colleges, mostly with students and a ragtag group of his theater friends. He categorized his plays as 'experimental.' None of them made sense. Let alone a profit. His friends seemed hell-bent on performing, though. So they recycled costumes and hammered together sets regardless of where or when Glenn's stories were set. I don't think any of his plays ran for more than two or three nights.

"What I did know was that each production soaked up whatever money Glenn made tending bar and painting apartments during the week. When we were kids, I had been his default lead in every play, from his fourth-grade interpretation of *Wonder Woman, the Prequel* to his send-up, *The Cadbury Tales,* which he'd staged in the community room of our Park Slope apartment building when he was in tenth grade. His cast actually raised funds for that one.

"I do believe that most of our audience had come for the free candy we passed out during intermission.

"I had been his willing accomplice. But that was then. Once I got into Pratt, I needed to work at least two jobs every semester. Whatever financial aid I was able to get barely covered my art supplies. I had little money and less time. And I made it clear to Glenn that I was *not* an actress . . . I was so into my art then. So, sure . . . ." Shrugging her shoulders, the Lady with the Rings shook off the thought.

"When Glenn's leading man dropped out at the very last minute, leaving him stranded, what could I do? The guy had chosen a 'real' job over the glittering lights of Red Hook. And it was only one night.

"Once the applause died, I made a beeline for the storage room that Glenn had set aside for me, his star. I didn't mind playing a man, there was very little I wouldn't do for him, but I needed privacy to get into and out of that butler costume. I'd even cut my hair short so the wig would fit and added that nasty mustache to make me look more masculine. I had mixed pastel shavings . . . my good Caran d'Ache pastels that I skipped lunch for a week to afford . . . I mixed them with Vaseline, glazed my chin and throat with the mess and, voila! Stubble and an Adam's apple. But flattening my chest? That was exhausting. I needed to breathe.

"Before I reached the storage room, I heard Glenn calling, 'Hold up!' He was grinning and giddy, flanked by the two guys I'd seen sitting with him in the audience. There was no way his investor talk had been serious. This was still Red Hook. And my sweet, determined, delusional Glenn, the brother I adored and encouraged, had written a real stinker this time. But I'd never tell him. So I might wrap myself in gauze, slap on a mustache, and play along like I had in grade school. And somehow he had convinced others—*non*–blood relations—to take on roles this time. But luring in someone who'd spend actual money on this play? Not possible.

"'Jeremy, Chaz, I'd like to present my star,' Glenn said proudly. He gave me a curious wink.

"Heads nodded, hands were shaken, compliments were paid. My accent, timing, my presence . . . just masterful, Jeremy gushed. Seriously? His friend Chaz had said nothing, but simply studied my face. I felt suddenly aware of how dank with mildew the walls were in that hallway, how close together they seemed. Honestly, if I couldn't get out of that costume soon, I worried I'd use what little air I had left to scream.

"Glenn knew me too well; he knew I was ready to bail. 'We'll meet you out front in ten, cool?' he said to his new friends, either missing or intentionally ignoring the side-eye I was giving him.

"'I gotta get out of this thing, Glenn,' I insisted the minute they'd left.

"'No. C'mon, Alex,' he said. 'You gotta come with us. Please? That guy, Chaz, is loaded. Like, serious, old, big-time money, okay? He can take this straight to off-Broadway!'

"I was happy for him. Happy he had such faith. And I told him so. 'But tell me about it after I change, all right?' I remember saying. Just talking was a strain.

"Glenn had leaned in close even though the exit door had firmly closed behind his new friends. 'Listen, sis. Chaz, the guy with all the money? I think he thinks you're a dude. Really. Like, kudos, hats off to you kid, you nailed the part!'

"''Kay, so? I get the lead when he brings your play to Broadway . . . seriously? No offense, brother dear, but the fuck do I care? Not an actress, remember? And don't wanna be.'

"Glenn rolled his eyes. 'No, c'mon. Course not. He's got a job for you. For big bucks I think,' he added. 'Hey, you know that's gotta be good news. Just come with us to this thing in the East Village.'

"I studied my brother. Yes. I needed money. I had one semester to go at Pratt and no job prospects in sight. I had a hundred and thirty-eight dollars in my savings account and not enough in checking for an ATM withdrawal. Plus, rent was due. So there was that. My internship at WE Press Books hadn't paid me in two weeks, so I had stopped going. Which made it highly unlikely that they would pay me what they owed me anytime soon. Yes, money would be nice.

"Still, I leaned in close to his ear to make my point. 'I. Can't. Fucking. Breathe.'

"'You are such a drama queen' was all he said.

"We took a taxi, following the car service his new friends had taken, so Glenn had time to brief me on how Chaz was ready to finance his play, to make it 'real.' I remember thinking about how many good and well-intentioned lies we tell others. His new friend's offer set off an alarm in my brain. I watched Glenn's face. I wanted to warn him. But being honest seemed cruel. My brother was too excited to entertain the truth about his play. Crossing the Manhattan Bridge, the lights overhead kept stroking his face on, off. On, off. He believed this was his beginning. And I wanted that for him. Hell, I wanted as much for myself. But when others said I had talent, I had enough sense to question it. Others could be well-intentioned liars, too.

"How many times had I railed against situational ethics? But this was different. This was Glenn. And situational ethics sounded better than lying.

"Every bump that we hit on the bridge, every pothole

we caught as we headed up the Bowery had a curative effect, each jolt loosening the fabric I had wound around my chest. I tried to focus on breathing. This had better be worth it.

"The party turned out to be on the rooftop of a nondescript walk-up building on East Third Street."

The Lady with the Rings looked meaningfully around the rooftop, at all of us staring breathless back at her, trying to figure out where this story was going.

"Anyway, strings of lights outlined the borders of the roof, and most of the crowd stayed clustered in the shadows, their silhouettes merging and pulling apart, defined by the city lights behind them. There was a makeshift bar, blankets, pillows, and chairs set in one corner, and someone was playing what sounded like a weird mix of rap and sitar music.

"Glenn left me and returned with two plastic cups of very bland wine. Then he took off in search of his friends. I found a spot on the ledge of the building that abutted the roof next door, the side that didn't offer a seven-story drop to the sidewalk. I parked myself and sipped my wine.

"'Glenn told you I have a job for you?' Chaz was suddenly above me, holding a half-filled champagne flute. Clearly, Glenn had missed the bar with the good stuff.

"'Yeah, he did mention that,' I said, hoping I

sounded husky despite being taken by surprise. With enough distance and makeup, I had pulled off being a man onstage and in that shadowy hallway. But now I was worried about the streetlamp a few floors below. How much was revealed in this light?

"'What I've got is a, well . . . it's not, uh . . . not a conventional acting job, exactly.' Chaz let out a choked, heh-heh, phony sort of laugh. His eyes narrowed, and he studied me as though he was unsure about telling me more.

"I stared at my plastic cup and slowly swirled what was left of the wine, keeping my face turned away from the light. Jesus. What did that mean? Birthday clown? The back end of a horse? Some weird sex thing? Had Glenn known what the deal was and not wanted to tell me? Did that even matter? Rent was due in two days.

"'What's involved?' I asked.

"'Well,' Chaz said, sitting down next to me on the edge of the roof, 'you'd have to lose that mustache for starters, *Alexandra*.'"

We were leaning forward intently when suddenly we heard a crash at the far end of the roof. Someone began yelling, and a man, disheveled, unmasked, covered in sweat, his eyes wild, rushed into the center of our gathering.

"Hey, I wasn't expecting anyone up here. Yeah, I thought I'd be alone."

"Who are *you*?" demanded Florida, half rising from her seat. I saw Vinegar and Eurovision exchange an alarmed glance. We were all half frozen with surprise.

"You haven't seen me before, have you? You don't know me. Of course you don't. Who knows me? No one. That's why I came up here, see. Since you're staring at me like I'm some new kind of animal species, I'll tell you the truth. I came up here to jump. Yeah. Like a nosedive. Off the roof. Ha ha. I'm laughing at your faces. Such horror. Like in a bad movie. You can close your mouths. I was probably joking, you know. I mean, that's what I do. I'm a joker. None of you have ever seen me, have you? Morty Gund. The stand-up. Anyone been to Stewie's on Second Avenue on open-mic night? Of course you haven't. How about the Comedy Shack on Ninety-Sixth Street?"

Nobody was even attempting to get a word in edgewise. I glanced at the Lady with the Rings, who had been so rudely interrupted. She was as stunned as the rest of us. Who was this guy?

"Morty Gund. The name doesn't mean a thing to you. And, of course, it's phony. Martin Grunwald. Who would come see a comic named Martin Grun-

wald? Martin Grunwald would have to be the funeral parlor manager who tells everyone he's sorry
for their loss.

"So that's why I'm Morty Gund, not that anyone
asked.

"Morty Gund, fastest comic in the west. Ha ha.

"My ex-wife didn't think that was funny. She didn't
think I was funny. My ex-wife is the main reason I'm
up here joking about jumping off the roof.

"Here's more you don't want to hear. Her name is
Annie. But I call her Annie the Anvil. Because she's
been like an anvil, a heavy weight pulling me down my
whole career.

"Hey, a lot of people think I'm funny. I killed at Ray-
Jay's in Hackensack. A talent scout for *The Tonight
Show* was supposed to be there, but I think he had car
trouble. I played that club three times and got screams.

"Not from my ex-wife, of course. She screamed
okay. She screamed at me day and night about why
don't I make a living. She never stopped screaming
about how I'm not funny.

"She hurt my confidence, but I know I'm funny. You
don't know me, but maybe you know my catchphrase.
Every stand-up has to have a catchphrase, right? Like
Rodney Dangerfield—'I don't get no respect.' Even
you folks must remember that one.

"Well, my catchphrase is, 'Really for real, folks.' I say that ironically, you know, after a joke. Like I'll tell a crazy joke about my ex-wife, and then I'll say, 'Really for real, folks.' It makes people laugh.

"Listen, this is a hard time to make people laugh. I'm not the only one who is striking out. People don't want to laugh these days. They just want to be offended.

"Everyone is offended all the time. People just walk around being offended by everything they hear and every joke someone tells.

"My gay dentist routine used to kill. I mean, really for real, folks.

"But try to do a gay joke today. They just stare at you like you committed a crime.

"Everyone is so uptight.

"I had this great bit about my ex-wife. I'd say, 'She's so fat, when she stands on the corner, people drop envelopes into her mouth.' Ha ha. That's a riot, right?

"I always loved it when a fat woman came into the club. I'd go to town on her, and everyone would go nuts. Then I'd say, 'Just kidding. Just kidding. Not.' And the laughs just boomed off the ceiling.

"You can't do that now. No one has a sense of humor.

"I mean, what kind of world is this where you can't do fat jokes?

"It's tough out there. Take it from me. And I've been funny my whole life.

"When I was in second grade, I was in some kind of stupid play. And I was onstage in front of all the parents. And my costume fell off. As I bent down to pick it up, I heard a roar of laughter ring out over the auditorium.

"I still remember that laughter. And I remember thinking, 'That's fun. Making people laugh is fun.' All those years ago. And so I tried to be funny ever since. And people laughed. Really for real. Everyone except the anvil, my ex-wife.

"I came to the city to do stand-up. My ex-wife did everything she could to discourage me and make me doubt myself. I knew it would be hard work. I knew it would be two hundred open-mic nights and dozens of shabby clubs in terrible little nowhere towns. But I was willing to do all that because I knew I was funny. I knew I could be big-time.

"And yes, early on I had a mentor. Someone who helped me define my personality and carve out my act until everything worked.

"Buzzy Gaines.

"You know Buzzy Gaines, right? You have to know Buzzy. Buzzy is big-time. He had his own half-hour on Netflix last year.

"Well, I met Buzzy at The Jokery in San Jose, and we became fast friends. I was flattered when he offered to give me tips and help work on my act. I mean, he was a pro. He studied comedy and audiences, and he had a great eye for what worked.

"It means a lot when an old pro takes an interest in you and tries to give you a boost. Buzzy and I were close for over a year. And then came that night in Hoboken.

"He was headlining at Sammy's Joint, and I decided to surprise him. I sneaked into the club and sat at the very back table. It was really dark there by the bar, and I knew Buzzy couldn't see me.

"My plan was to heckle him. You know. Give the guy a hard time. I knew he'd get a kick out of it. But when he came onstage, I changed my mind. And I just sat there in stunned silence.

"You see, Buzzy was doing my act.

"He stole the whole thing. Every word.

"I never spoke to him again.

"I guess I became bitter after that betrayal. I changed my act. The act was now all about my ex-wife. But I couldn't do fat jokes anymore. So I did thin jokes.

"'My ex-wife is so thin, I turn her upside down and use her for a broom. My ex-wife has no tits at all. When she turns sideways, you can't see her!'

"Great stuff. But audiences don't want to laugh anymore. The women would start to hiss at each joke, and then the men started booing and hissing. And Stewie asked me not to come to open-mic night anymore.

"Annie the Anvil said, 'I told you so.' And that's when I decided to make Annie my ex-wife. That's when I decided to kill her.

"I dreamed up all kinds of plans, but then I decided they wouldn't work. I didn't think I had the strength to just plain strangle her.

"Annie had taken away all my confidence. I had no faith in myself.

"But I surprised myself. I did have the strength.

"And that's how she became my ex-wife.

"No. Don't get up. I'm leaving. I'm not going to jump off the roof.

"Let me just say, 'Thank you all for being such a great audience. Good night, drive carefully, and God bless.'

"And don't worry about me. I'm working up a whole new act, and I think it's going to kill."

Just as fast as he'd come, he was gone. We were surrounded by vacant lots, so he couldn't have jumped to an adjacent roof. He had to have gone out the door, but none of us had heard it rattle. People were breathing loudly behind their masks, freaked out.

"What the fuck?" Eurovision finally exploded. "Who was that dude?" He turned to me almost accusingly. "Is he a tenant?"

"I've never seen him before in my life," I said defensively. "The doors are locked. He must've broken into the building."

"Where'd he go?" Eurovision cried, lurching to his feet. "Did he jump?"

"He said he wasn't going to," said Wurly.

"He *must* have," said Eurovision. "He's not here and he didn't leave by the door! He was over there when he disappeared. For fuck's sake, somebody look over the side." He fixed his eye on Darrow, who was closest.

"Hell no," said Darrow. "I'm not looking. I'm not going to end up on a witness stand. Somebody else look."

"We would've heard him hit the ground," said the Lady with the Rings.

"How would you know?" asked Vinegar. "Don't tell me you pushed Chaz off the roof?"

"That's not funny," said the Lady with the Rings.

Finally, with an irritated sigh, Hello Kitty got out of her chair and went over to the parapet and looked down, while the rest of us watched in a stasis of dread.

"It's too dark to see," she said, returning to her cave chair.

"What do we do?" asked Wurly.

"Nothing," Hello Kitty said with a shrug. "A bat-shit crazy trespasser invaded our roof and disappeared. Not. Our. Problem."

"It *is* our problem if he's dying on the sidewalk down there!" Vinegar said.

"If you're so concerned," said Florida, "why don't you go down and give him mouth to mouth?"

"But how did he get in?" said Whitney, turning to me again. "Isn't the lobby door locked?"

"Of course it's locked!" I repeated. "Someone probably buzzed him in." I looked around to see if I could catch the guilty party. "That's how most people who aren't supposed to be in the building usually get in."

"Maybe he's *still* in the building," said Wurly. "Someone should go check."

I felt their eyes resting on me and my resentment mounted. "I'm the super, not a fucking door shaker."

The big silent Iraq veteran, Blackbeard, stood up. "I'll do a sweep."

He left. For a moment no one said anything, and then Amnesia said, "We might as well hear the end of the story about Chaz while we're waiting?"

The murmuring seemed to be in favor of the Lady with the Rings finishing the story. Everyone was too upset to just wait around and think about what had just happened.

"Where was I?" said the Lady with the Rings.

"Chaz had a job for you."

"Yes." She gathered up the ends of her scarf and pulled it tighter against the encroaching cold. "When Chaz Cavanaugh called me Alexandra and said to lose the mustache, I peeled it right off and relaxed a little . . . And when he showed me his photos, I finally understood what he wanted me to do. To *become*."

She patted her hair with a beringed hand. We waited.

"**So. Let** me paint you a picture: thirty years later. Another night, in another world, I was throwing a party. The caterers had come highly recommended, but they were running behind schedule. So was Glenn. He had promised to come directly from the theater with a star or two in tow, and his show should have ended forty minutes earlier. My hair had been styled, I had dressed, gone through five shoe options, changed my jewelry, changed it back, and even had time to instruct Herve on how to arrange couches on the terrace to encircle the firepit: close enough for conversation but not so near the fire as to make anyone hot. It was a cool night like this, I recall.

"I had wandered onto the balcony to watch, as a stream of taxis sailed along Park Avenue, far below. Traffic noise never fully reached me up there. From high above, leaning over the railing, it was easy to admire the artistry of the gardens that graced the center of the avenue. Someone must coordinate the blooms and the shrubbery, decide which trees to incorporate and where to place them. Someone had to curate the sculptures that change with every season. I would've been good at that. Choosing colors, themes. That's what I'd always been told: What a great color sense I had. I rarely looked over that railing without thinking back to the rooftop on East Third Street, back to that one night so many years before.

"'The caterers have arrived, Ms. Cavanaugh,' Herve had announced from the terrace door. Indispensable Herve. The irony of having a butler never escaped me. Behind him, my housekeeper was ushering in a small band of workers with their trays and carts, pointing them toward the kitchen.

"You see, as intricate and improbable and shady as it had all seemed, I realized then how well it had worked out. Chaz Cavanaugh hadn't blinked when I removed that mustache. He had simply stared. It was a long, hard, unsettling stare, to be honest. When he showed me photos of his sister, though, I understood what he wanted. Jessa Cavanaugh could have been my twin. It felt as if I were looking at photos of myself, but dressed differently and in locales I didn't remember visiting.

Everything happened quickly after I agreed. For the next couple of days, Chaz schooled me on every pertinent detail of his and his sister's childhood. He produced documents for me to study; I read and reread letters she'd written. I sat at an antique desk in his sister's apartment, a desk that would've paid for my last year at Pratt, and practiced her handwriting. We rehearsed the story of where Jessa had run off to, when she had returned, and why she had kept to herself when she returned. These were not lies, I told myself. These were *possibilities*.

"Now and then, it nagged at me, of course, how certain Chaz had been that his sister would not return. But who was being hurt by this? The lawyers got paid. Chaz got his inheritance. I made sure that Glenn got Broadway. I got Jessa's lifestyle.

"Chaz is gone now. Since he'd never married or had children, I inherited from him as well."

The Lady with the Rings took a long look at her neighbors. "Of course, I often think about him and that night when everything changed. What I remember most is his eyes. And the relief I felt looking into them: relief that I *thought* I could stop pretending . . . and relief that I wasn't perched on the side of the roof with a seven-story drop."

"So what happened? You just *lived* as Chaz's sister

for thirty years?" Darrow asked. "Did you find out where she'd gone?"

The Lady with the Rings smiled again.

"Back in those days, there weren't photos all over the internet, tracking everyone. Glenn was my only close relative, and he was in on it. So there was no one to call me out or wonder where I went. We weren't close to our parents. A change of address, even my name change they chalked up to our 'artistic' lifestyles. But the money put me through the School of Visual Arts' graduate program in fine arts. I opened a small gallery downtown, hired staff, and mostly showed art by Black conceptual artists . . . David Hammons, Senga Nengudi, even Elizabeth Catlett. Once a year, I exhibited my own work. Ha! How delicious to thread through the crowd and listen to comments about the mysterious artist Alex Chimère, who never attended her own openings. Actually, Alex became something of a sensation for a while. Chaz loved that. A little theatrical paint, a couple of wigs . . . and voilà! I would have headshots of the elusive Ms. Chimère for each exhibit. The 'shy' artist never gave interviews.

"My forgery of Jessa's life went on without a glitch. Only the three of us knew, and it was in our best interest to keep up the charade. There were moments . . . but, I just played through, you know? Even when Chaz passed away, and I worried an old friend or some long-lost relative might expose me at the funeral. To answer your question, no. I never learned what became of Jessa. I could have pressed. I certainly had the resources to find out. But . . ."

The Lady with the Rings paused. Her back stiffened and she looked away. "I never tried."

The door to the roof banged loudly, and we all jumped. Blackbeard came out. "Building's clear," he said. "Front door is locked, everything seems secure. Unless he's gotten into an apartment and locked himself in, the guy's not here."

"Did you look out on the sidewalk?" asked Vinegar.

"Fuck no. I'm not going outside."

At that, it was clear everyone was ready to get back to their apartments, doors safely locked behind them. Before she left the roof, though, I walked over to where the Lady with the Rings was gathering her wineglass, because a suspicion had been building in my head. I finally voiced it. "Chaz killed his sister, didn't he. That's why she never showed up."

The Lady with the Rings hesitated, and a look close to pain crossed her face. "Chaz told me that people really do just disappear: They travel to remote places with someone they trust . . . but *shouldn't* . . . and meet with a tragic end that is never revealed. He could be curiously precise when it came to what may have happened to Jessa. But that was Chaz, cryptic as hell. The man changed my life." The Lady with the Rings shook her head slowly. "No, I would never say he killed his sister."

But I could still hear doubt in her voice. She had the face of a person satisfied with how things in life have turned out—but I wondered just how at peace she really was, having built a life maybe, just maybe, on the back of a murder. Not that I was one to talk.

"So with all that wealth," Eurovision said, surprising me from over my shoulder, "how on earth did you end up *here*, at Fernsby?"

"That," she replied grimly, "is a story I think I'll save till the next pandemic."

We broke up for the evening. I made my way downstairs to my apartment, but instead of transcribing tonight's wild stories, which I was still having trouble wrapping my mind around, I felt so wiped out that I decided to do it in the morning. I lay down on my bed, but couldn't sleep. God, how I hated this recent bout of insomnia. I couldn't stop thinking about the Lady with the Rings. If she had all that money, why was she living in this shithole of a building? Was she even who she said she was now, or was the whole story just something she made up? But I liked her. I liked her a lot. I wondered how many of us up there had something to hide.

The creaks and ticks of the old building filled the silence, and then the footsteps came, right on schedule. A soft brushing sound, like someone in thick socks sliding his feet across the floor. I had a sudden, chilling thought: *Maybe that's where the crazy guy, Morty Gund, has been hiding.*

After a few moments of wrestling with my conscience, I got up, grabbed my master keys and the old super's Louisville Slugger that he kept by the door, and snuck out into the hall. The basement was dark and cold, half the lightbulbs in the ceiling burned out, but with my cell phone light there was enough to see by. A few roaches scuttled away—which reminded me of another thing I'd run out of: Roach Motels. I ascended the stairs to the first floor. The long hall was quiet.

I crept up to the door and listened. All was silent.

I slipped my key in the lock, turned it, and shoved the door open with my foot, cocking the bat and flicking on the light switch at the same time.

No light. Of course, with no tenant, the power was shut off. I backed away, lowering the bat, fumbled out my phone, and turned on the light, which cast a feeble bluish glow about the room. Empty except for the shabby furniture. The dust on the floor lay undisturbed, only marked by the previous footprints I'd made while checking for leaks. I moved across the living room holding the bat in one hand, phone in the other, past the Pullman kitchen and into the bedroom and bathroom, shining the light back and forth. There was a strange smell in the place, moldy like damp leaves. The bedroom window, shut and locked tight, looked out over the empty lot next door, covered with rubble and broken bricks, and beyond that a chain-link fence and a stretch of the Bowery. I paused to listen but could hear only the muttering sounds of the old building, which never seemed to settle down.

The apartment was clearly empty. I lowered the bat, feeling foolish.

Back in my own apartment, I dropped back onto the bed, fully clothed. I could swear I still heard those sliding feet.

I lay awake in the darkness until first light, when I finally fell asleep.

Day Twelve
April 11

The days were getting longer, and the seven o'clock commotion was now happening just before sunset instead of at dusk. This evening was the most beautiful I could recall in years, with bloodred clouds overspreading the city that cast a fierce glow downward into the streets as we banged our pots and cheered. It was like being underneath a huge fire.

After the city went quiet, as the lightshow reached its peak, a commotion came from the street below. Out in the Bowery, a man was shouting into a cell phone. At first I wondered if someone had just discovered Gund's body after all. But from the disjointed phrases floating up, it appeared the man's partner in an apartment nearby was dead or dying of Covid and he'd fled to the street to call

911. Everyone's faces on the roof were imprinted with horror as we realized what was happening, as the faint, desperate voice drifted across the rooftop. Soon enough, we heard an ambulance siren coming up the Bowery and halting nearby, and then the blare of radios and EMTs shouting to one another. Nobody went to the parapet to watch. Ten minutes later, the siren started up with a series of whoops and faded away down the Bowery, and all was quiet again.

La Reina said, quietly, "God just gave the rabbit box another turning over."

Monsieur Ramboz eventually cleared his throat. "I think we're doing something extraordinary up here by telling stories in the face of this goddamned disease." He added, "Maybe we should start recording them for posterity."

"Record us?" said Vinegar. "No way."

"I appreciate that sentiment," Prospero said. "But what's happening on this rooftop is an assertion of our humanity against the terror and banality of a virus. It shouldn't be forgotten."

"Oh, hush," said the Lady with the Rings. "I, for one, am going to boycott this rooftop if anyone starts recording." I couldn't blame her, after the story we'd just heard.

"If Boccaccio or Chaucer hadn't written down the

stories they'd collected during his lifetime," Ramboz insisted, "we'd have lost some of the great works of the Western canon."

There was some eye-rolling at the words "Western canon." No one else stepped in to agree with Ramboz's proposal. I, of course, kept my mouth shut—and my recording going.

"I don't give a la di da about your Western canon or your Chaucer," said Vinegar. "If you want to leave something permanent behind, write or paint on the wall. Leave our stories alone."

"The *Decameron*," announced the Poet loudly, lounging back in his chair. Heads turned in his direction. He smiled, looking a bit smug. "That's what's going on here. I've been sitting here, listening to all of you up here, hiding from the plague, telling stories. How could this whole thing *not* remind us of the *Decameron*?"

"Okay, but what's the *Decameron*?" La Cocinera asked.

"One of the classics in the Dead White Man canon," said Amnesia.

At this, the Poet let out a long, low laugh that sounded almost like a whistle, which had the effect of shutting everyone up. "Yes." The Poet looked around.

"Let me tell you a story about the *Decameron*. It happened earlier this year, when no one really expected the pandemic to hit America the way it has. We were all just starting to hear the news from Wuhan, and a global disaster was more of a sci-fi theory than this pathetic reality we're trapped in. Anyway, that's when the *Decameron* came up.

"The semester had begun at the downtown experimental college where I teach, and my poetry course had assumed a rhythm. About a fifth of the students had dropped the class. One half didn't turn in their assignments on time. Two or three would be published. About every five semesters, a student enrolled in my class might become famous. Some of my students had graduated and authored bestsellers, while I, at fifty, am still an experimental poet, a sort of upper bohemian member of a family of workaholics where family members compete with one another over who would put in more overtime. Only in the arts can one be 'experimental' without achieving a result. If I were a scientist, I would have lost my funding years ago.

"My brothers are successful. Professionals. So are their wives. Their children have high IQs. They have vacation homes in the mountains outside of New York. They have good connections because they belong to the Anglican Church. One is even a deacon. They own property in Harlem. One brother, Jack Caldwell, is extremely wealthy and teases me about my occupation. He's been frequently photographed by Bill Cunningham when appearing at charity balls and museum openings, the only time he's set foot in a museum. Jack's idea of poetry is 'Roses are red / Violets are blue. . . .' My mother, who had bought the property in Queens before those who couldn't afford New York were driven there, asks me when I am going to get a real job. When will I get married? Should she send her hairstylist to cut my hair? When will I move from my apartment, which had the kind of space my brothers would allot to a closet? My mother and my brothers had my father put away. No, he didn't have dementia. He couldn't keep up with their fast pace. What was wrong with him? They consulted a psychiatrist friend of theirs, and between them, they cooked up something based upon the *Diagnostic and Statistical Manual of Mental Disorders*, which deems every act of behavior an expression of a mental illness, and placed him in one of these country-club assisted-living homes. He seems to like it there.

"With my teaching salary, which requires me to teach every other semester, I can barely keep my head above water in the expensive town that Manhattan has become, a trend that began in the 1980s. (I am one of these 'cult' writers, which means my books don't sell.)

"My agent said that the market demanded 'girlfriend' books from Black authors and, over drinks uptown, said cynically that white feminist editors and book reviewers were pushing these books as a form of literary reparations because these white women were guilty about the conditions under which the Black domestics were treated by their families. These Black women domestics had paid more attention to these future book reviewers, editors, and bookstore owners when they were infants than their parents had, who were the types that Woody Allen satirized in movie after movie. People who spend more time in therapy than with their kids. One of these women had written that she'd had a 'nurturing' experience with a Black woman and was answered by one of these unpredictable outlier Black feminists, who asked, 'Did this mean that she grew up in a house that employed a Black maid?' For her impudence, the Black feminist was condemned by the movement, whose leaders, white women, pushed the line that there was solidarity between Latina, Black, and white feminists. She had trouble finding a job until one was available. A low-paying assistant professorship at a community college in Down Creek, Alabama. Things had gotten so bad after salespeople at big publishing

companies began to dictate the trends in Black literature that an excellent poet, Rita Dove, a former US poet
laureate, came in ninety-ninth among the one hundred
best sellers in Black poetry. Ninety-ninth! Like weeds
depriving an orchid of water and nutrients.

"My agent is a hypocrite. He could afford a big house
upstate due to the best-selling Black women on his list.
And his prating about the success of Black women
writers was off the mark. Most Black women writers
I know are either broke or had to take teaching jobs,
like me, to support themselves. But unlike them, I had
some support.

"Two of my students, a married couple who were
arts administrators, suggested I seek a foundation grant
to give me a year off from teaching. I could write a nonfiction book whose subject would instruct whites about
how to get along with Black people. Life coaching.
(The Black genre—besides 'girlfriend' books—that
sells.) This was a variation of the old indulgences hustle
that helped to build the treasury of the Catholic Church
in the eleventh and twelfth centuries. If you buy my
product, you'll only have to spend a year in Purgatory.
The new indulgences pitch was, buy my book, and I
will absolve you of your racism, a sales pitch marketed
brilliantly by the late James Baldwin. Nowadays, there
are more Baldwin imitators than those imitating Elvis.

They just don't have his velvety rage and his painter's eye for detail. Having taught Baldwin's books, I could tell that most of his fans knew him by his performance rather than the perusal of his books. He studied at Actors Studio, and in the book that lost his sponsorship from 'the Family,' the New York literary establishment, the chief character is an actor. It was his best novel. *Tell Me How Long the Train's Been Gone.*

"I was entering Starbucks on Delancey Street to buy my usual grande with a shot of espresso when I ran into the students. It was this past January, a month or two before the government declared a national emergency—the same government that has told us that Covid-19 was nothing to worry about. That it would go away. Of course, the first signs of the infection occurred in December, as we all know, but leaders of the government assured us that it was no threat and would only happen to Blue states. This is the kind of thinking that happens when you put your son-in-law in charge of things.

"The grant application, which my students submitted on my behalf, was a masterpiece. They had navigated the complicated eligibility questions, a maze on paper, done to discourage poor arts organizations from applying. All I had to do was to describe my project. And if gyms closed due to the national emergency, reading books about how to get along with Blacks would replace aerobics. I submitted an outline and a budget to the couple. For example, (1) On your first meeting, don't bring up Black athletes; (2) Don't ask Black women how much they charge to do laundry; (3) Don't ask Black men if they had ever used Konkaline; (4) Don't bring up Elvis Presley. Don't bring up Oprah; (5) Don't tell the story about the first Negro you ever met; (6) Instruct your child not to say 'poopy face' to describe a Black person; (7) Don't ask Black women to be your psychiatrist. If you do so, pay them two hundred dollars per hour.

"Where in an earlier time, fledgling organizations were provided with seed money so that they could grow, now an organization has to have a large budget to receive grants. This favored arts organizations like the opera and the ballet. But with the help of my students, all I had to do was sign or initial my name in several places.

"They were carrying huge containers of coffee.

"'Where are you guys going with all of that coffee?' I asked.

"'We're holding classical readings about the plague now that it has been declared a national emergency.'

"I figured this must have been the husband's idea. Every time I'd try to introduce Latinx, Black, Asian

American, Native American, or feminist poets to my students, he'd object and accuse me of lowering standards or practicing political correctness. I think he was gunning for a job as a critic at *City Journal*. The guy is one of those Manhattan know-it-all-niks. Kept interrupting the other students and doing a lot of intellectual hotdogging. An obnoxious name-dropper as well. You wouldn't know that both of his great-grandfathers were radicals who arrived here in the early 1850s. They signed up for the Civil War and were part of a group of immigrants who fought the Confederate army at Gettysburg.

"He submitted poems that were so abstract and dense that they were unreadable. If you asked him to translate, he would say snarkily, 'That's for me to know and for you to find out.' The husband's poems were more like riddles, but unlike riddles, if an exasperated reader said, *O.K. I give up*, they'd look like a Philistine. Meanwhile, his spouse used poetry to get even with her father, who is the head of a social media company. One of her poems scolded him for forgetting to send the limousine to take her to an elite school. The school was located three blocks from their Park Avenue apartment.

"'Why don't you join us, Professor Caldwell? We're serving lunch.'

"Why not, I thought. I was supposed to have lunch with my agent, but he'd canceled. He said he had a meeting with an 'important' client. I doubt my agent even read the books that afforded him a very handsome living. He'd become an agent by accident. He'd begun as a waiter in the town house where publishing executives had lunch when 'riot books' were popular, named that by a publisher's cynical sales department. They were looking around for Black editors, and as he was pouring water into the glass of one of the executives, a famous publisher, who'd had too much to drink, said, referring to him, 'How about Jake?' They took him out of the dining room and made him an editor. He quit publishing after a while and became an agent. He was now in his sixties.

"I asked my student where the readings would be held. He said Kenkeleba House, an art gallery located on East Second Street.

"The building in which the gallery was located has a fabulous history. 'Known as Henington Hall and located at 214 East Second Street, it was built in 1907 as a six-story *and* two-story building, according to the building permit. Designed by architect Herman Horenburger for Solomon Henig, the community space was likely created for the area's Jewish residents. Since 1974, it has been home to the Kenkeleba Gallery.' The curator of Kenkeleba said that the students could use some space in the gallery to hold their sessions. They were apparently instrumental in getting grants for the gallery.

"These would be after-lunch readings, the model provided by the storytellers who had fled plague-ridden Florence for the countryside from where they conducted the original after-lunch storytelling.

"Lunch would even be provided. Vegetarian pizzas, avocadoes, cucumber sandwiches, broccoli, carrots, celery, cheese, green tea, and Starbucks. There were pound cakes and strawberries for dessert. I decided to attend a meeting. Seated around a long table were attendees who reflected the racial and gender complexion of our Lower East Side, which could be called Nerd City. The couple distributed texts of the readings, which included footnotes that sometimes took more space than the stories.

"The wife spoke first. 'This was me and my honey's idea. With the news coming out of Wuhan, we decided that we could read classical literature about earlier plagues—Boccaccio's *Decameron*, along with Chaucer, Shakespeare, and Defoe—and become acquainted with one another at the same time.' Turning to her partner, she asked, 'Honey, did you want to say something?'

"Of course, there were earlier plagues that had

ravaged New York, but as recipients of a Eurocentric education, these two believed that only Europeans produced classics.

"'We'll begin with readings from the *Decameron*.'" He then talked about Boccaccio and his times and the history of the Florence plague. The husband yammered on and on while aiming lecherous glances at the women who were present. After we were given instructions, some attendees hung around to talk. I inspected some of the paintings on the gallery's walls.

"By the time of the next session, the others had read the sections from the *Decameron* that the couple had assigned. The husband asked, 'Is there anything you want to say about what you've read?'

"A Black gay playwright spoke up. 'It's homophobic. Gay love is called "unnatural."'

"Where did you find that?

"'"The Second Story, Day the First." And when he sends Abraham, The Jew, to Rome, Abraham finds a papal court, "shamefully given to the sin of lust, and that not only in the way of nature but after the Sodomitical fashion, without any restraint of remorse or shamefastness." This text says that being gay is something to be ashamed of?'

"'From "The Third Story, Day the Second,"' a white transgender curator for a major museum added, 'when the abbot prepares to make love to Alessandro, thinking that Alessandro is a man, he finds that he is a woman. In Boccaccio, some characters are cross-dressers who conceal their identities. We've fought hard for the right to our true identities, and you accost us with a story where the characters are afraid to reveal theirs.'

"The husband tried to speak up. 'Ma'am, we were not aware that—'

"'My pronouns are they/them. You're as backward as Boccaccio, you asshole.'

"Seeing this smart-ass squirm as he was fired questions, I thought to myself, 'This will be fun.'

"A dancer in a wheelchair rolled into the gallery. He was a protégé of David Toole, who championed greater visibility for disabled actors and dancers. His face was red. He could hardly talk; he was so angry. 'I was disgusted by his using the word "cripple."'

"'Where?' the wife asked.

"The dancer quoted, 'The First Story, Day the Second':

"'Martellino answered, "I will tell thee. I will counterfeit myself a cripple and thou on one side, and Stecchi on the other shall go upholding me, as it were, I could not walk of myself, making as if you would fain bring me to the saint, so he may heal me."'

"'In his story—in this passage—disabled are mocked. Having chosen this passage, are you agreeing that the disabled are funny and that people can disguise themselves as disabled to deceive? Do I look funny to you?'

"Before the two arts administrators could defend themselves, a director of a downtown radical theater protested.

"'The stories are all about rich people. Kings and queens, people with money. Just like today, if this novel coronavirus hits our shores, the rich will flee to the Hamptons or their yachts and leave the poor to suffer the plague. The wealthy will receive experimental cures that are unavailable to the general population. While these few told their stories in a villa in Florence, wheelbarrows full of corpses filled the streets, and families had to keep their distance from one another. Boccaccio favors the rich. Why did you choose this toady for wealthy people? I guess you chose these characters because they reflect the libertarian values of your generation. You have the luxury of wasting our time reading stories.' He sat down.

"The editor of a Brooklyn arts weekly spoke up. 'I just came to tell you that I won't be attending more of these readings.' He walked up to the graduate students and stood before them. If they were the designated 'king and queen' of the gathering—which were the titles given to those who moderated the original *Decameron* readings—a revolt was already underway. The editor was shaking. 'Boccaccio, Dante, Chaucer in his *Prioress's Tale*, in which Jews murder a young schoolboy for singing a song in praise of the Virgin Mary—all the rest of these bums were anti-Semites. In "The Second Story, Day the First," we find "that the soul of so worthy and discreet and good a man should go to perdition for default of faith; wherefore he fell to beseeching him on friendly wise leave the errors of the Jewish faith and turn to the Christian verity, which he might see still wax and prosper, as being holy and good, whereas his own faith, on the contrary, was manifestly on the wane and dwindling to nought."'

"'The errors of the Jewish faith? Christian verity? For choosing this reading, you must endorse this anti-Semitic view of Judaism.'

"'But this is the world's great literature,' the husband said as the director stormed out.

"An outburst of murmuring followed. I was enjoying this. I got myself a cup of coffee and leaned back in one of the chairs. It was turning out to be quite a show.

"The editor of the feminist journal *Représailles* spoke up. She was an excellent writer on paper but, performing before a large audience of women, she'd rip men to pieces, and the audience would call for the blood of the species, and there would be foot-stomping and jeers, and the men who were present would receive angry glares. Those who weren't heading for the exits. She said, her voice quaking, 'I find Boccaccio to be deeply misogynistic. Women are called "fickle, willful, suspicious, faint-hearted and timorous," or "men are the head of women, and without their ordinance seldom cometh any emprise of ours to good end; but how may we come by these men?" How dare you ask us to read such woman-hating trash? His *Il Corbaccio* is even worse in its misogyny. And then you plan to do Chaucer? Another writer who rages against women. He's the one who translated *Romance of the Rose*, in which women are, as one scholar put it, "contentious, prideful, demanding, complaining, and foolish; they are uncontrollable, unstable, and insatiable." He translated these diatribes against women and had to apologize in his poem "The Legend of Good Women."' Turning to the wife, she asked, 'How can you live with this man who would ask us to read such woman-hating rubbish?'

"A Black woman, a costume designer whose works had been used in Broadway plays, spoke up. 'Why couldn't you have chosen something American? Like William Wells Brown, a Black playwright who wrote a play called *The Escape; or, a Leap for Freedom*, about doctors making money from the epidemic of yellow fever. Isn't that what's happening with Moderna, Pfizer, Kodak, Johnson and Johnson? Competing to create a vaccine. One that will make their investors profits. Instead of choosing Wells, you choose this *Decameron*, which is racist.'

"The husband spoke up again. 'How can that be—there are no Black people in the story.'

"'That's just the problem. There were Black women in Florence at the time, yet they don't appear. Boccaccio didn't care about Black women.' She sat down.

"Others objected to the way Boccaccio treated their groups. Lunchtime became dinnertime. It was five p.m., and a Nuyorican muralist was criticizing the couple. He was complaining about the lack of visual representations of plagues. 'What about Indigenous portrayals of the consequences of the plagues brought to the continent by Europeans? You can find the sick and dying in Aztec drawings.'

"The couple was withering under the assault. The wife looked defeated. Her arrogant husband continued to defend the readings. He termed the gatherings' criticism of his reading list as part of a cancel-culture literary coup whose effort was to undo the Western canon. One after the other, the protesters explained that their cultures were the ones that were being canceled.

"One Black male writer spoke up. 'You take a look at the catalog of, say, Princeton and Harvard, and the faculty devoted to Western culture is as big as the personnel for General Motors. Yet you guys are always pretending to be on a mission to salvage Western civilization, which would be nonexistent without Muslim scholars saving works considered pagan by Christian vandals.'

"After all of this, I'd begun to feel sorry for the 'king and queen.'

"I thought about how they'd prepared that grant for me to take off a year from teaching to write my nonfiction book. My life-coaching book. Telling white people how to get along with Black people. They weren't charging me anything. I'm the guy who believes that if you rub my back, I rub yours. That's how things are done in Tennessee, the ancestral home of my parents. I rose.

"'I think all of you have been unfair to these young people. Why blame them? All of their lives, they'd been led to believe that no civilization exists outside of what American professors call Western civilization. This was the realm of all that was worthy of study and thought. With the "woke" generation, there has been what might be called a recall of Western civilization. Just as a manufacturer would recall an automobile whose brakes were unreliable. We don't want to get rid of the whole car because of defective brakes.' Addressing the 'king and queen,' I tried to become a mediator. 'Your critics say that our examination of your author's bigoted stance against Jews, Blacks, the disabled, and queers shouldn't exempt them from the kind of criticism they'd receive if they were around today.' Some members of the gathering nodded.

"'But isn't that censorship?' the husband asked.

"Here I was, throwing him a life raft. Why couldn't he shut up? I said, 'Well, if some of our members are into censorship, the *Decameron* is loaded with didacticism. Lots of proselytizing for Christianity.'

"'He's right,' came a voice. The speaker identified himself as a Russian poet who was here on some kind of artist exchange program. He spoke with an accent.

"Standing, he said, 'The professor is correct. This *Decameron* is full of didacticism. The couple that organized this reading can recognize the didacticism in the works of others but not in books adopted by your Western canon. They are immune to such accusations, which is why you did not include in your readers' list the works of one of the great plague writers, Marina Tsvetaeva.' He held up her book of poems, *Moscow in the Plague Year.* 'You westerners believe that Russian artists are confined to propaganda posters about five-year plans. Unlike Boccaccio, with his beautiful education and middle-class upbringing, or Chaucer, who always had a good job, or Dante, who was city prior to Florence. Not only did she write about the Moscow plague, but she lived a life that was a plague, something that privileged Americans will never understand.

"'Our people have been tested while you have become soft and flabby. Even if this coronavirus takes root here in America, let's be realistic. Sacrifice never comes to American shores. In a global pandemic, you will continue to enjoy life in restaurants and taverns and crowd the beaches while swapping breaths filled with bat fluids. Could you have taken high casualties as we did during World War II, our cities surrounded by enemy troops during a cold winter at Leningrad, where we stood fast for over eight hundred days? No, for you Americans, nothing should interfere with your right to party. To observe one of your sacred Capitalist holidays like Black Friday, a perfect image for your society, where, if you are not fast or greedy enough, you get trampled. You Americans don't know hardship. You've become bloated. The airlines have had to create bigger seats to accommodate your fat asses, yet you're always telling pollsters the country is moving in the wrong direction. Slothful. Pampered. Life has never been a spring break for us Russians. Life was not a social for

Marina, yet she produced four-to-six liners that were like little jewels. Her Palm Sunday poem, "1920" for example.' Reciting the poem, he closed his eyes like Andrei Voznesensky when reciting a poem. He had Voznesensky's tight, intense face.

"'"I've sunk so low, and you're so wretched / so isolated and alone / Both of us sold for a farthing despite our good characters / I don't own so much as a stick / She used the note to light the stove."'"

"'Unlike the bourgeois men whom you have chosen, men who had patrons like Petrarch, she was so poor that, in 1919, a man who was about to rob her, seeing the miserable conditions under which she lived, offered her money. While your heroes Dante, Boccaccio, and Chaucer had connections to aristocrats, Marina writes about owning one dress during the Moscow plague. She joked about it.' He began to recite once more.

"'"My day: I get up—barest glimmer from the window in the roof—cold—puddles—sawdust—buckets—pitchers—dusters—little girl's skirts and blouses everywhere. I saw wood. Light the fire. Wash potatoes in icy water and cook them in the samovar, which I keep going with coals taken from the stove. (Day and night, I wear the same dress of fustian, made for Asya in Alexandrov in spring 1917 while she was away, and which, one day, shrunk horrendously.

It has burns all over, from falling embers and cigarettes. Before, I kept the sleeves in place with an elastic band. Now they are rolled back and fastened with a safety pin).'"

"'Marina could not keep her children. She sent her girls to an orphanage. One contracted malaria. The other died of starvation.

"'Next time you choose an author who wrote about a plague, choose an author who was a victim of one yet found joy and humor. Not one of these men who hobnobbed with royalty. And by the way, women's rights?' He looked over at the feminist who had objected to the misogyny of Boccaccio and Chaucer. 'We were way ahead of you. What better way to empower women than to arm eight hundred thousand with weapons, the number of women who fought alongside men in the war against the Nazi invasion. Russian women fought side by side to repel the enemy at Stalingrad. The Germans, who put German women on a pedestal and treated them in a chivalrous manner while murdering millions of women who were "non-Aryan," were shocked to see these men and women fighting side by side. One of them, Lidiya Vladimirovna Litvyak, the "White Rose of Stalingrad," brought down ace German pilots and fought them even when she was heading for the crash that killed her. But some say she wasn't killed and was last seen escaping Nazi planes in fast pursuit. She was one of the world's two female fighter aces. You Americans who sacrificed during World War II have forgotten how to suffer. How to go hungry.'

"He sat down. There was silence. I was thinking of Litvyak. Would people in our selfish nation defend each other against the virus as much as the men and women united to defend Stalingrad? I'm sure that others were thinking about that one dress that Marina owned. It became a kind of objective correlative for the meeting. Maybe that's why the feminist who'd given the husband such a hard time was looking down at her shoes, which she'd probably bought at a seventy percent discount at Saks Fifth Avenue. The men's wardrobe included wares from Calvin Klein, Ralph Lauren, and Nike. The clothes were likely made by child labor. Hearing of Marina's condition, maybe the Black costume designer was thinking of the beautiful health insurance that she received for belonging to a union. Her children would never contract malaria or die of starvation. The disabled dancer must have known that he was in demand to book performances in both the United States and abroad, in part because of the movement to promote disability rights, which was also helping to draw attention to excellent poets like Jillian Weise. The university buildings all had ramps and elevators. Like the others who were reading about the plague, he was comfortable.

"Hearing Marina's powerful words, some of the audience had been left sobbing, quietly. The husband showed signs of compassion as he held his wife's hand. The molasses-colored sun was descending into the Hudson River, and, as I'd predicted, a few attendees were suggesting we needed dinner. I'd called Grubhub earlier in the evening, and now the deliverer finally arrived. He set three large bags on the table and left. There were what appeared to be TV-dinner-type pies, but instead, these pies had different ingredients. Poi. Poi is a Hawaiian dish made from the underground stem (corm) of taro. The participants began to dig in and, having tasted some, the gathering gave their thumbs-up of approval.

"'Why did you order this?' someone asked.

"'Well, it applies to our discussion,' I said.

"'How is that?'

"'One person's poi is another person's poison.' Groans. 'I know this might be a hokey metaphor, but it applies to art, don't you see? One person's censorship is another person's didacticism.'

"The smart-ass husband interjected. He said, 'But shouldn't art be universal?'

"Quoting T. S. Eliot, I said, 'All ethnic writers may not be great, but all great artists are ethnic.'

"That sat him down, but then his spouse spoke up. 'We can't apply the values of our enlightened times to Boccaccio, Chaucer, and Dante.'

"That remark drew laughter. Someone said, 'Our enlightened times? Millions elected a man who believes that water flows from the oceans to the mountains and that the way to end forest fires is to sweep the forests.'

"Someone else said, 'One quarter of Americans believe that the sun revolves around the earth.'

"Another person began to talk, but he was interrupted by the sweet strumming of a guitar. The resident blues musician had begun to sing after reminding the gathering that the original daily *Decameron* readings ended with a canzone. A song. He began a song by Blind Willie Johnson. The blues musician had a voice like Taj Mahal's. Raspy, and robust. He started singing.

"'*Well, we done told you, our God's*
done warned you, Jesus comin'
soon
We done told you, our God's done
warned you, Jesus comin' soon
In the year of 19 and 18, God sent a
mighty disease
It killed many a-thousand, on land
and on the seas

We done told you, our God's done
    warned you, Jesus comin' soon
We done told you, our God's done
    warned you, Jesus comin' soon
Great disease was mighty and the
    people were sick everywhere
It was an epidemic, it floated
    through the air
We done told you, our God's done
    warned you, Jesus comin' soon
We done told you, our God's done
    warned you, Jesus comin' soon
The doctors they got troubled and
    they didn't know what to do
They gathered themselves
    together, they called it the Spanish'in flu
Well, the nobles said to the
    people, "You better close your
    public schools
Until the events of death has
    ending, you better close your churches too"
We done told you, our God's done warned you, Jesus
    comin' soon
We done told you, our God's done warned you, Jesus
    comin' soon
Read the book of Zacharias, bible plainly says

Said the people in the cities dyin', account of they
  wicked ways'

"He ended by reaching for one of those deep bass notes reached by Paul Robeson.

"The gathering continued eating their poi as the musician sang another plague song. That poi was a real hit. People began to reach into the Grubhub bag for seconds and thirds. A dark cloud passed over the moon, which hung above Union Square. It began to drizzle. I stood up and stretched. Others took a bathroom break. I glanced at the Kenkeleba office. Corrine Jennings, the curator, was at the computer, sitting among piles of paper. She was determined to continue a legacy begun by her and her partner, Joe Overstreet, the great painter.

"There were paintings by Haitian artists on exhibit. Some of the painters were autodidacts; others, like Jean Dominique Volcy, Michele Voltaire Marcelin, and Emmanuel Merisier, were trained. One painting caught my attention. It was about the seven-point-zero magnitude earthquake, which struck the island on January 12, 2010, at four fifty-three p.m. The faces express horror. Their sticklike arms are held aloft. A dark matronly figure is at the center, surrounded by two children, set against a yellow background.

"The Americans will overcome Covid. We have the science and the money. While Haiti will continue to suffer like Job."

As the Poet brought his story to a close, Prospero was nodding. "Just like the original *Decameron*," he said. "The princes and princesses fled the city to a villa in the hills and told stories while half of Florence died with suppurating buboes."

Florida added, "I wasn't sure where you were going with that—those arts administrators sure sounded like asses, and the way I see it their critics make a damn good point. But in the end, God's done warned the *poor*," she said. "The rich just went to the Hamptons. That's what this pandemic's done—the rich shagging ass out of town and leaving the rest of us to die. Whatever our differences, as the New Yorkers who stayed, we're all in this one together."

"This is a day of reckoning," agreed Vinegar, acid in her voice. "This pandemic's ripped back the curtain, hasn't it? Nothing like a plague to show how the poor are trashed in this country. I bet half the Upper East Side is empty. Abandoned. All those mansions and town houses and floor-throughs stuffed with antique furniture and paintings, empty and dead. While their owners have parked their fat asses on five-acre lawns in Southampton, drinking vespers and talking about Damien Hirst."

Nobody asked who Damien Hirst was. Finally, Whitney spoke.

"I know those town houses," she said. "When I was in my twenties, I worked at an auction house on Madison Avenue. We sold fine art, but we also appraised it, sometimes for sale, sometimes for insurance or probate. So we went to those houses and looked at great collections. Sometimes these had been carefully put together by someone who loved the material, and sometimes they had been made by a hired curator, for someone who wanted the status. When the collector died, the estate would be sold through us, and the collection would be broken up, and all the pieces would go to other collectors, or dealers and museums."

"There's a lesson in that," said the Lady with the Rings. "All those possessions gathered together—to what end?"

"Well," Whitney said, "I think art is important. It enlarges your life. Loving art is important. Collecting anything you love is important. But collecting isn't everything."

"God takes everything away in the end," said Florida. "'Go to now, ye rich men, weep and howl for your miseries that shall come upon you. Your gold and silver is cankered; and the rust of them shall be a witness against you, and shall eat your flesh as it were fire. Ye have lived in pleasure on the earth, and been wanton; ye have nourished your hearts, as in a day of slaughter.'"

This sudden Bible quotation, delivered by Florida in the energetic voice of a prophet, shut everyone up for a moment—even Vinegar.

But Whitney smiled. "That's a fitting introduction to my tale, which is a horror story about cankered wealth very much along those lines."

"**The auction** house's offices were in a handsome building that took up the whole block.

"Overlooking our wide entrance was an Art Deco bas-relief sculpture: a muse hovering above a yearning artist, to show that art, not commerce, was our god. At that time, we had just been acquired by an English house, which gave us a certain international cachet, but we were already old and distinguished, and our stature was considerable. Virtually all important public art sales went through us. We handled Rembrandts, Fabergé eggs, Louis Quinze furniture, Gutenberg Bibles, and Aubusson carpets. Our important sales were held in the evening, black tie and by invitation only. We sold objects of great beauty and rarity to connoisseurs of great knowledge and wealth; we dwelt at the pinnacle of culture and affluence. On the wall in our department were four clocks labeled Tokyo, Los Angeles, New York, and London. We had a place in the world, and it was right in the thick of things. We thought quite highly of ourselves.

"I worked in the American Paintings Department. Each department provided estimates to their own clients, but there was also a separate Appraisals Department, which dealt with corporate clients—banks or law firms or museums. The Appraisals Department would assemble a team of us and send us out to do an estate or collection.

"Grant Tyson was the head of Appraisals. He was a tall, handsome Brit in his forties, solid, with a roast-beef complexion, dignified, knowledgeable, and impeccably courteous, with a wicked sense of humor. His assistant was Priscilla Watson, who had gone to Smith and came from an old Philadelphia family. Her hair was in a perfect bob, held in place by a velvet band, and her shoes always matched her handbag. She was prim, fussy, and very smart, with a diamond-sharp tongue. She was in her early thirties: Though the auction house was old, the people in it were surprisingly young. Many of the department heads were in their forties, and many of the junior staff, like me, were under thirty.

"An appraisal came in from Grant: a big collection at an estate in New Jersey. It was mainly nineteenth-century European bronzes. There were also a few American bronzes and pictures, which is why I was sent. Everything was to be appraised, though we didn't expect to see anything good except the bronzes. Collectors either had good art or good furniture, rarely both.

"Grant's specialty was Old Masters, and Priscilla's was porcelain, but they were also generalists, and could do a wide range of things. Rex Miller came along, too, from our sister house. (Rex Miller had a peremptory manner, very patrician, and a deadpan sense of humor. Once, when Grant was giving a talk on Old Masters, Rex slipped a pornographic slide into the carousel. The darkened room was filled with scholars and collectors, who were suddenly treated to a bright flash of pink flesh. Grant said, imperturbably, 'Next slide, please.')

"The sister house was where we sold minor things, decorative rather than fine art. Estates always contained the unexpected oddment: an eighteenth-century ostrich egg embossed with the Lord's Prayer in Dutch, or a crude little wooden trencher that had belonged to an ancestor during the Revolution. And every estate included objects too minor to sell. Some of these we simply took home: We called them 'haggies,' from the Scottish word 'haggis,' named for the offal given by a chief to his clansmen after an animal had been slaughtered, and after he'd taken the good cuts for himself. For us, a haggie might be clothes, kitchen utensils, shoe trees, or something fragile and irreparably damaged. One estate had contained a trove of bespoke silk boxer shorts, in dusky rose and lime green. I took home a pair in dusky rose. They were both elegant and creepy: beautifully made, but still dead man's underwear. I thought I'd wear them as a joke, but the occasion never arose. For a long time they were in a drawer in my bureau, and then I couldn't find them anymore.

"That morning we waited by the glass doors at the entrance. We were picked up by the lawyers in a long black limousine, and we all set out for the rich part of New Jersey. The owner of the collection was a widow, Grant had told us. She'd been the sole heiress of one great American fortune and she'd married the sole heir to another. You'd recognize their names. They were unthinkably rich. They had a mansion at Fifth Avenue and Sixty-First street. It's gone now, but it was a big six-story Federal house, somber and forbidding, the windows sealed with dark metal shutters. Mrs. Heir lived on the estate in New Jersey. There were no children.

"During the ride we were quiet because of the lawyers. They had short hair and wore pin-striped suits and narrow rep ties. We thought they were dull, trapped in a tedious maze of legalities. Not like us, who were so lively and interesting, swimming in our sparkling current of art and wealth. We didn't want to talk to them. We condescended to them as we condescended to everyone: We held our erudition over rich people, and our social standing over scholars.

"We had reached the part of New Jersey which is full of old stone houses, wide pastures, and grazing horses. At the entrance of the estate were tall stone pillars, and beyond them a pastoral landscape. As we drove through rolling fields, the lawyer pointed at a group of low buildings.

"'Those are the kennels,' he said. 'Whenever I come out here to lunch, I always find out first what they're serving at the house, because if I don't like it I can just eat at the kennels. They always serve steak.'

"We smiled politely, but we didn't laugh; we wouldn't allow such familiarity.

"The Heirs bred show dogs, as glamorous people did in the 1930s and 40s. I was a dog lover, and I wondered what breed the Heirs had chosen, but I didn't want to have a conversation with the lawyers. Anyway, by now we had passed the kennels, where the dogs were invisible, inside, eating steak.

"We saw the house from a distance: massive and baronial, with towers and chimneys. The driveway wound toward it through wide lawns, ending in a huge circular sweep before the front door. The lawyers led us into the front hall. This was large and gloomy, paneled in dark wood, with high ceilings and a staircase curving upward. A man in a suit came forward to greet us and take our coats.

"The lawyers explained that the collection was scattered throughout the house. We should go into every room, upstairs and downstairs, every hall and every closet. They would meet us for lunch at one, in the dining room. We nodded and set out with our clipboards and measuring tapes.

"The house was large and grand. The formal rooms downstairs were paneled, with ornate moldings and huge carved stone fireplaces, and big gilt-framed paintings on the walls. Most of the art was European, though there were a few minor American Impressionist landscapes, and some American bronzes.

"I started out in the living room. The paintings were undistinguished. Often pictures were easily identifiable—George Inness's dreamy river landscapes, or John Marin's fractured cubism—but sometimes you'd get wrong-footed. It's surprising how hard it is to identify an unsigned work—if it's an early or late work by a known artist, or a very poor example, or a fake. Sometimes a European drawing would be tucked into an American collection, or one by an American working in France. Sometimes a favorite picture by an important artist would turn out not to be 'right,' that is, not by him at all, which would cause considerable consternation.

"Sometimes these appraisals did reveal unexpected treasures: A huge Albert Bierstadt landscape had been discovered in a back hall at a school in England. Usually the discoveries were more modest: On one appraisal, I had gone through a carton of small framed pictures down in the cellar to find an etching by Whistler, with his butterfly mark. When I told the clients, they seemed uninterested; I wasn't sure they knew who Whistler was. But I was happy. It was always exciting to deal with masterpieces—thrilling, really—but this collection had none of those, at least none in my department, and I wasn't expecting any sort of excitement at all.

"The living room furniture was French: stiff upholstered sofas and spindle-legged chairs, marble-topped tables. Grant was behind me; Priscilla had gone upstairs. Rex came through, and paused near me, picking up a gilt-trimmed vase. He turned it upside down to see the mark.

"'Nicholas II,' he said. 'Very nice, isn't it, to have a murdered man's china in your living room.' He talked in an exasperated undertone. He liked saying shocking things.

"'Did it actually belong to the czar?' I asked. 'Or was it just made during his reign?'

"'There's the mark.' He held out the vase, but I didn't look. I don't do porcelain. 'I certainly wouldn't have a murder victim's things on my table,' he said.

"Shaking his head, Rex set down the vase and moved on. I thought of the silk boxers that I had in my bureau, the things we'd all taken home that had belonged to dead people. Not murdered ones, though. Provenance was important in our world; a long history of known ownership increased the value of an object. Why was it distinguished to own something that was centuries old, pre-owned by generations of people who were all now dead, but distasteful to own something that had come from one person immediately dead?

"Was it useful to wonder about?

"Mrs. Heir had bronzes everywhere, on every table, tucked into every bookcase, in pairs on every stone mantelpiece. They were dark heavy shapes, animals locked in death grips, tortured humans in contrapposto, either dull, depressing, or sentimental. Rosa Bonheur and Louis Barye. I checked each one to see if it was American, but most were European, and I left them for Grant.

"I finished the downstairs reception rooms and went upstairs. Grant was standing by a table in the hall, and he held up a small statue as I arrived.

"'Here you are,' he said. 'If you want to see how an ox reclines, it's like this.'

"'Is that *Reclining Ox*?'

"'*Reclining Ox*,' he said, nodding. 'She went to the abattoir to see how they looked.'

"'I can't imagine there was much reclining done in an abattoir,' I said. 'It's probably actually *Dying Ox*.'

"'Whenever it happened, Rosa Bonheur was there taking notes,' Grant said. 'Just so you know.'

"I walked to the far end of the hall, where there was another bronze. This was a nymphlike nude woman, prone. She had raised her torso off the ground, pushing off with her hands, and pressing her toes against the back of her head. Her pose was overtly romantic and covertly erotic. It reminded me of an American sculptor I knew, and I picked it up and looked at the bottom, but there were no marks. I looked for Grant, but he had moved in the other direction. We were now nearly at opposite ends of the hall, so when I spoke, it was quite loudly. The lawyers were downstairs, and there was no one else in the house to disturb.

"'Have you seen this soft-porn naked lady? It looks like Harriet Frishmuth, but I don't see a mark.'

"Grant swiveled, and instead of answering, he came swiftly down the hall. When he reached me, he took the statue.

"'European' he said, 'I've already done it' He put it down and moved closer, leaning in, his voice private and urgent. 'She's here.' He looked at me intently.

"'Who?' I asked, but from his manner I realized who he meant. It was a shock. 'Here?' I pointed at the floor. 'Here in the house?' Now I was whispering.

"'In the bedroom,' Grant said.

"'In the bedroom,' I repeated, taking it in.

"'On oxygen. More or less life support.'

"I had thought Mrs. Heir was somewhere else, I don't know where. I had thought we were free to roam through this big mausoleum filled with the spoils of family wealth, free to judge her collection, her taste, her house. I felt my chest contract.

"'Is she—' I didn't know how to finish the sentence.

"'No,' he said. 'In a coma.'

"She was here, lying in her own bed, in her own room, silent but present in this house where she had lived for decades, reigning over it all, the kennels and their menus, the rolling hills, the big gravel sweep by the front door, the living room with its massive stone fireplace, the Westminster show ring—all of that had been part of her life. All these things were still hers, as she lay now with her eyes closed, her mind darkening, the oxygen hissing into her lungs, a needle set deep into her slack flesh, her motionless body barely a rise in the sheets in her ornate bed. How long had she been lying like this? When had the lawyers decided it was time for us to come? This was an appraisal for the estate of a woman who was still alive. The idea was gruesome.

"'Where?' I asked, whispering.

"Grant pointed at a door halfway down the hall.

"'Is there art? Do I have to go in?'

"He nodded. 'A few watercolors. It won't take long. There's a nurse.'

"Grant held my gaze until I nodded. Then he set down the bronze nymph again and went back down the hall.

"I dreaded going into the room.

"I did the rest of the hall first. I did the pictures—French engravings, mostly—and checked the occasional bronzes on a table. Then I braced myself for the bedrooms. There were only three doors. The first opened onto a guest room. Twin beds with headboards done in that French canework, fussy lamps with shirred shades. A big French bureau, a chaise longue. The pictures were European, watercolor, landscapes, two French, one Spanish. I felt my pulse rising as I opened the next door. Inside was another guest room:

a double bed, with a carved French headboard, a mahogany bureau, and a French writing table, strict and elegant. On the walls were watercolors. They were all French, nineteenth century, except for a print by the American Joseph Pennell. I took it down and measured it and wrote down the information. I was done here, but stalling. On the bureau were several photographs, and I leaned over to examine them. I always looked at family photographs.

"The first picture showed a small boy on a pony with its ears laid back. The little boy was squinting against the sun, his fat legs barely long enough to bend for the stirrups. The next picture might have been the same boy, now older, wearing tennis whites and a V-neck sweater, holding a wooden racquet. Then a formal graduation picture, black gown and mortarboard. I leaned close to see where he'd graduated from. Below the image was the printed text: Princeton University. *Dei Sub Numine Viget.*

"Beside the bureau was a bookshelf. Nosily, I scanned the titles. *The Cruise of the Cachalot. Roughing It. Moby-Dick.* Hemingway and Fitzgerald. Lots of titles I'd never heard of, old dark jackets from the thirties and forties. A few books on engineering. I moved to the desk: more photographs. A rowing team in their T-shirts and shorts, each holding a tall oar, standing barefoot on a dock. A formal picture of a rowing team, older, seated, now wearing white blazers and boaters. This was at Oxford, according to the text, and their boat had been called, impossibly, the *Torpid*. This must have been Mr. Heir as a child. The room seemed frozen and unused, but of course Mrs. Heir was very old, and her guest room would not have been used in decades. I thought of her, motionless under the sheets, the whisper of oxygen, and I shivered.

"There was only one door left. I turned the handle carefully. It opened noiselessly, and I stepped inside. A large bed stood against one wall by a bay window overlooking the lawn. A dressing table stood in the middle of the window; at the edge of it was an armchair. A uniformed nurse was sitting in it. She looked up when I came in, and we nodded silently to each other. She held a magazine in her lap. Carefully avoiding looking at the bed, I began to examine the pictures. There was a tall bureau against the wall opposite the bed, a low bookcase, and a chaise longue covered in blue toile. I went slowly along the walls, checking each picture. There was one that looked like Childe Hassam, but when I looked at the back, it was by a French artist I'd never heard of. I had to step behind the nurse to look at it, and I excused myself in a whisper. She nodded briskly and looked down: She was doing a crossword puzzle.

From above I could see that her dark hair was covered in a fine net, I could see the crisscross web.

"There was a watercolor hanging over the bed, a big landscape signed Harpignies. It was French, so I wouldn't have to take it down. But as I looked at it, I couldn't help seeing what lay below it. I tried not to look directly, but I did glance downward, glimpsing a head on a pillow, silver hair and closed eyes, a yellowish face. It was partly obscured by a tall metal stand holding a bag of fluid, a pale hose snaking down from it to the body. Some kind of machine was hooked up to her as well, giving out a periodic gasping sound. It was like an infernal cross between a hospital and a laboratory. My heart pounded in my chest. Frightened, I looked at the nurse again. She nodded at me, and I turned from the bed. As I turned, I saw the hand, crumpled and yellow, terrible, motionless on the crisp sheet.

"I finished the pictures on the other wall and pressed my yellow pad to my chest. The room was silent except for that gasping wheeze. The room was now filled with what was happening in it. The pictures, the furniture, the carpets, all the reasons that I was here had become meaningless. What was important in here now was a slow somber march that could not be stayed.

"I moved quietly to the door and put my hand on the handle. I looked at the nurse, and we nodded to each other once more, as though we had become silent partners in some endeavor. I opened the door and stepped outside. I closed the door soundlessly behind me and moved away. My pulse was thudding, as though I'd narrowly escaped something.

"It was past one o'clock. I hadn't dared look at my watch while I was inside, but I knew I was late for lunch. I hurried down the curving staircase, moving quietly, as though this was necessary. I could hear the others in the dining room. I went through to find them all there, Grant and Priscilla and Rex. The lawyers were there, too, so whatever we were having was better than steak.

"I sat down in the empty seat beside Priscilla. The four men sat in a row: Grant and Rex side by side, flanked by the lawyers. Of course the lawyers wanted to sit with the important people, who were men. I had once come out to see a client who had brought in a painting to be appraised. When she saw me, her face changed, and she asked if she couldn't see a gentleman.

"Grant was being professional. 'It's a very important collection,' he said to Lawyer #1. 'There are some very good pieces. Excellent casts.'

"Of course, these were just lawyers, not actual collectors. They wouldn't know the difference between a cast and a play.

"'Yes, so I've heard,' said Lawyer #1. 'Several museums are interested.'

"Grant nodded. 'And so they should be,' he said. We wouldn't have been there, though, unless the deal had been signed. But maybe we were just doing the appraisal for probate, and not for sale. 'Of course a museum wouldn't take the whole estate, only the bronzes.'

"'Probably true,' said Lawyer #2.

"'And we probably, we wouldn't be interested in the estate without the bronzes.'

"The lawyer nodded.

"'How is the furniture?' I asked Priscilla. 'Any good porcelain?' I wanted gossipy distraction. I didn't want to think of the form lying in bed upstairs. I didn't dare mention this in front of the lawyers.

"'Some very good French furniture, some excellent German porcelain, and some perfectly dreadful stuff.' She made a tight mouth and shook her head in little tiny rapid snaps. We were scornful of people with money and taste who could buy exquisite things but who chose instead to buy dreck. 'A beautiful set of Meissen, a superb dinner set of Sèvres, I counted one hundred seventy-eight pieces. And then some imitation Louis Seize straight out of Sloan's Department Store.' I shook my head in agreement.

"The food was delicious. First we had a velvety cucumber soup, then herby roast chicken. I was still aware of the form lying in bed upstairs, but I was grateful at being drawn back into this easy world of art and gossip. Priscilla's cousins lived near here, and she began talking about the politics of the local hunt, how difficult it was to become a member, and how scandalous the efforts were to do so.

"'These newcomers can't even ride, you know,' Priscilla said, confidentially. 'They put themselves up for membership, and they can barely ride a bicycle.'

"'What kind of dogs did they breed?' I asked. 'Here. The ones who get the steak lunches.'

"'Schnauzers,' Priscilla said. 'Those awful jumpy dogs that bite you if you look at them. Can't stand them. Also Rottweilers and Dobermans. She liked German breeds.'

"'Schnauzers,' I repeated.

"'Give me a retriever,' Priscilla said. She talked rapidly and with absolute certitude. 'Or a sheep dog. Not some jittery creature that barks incessantly, and when they're not barking they're biting.'

"I didn't like schnauzers, either, which was another way to distance myself from the room upstairs.

"'I like border collies,' I said. 'Or standard poodles.'

"'Well, if you don't mind paying your entire salary

to the dog groomer,' Priscilla said at once. She had views on everything.

"I didn't want to argue with her.

"'No, they were famous for schnauzers and won zillions of prizes with them, but they had some house dogs as well. Some mutts, and some—what else, corgis? I can't remember. We came out here some years ago, and there were dogs here in the house. Some kind that the son liked.'

"'The son?' I said. 'I thought there were no children.'

"'Oh, no, there was a son,' declared Priscilla. She said a brisk thank-you to the maid, who was clearing the dessert plates. 'No, they had one son. Who died.'

"So that was the boy on the pony, the graduate. That had been the son's room.

"'What happened to him?' I asked.

"'He died,' said Priscilla again. 'He died, and they never got over it. He wanted to become a pilot and go into the air force. They wouldn't allow it—she wouldn't— she thought it was too dangerous, and they sent him to France, instead, to become an engineer. They loved France—you can tell that from the collection.'

"'How did it happen?' I asked. 'Did he die in the war?'

"Priscilla shook her head. 'Nothing so grand. Car accident. He drove into a tree. He was killed instantly. It nearly destroyed his mother. She got the news in

French, in a telegram. They said she read it over and over, trying to make it mean something different. She never really recovered. That's when they closed the house in New York.'

"She looked around. 'Do you think we could have some more water? I don't want wine; you can't drink on an appraisal.' As she spoke, a man appeared behind her with a pitcher of ice water. He leaned over her shoulder and filled up her goblet.

"'Thank you!' Priscilla said, giving him an instant smile. 'Perfect.' She turned back to me. 'It absolutely shattered them, and it was a national story, because they were so well-known. In those days, you know, the public loved the rich. All those movies about men in top hats and women in emerald necklaces. Fred Astaire and sable coats. So everyone knew the family, even though they were discreet and hated publicity. Except when their dogs won at Westminster. They were proud of that. But when the son died, they didn't want anyone to know. But everyone in the country knew. They went into seclusion.'

"This was all terrible to me, shocking.

"I thought of the mother reading the telegram over and over, that strip of typed French words refusing to be resolved into any other message. The boy with his oar, standing on the dock. Those books in the bookshelf: I had already gotten to know him as a person.

"'And you know,' Priscilla said, lowering her voice, 'the top of the coffin is here.'

"'What?' I asked.

"'Here in this room,' Priscilla said. She tapped the table with a manicured finger. We had finished the crème brûlée, and it was time to go back to work, walking through rooms and passing judgment on things.

"'What do you mean, here?' I asked.

"'I'll show you,' she said. 'No, thank you so much," she said, smiling brilliantly at the man with the coffee.

"No one wanted coffee, no one wanted to linger, everyone stood up. As the others moved out of the room, Priscilla drew me briskly over to a door that led to a sort of sunroom. We both went through, and then she shut the door behind us. On the back of the door hung a large slab of polished wood. The shape was unmistakable: narrow at the top, slanting outward for the shoulders, then slanting inward, a long slope toward the bottom. The feet. On the wood was a metal plaque, with the name and dates. He was twenty-two.

"This slanting lid had hung on the door. At every meal it had been there, hidden, present. It was the only object in the house that was truly theirs, irreplaceable, priceless.

"For what seemed like a long time I stood looking at it. The terrible soft sheen of the wood—it was oak—the quiet burnish of the brass. This object represented her whole life, really. This was the thing that meant everything to her. All these animalier bronzes and French furniture, our clever, demeaning comments. All of that slid away, like foam on the current. I couldn't speak, and I didn't want to look at Priscilla because there were tears in my eyes.

"Afterward, I got my things and went into the back rooms and finished the appraisal. There was nothing much to see in the kitchens, the pantries, the china closets. There were only framed reproductions on the walls. But my mood was different. What was wrong with hanging a beautiful image on the wall? Who cared if it was a reproduction? And all afternoon, as I walked from room to room, opening doors, examining pictures, I was aware of that polished piece of oak. The chilling implacability of its shape. The dates. I thought of the house on Fifth Avenue, its metal shutters.

"For years, after that, every time I went on an appraisal, I thought of the woman lying upstairs in her bed, the gasping wheeze of the machine. Her yellow hand, and the piece of polished wood that hung on the dining room door."

The sound of Whitney's voice hung in the gathering twilight.

"Oh my God," breathed Eurovision. "That coffin lid."

"Do you think they buried him without the lid?" drawled Hello Kitty. "How messy."

"*Please*," said Eurovision, spinning on her. "Do you have to have a sarcastic reply to everything? That was a very tragic story. Do you even understand what it means not to subject everything to your *judgment* all the time?"

I thought of all the stuff the super had left behind, and it suddenly and shockingly occurred to me—I don't know why it hadn't before—that maybe the previous super hadn't left the building: Maybe he'd *died*. Otherwise, wouldn't he at least have taken the ashes of his pet? I looked around. Did I dare ask the question? Most of them would have to know about his death. But before I could decide whether or not to speak, Prospero let out a laugh.

"Denial. Denial of the meaning of the words in the telegram. Denial of the son's death and burial. Denial of death itself. Just like now. The morgues are full, and the bodies are piling up on Randall's Island in refrigerated containers on the soccer fields. No bedside deathwatch, no funerals, no burials. All about denial."

"Covid is erasing our ceremonies of death," said the Lady with the Rings, nodding at La Reina, clearly thinking still of the story of her father's long-ago death, the grandmother's whispered somos.

"But what a vision of the old woman up there in a coma," said Darrow, "surrounded by her stuff, her money and art and all the things that padded and protected her life. But the most important thing she had is gone: the memory of her son. It vanished from her ruined brain. Where did it go?"

"The physicists say that information in the universe can neither be created nor destroyed," said the Poet, eyes narrowed. "So it's still out there, somewhere. Her son, her memories of her son, his memories of her— out there somewhere among the stars."

Florida shook her head. "*Santo cielo*, what a silly discussion! You make it so complicated! Go to church if you want answers. It's as simple as that."

"Out there somewhere," echoed a young woman in the dimness of the edge of our gathering. She said it again, louder. "Somewhere out there."

Eurovision shot an accusatory glance at me, as if I'm the one somehow inviting in all these strangers. He rearranged his face then, and turned to the newcomer. "Yes, welcome. What . . . er, which apartment are you in?"

"6E. Pardner. I think y'all know my mama." Her voice was low, calm, and dreamy.

"You're the daughter?" asked Eurovision. "From Pardi's stories?"

The young woman nodded.

There are stories inside of the stories in Mama's stories. And stories in the apartment where we lived. Jericho, my father, hid journals in the walls. I found at least three of them. And I found a note he had written Mama but didn't leave out for her to find. It read, 'I am ashamed of what made me. Loving a Black woman does not change this. Singing the blues does not change this. Thank you for not holding my people against me.' Then he told a story about his grandfather, and water hoses.

"Finally he wrote: 'I asked you about the rifle, because I knew what you didn't know, what your daddy was thinking about that night on the pier. But he leaned into you and died of natural causes in his bed. I'm not going to do that. I can't separate you from my want to be Black. It's hard to be a Texas blues singer and not be Black. And so much easier to be a Texas Blues singer and be white. I am fucked up.' I am glad he didn't leave her that note. If Mama were here, I wouldn't tell you any of that.

"And I wouldn't tell you about the ghosts.

"You see, there are two ghosts in my apartment.

One moved with me from Mississippi. One came with the place. Rosie talks in poems, and she's tired of white people. She was born tired of white people, in Mississippi, probably ninety years ago. The other one, I call Ghost Cracker. He's a kind of prophet. White, and country as hell, and also, somehow, tired of white people. Thinks sometimes he's the blackest one in the room. Rosie hates him.

"Ghost Cracker says it's hard being born into a world where just having white skin and a dick used to give you a leg up, then you wake up one morning and people with pussies have the advantage. Or people with brown skin have the advantage. People with brown skin and pussies? Well, don't get him started. Wondering on that, how people who start behind you end up ahead of you, will get your teeth rotting out of your head. Or if you are Ghost Cracker, will get you dead.

"Rosie says he's just a ghost who wants to be an angel, who thinks I'm his train out of town. I love Rosie. She sticks to the gut-bucket truth.

"The other night I knocked a glass of red wine to the floor—Ghost Cracker was wild prophesying again—and Rosie sank into a kind of reverie. Started asking questions.

Do a sound turn the lights on?   *Ha!*
Do the light
      bend   *across her body long*   *enough*
to take the measure of her   *there?*
O,   *do wood keep*

                        a taste?

"Ghost Cracker loves Rosie. He thinks he's at blues church. He thinks this is call and response.

"'Keep talking bout the taste of wood, girl.' His gold tooth sparkles. He thinks he's charming-dirty. I just scrub and listen.

"Rosie pitches her voice lower and comes for him.

How much southern wood carries the taste
of black girl   *thigh sweat?*   *What wood*
wouldn't want it?

"Now I'm thinking about the drip down the back of my leg while I clean the wine—working the same red spot and thinking about how far we've come and haven't, me and Rosie, from Mississippi to this white man's New York gaze. Am I leaving my salt on this floor? Did I inherit some kind of survival sweat from my mother? Does it flavor me different when I'm outside the South? Does the wood taste different in the North? Imagine Ghost Cracker could tell me, see him press the flat of his tongue to the grain, to the inside of my leg, if I let him—

"*Ooh land and flesh*—Rosie says.

"*Ooh wood and water*—now she's going at it good. Her eyes are closed. Flower in her hair. Dress hanging, coming correct around her hips, and she sways her sermon. Ghost Cracker hangs his head. He always does this when he knows she's about to start preaching past her own voice into the Delta itself—the name of that place means change.

> *Happen that I sag all polished under her bent knee*
> *happen that I fill up on her shoe-footed press*
>   *and sway   happen*
> *that her pain red hands   stay   singing blood*
> *into my waters—happen that*

> *I   need   Miss Rosie,*
>   *Don't it?*
> *She. my. victual.*   *Don't it?*

> *Her sweet funk/season/my vitals. Sustain them.*
> *Can a place have a preference? Lord*
> *know this place ain't like God—*

even sided—
Yea though I do eat of her,
Her toil aches me, still and all.

"**By the** end me and Ghost Cracker are leaning together on the couch, and both of us wiping a tear or something. Wishing we had the words or something.

"Rosie lets a small, sharp, 'Ha!' loose from her mouth.

"Ghost Cracker shudders and stretches his legs. 'Well I'll be dipped in shit.'

"Rosie is still leaning in the door to my bedroom, looking like every right thing that survives in a red dress, and she's smoking now. 'You don't deserve us, white boy.'

"'Like hell I don't. Ain't that my guitar—ain't that a white boy guitar gives little miss light-bright-damn-sure-ain't-white all her tunes? The sounds to keep the light on, like you say?'

"Now my ghosts are laughing together, at me. I wouldn't mind but for the way I get all my words from them, and I don't want to be scared or hurt by my own voice.

"'Rosie,' I say. 'Can I be the land now? Can I speak for it some?'

"'What you know about the land, high yellow?'

Ghost Cracker thinks because he's country he knows more about Black bodies than he could or should. More than I do, anyway. Lord but he's long wrong about it. 'What you know about that, city girl?'

"'She know enough.' Rosie sends me. 'Go on then, baby girl. Tell us what you brought with you.'

"It came from somewhere outside of me, or some part of my bones and blood decided before I was born. Maybe in Meridian, like Mama tells it. Behind the beat, like Ghost Cracker taught me. Like he learned from Rosie when he was still alive—he needed the idea of her all his slip-slid days—I think she haunted him without knowing. Most times I'm their way back and forth. A psychopomp, in house shoes. Tonight I'm a different kind of witness.

> *Call me*
> *a cradle*
> *and a nest—*

"'It's a start, it's a start.' Ghost Cracker thinks he got a right to say something about it.

"'Hush boy.' Rosie knows he don't, and I do, too. I keep on.

> *Call me*   *Mississippi*

"'**Goddam!**' **he** whispers.
  "'Mmm. Shh.' She feels him.

I am
everything   wrong
with Eden
and I am every hope for it   before
and after—

            they fall,
say,
Feed me, Mississippi

say,
Rest me, Mississippi.   See this,
my fist? See this, my raging growth?

"Ghost Cracker shakes his head. Lights a cigarette.

Say
Can't see to can't see,
Mississippi—Watch me
grow me these
can't see
beans. I mean
white beans

and salt pork
gone smooth   sweet almost
and with pepper.
Slick down your tongue

                    can't see

"I feel my feet start to go a cadence, my hands play
my breastbone, the side of my thigh.

to stop the belly
from knocking her backbone

                    can't see
for a spell.   Say
Oh God, help me eat
to survive
Say
Oh Lord, let this spoon sustain me
this cupped lip
holding
its small covenant—I will
eat today.
Yes I ate them all
I eat them all
up.   I have

let the kudzu grow
and grow and grow
and grow and
this green plant

        adores me,
        adorns me,
and I let it   live,
live and eat things
people try to keep
safe.
This house—ha!
Its foundations—nothing.
I let it eat
these black bodies—yes

        watch me breed
a mosquito—yes
that will eat and eat and eat
a man alive
and yet
let live and live
and live.

"**Ghost Cracker** has slid down the couch all lean and loose while I was talking.

"'Y'all middle-brown-skin girls,' he says from the floor. 'It's your time.' He lays at Rosie's feet.

"'What's he talking about, child?' She lets smoke from a cigarette roll out her mouth and down over his shut eyes—a long ghost shotgun.

"'Y'all caramel-colored girls. I mean not the light-light brown but the medium'—he opened his eyes and shook a drink at us both—'it's your time. The world is ready. Time to show the world what it can't see. Say it with me girl. I know you can feel it coming.'

"And he is right. He can send me, too, when he wants to. We find a word together—

> Give me some fresh salt, Rosie—
> I said drip me that good sweat, Rosie—
> Yes, send it from your top lip, your bent knee,
>   your bosom's between—
> Keep me salt rich from your hard work to your
>   blue moan, Rosie—
> Keep me full fed on your hand's blood, clean in
>   my river—

"**Ghost Cracker** rises up to his knees. Clings to Rosie's dress. Looks her in her face and leaves me to speak the last.

I know you, girl. I am you, woman. Come and see.

"**Rosie puts** her hand to his cheek then steps out from the ring of his arms.

"'Don't be like me, doll,' he says. 'Can't sit still and can't stand anywhere nice for too long.'

"Rosie doesn't say anything, but I know she heard him. She pours herself a drink and takes a long time stirring it.

"'Nope. Nowhere nice for long. Not even my own mind or heart. See, first you run home, run here, away from the outside places and faces. Then you chase yourself away from the nice parts of your own head.'

"'All the vice and nothing nice,' I smile. 'That'll get you killed, chasing death like that, not living right.'

"For once Ghost Cracker has nothing to say, to either of us. He just bends his limbs up off the floor and reaches for the guitar.

"It's a thing to watch him play, the way his hand moves on the neck. He's right—nothing of a stillness in him, sometimes. Can't even keep his fingers still long enough to play any chord its old-fashioned way. Always a bent note in it, a blue note in it, and almost, sometimes, I think even Rosie knows he knows the blues.

"Tonight she starts singing, gives him her blessing in bars:

Do as I say, little gal, no not Lord as I do,
Do what I tell, honey child, and not just as I do,
You need your pardons in this life,
Go on and take the one I'm handing you

"**Ghost Cracker** finishes the lick but keeps hanging on to the box like it's a tender thing, and Rosie wets her lips with her glass, and I love them both. This living haunted means you'll never fear, or be, your first ghost."

She was done. As her voice faded away, one line stuck in my mind: *Living haunted means you'll never be your first ghost.* I was living haunted. Maybe all of us were, up here sharing these memories.

"Now, that's a different kind of ghost story," said Vinegar, when no one else spoke. Maybe Rosie and Ghost Cracker had been squatting in 2A at night. It almost made me smile to think of it.

"This Rosie," said Wurly suddenly, "is that the Miss Rosie your mother talked about, from the Leadbelly song 'Midnight Special'?"

"She is," said Pardner.

"And this Ghost Cracker of yours, this white dude, you say he knows the blues? That's not a compliment handed down lightly."

"No, it sure isn't."

"'Midnight Special,'" said Wurly, "I can't think of another song that's traveled so far around the world and into people's hearts. Paul Evans. Johnny Rivers. Creedence and Little Richard. Even ABBA."

Pardner said, "It's a human thing. We're all in prison, waiting for that light to shine on us. Leadbelly learned that song when he was locked up in Texas Sugar Land prison next to the railroad tracks. If the train light shined on you through your cell window, it meant Miss Rosie was coming to save you with a pardon and take you to freedom." She paused and then took a breath and sang, her voice low and rich:

Yonder comes Miss Rosie, how in the world do you
    know?
Well, I know her by the apron and the dress she wore.
Umbrella on her shoulder, piece of paper in her hand,
Well, I'm callin' that Captain, "Turn a-loose my man."

Let the midnight special, shine the light on me,
Let the midnight special, shine the ever-lovin' light
    on me.

"I've heard enough stories about ghosts," said Eurovision crossly, starting to pack up his speaker and drink as the bells of Old Saint Pat's began to ring. "Let's have some stories tomorrow that don't have dead people or ghosts in them, shall we?"

"Like you have room to talk, with all your 'importance of trauma' crap." Hello Kitty rolled her eyes. He ignored her.

As we packed up, I heard Pardner say, to no one in particular, "Gotta find my mama." She seemed to disappear into the shadows. I shoved my thermos and notebook into my bag, turned off my phone, slipped it into my pocket, and just hurried up to leave with the rest. I was as anxious as Eurovision to get off the roof tonight. I think we were all feeling a little haunted. We filed down the narrow staircase six feet apart, back into the ramshackle building, to do whatever we all do in these long Covid nights.

Maybe we were all returning to our ghosts.

Day Thirteen
April 12

Sick and tired of my basement tomb, I was the first up on the rooftop this evening, carrying a thermos of Moscow mule, mixed strong. Spring should have been blooming, but instead a dark rainy day had given way to a darker night, and a fitful wind licked across the roof, which was covered with puddles and smelled of damp tar and earth. There was a piece of loose metal somewhere, and every gust made it rattle.

I felt off-balance. The wind had been blowing all day, every bluster wracking the building with creaks and ticks. I had forgotten it was Easter Sunday until I saw that someone had painted on the mural wall next to God and His bunny box another bunny, this one with big eyes sitting on an Easter egg. My father had always made a big deal about Easter. It was usually just the two of us, but we ate roasted lamb and then had egg-knocking contests. It's a Romanian tradition, where you decorate hardboiled eggs and then rap them against each other, and the one that didn't break won. Dad said that tapping eggs with loved ones on Easter ensured that you'd see them again after death. It seems silly, and I wish I'd asked him why. I felt awful thinking about Easter without my dad. But after yesterday's stories of death and ghosts, and a long night of insomnia, I'd decided today on a new mantra: *Dad is dead.*

I guess this is where I should tell you that I've finally stopped trying to call Evergreen Manor. I mentally couldn't hack it anymore, the endless sound of ringing on the other end, the robotic voice: "The party you are trying to reach is not available . . ." The news just keeps coming out about the staggering toll of nursing-home deaths. Maine had been trying for me this whole time, too, and she's just as distressed as I am that she hasn't been able to get through, either. We're all of us cut off, lost, adrift, atomized, and apart.

So since Dad was either dead or alive, and I couldn't know which, I had to make a choice. This morning, I decided: He was dead. If he was dead, he was safe. I hoped it would stop those hours of staring at the ceiling fighting the awful images in my head. *He is dead.*

Simple and staggeringly awful, but at least a fact, something I could cling to. I tried to imagine him walking around that ridiculous Romanian Orthodox heaven that the patriarch always talked about, with clouds and singing angels and everyone gazing on God with infinite adoration—that world my father believed in so fervently. I couldn't quite get there. Another problem was that he didn't *feel* dead—he was such a vivid presence in my head. But before I lost my mind with worry, trapped here without any way to reach him, I had to do something about it, tell myself something that worked. Judge me for it, if you want.

On the roof, Eurovision stood by the freshly painted bunny and received everyone's compliments, nodding and smiling like the priest at the door at Sunday liturgy. I had no idea he celebrated Easter. But maybe he just liked bunnies. In a box or otherwise. Florida gave him a particularly friendly greeting and even crossed herself in front of the mural.

The Lady with the Rings wore a new scarf wound around her neck, not Hermés like the one she'd sacrificed for her mask, but a cheap tourist "I [heart] New York" bandanna. Instead of sitting down, she made her way to the parapet and looked out. She gestured at the rubble-strewn vacant lots surrounding the rooftop, on which new high-rises would be built.

"Look at this," she said. "They're tearing down everything. Got a brave new world coming."

I took a gulp of the banana daiquiri, and another, and soon felt the first flush of alcohol in my head. It had been another day of death and sirens: at 188,694, the state of New York now had more Covid cases than any *country* in the world. More even than Italy or China. Cuomo ordered all the flags to half-mast. He didn't say when they would go up again. He and everyone were claiming the outbreak was starting to level off, that it had peaked, that it would now fade away. I wondered how much longer we'd be banging pots and pans. I was getting sick of it. Of all of this.

I looked around but couldn't see the young woman, Pardner, who told the ghost story last night, or Pardi. I was worried about her, if I'm being honest. Besides, I wanted to ask her about 2A's low footfalls. Did her ghosts tiptoe around in socks?

"Greetings to everyone—welcome to the roof," said Eurovision, when the compliments on his bunny were dropping off.

"Anyone else think the building's haunted?" asked Darrow, suddenly.

That got everyone's attention.

He shoved his hands in his elegant suit pockets, looking unusually awkward. "I, ah, finally got out my binoculars and checked out the construction site down there, where I think that Gund guy might have fallen," Darrow went on. "Nothing there. But he came and went without using the stairs, right? Which leads me to think he might have been . . . a ghost."

"I thought we weren't going to talk about ghosts," said Eurovision.

"I hear footsteps and water running sometimes in the apartment below me, which I'm pretty sure is supposed to be empty," said Wurly. He lives in 3A. He noticed when my head snapped up, startled. "Hey, now isn't the super's apartment 1A? You ever hear anything above you at night?"

"I do," I stammered. "But I've looked in there a few times. It's definitely empty."

"Maybe it's the ghost of that old man who died in 4C," said Hello Kitty.

"I sometimes feel a cold presence passing by in the halls," said Florida.

"That's because they're drafty," said Vinegar.

Eurovision scoffed. "Please. There are no ghosts in the building." His eyes fixed on me. I felt a surge of panic. Why had I responded? Why couldn't I just keep my damn mouth shut?

"We haven't heard a story from our super yet," he said.

"Yes! You did. I told a story."

"You read a letter you found. I want to hear a *story*."

"I already told you, I don't know any stories."

"Of course you do! You must have a trunkful of stories."

I pulled out a document I'd found in the old super's accordion file. "I don't have a story, but I've got this."

"What is it?"

"A scientific report about a rare animal. It's really bizarre—"

"No, no, *no*," said Eurovision. "A story. About you. I mean, you sit here every night taking in our stories but never telling anything about yourself. You can go into our apartments anytime you please, and you know all about us. But you? Nobody here knows anything about you. You just showed up one day."

"I'm not hiding anything," I said quickly.

"I'm not saying that. All I'm saying is, you're the only person on this roof who hasn't told a real story." He crossed his arms and sat back, waiting. I looked around to see suspicious faces looking back at me. I knew I hadn't made a good impression on them. Maybe it was the crappy state of the building, or the fact that strangers seemed to be getting in, or because I keep to myself. I considered just telling them all to fuck off, but knew right away that would be a bad idea, given that we were going to be locked up in this coronavirus cattle car for God knows how much longer. I was suddenly mad at myself for having started to like these assholes, to look forward to spending time with them. Maybe it was because I was half drunk or resented being looked down on the way my father was his whole life, but a savage impulse came over me. I wanted to shock them. To see their horror, and to tell this story at last. So, yeah, I had a story.

"Fine. Here's a story," I said. "Not about me, though. Just a story I heard. It's actually a story about a storyteller. I mean, the storyteller tells the story, that I heard, so this is actually a story about a storyteller telling a story."

"Just spit it out," Eurovision said.

I took a deep breath. "You know those events at bars they have sometimes, where people get up and tell stories?"

"Sure," said Vinegar. "Each person has ten minutes, can't use notes, and the story has to be true. That kind of thing?"

"Exactly," I said. "Well, I'd never been to one of those before, and then about a year ago, a friend of mine . . . A friend told me to meet her there. It wasn't far from here, actually, I think. Remember when the bartenders over at Burp Castle used to dress like monks and didn't talk? For a while there was a pop-up place next door, and that's where the storytelling thing took place—like it was set up to be the antithesis of the shush bar. You had to bring your own drinks. So I got there and brought along a Moscow mule in a thermos. Same one I've got here." I held up my thermos and wiggled it like an idiot. Pull it together, Yessie. "But by the time the event started, I realized my friend had stood me up. I was about to head back to Queens, but this woman got onstage, and I figured each story had to be ten minutes or less, so I might as well listen."

"Wait. At least describe her a bit. Tall, short, old, young?" Eurovision asked.

"She was very tall, probably six feet," I said. "Her hair was longish, but more like a shaggy mullet than a mane. Jesus hair, really. She wore a plain long-sleeve T-shirt, which just said 'Beach Vibes,' and then jeans. I remember thinking she'd look just as natural holding an acoustic guitar as she would a lasso. She had a hippie-cowgirl aura that was really endearing. She said her name was Priya."

"Really? A cowgirl named Priya?" Eurovision asked.

"Shush," Vinegar said. "No more interruptions."

"The storytelling event had a host," I went on.

"The host was a very energetic person named Senga. She wore a bright blue patterned dress I remember feeling was very out of place in the Lower East Side. She was in charge of keeping the time, and generally making sure nothing went off the rails. Sometimes, I'd heard, the storytellers were drunk, or were intent on libeling someone, or just went on too long. So Senga was there in the wings to keep the train on the tracks.

"With a very warm glance her way, Senga introduced Priya as someone new to the venue and the series, and Priya stepped shyly into the spotlight. She took a second to bring the microphone up a foot or so to accommodate her height, and I think all the while, the audience was taking her in. She didn't look like many other women in Manhattan.

"'Hello,' she finally said, lowering her voice, as if mocking herself, mocking the idea of saying hello. Then she looked up, into the gentle spotlight, and her face delivered on the promise inherent in the emcee's happy glance.

"She was a strikingly handsome woman, with light hair, somewhere between blond and brown, with dark eyes and angles everywhere: a sharp jaw, sharp cheekbones, a long neck, and wide, planed shoulders.

"Then she smiled. And it was her smile, more than any other single factor, that sent heads together whispering. It was a cowgirl's smile, guileless and somehow making her seem stronger than before.

"'Thanks for having me and for listening. Thanks in advance,' she said, and cleared her throat in a way that was just short of disingenuous. 'As I think I mentioned, my name is Priya, and I'm going to tell a story.' She cleared her throat again; this time it seemed performative. 'I want to warn everyone that this starts kind of dark and then has a happy ending. So bear with me. I know everyone's here to have a good time, and I don't want to bring anyone down. So just know the ending is a good one.'

"She said this in a way that made much of the audience smile. I remember thinking, 'They'll love anything this woman says.'

"'Okay,' Priya said, 'a long time ago, I was seeing a young woman. I was a young woman myself, so it was perfectly, uh, appropriate.' This provoked a cautious wave of laughter.

"'Let's call her Lynn. About six months into our relationship, while we were taking a walk in the woods near where we lived, Lynn said she had something to tell me. It was fall, everything orange and brown, and she was very upset right away, just at the thought of telling me this. I made the assumption that anyone would have—that she was breaking up with me. It would not have surprised me. She was beautiful and far more accomplished than I ever would be.

"'But instead, she told me about a man she'd once known, a teacher of hers in college. I would say professor, but he wasn't that, and never would be. He was there as a visiting lecturer, and Lynn took a class with him. One night, at the end of the first semester, he invited all his students to his house. She went, and there was pot and booze at this gathering, and everyone was very happy to be in college and to be finished with the semester, and to be so well liked by this visiting lecturer.

"'As the night was winding down, while everyone was leaving, this lecturer asked my girlfriend to stay. And she did, because she liked him. Any nineteen-year-old student, she said, would have stayed afterward to have the attentions of this man.

"'They had another glass of wine, and then this man forced himself on Lynn. When she protested, he laughed, and held her down, and told her to get with the program. Those were his words—get with the program. She struggled, but he was very strong and was able to hold her two hands over her head with one arm. She cried through it all, crying at what she called her own stupidity.'

"There were nods of recognition in the audience, and there were quiet gasps, but most of the room had forgotten to breathe.

"'After that, Lynn and this visiting lecturer saw

each other on campus, and he greeted her profession-
ally. He didn't seem at all ashamed of anything he'd
done, but he didn't pursue her in any way again. It
had been a transaction for him. He'd invited her over,
he'd taken what he felt he deserved, and she was left
to sort it out.

"'Lynn did not handle it well. As summer approached, she was struggling so much that she skipped
her finals and eventually she left school. Even though
the lecturer wasn't returning, she decided she couldn't
come back to that campus. She spent a year at home, in
the blackest depression, and only through the miracle
of her parents was she able to recover and return to
college, a different one, very far away, almost two years
after the assault by this visiting lecturer.

"'Lynn told me all this as we walked through the
woods, and by now, we were sitting on a fallen tree,
and she was sobbing. I held her head against my chest,
and told her I was sorry, and told her what I wanted to
do to this man, which was murder him in the light of
day, in front of everyone he knew. I thought this might
please her, but she only got more upset. I asked her
why she was getting more upset, and she told me that
she was afraid, having told me about this, that I would
leave her. That I would see her as damaged, spoiled,
unwantable.

"'I told Lynn that this was not the case. That it couldn't possibly be the case. We walked back home, and I tried to hold her next to me, uninterrupted, for the next twenty-four hours. I didn't want her to feel fragile, or alone, and wanted to make sure she knew, if anything, I loved her more than before, because when you tell someone about something like that, you do so out of love, and this can only deepen love.'

"Priya looked at her shoes, and I assumed the story was over. It was not the kind of story I'd expected to hear at an event like this. Usually the stories involved some comedic self-embarrassment. A few people clapped for Priya, but she raised her eyes again, and made the gentlest gesture with her hand, indicating she was not done.

"'But as I held her,' she continued, 'I was also thinking of harming this man, and how I might do it.'

"There were scattered laughs. But Priya wasn't smiling.

"'This experience with the lecturer,' she continued, 'had happened five years before Lynn told me about it. And so finding this lecturer took some doing. I started looking the next day. This was before the internet tools were where they currently are, so I had to make some careful inquiries, and had to do so without her knowing. Eventually, I did find him, and learned he was in

New York City, doing the same thing he was doing when she met him, acting as some kind of guest lecturer at one of the colleges in the city.

"'At the time, Lynn and I were living a few hundred miles north of New York, in the Vermont woods I was mentioning earlier. So for a few days, I sat on this knowledge, thinking it was not the same as knowing he's in the next town. There was something dampening about knowing he was so far away.

"'Or at least there was at first. Then, the very fact that he still existed, and existed on a college campus, with access to the same sorts of young women that my girlfriend had been, began to focus my anger again.

"'So . . .' And here, Priya began to smile, like a cowgirl describing a crazy calf she couldn't quite rope, 'the next thing I know, I'm in my car, and I'm halfway to New York, having driven nonstop for hours. Lynn was in Australia for work and would be gone for ten days, and so I thought this would be the perfect moment to, well, I don't know what I had planned. I had some ideas, but nothing concrete.

"'So I remember driving over the Tappan Zee, just a few minutes from the city, and thinking, "What will I actually do when I see this guy?" I mean, I've been in one or two fights in my life, and those were in junior high, and I lost. I got tall later in high school, and I filled out, but I'm not a violent person. And anyway, was I really going to stalk this man?'

"And here the audience seemed to relax. Everyone assumed that Priya's story was about to wind down and end with some kind of thwarted interaction, some inner peace reached, acknowledging what one can and cannot change or rectify.

"'But then I saw the guy,' Priya continued. 'I found him that first day. It was too easy. I looked him up online, found where he was teaching, saw his class schedule, and went to the building. So I waited outside the building, and sure enough, he came out ten minutes after the class let out. I knew from my quick internet search that he lived only about twenty blocks away, in a nondescript apartment building near the East River. So I assumed he was walking that way.' Priya shrugged. 'So I started following him. This was the first time, mind you, I'd ever followed anyone anywhere.

"'It's a rush, I have to say. At least at first. You have this knowledge they don't have. You're walking, and they're walking, but you're living on two levels at once. You have a purpose he doesn't have. He's just puttering home, but you're a missile. You're both walking, but your life at that moment is far more interesting than his. He's just walking home to watch half a movie and sleep. But you have a purpose. You plan to do something operatic in scale. So I was walking, feeling electric everywhere. I followed him for a few blocks until I realized he was going home. Which was my hope.

"'So I just have to remind everyone that I'd driven hundreds of miles to find this person. But I hadn't decided what to do with him once I did find him. I guess there was something in my heart that believed that, once I did find him, I'd know what to do. Or I'd chicken out. But I'd been following him for about twelve blocks and my heart hadn't given me any clarity yet.

"'And then something happened. And this will sound to you like the part where I embellish, but I swear this is true. This guy stopped to talk to someone on the sidewalk, and I stopped, too. It was a young woman. She was wearing a backpack, two-strapping it, so I had to assume she was a student. I was hidden behind a moving van, and I listened and watched as they talked for a few minutes. And when he continued, walking away from her, he had this smile on his face. Even across the street I could see this smile, this guarded, private, terrible smile—a smile of plans and privilege. He was walking along, smiling to himself about this young woman he'd just spoken to, and that's when the answers I had hoped for arrived. The plans filled my heart.

"'The next thing I know I'm crossing the street, and he's seeing me heading toward him. I was moving very fast, and seeing my approach, he stopped. I could tell he was wondering if he knew me, because there was no one else on the street, and I was coming right to him, staring right at him. There's no chance I'm just crossing the street there for some other reason. So he was thinking, "Who is this? How do I know this lady coming toward me?"

"'And then, when I was about ten feet from him, something else came into his eyes, which I felt was recognition. I can't explain how I knew, but I knew. I saw it. The recognition that retribution was coming. The recognition that I was an agent of retribution. In just one moment, I saw in his eyes the sins he carried with him, and in his eyes I saw the knowledge that I was coming to hold him to account. I will never forget that moment. It confirmed that we are all highly intelligent and intuitive beings for whom a great deal can be communicated in one look. We so often pretend we need things explained, verbalized, clarified, but nearly always we know exactly what's on someone's mind.

"'Now, remember I had told you that I didn't know what I would do if I actually saw him. But now, before I had even had a mental reckoning, before any plans had been made in my mind, I'd taken my two hands, and with them I'd formed them into the shape of a great hammer, the kind you would use to strike an anvil.'

"Priya had entwined her fingers into a massive fist, her forearms fused.

"'And I swung high and because he cowered in the shadow of my hammer, my arms and fists came down on the back of his neck.'

"Onstage, Priya swung down, and then stared down at the imaginary victim at her feet.

"'The force was far greater than I thought I was capable of. And from that first blow, the lecturer crumpled like a coat slipped from a hanger.'

"Priya paused for a long moment, then looked up and smiled her cowgirl smile.

"'Remember that this man was about five feet nine. I'm taller than that. He was probably one hundred fifty pounds. I weigh more than that. He's a man who types at a computer most of the day. I . . . do other things. So it was not a fair match. And he was already on the ground. But I couldn't stop. Something about his cowardice angered me more. So in a repetitive motion that I would compare to the hammering of railroad ties, I swung my hammer into him six or seven times as he shrank in on himself, on the sidewalk.'

"Priya glanced again at the clock. She had four more minutes left, but it seemed the story was winding down. The audience assumed she would explain how she walked away, or what she said as she walked away. How the lecturer apologized.

"'Soon, I knew he was unconscious,' Priya continued. 'He was breathing but out cold. And it was then that I had an idea. The hammer strikes hadn't been an idea—that was just my fury speaking, and it all happened before I could think. But now I had a plan forming. So I left him where he was and went to get my car. I hoped no one would find him in the meantime. My hopes were rewarded. I came back and he was there, half conscious, so I put him in the back seat of my car, and I drove the two of us out of New York and into New Jersey. I was looking for a Walmart or some store that might have hardware and be open late. It was about nine o'clock then, and I found a Target off the highway near Middletown. Again, I hoped he wouldn't wake up and leave the car as I shopped.

"'I was quick in the store and came back about ten minutes later with duct tape, ten yards of vinyl rope, a length of rubber tubing, a flashlight, a small cooler, a bag of ice, and a handsaw, the kind you'd use for pruning a tree. When I got back to the car, he was still there, just waking up. There in the parking lot, which was nearly empty, I used the duct tape to cover his mouth, and used the rope to hog-tie him. When he was secure,

I got back on the highway, looking for an area where I could carry out my idea undisturbed.

"'After forty minutes, I found a rural area,' she said, 'and drove down a narrow road for about three miles. Wait, how am I doing with time?'

"Priya looked to the host, Senga, whose imperturbable face had paled. She seemed half ready to end Priya's story before it took an even more disturbing turn.

"Priya checked the clock. 'Oh shit, I have only forty-five seconds. Should I go on? It'll take a few more minutes to finish.'

"The crowd urged her to finish. Someone yelled to Senga, 'You better let her finish!'

"'Okay, okay,' Priya said, raising her hands, as if she'd been urged to play an encore on her guitar. 'So I found a good spot, pulled over, and turned out the lights. I arranged the flashlight in a tree such that it shone down on a small area where I could see. I dragged him to the light, and told him that I was about to saw off his right arm. I told him that this right arm was the arm he used to hold my girlfriend down as he raped her. I told him that I would saw off the arm below the elbow, and that, if he behaved, I would put the arm on ice, in the cooler, and I would tie a tourniquet such that he would likely survive the wound. Then I'd give him the flashlight, and allow him to walk with the cooler to the hospital. Chances were they would attach it in time. Sounds fair, right?'

"No one in the audience said a word.

"'I'd never sawed off an arm before,' she said, and now there were titters from the audience, as if a swath of them had come to the realization that this story was fabricated, and that she'd masterfully led them into the realm of the impossible.

"'But I will say two things about sawing off someone's arm,' she continued. 'First, there is so much blood.' Priya laughed, and the audience, or half of it at least, laughed, too. This was surely a joke.

"'It's like sawing through a water balloon!' Priya said, chuckling. 'I got blood in my face, my eyes, all over my clothes. And I hadn't prepared for that. I knew there'd be blood, but just not quite so much. Second, the bone part wasn't that difficult. The bone is tough, sure, but after a few seconds sawing, which was tough going, I decided to break it first. I just stood up and just came down on it with my heel, and that did the trick. It snapped pretty close to where I was sawing, so I just cut the shards down a bit, and then finished the rest of the flesh and cartilage.

"'I guess you're wondering if he was screaming. Oh, he was screaming! But I had all that duct tape around him, and so it was pretty muffled. And remember that I had the car radio on, just in case someone was out in the woods that night. They'd hear the oldies station I was listening to, and the muffled sounds, and figure it was some people having relations in the back seat.

"'I tied that tourniquet, and the blood stopped. Then I put his severed arm and hand in the cooler, which was funny, because it turns out the one I bought wasn't quite big enough. I should have bought the eight-gallon one instead of the four-gallon one. So I had to rearrange the ice and then angle the hand and arm so it was kind of diagonal inside.' Here, using her own right forearm, Priya demonstrated the position of the severed arm.

"'So I made sure he was okay to stand and walk. He still had the duct tape over his mouth, but when I asked him if he could walk, he indicated that he could. I reminded him that this had all happened as retribution for what he'd done to someone I knew, and he seemed to understand that, too. I told him that it would be unwise for him to report me, or this incident, because that would likely bring formal charges from my girlfriend, and no doubt many other students he'd assaulted. The recognition in his eyes proved to me, at that moment, that I was right—that my girlfriend had been one of many young women he'd raped. All of them had been afraid to accuse him, for fear of altering their lives, not wanting to give him more of their lives than they already had.

"'So my hope was that he would get his arm reattached, and that every time he looked at it, at its gnarled shape, its restricted functionality, he would know why this had happened. Every time he was alone with his mangled arm, I would be there with him—just as every time my girlfriend and I were alone, he was there with us.'

"The audience said nothing.

"'Thanks, everyone!' Priya said brightly, and then stepped off the stage. There was scattered applause, followed by darting glances between us all, as if everyone were deciding whether it was appropriate to applaud, and whether we'd just heard the confession of a serious crime, or just a gruesome and made-up tale.

"Then, as if knowing our thoughts, Priya jumped back onstage, took the microphone, and said, 'True story!'

"And she left through the back door."

I stopped and gulped down even more of my drink, then raised my head. I was met with a wall of staring, frozen faces. Especially Darrow, who looked sick. *Well, they asked for it*, I thought.

"Did anyone at that place call the cops?" Whitney asked.

"No!" I realized too late that it came out as a kind of yelp. "Why? It was just a story."

"*Why?*" said Whitney. "A story about a serial rapist,

assault, and possibly even a murder? Someone should have called the cops. You should have reported it."

"It had nothing to do with *me*. Or anybody else in the place. It was none of my business," I said.

"Call the cops," said Hello Kitty, "right. Great idea. Always call the cops." She blew a lazy smoke ring with her vape.

Darrow suddenly made a sound, like a throat clearing for attention, but it was strangled. "Calling the police was precisely *not* what she should have done."

"How so?" said Whitney.

"Our super here heard a story describing multiple felonies from someone she doesn't know, without a scintilla of evidence supporting it. It's unsubstantiated hearsay. It has no legal value. It could be—in fact, probably is—a fiction. If she *did* report it, and it's false and defamatory, or causes harm, she might have serious legal exposure. So my advice is definitely do *not* report it."

"Thank you," I said to Darrow. I was already bitterly regretting telling the story.

"You ask me?" said Florida. "I think it *is* just a tall tale. If it were true, she never would have confessed to it in front of all those people."

"As a matter of curiosity," said Darrow, "did he make it to the hospital, or did he die in the woods?"

His glance lingered on me a little longer than was comfortable.

"How would I know?" I said. "She didn't specify."

He shrugged and turned to Maine. "What's the prognosis, Doc? Do you think the dirtbag could have survived with his arm cut off like that? Hypothetically speaking, of course."

My head was now spinning, the tall dark buildings surrounding us moving in a horrible, sluggish fashion. I wondered if I needed to run to the parapet for a good vomit.

"If the arm was taken off just below the shoulder, that would be pretty serious," Maine said thoughtfully. "But given it was below the elbow, he might have survived with a good tourniquet. And Priya sounds pretty capable. A lot depends on how far the man had to walk, how much blood was lost before the tourniquet was applied, and how severely he experienced shock. The man might have staggered a few hundred yards before collapsing, or he might have been able to walk a mile or more. I would give his chances at around sixty-forty."

A silence settled on the rooftop. I took another gulp of daiquiri. "Let's move on to the next story," I mumbled.

Eurovision, who had been looking at me curiously, said, rather slowly, "I remember the Burp Castle."

"Cool." I avoided his gaze.

"There never was a pop-up story place next door."

"Huh. I guess it was somewhere else then," I said. "I've forgotten."

"Also . . ." his voice dropped in timbre, "I just can't see Priya or anyone telling that story to a group of strangers."

"Just what she said: It's a made-up story," said Florida. "Told for shock value."

"I . . . actually don't . . . think so," Eurovision said slowly. His gray eyes were fixed on me.

"Let her be," murmured the Lady with the Rings.

Eurovision didn't take his eyes off me. "Which woman in the story . . . is you?"

"Neither one! Go fuck yourself."

The Lady with the Rings snapped at Eurovision. "Shut your damn mouth." She turned to me. I was trembling all over. "Sweetheart, you don't have to answer these questions."

I stared around at the group, with a feeling of tightness inside my chest so painful I thought it would kill me. *What the fuck*, I thought. I suddenly wanted them to know—to make them all finally *see* me. "*I* cut off his arm."

This was met with a stunned silence, so I added, "He didn't die, okay. I checked. But he never told. They couldn't put his arm back on." With this, and a sudden wrenching feeling in my gut, I staggered to my feet and stumbled toward the parapet. Eurovision, who was already standing, shot over as if to grab me—he must've thought I was going to jump—but then halted awkwardly about four feet from me, and took a couple of apologetic steps back, adjusting his mask. I didn't quite make the parapet and vomited just before it. I remained hunched over, horribly ashamed, heaving.

"Don't . . . jump," Eurovision said, his voice hoarse.

"Fuck off," I said, finally straightening up, spitting and wiping my mouth with the back of my sleeve. "Why would I jump?"

I leaned another moment or two on the parapet, steadying myself, and then returned to my couch and eased myself down. I could feel everyone's eyes on me. This was it: Some righteous do-gooder would turn me in to the cops, just like they'd turned in my dad when his mind started to go. When you're a super, you can't ever forget your place. What the hell had I just done?

But when I finally looked up, through my veil of turmoil, shame, embarrassment, I discovered that most faces were filled with sympathy and concern. A few people still seemed shocked and suspicious, but the majority of the tenants appeared to believe this wasn't as bad a crime as I had always felt.

For his part, Eurovision was managing to look

positively guilty. "God, listen, I'm so sorry," he said to me. "What was I thinking? I'm such an idiot—"

"You *are* an idiot," said the Lady with the Rings to him, then turned to me. "No harm, no foul, right? The guy lived. I think a lot of us would agree he got what he deserved. And you? You told that story because you had to. You *needed* to."

"What a burden you must have carried all these years," said Vinegar.

I just didn't have words. I sat there, leaning against the back of the couch, trying to control the spinning and unable to respond.

"Listen. Your secret," said Eurovision, "is safe with us. I swear."

"Absolutely," said Darrow.

The tenants on the rooftop murmured their promises.

Eurovision went on. "That bastard deserved it. You probably saved more women from being raped. He won't do that again, not with one arm and that awful memory."

I found, after a moment, despite my mental confusion, that there was more I wanted to say. "I never told Lynn," I said. "When she came back from Australia, I never said a word about what I did. But it was always there, in my head. It ate away at me and finally ruined our relationship. It was all my fault. My love for her couldn't hold up against . . . what I now knew I was capable of. I left her—and we lost touch."

No one had much to say about that. Finally, the Therapist said, "Thank you for sharing." She added, "We're here for you, anytime."

The phrases were trite, but there was so much feeling behind them that I felt my defenses pricked. I said, to her, to everyone and no one in particular, "Can we please just . . . move on?"

Before Eurovision could call on someone, Darrow did that throat-clearing thing again. He looked pale, and there were beads of sweat on his brow, even in the chilly night. "As long as we're in confessional mode," he began, "I've got one. Similar, but worse. *Much worse.*" His voice was slow, measured.

Everyone waited. What could he possibly have to say that would be awful enough to eclipse my story?

"**Before I** moved to New York, I lived outside of Stockton, California, with my family. This happened out there.

"It was no secret that I liked to run. But what do I mean I liked to run when I averaged eight miles a day? It was an obsession. I needed it. An addiction? I tend to think of addiction as detrimental, and, while I might suffer from arthritis one day, the runs were generally good for me physically, psychologically, even spiritually. All but for this one time.

"We lived in the mountains then, so it felt pretty private for anyone other than those who lived near us, who knew it was something I did pretty much every day, based on the fact that they'd see me, be forced to slow down, to wave, to acknowledge that, yes, I was out there again, sharing that one-lane, patrolless stretch of road they hated to have to slow down on. Most of the time I ran with our dog Seidon, who was still young enough to run that many miles, not like our older dog, who had to retire from running, having aged out of it due to an arthritis supposedly common to older boxers. We loved Seidon so much. Still do, in the way you can love the gone. Got him from the pound in Stockton. I'd come to love the city of Stockton because the more familiar I got with it, the more it reminded me of Oakland, which was the same reason my wife loved Oakland, where we'd met, because of how much it reminded her of Stockton.

"Poseidon was the name he came with, the god of the sea, but we never called him Poseidon, only ever Seidon for short. Sometimes Sides. Sometimes Bardy. Sometimes Papa Seides. Sometimes Sapa Peides. That's how it gets with names for dogs, for every kind of thing you love, names abound. It was the same with our boy, our son; there'd been countless names between when he was a baby and when he began to find it embarrassing for us to call him anything but his legal name.

"Living in the mountains was great for so many reasons, including the beautiful runs, the clean air, and the lack of complications relating to cities, to crowds, to what crowds boil down to, people. We were mostly removed from any people-related problems. The only people-related problems we had were the tweakers. I couldn't say for sure what they were on, likely it was meth, or whatever other kinds of highs they could scrape together, these strange, bearded, mountain men who lived out of their cars. There was unattended shit to steal up and down our country road. Enter the frequenting tweaker in the Ford Escort with Washington plates. I'd first seen him charging stolen car batteries with a single solar panel—also stolen—on a country road even more country than our country road, which was called Esmerelda on the map on my phone but there wasn't a single sign with that name to be found anywhere, up and then down a hill where the road went to reddish dirt and you couldn't see signs of where people lived but from their gates and mailboxes. The tweaker was fixated on what he was doing, with his tongue sticking out slightly, stealing and converting energy from the sun with stolen hardware for both the stealing and the storage. He wore overalls and looked like Charles Bukowski, if he'd found meth instead of booze. He didn't notice when we ran by, that first time I saw him. The next time he raced by us in his mufflerless Escort, going dangerously fast just inches from me and Seidon. I stuck my middle finger up almost instinctively, which I saw him see in the rearview. I could see even then that my finger had pushed a button.

"I was running with Seidon not long after the middle-finger incident with my noise-cancellation headphones playing music at possible peak volume, going up a steep hill—that was when I tended to need to play high-energy music to get me up hills and not podcasts or audiobooks, which were more for downhills and straightaways, but where we lived there was pretty much only uphill or downhill so I was constantly switching back and forth between audio mediums and volumes. It's obviously a fucked-up thing to lose a beloved dog, period. Worse was to lose one to a tweaker driving a loud-ass car who couldn't have been paying enough attention. But to lose a beloved dog to someone who might have done it on purpose, and to have that dog die on the leash you were holding? It was of course the tweaker in the Ford Escort with the Washington plates who got him. I'm not sure why he stopped and got out. That's the only part I can't understand about him doing it on purpose because of the middle finger. Was he trying to pretend it was a mistake to save himself from possible prosecution? I'll never know. Because there he came at me waving his hands like, *Sorry man, sorry man, you okay, you okay?* My face must have shown what I was feeling for him to be asking that, or it showed something pitiably approachable, in need of consoling, but that's not what was going on inside. Seeing Seidon there on the road clearly gone, eyes still open, I felt a rage so pure it was almost love I felt, going at the man with everything I had in me. The best kinds of dog leashes are durable, but more than that, they're hard and don't break easily. The first hit was with the plastic bulk of the nonleash part of the leash, the part that retracts the thing and holds the reel of it, that first hit just sort of stunned him. Then his eyes went wide and focused on me in a way I knew meant I better move fast, so I went at one of his legs and pulled off this move my son learned in karate, that he showed me how to do once. The way I did the move was in no way clean, or with technique, but it worked. I landed on top of him with the leash still in one of my hands. I then, without hesitation, proceeded to beat him with it over and over and over and over, the plastic leash not cracking, and definitely not retracting as the dead lump of beloved dog was still hooked to the other end of it. That the tweaker's body went still didn't scare me at all at first.

"It was with suddenness that I found that I was crying and calling my wife, but she didn't answer. I called again and she didn't answer again and, in the meantime, I gained some panicked form of clarity regarding the immediate future and what to do. Thinking about the idea of carrying Seidon's body down the hill, so we could properly bury then mourn him, made the reality of the tweaker's body take on a weight I hadn't felt until just then. The phrase 'tweaker's body' even sort of clanged in my head, and you'd think I'd done it before how fast I moved after that.

"No one ever came to investigate the missing tweaker or his car with the Washington plates. My wife and son were gone long enough that day that I had time to hide everything. We lived on seven acres with lots of trees and bushes to hide things, if you wanted to. I rolled the car deep into these bushes we didn't ever even go near. Well, first I dug a hole and buried the tweaker in it, then rolled the car on top of the hole. There was a chance one day my wife or son would find the car, but what then? We'd have it towed. Nothing more. When they got back home, they cried at the sight of Seidon's body. Then we buried him and cried and talked about all that we loved about him. My wife kept rubbing my back, thinking I was taking it pretty hard.

"I stopped running up and down the hills around our house and found a different run a couple miles away from us. That run was longer, and you pretty much never saw anyone else on it. But then this one time, maybe a year after I killed the tweaker with the dog leash, I saw a guy with a truck move a garbage bag that looked like it could have had a body in it over to this tree-and-trash pile he then set on fire. I saw most of the action from far off; I was running back to where I parked my car and had to pass him on the way. By the time I passed him, he was at his truck, now smoking a cigarette, watching his fire smolder, to make sure it all burned all the way down, or I didn't know. We caught eyes as I passed. And he really looked into my eyes. I didn't want him to, but you can't control that kind of thing. It was like he was searching for something in me, some sameness I didn't want him to have found there, the sameness that he found in me about having secrets that need burning or burying, and once he did find that thing in me, he winked at it, or at me, like we had that something between us, our secret, that we country folk, where no one could see us, could do and get away with things if we had to, if it came down to it, and that I better just keep quiet about his fire and finish my run, go back to my quiet mountain life with my wife and son and our other two dogs, safe from reckless tweakers, pretend it didn't happen, the killing, the burying, let his fire have consumed it all, then let the embers have settled, then let the ashes blow off in the wind those foothills got there, up at the snow line of the Sierra Nevada mountains, where fire was becoming more and more a concern, what with global warming, and wasn't my wife having the land cleared for fire safety, and wouldn't they uncover the tweaker's car, which would then prompt my wife to ask again, as she had the day we lost Seidon to the tweaker, 'Who did you say was the hit-and-run again, what kind of car was it?' I would know she was testing me, having suspected all along that I made up a different car having hit him, and here, I would forget which car I made up. It was all in the old man's eyes as I passed him and his fire, there on that country road, the unraveling, the unburying of the body of the tweaker that I killed out of a rage so pure it was love."

He was done, and a feeling of actual horror did accumulate in the air. I was infinitely grateful. Darrow had told that story for me. I felt exorcised.

"How long ago was this?" Hello Kitty asked.

"Ten years."

"Did your wife clear the land?"

"Yes, she did."

"Did she ask the question?"

"Yes."

"And did all that unraveling come to pass?"

"Yes."

"Aren't you worried? Like, every day?" Hello Kitty asked. "Whoever owns the property now might dig a foundation or make a garden or something."

"I never sold the property. The car is still there, the house falling into ruin. Am I afraid? I was. But the older I get, the less afraid I am. As far as what I did to the tweaker—no regrets." He gave me a significant look as he said "no regrets," and I felt a quiver of something inside me, I'm not sure what.

"Well," said Eurovision weakly, "good God and all that."

I wasn't sure what time it was, or when the bells of St. Pat's would ring, but I couldn't bear any more stories, any more secrets. All I could think was, thank God my dad would never get out of Evergreen, never have a chance to learn what I had done. I lurched to my feet, mumbled something about being tired, and fled the roof. I staggered back to the basement and crawled into bed, purged to the bone.

Day Fourteen
April 13

We took our seats. I almost didn't come, after last night, but I didn't want a gap in my recording, and I didn't want to look like a deserter. I started my phone recording and reclined on the fainting couch. I assumed I could once again become invisible and ignored. But the excessively cheerful greetings, the little looks from everyone on the roof as they took their seats, the sympathetic smiles, confused me. Were they really concerned about me? Do they weep at night for me? Ha ha, of course not. Nobody ever cares about the super.

My drink was Pastis, from a fly-specked bottle that looked half a century old. I never liked the taste of licorice, but this did the job. I'm giving up on my daily effort of piling up charnel heaps of numbers in my bible, for the same reason I stopped trying to reach my dad. We've been up here on the roof for fourteen days, the quarantine period the government told us was necessary to no longer be contagious, but even still, there's no end in sight. It's starting to feel like we'll be trapped on this rooftop forever, banging our pots and pans until hell freezes over. At the same time, during the daytime I keep finding myself weirdly looking forward to the rooftop gathering, the outlandish stories of these random New Yorkers.

Tonight there was another addition to the mural: Someone had scribbled a quotation below the picture of God holding the box of bunnies.

Is He able, but not willing? Then He is malevolent.
—Epicurus.

Hello Kitty read it out loud and laughed. "Who gave us that little tidbit?"

The Poet raised his hand with a slight smile.

"I approve." She curled into her chair, caressing the vape with her lips. "Those idiots who believe in God," she said, "should be required to explain why He won't help us with this virus—why He's able, but not willing."

"The Lord moves in mysterious ways," said Florida. "'For I consider that the sufferings of this present time are not worth comparing with the glory that is to be revealed to us.'"

"Lord save us from Bible quoters," said Vinegar, acidly.

It had rained hard again in the afternoon, and it had turned into the kind of evening where the overcast sky just fades from gray to black. I had put a fresh candle in my lantern, which cast a little pool around my red couch. The other candles and oil lanterns were like dewdrops of yellow light in the darkness. We made the usual clamor at seven, not very enthusiastically, and then lapsed into muteness. Nobody wanted to tell a story. People looked uncomfortable. I guess they were still shaken by my story and Darrow's yesterday. Was everyone now just looking around our circle, wondering what other crimes their neighbors are capable of?

"And how is our super this evening?" said Eurovision gently, startling me out of my cynical reverie.

"Uh, a little hungover," I mumbled and lifted my Pastis. "Cheers."

"I would guess quite a few of us these days are hungover."

The Lady with the Rings rattled her hands as a way of getting everyone's attention. "I think it's a shame," she said, "that we don't have a priest up here to tell us how many Hail Marys we need to recite as penance.

Because that's what our little rooftop is turning into, isn't it: a confessional booth. It's given us all a chance to expiate our sins. Mine among them." She turned to me, sweeping Darrow into her gaze as well. "I hope you feel better, sharing with us your story."

"I've no idea how I feel," I said, brusquely, in a tone that I hoped would shut down further commiseration. And then I felt badly, because I'd really come to like the Lady with the Rings. "What I mean is, I just don't want to be fussed over."

"Very understandable," said Eurovision. "So does anyone want to start us off with a story? Or a confession?"

No one spoke.

"Come now, people!" said Eurovision. "Anyone?"

"Maybe we should take a break from stories," said Maine.

"Nonsense," said Eurovision, canvassing the group with his hands clasped, trying to hide an air of desperation.

"The old super had some good stories," suggested Darrow. "When he came to fix something, he always had juicy gossip."

"Too many stories," said Florida. "That man talked nonstop. You couldn't turn him off." She turned to me. "I prefer our new super. She's quiet and doesn't stick her nose into other people's business."

I felt grateful for this, hoping she'd never notice my recording phone. And here was my opportunity to ask the question I'd been wanting to ask for a long time. "What happened to the old super?"

There was an uncomfortable silence. "It was strange," said Eurovision. "He left right at the beginning of Covid, just gone one day. I figure he fled the city like everyone else."

"What was he like?"

"Well," said Eurovision, "he was fat, short, cheerful, and Greek. He talked fast and asked a lot of prying questions and doled out advice. I swear, if he hadn't been a super, he would have made a great therapist. He was everywhere in the building, bustling about. Like Florida said, you could never quite get rid of him."

"He had sticky fingers," said Florida.

This intrigued me. "Really? How do you know?"

"Once, when he'd come to do some work in my apartment, I found later I was missing my prayer hands. After that, I watched him like a hawk."

I had those hands! But if I said anything now I'd never be able to learn the rest. "What was his name?" I asked.

"Zynodeia," said Florida. "Virgilios Zynodeia."

So much for the totally wrong image I had created of

Wilbur P. Worthington III, which had grown so real in my mind's eye.

"Funny you should mention sticky fingers," said Whitney. "I always wondered what happened to my *Morpho didius* butterfly. It just disappeared one day."

"I was very attached to those hands," said Florida.

"My childhood Elvis collection of forty-fives went missing," said the Lady with the Rings. "I wonder if he took them? He was such a nice man, though. Perhaps he had a mental disturbance."

I was heartily sorry I ever brought up the subject.

Before I could think of what to say in his defense—or even wonder if it was my job to defend him—we were interrupted by the late arrival of La Cocinera. She held up her phone with a delighted smile. "It's now fully charged. I feel sure that tonight you'll see my angel."

Hello Kitty said, "Take two on the angel, *clack*."

"I've been waiting all week for this," said Florida.

I was sure it would be another no-show, but La Cocinera's enthusiasm was infectious.

She held up the little phone for us. We strained to see. There was the view through the San Miguel cam of the garden and behind it, the pink church with the wedding-cake towers. It was sunset there, and the scene was suffused with a golden light, so different from the gray skies here, thousands of miles away.

"Come closer," La Cocinera said. "You'll see better." She checked her watch. "Seven twenty nine. One minute."

Some moved their chairs to see better.

There was movement in the bright rectangle. A figure in black appeared from behind the trees—small, bent, ancient, wrapped in tatters, balancing on two canes while awkwardly carrying a mesh bag with an orange in it. La Cocinera gasped in joy, and we all leaned closer. The woman tottered with agonizing slowness over the rough cobblestones, walking toward the camera, high up on a building. As she reached a spot below it, she stopped and slowly raised her head. Her deep-set eyes locked on ours, somehow straight through the screen. She gazed at us steadily from an impossibly wrinkled face, her white hair peeking from under her scarf—and then she smiled. I saw her mouth move as she spoke some phrase. Then she lowered her head and resumed her painful walk, heading toward the church, vanishing beyond the frame.

La Cocinera retracted her phone and put it in her pocket.

"What did she say?" Eurovision asked.

"*Mis hijos.* My children." She looked triumphant. "I promised you'd see the angel!"

"Um," said Eurovision. "No offense, but she just looked like an old lady to me."

"You think angels are all beautiful young creatures with wings," she scoffed.

"No—" Eurovision fell silent.

"You all saw her, right?"

We all agreed that we saw her.

"Then I'm happy."

All of a sudden, the broken door to the rooftop banged open and a couple emerged. Strangers. Again.

Above their red homemade masks, two sets of exhausted eyes took in the scene on the roof. They were dragging luggage.

"What's this?" Eurovision asked, rising from his seat, alarmed. "Who are you?"

The woman took a step forward.

"We're from the building down the street," said the man, glaring.

"Me, my husband, my mother-in-law, and our kids," said the woman. "Jesus, we can't get back home!"

"How'd you get in here?" Eurovision said.

The couple looked at each other. "The door was open," said the man. "It was raining. So we came in."

The woman propped up her roller bag. "We don't have anywhere else to go."

I braced myself for an onslaught of accusations. But I knew, I *knew*, that I'd locked the door up tight. Someone had left the door wide open again, but how? I wondered if it was deliberate—if there were a saboteur in the building.

"But—you can't be here!" said Eurovision, with an edge of desperation. "We're in a *pandemic!*"

"And we're not?" the woman yelled back. Her husband put a hand on her shoulder. After a pause, she sat down on her suitcase. She looked like she couldn't take another step.

There was something crazy going on with this building.

The Therapist spoke up. "Please, rest here until we get this sorted. I'm sorry we don't have any extra chairs to offer. But if you wouldn't mind, just keep your distance? For all of our sakes."

"And ours, too." The man rested his hand gently on his wife's back. "You rest here," he said to his wife, "and I'll go down and fetch my mother and the kids."

I could tell that attention was about to turn back to the question of the "open" door and this sudden intrusion, but Eurovision saved me.

"What do you mean you can't get home?"

"Our neighbors turned against us." The woman sighed. "We're locked out."

"Locked out?" said Vinegar. "During a pandemic, in the rain? How in the world did that happen?"

The woman took a deep breath, then exhaled as if releasing her own pent-up storm.

"There we were, on a darker and stormier night than this one, locked out of the apartment building. We stood shivering and sneezing in the lobby, suitcases soaked after a three-hour flight from the Dominican Republic, endless lines at Customs, the long cab ride home.

"Our code to the main door didn't work. We figured the super had changed the combination on the lock. We figured the super had finally done something about all the package thefts in the building besides shrugging and saying, 'I'm just the super, man, not a cop.'

"Maybe a robber, too. Maybe El Superman was that seller on eBay whose merchandise always happened to match the missing items the tenants ordered from Amazon. Maybe it's true what our neighbor told us, that El Superman is the one swiping other people's food deliveries.

"At that witching hour, though, El Superman was the only person in the building we'd dare to bother. Sure, there's our neighbor, but she's on antidepressants on account of her no-good son, and we figured the meds had knocked her out to Mars. Besides, El Superman owes us a favor. And supering, or whatever it is he does around here, is what building heroes get paid to do.

"We rang and rang and rang his buzzer.

"As we waited, our eyes fell on the poster taped near the buzzer panel. We recognized the same graphic style on all the instructional posters El Superman puts up in the elevators and hallways. The art is worse than ever.

"Weeks ago, we'd risked our lives to help him lug a drafting table into his apartment, along with other furniture belonging to that political cartoonist from 4C, the one who got kicked out of El Salvador, then got deported back to his country by ICE, may God conserve his soul and that of too many others. He has no family in the States to claim his things. So El Superman begged us to help him relocate the cartoonist's art supplies to 'Krypton,' as El Superman calls that huge apartment the management company placed him in to compensate for the 'shitty super salary.' He always puts on a good show of begging, making requests right after reminders that we're late with the rent yet again. We of course made excuses, that we're a family of five, including an elder and two well-mannered, clean, smart, English-speaking children with American citizenship. Then El Superman apologized, sniffing that, of all the tenants in the building, he just thought he could count on people blessed with the likes of our Family Name. Good Samaritans that we are, we relented, lined our homemade masks with paper towels, and agreed to do him the favor.

"Krypton looked like a warehouse; we had to maneuver around everything from old chandeliers and ceramic tiles to boxes of two-ply toilet paper and organic hand sanitizer. 'Pandemonium emporium endemic to pandemic,' El Superman recited between tokes of a joint. Instead of offering us beverages for the trouble, he gave us an autographed sketch of his latest poster in progress. 'This pandemic's gonna make my poetry and art go viral,' said our antihero, popping open a can of Corona Hard Seltzer, mango-flavored.

"And now in the lobby, we instinctively stepped back six feet from the completed poster: a masked Uncle Sam giving us the finger above the words 'Fuck YOU, Covid.'

"'Well, fuck El Superman,' said our eldest.

"With the tip of an umbrella, our youngest rang and rang and rang the buzzer labeled 'S.'

"Then we noticed the ultimate fuck-you-back: Our Family Name had been crossed out from the label to the buzzer for apartment 3A. Wite-Out would have been less violent. The thick black line was probably drawn with one of those damn Sharpies we'd rescued from 4C.

"Across what we most hold sacred.

"Across the very reason we'd broken quarantine to travel to the land of our birth, heeding the messianic call of the Teller.

"Across a history paved with gold centuries older than this godforsaken country.

"Our youngest lifted a leg and, with the tip of his sneaker, rang and rang and rang the super's buzzer.

"Through the glass door, we finally spotted El Superman. He appeared at the farthest end of the hallway, illuminated by fluorescent light. A mirage in long johns, blue face mask, and dusty yellow Crocs. When he was close enough to the lobby door, we smiled, waved, held up the bag of duty-free island rum originally bought for relatives in Brooklyn.

"His flaring red cape gave us hope.

"In an alternate universe, El Superman would have opened his arms and belted out: 'Welcome back! How was your trip? Did you meet the familia you were searching for? One day I'll visit your country, find me a Lois-a to do all this work for me. Fuggetabout the rent due—Black Lives Matter, man! Ah, and I changed the door code to keep out the POTUS and his den of thieves. The new code is 440. Heh, heh, heh. Open sesame!'

"But in our present universe, he did not say a word or meet our eyes. With a rubber-gloved hand, El Superman slipped an envelope under the door.

"Dumbstruck, we watched him shuffle back to his apartment.

"We banged and banged on the glass.

"Once El Superman had receded from our view, we took turns ringing and ringing each and every buzzer, including our own.

"Crackled responses soon echoed in the lobby.

"'Who is it . . . *quién es* . . . who is it . . . *qu'est-ce* . . . who the . . . ?'

"Over and over, we shouted our Family Name.

"No one buzzed us in."

"Typed on the envelope was our Family Name in bold Times New Roman.

"The letter was to inform us that, pursuant to whatever agreement we'd signed with Rivington Management over a decade ago, we were hereby barred from entering the building until we met three conditions. We were to kindly take further notice that these would be impossible to meet: (1) quarantine for a month—yes, a month; (2) test negative for the alpha, beta, gamma, delta, and all other possibly forthcoming alphabetical strains of the novel coronavirus SARS-CoV-2; and (3) remit in full months of past, present, and future rent. Failure to comply with all of the above would result in forfeiture of our VIP rent-controlled status and institute summary proceedings under the Statute to recover the possession of said apartment 3A.

"Listed at the bottom were the signatures of people whose autistic dogs we'd whispered to, people whose laundry we'd folded and unfolded, people who'd sobbed in our kitchen after the death of their dancing-lady orchids.

"Typed in italicized Helvetica above these signatures: 'Love, Your Neighbors.'"

"So there we were, on a night darker and stormier than this one, facing eviction during a pandemic in a neighborhood already eager to erase us.

"Three weeks. We'd only been gone for three weeks. On family business. We'd been careful. We hadn't hugged or kissed relatives, even the long-lost ones we'd gone to consult. We'd socially distanced while recording interviews, used hand sanitizer after handling birth certificates. American hand sanitizer. We'd made extra masks, washed our hands, said our prayers. Red masks, white soap, blue prayers.

"We called ourselves another Uber, this time to Brooklyn, across the bridge to a relative's in Williamsburg. Ten minutes later, a driver wearing a gas mask was loading our suitcases into the trunk of his SUV. Our youngest stared at him in terror, and we had to wrestle the wailing kid into the vehicle.

"The interior reeked of fake lavender.

"We sneezed and argued all the way down Delancey Street.

"That we should call before showing up at a relative's doorstep, to hell with our Family Name. That, well, this is what we get for listening to the Teller in the first place, for spending the rent money to hunt for the fool's gold he promised. That we're hungry. That, please, not in front of the kids. That, oh, our homeless kids? That, come on, we have to have faith. That we need to pee . . .

"Our eldest sucked her teeth and grabbed the phone.

"Our relative picked up on the second ring.

"'Just come,' she said.

"'See,' said our eldest after hanging up. 'Told you bar people don't sleep.'

"The driver screeched us to a halt at the red light before the bridge. When he turned his head around, we could hear labored breathing through the gas mask.

"'Once upon a time,' he said in a muffled voice, 'there was a bar owner who had many servants and cattle and acres of land.'

"'Just drive!' we yelled.

"The light had just turned green; the driver wouldn't budge.

"'One afternoon, while reaching for the top shelf at

the bar, the owner dropped all the bottles of Johnnie Walker Gold Label Reserve he held in his armpit.'

"He then drove us across the bridge in silence.

"We would later give him a five-star rating not for the quality of his service but for telling us what the Teller would not."

"Our Family Name may mean little in this neighborhood and in this country, but it's worth a fortune on the island.

"We can't say the Teller didn't tell us.

"Perhaps he was right to proclaim: <Even among your neighbors, there will be enemies against those with your Family Name.>

"Long before this pandemic, the Teller had spoken of an epic inheritance due to us.

<Infinite gold,> he said, first in living rooms, later at press conferences. <Colonial gold so yellow it's green.>

"The Teller is a lawyer. He may not carry the Family Name, but he was born with a gold tooth in his mouth.

"His Mother told the story on TV Orovisión:

"'When he was fourteen years old, lightning struck his left eyetooth, right after he'd smiled up at the rain. Thereafter, his ears would not stop ringing. Through the sounds of brewing coffee or honking cars or barking dogs, his ears would not stop ringing with a thousand and one stories. Each time he told one, the ringing would stop.'

"When he was fifteen years old, the Teller told this story at the birthday party of his father:

<Once upon a time, there was a deaf parakeet that liked to eat sugarcane at the train tracks. 'Get out of the way!' people yelled, but the deaf parakeet would keep pecking at his cane. 'Don't say no one told you,' they'd say and go merrily on their way. One day, a train sped by, leaving a smear of colored feathers and cane juice in its wake.>

"When he was sixteen years old, the Teller told this story at the birthday party of his mother:

<Once upon a time, there was a woman who had no face. But her hands knew the language of dirt. When her hands said, 'Turn into clay,' the dirt would turn into clay. When her hands said, 'Turn into me,' the clay would turn into little faceless women. Soon, people came from far and wide to buy her ceramic dolls. 'How much?' they'd say. 'Too much,' she'd say and give her selves away. One day, a man put a roof, a sign, and a price over her head. 'I will be a rich man,' he thought. But when he put a ring on her finger, her hands forgot the language of dirt, and the man lost half of his face.>

"When he was seventeen years old, the Teller told this story at the birthday party of his brother:

<Once upon a time, there was a village where girls turned into boys on their thirteenth birthday. A train came to the village each month to collect salt and gypsum. One day, a twelve-year-old boy secretly hopped on the train right as it was leaving the village. He wanted to go to the capital and become a rich man. He planned to return with a gold ring for the girl he wanted to marry. During the three-hour ride to the capital, he sucked on salt and sugarcane. By the time the train arrived at the capital, the boy had become a woman. She returned to the village years later, poorer than dirt. But she married the girl, who by then had lost a hand and become a rich man.>

"When he was eighteen years old, the Teller told this story at the birthday party of his sister:

<Once upon a time, there was a cane field infested with parakeets. While the cane cutters chopped away, the parakeets perched on the stalks and sang this story each time a train whistled by: 'Once upon a time, there was a cane field infested with parakeets. While the cane cutters chopped away, the parakeets perched on the stalks and sang this story each time a train whistled by—'>

"It was at this party that the Teller was interrupted by a toothless musician, who gave him this advice: 'Don't play the music you hear, boy. You gotta play the dancers.'"

———

"'**A la** mar' by Vicente García was playing when we arrived at the bar-restaurant. Its awning was emblazoned with our Family Name, which our relative had married into and from which she was in the middle of divorcing.

"Under the sheets of rain, we sensed that the sun was rising.

"In our universe, people receive you with music. They inquire about your health after the kiss and hug. They bring fresh towels from their apartment upstairs and coffee with a hint of nutmeg. They rearrange tables and chairs, making the dance floor quarantine-ready. They fluff pillows on the four extra cots they happen to have at their place of business. They write out the Wi-Fi code on business cards so that the kids won't miss their classes. They make runs to the bodega for extra gallons of milk and that quart of almond for the lone vegan among us. They can divide fractions by fractions in their heads to somehow yield whole numbers.

"We ate and slept like royalty. Each day after dinner, at seven p.m. sharp, we stood in front of the business, banging pots and pans. To the embarrassment of our kids, we whistled and clapped in honor of the workers, who smiled wearily on their way to or from work. We filled our idle hours catching up on family gossip over duty-free island rum.

"'A gift,' she called us after three days, 'not pandemic refugees.'

"Fearing we were beginning to smell, we asked for cleaning supplies to earn our keep as guests. We dusted the bar, bottle by bottle, and mended chairs long broken by jealous dancers. We mopped every corner of the floors, fixed hinges, rewired lighting. We leveled the jukebox, playing the rest of García's albums on loop. Each night, we took on the duty of turning away the regulars who ignored the 'Sorry, We're Closed' sign, begging to be let in. In anticipation of a grand reopening, we bought wood and paint in tropical colors and constructed a paradise in the small lobby, complete with Christmas lights and plastic palm trees.

"'A gift,' she called us now, 'genies from a streetlamp.'

"Indeed, her life had been looking rather dim before our arrival. She was tired. For decades, she had worked in this country so that her kids could get ahead and one day take over the business. Then came the marital discord, the arthritis and insomnia, the three kids in college. One was studying infodemiology, another thanatology, the other numismatology. Useless, she said. She was training them for the family business under her DIY-MBA degree program. Ay, the neighborhood, her kids, the world—everything changing too fast! And for God's sake, here she was, an old divorcée macrodosing CBD. For the inflammation, she insisted, for the insomnia.

"We declined. We listened. We empathized. We told her about the Teller.

<Disbursement Day is just around the corner!> The Teller reassured us over WhatsApp messages we forwarded to her daily.

"Ah yes, she'd heard about that scam.

"Not at all, we insisted, showing her the banking PIN numbers assigned to us by the Teller, the key to our financial freedom.

"Despite all her troubles, her initial response was, 'Thanks, but I've got God.'

"'Stop hoarding,' we said, 'and leave some God for the others.'

"She declined. She listened. She empathized.

"Because churches had closed in those days of unanswered Hail Marys. More and more prayer beads dangled from rearview mirrors. We also saw prayer beads in the garbage. These we rescued and scratched the letters of our Family Name into the beads, for quarantine had also given even the skeptics among us renewed faith in the Teller. We soon transformed the bar into an altar, where we convened before each meal to pray. The prayer beads helped us keep track of our days, which we subdivided with retellings of the Teller's stories by themes in sets of five: the joyful, the luminous, the sorrowful, the glorious, the reborn. Bead by bead, we recited our holy Family Name to help us remember the sequence of our stolen history.

"Because if there's no method, there's madness.

"And even then, there's madness."

"Following the musician's advice, the Teller began to listen to his listeners. He stopped telling his stories, and the ringing in his ears returned. He let it ring, determined to find his Master Story. And the less the Teller told, the more we his listeners told.

"In no time, he learned the five things we most value: names, gold, land, dreams, and God. In no time, he learned the five things we most fear: documents, dirt, law, silence, and God.

"When he was good and learned, the Teller went and earned a law degree. He spent days at the Pedro Henríquez Ureña National Library, which was often empty. Besides legal cases and ethics, he studied the stories in the Bible, the Torah, the Koran, and every other holy book available in translation. Bribed with food, the staff sometimes let him pitch his tent in the stacks, where he read himself to oblivion.

"When he was good and lawed, the Teller joined a real estate firm. He bought a beige suit and gold watch. He memorized maps of the north, the east, the south, and the west. On his few days off, he took short naps and long walks. He befriended washerwomen and shoeshine boys. He memorized their names, visited their houses of worship. He carried a briefcase full of newspaper clippings, lollipops, and extra ties. He attended naming ceremonies, weddings, and funerals. He donated to orphanages, extended his arm at blood drives. He befriended the mayor and the mayor's friends, including the bishop.

"Not once did he tell a story.

"When he was good and peopled, the Teller went to the dentist for a cleaning. Some said that his gold tooth had turned to lead, a curse by the musician. But a good many of us had faith that the Teller's stories would return, and we were ready to dance to anything."

"'We're hungry people because we're not in charge of our story. We're a people whose story has been abducted.'—Haile Gerima

"Two weeks into quarantine, our relative responded to one of our WhatsApp messages with this quote. Ours had been a message about Disbursement Day, so we were confounded by her response.

"She later came down while we were at the tail end of our daily prayers and leaned with her arms crossed against the jukebox. When we had finished reciting the last round of our Family Name, she uncrossed her arms. She lifted her mask, tilted her head back, and squeezed multiple drops of a tincture under her tongue. A few deep breaths followed.

"Was her ex-husband okay? we wondered. Had one of her employees passed away? The death count was steadily rising in the city.

"She asked to read our eviction notice.

"The directness of her request coincided with the jukebox's shift to blue light.

"Our eldest rapped her cane against our youngest, 'Papers, boy! The woman's asking us for our papers.'

"In no time, he was presenting the water-stained envelope to the relative with the solemnity of an imperial page.

"'Bullshit,' she said after scanning the letter.

"We took offense, offense at her insinuation that we were pandemic panhandlers.

"She clarified: 'The writer of this letter is full of shit. Can't you smell a rat?'

"We took offense, offense at her insinuation that we'd lost our sense of smell.

"She asked why we hadn't thought to return to the

building or to contact Rivington Management. At the very least, we should check up on our tenant status. Not for nothing, she said, but our eldest and youngest needed stability.

"We took offense, offense at her insinuation that we were as unstable as the president.

"The truth was that we'd enjoyed our time in this pod of the Family Name. It was more than an extension of our trip back home, where we'd spent three weeks tangled up in documents and meetings and bureaucracy. Here at the bar-restaurant, we had gotten to know her and her children in a way we never had since immigrating ages ago. We delighted in setting our nightly storytelling sessions to music from the jukebox and watching videos from our cell phones on a big screen. We enjoyed conjuring up new recipes from leftovers, which we turned into feasts in the restaurant's spacious kitchen. And from the seeds of these labors, we were able to line the windowsills with plants, whose growth we measured by the hour. For the first time in a long time, we felt useful, alive, essential.

"If we briefly forgot the Rivington, it's because we were beginning to remember ourselves.

"She was touched by our sentimentality, of course. And yes, she loved us, too. Our presence had helped her glue back together the pieces of her life. But fairy tales have to end. She had a business to run, divorce lawyers to consult, children to train. And people to date. So with our permission, let us get back to this business of the notice.

"Then she texted one of her -ology kids.

"Her son appeared downstairs as if already waiting in the wings. He was the one we'd overhear her berate for flunking remote exams and smelling like cannabis.

"'DIY-MBA session,' she said in drill-sergeant voice, and he stood at attention. She handed him the notice. 'What's wrong with this document?'

"He glanced it over, then looked up at us and grinned.

"'Duh, there's no letterhead.'"

<There is no 'once upon a time,'> said the Teller, <because I am not telling a story.>

"He first convened these meetings in our living rooms, then at the grocer's, churches, union meetings, antigovernment protests, press conferences, and finally in our dreams.

<What I am telling you is history. The history of two great ancestors who owned a gold mine in this land. They shipped part of the gold across the wide blue sea to the king and queen. The rest of the gold, they hid in banks across Europe during the war. Gold

engraved with the very Family Name coursing through your blood. Here's to God, to nation, to liberty!>

"So we're not bastards after all, we thought. We come from people.

"To prove it, we had set to digging up birth certificates and land titles in a country whose climate and government officials devour paper. Those of us living abroad begged and borrowed to secure flights out of various points of departure to the airport named Las Américas, where, centuries earlier, our Indigenous ancestors had been visited upon by a different breed of gold seekers, some of whom also bore the Family Name.

"'Ha, the colonized claiming the name of their colonizers,' said enemies of the Family Name. They laughed at us in person and in print, on air and online.

"Still, we were patient and civilized in our quest. The pandemic had bought us enough time to stake claim on our DNA before any virus could. Hundreds of our compatriots interviewed elders, combed through church archives, visited the country's National Library in search of the origins of our Family Name. The least fortunate of us wept after hearing the never-told story of the grandfather who had actually been an orphan, the Family Name only pinned on him, as if on a donkey, by a benevolent landowner. The luckiest of us rejoiced upon finding a grandmother's signature in Spanish colonial ship records at the National Archives, never mind her luckless trade.

"To pay for the Document Fees, many on the island bearing the Family Name had saved up or sold cows or driven cabs. Then we stood out in the sun for hours, waiting to present our damp manila folders to the Teller, whose staff army anointed us with Pin numbers.

<For Disbursement Day,> he pronounced over social media, making the sign of the cross.

"'For Disbursement Day,' we later bragged to others, uploading blurred images of our magic numbers, along with prayer-hand emojis.

"Back in New York, when Disbursement Day came and went, we kept the faith. The Teller gathered the faithful at his offices in the Capital or on Zoom, and announced:

<Have faith!>

"And we prayed.

<You will inherit the earth!>

"And we breathed, 'Amen!'"

Early this morning, we called ourselves an Uber, this time back to the Bowery.

"Ten minutes later, we were face-to-face with a driver wearing a mask printed with a selfie. As she loaded our suitcases and plants into the trunk of her

SUV, our youngest climbed inside on his own in a fit of giggles.

"The interior reeked of fabric softener, and we sneezed all the way across the Williamsburg Bridge.

"At its midpoint, our youngest leaned in to ask the driver why she was wearing her face on her face.

"'And how do you know this is my face if you haven't seen my face?' she asked, eyes glued to the road.

"'So sick of all this shit!' our eldest said, removing her dentures. She rolled down the window and tossed her prayer beads toward the East River, yelling out our Family Name and a string of curses: her PIN number, her Social Security number, her Lotto picks, and the Teller's future date of death.

"No one else said a word for the rest of the ride back home."

"**In the** building lobby, we came across our neighbor. She was hunched over, fiddling with the combination to the inner door, her back to us. The rush of cold air made her turn around. She nearly screamed before realizing it was us.

"Her sigh of relief was heartwarming.

"Excuse her. There had been muggings in the building. But silly her for not giving us a proper welcome. How was our trip? Did we deliver her letters and the masks to her sisters? Ay, how she missed them. Her son promised to buy her a plane ticket once this pandemic was over. But listen, so much had happened while we were gone. We should come by for coffee—no, call, better. That racist from 3A? Well, he's now dating a Black Lives Matter guy, and she hears them through the radiator. Oh, the new code? She can't tell us, sorry. 'Because no good deeds go unpunished,' spat our elder. And as we speak, she's sitting on her suitcase in the lobby, cursing up a hurricane in front of the kids.

"We chose to ask for asylum here at Fernsby Arms only because our kids insisted that 'Arms' after this Family Name means embraces rather than weapons. Those kids keep us believing in the goodness of human- ity. One of them even gave the Uber driver a five-star review 'for not staring us down in the rearview and fo- cusing on the rocky road ice cream ahead.'"

I'm not sure any of us knew what to make of this strange, heartbreaking story.

"Well—" Vinegar began.

"That landlord should be sued within an inch of his life!" said Florida, with a look of sudden outrage. "And that Teller."

The woman offered her a weak smile. "Thank you. But don't let us interrupt your little gathering," she said. "We just need to rest." Having told her story, the woman closed her eyes. "We just need rest now."

"Of course," said the Therapist. "You can remain here with us for as long as you need."

She didn't look completely convinced about this, but her voice was soothing, professional. I wondered what was going to happen to these people, and found myself wanting to help. But before I could think of what to do, Eurovision spoke up.

"Well, then," he said. "While these folks get their bearings"—he paused here, meaning to be respectful, though he was checking his watch—"we've got more time. Does anyone have another story?"

"Or another confession?" asked the Lady with the Rings.

"Actually, I have a sort of confession," said Ramboz. "Or, more like, a revelation. A childhood revelation that opened my eyes to the reality we live in. There's so much we'll never understand about the people who walk around us every day. If I may tell another story?"

"Please," said Eurovision.

"I grew up in Wellesley, Massachusetts. Back then, in the sixties, it was one of the wealthiest towns in the country. It probably still is. Just up the hill from my street, across from the golf course, was a private hospital called the Wiswall Sanatorium. It's long gone, but back in 1965 it was an expensive and exclusive place, a mansion set on acres of lawn surrounded by woods. Wiswall was where Sylvia Plath got her first shock treatments. She called it 'Walton' in her book *The Bell Jar*. She grew up in Wellesley, and her mother still lived at 26 Elmwood Road when I was growing up. She was a nice lady, quiet and sad. Anyway, Sylvia was sent to Wiswall in 1953 in hopes the doctors could cure her depression with electroshock therapy. It didn't work, obviously, and the fact is, Wiswall was a pretty awful place. It was repeatedly investigated by the Massachusetts State Department of Mental Health and finally shut down in 1975.

"Back in 1965, everyone in my fourth-grade class at the Hunnewell Elementary School knew that Wiswall was a 'buzz farm' where they zapped people's brains with bolts of electricity, turning them into drooling zombies. We were just ignorant kids and didn't know anything about mental illness, of course, but we had a lot of vivid ideas. Many times, my friends Petey, Chip, J.C., and I rode our bikes to the gates of Wiswall and stared down the winding drive, trying to hear the gibbering cries of the insane and the crackling of electricity as the lunatics were lit up. In school, when the lights flickered, the kids said it meant they were hard at work up at Wiswall. But no matter how long we waited at the gates, we never heard anything but the wind in the trees.

"One day, Chip suggested that we sneak in. We shoved our bikes into the bushes and clambered over the stone wall surrounding the grounds. We made our way through the thick woods and circled around toward the rear of the building. We soon came to the big mansion where the lunatics lived. We hid behind some rhododendrons and peered over a green lawn to a screened porch. Nothing was happening. The place was silent. There were no shrieks or cries or the distant popping of electricity. But we could see the shapes of normal-looking people in the interior shadows. They were calmly reading, while others were just sitting or watching TV. All was quiet. What had begun as a promising afternoon turned into disappointment and boredom. We decided to go home.

"That's when the real adventure began. In cutting back through the woods, we spied an abandoned building hidden in the trees. It was square and two stories tall. The lower part was made of stone, and the upper story was shingled in wood. All the windows were broken, and ivy had climbed up the drain pipes. Now this was a fine discovery. Petey wondered if this was where they took patients to be chained and tortured, and Chip suggested that if anyone had escaped from the asylum, he would likely be hiding out in there, armed with a scalpel.

"We crept up to it and spied two horizontal basement windows at ground level. We peered inside and saw something wonderful—two carriages and a real, honest-to-God horse-drawn sleigh. It was an old carriage house.

"Chip forced the window frame farther open, and we squeezed through. The sleigh had two bench seats, front and back. It was painted in red with curlicued gold tracery. On the wall, a wooden rack held leather harnesses and collars, adorned with sleigh bells. We shook the sleigh bells, laughing, raising a storm of jingling. J.C. found a bone he was sure must be from a patient who was accidentally electrocuted, his body dumped there. He later brought it to the police station to report the murder and got us all in trouble, but that's another story.

"We soon turned our attention to a scary, crooked staircase leading upward. We climbed up it and found ourselves in an attic, packed floor to ceiling with stacks of cardboard boxes, old oak filing cabinets, and heaps of medical journals. Light poured in through the broken windows and the roof had leaked over everything. A lot of the boxes had rotted and busted open, spewing their contents across the floor—tons of files and accordion folders. The rats and mice had been busy burrowing through the mess, chewing the files into fluff, and the air smelled of moldy paper and piss.

"Some of the boxes contained blue disks, each in its own sleeve. The disks looked like forty-five records, with a hole cut in the center, surrounded by circular grooves. I wondered what kind of music might be on these records. Meanwhile, Petey and J.C. and Chip were pawing through the files, reading out loud. They were old patient histories, written in an antique language of psychiatry no longer in use. There were phrases that sounded hilarious to us back then. I can even remember some of them: *High grade defective. Feebleminded individual above the idiot level. Psychosexual deviance. Spastic torticollis. Bulbar palsy.*

"We spent the next half hour reading excerpts of people's madness and misery, laughing uproariously, until we fell back against the heaps of paper, exhausted. I wondered aloud how all these boxes ended up in an abandoned attic. We pondered that question until Chip said: 'Because all these people are dead.'

"A sudden silence filled the attic room. Of course that was the reason these files had been dumped and forgotten. The realization smothered our mirth, and we decided it was time to go. On the way out I grabbed a handful of those blue disks.

"Back at my house, we decided to play one on my father's hi-fi. Written on the sleeve was a date, a number, and a first name with a last initial: Charlotte P. I slipped out the disk and anchored it on the turntable with scotch tape, because the disk's hole was too big for the spindle. We turned on the phonograph, put the needle on, and listened.

"A thin, matter-of-fact voice of a man came on, speaking in a dreary monotone—a doctor, talking about the admission of a new patient. He began recounting her symptoms and history, and it was anything but boring. This is the story the doctor told.

"Charlotte P. was a married woman who had been brought to the hospital by her husband. She had once been a normal housewife with three children. Her husband worked in Boston in a professional capacity. Over the past year, Charlotte P. had become withdrawn. She had ceased taking care of herself, stopped washing, wouldn't get dressed in the morning. And then she stopped eating. When her husband asked why, she said the reason was because she had made a discovery. After much thought and observation, she had come to the realization that she was dead. Not only that, but she was pretty sure her family were all dead, too, only they didn't realize it.

"When the doctor finished recounting these details

in that same blank voice, he assigned a diagnosis to the woman's disorder, and the blue disk recording came to a scratching end.

"None of us said anything. My friends were spooked. But I, on the other hand, was terrified. Halfway through this recital of madness, I suddenly recalled hushed talk in my family over the years of a certain great-aunt Charlotte, my grandfather's sister, who lived in Wellesley and was married to a banker whose last name began with P. Something shameful and incomprehensible had happened to her. They called it a 'nervous breakdown,' but it was all so vague and no one ever explained what that meant and they broke off speaking of her whenever children came around.

"I'll never forget the nauseating feeling that churned my stomach. Could this be my family? My great-aunt? Had they built an insane asylum right here, in the middle of my orderly little white suburban neighborhood, because *this* was where the sickness was?

"I never told my friends, and I never asked my parents. I was desperate not to know. I said to myself over and over that there were lots of Charlotte P.'s in the world. When my friends left, I stuffed the blue disks in a gap in the wall behind the hi-fi receiver, and those tales of madness stayed hidden in that wall until our house was sold twenty years later. They may be there still."

The city seemed to have faded into darkness as Ramboz told his story. The sirens in the city were quiet. I'll admit it: The story really creeped me out.

"That happened fifty-five years ago," Ramboz said. "That attic room was jam-packed with the stories of forgotten people whose lives were shoved into boxes and dumped there to be chewed up by rats." His voice got gravelly with emotion. "You know what's even more frightening than death?" He paused. "Being *forgotten*."

"I can't wait to be forgotten," said Hello Kitty.

"So you say now," said the Lady with the Rings. "Wait until you're seventy like me, and your brain is packed full of stories and people and loves—all those precious memories you don't want to lose, especially when you see death approaching to take them all away."

"We all need the Teller," piped in the woman with the Family Name, who wasn't asleep after all.

"I've often thought about the process of being forgotten," Ramboz said. "First you die. Then the people who knew you and can tell your stories die. Then *those* people die. When your stories die with them—that's when you're finally and truly gone."

It's true. I have no plans to have kids—I haven't

even had a girlfriend in ages—so when I die, my dad will die with me. And those few memories of my mom, wherever the hell she is . . . all of it will disappear.

As we were all thinking about this, the roof door abruptly banged open again, and the woman's husband returned, carrying a duffel bag on one shoulder and staggering under the weight of a sleeping child on the other, followed by an old woman, and a sodden-looking teenager with a wet backpack hauling two more large roller bags. The teen flopped down on the roof surface beside his mother, who turned to take the sleeping child from the husband, who turned, himself, to help ease the old lady down onto his duffel.

Sitting in our comfortable, familiar chairs, safe in our six-foot bubbles, we watched them with sympathy and a growing sense of pity. They all looked so bedraggled, the husband and wife, with the old mother and stupefied teen, his hair still wet. But no one moved to help them, of course, because what could we do? We couldn't even touch them, not safely. We've spent this whole damn lockdown being so damn careful.

Finally, the Lady with the Rings cleared her throat. "I'm sure I speak for everyone," she said, "when I say you're welcome to stay here at Fernsby until you get things straightened out."

I looked around to see if she was really speaking for

everyone and was surprised to find no obvious dissenters. Even Vinegar was nodding.

Before anyone could stop me—before I could stop myself—I was standing five feet away from them, holding up the keys to 2A, still in the pocket of my jacket from a few nights ago. "Here," I said. "It's an empty apartment—supposed to be, anyway. I'm the super. Stay there until you work things out with the Rivington. For now, the Fernsby Arms welcomes you."

"*You're* the super?" said the teenager.

The couple blinked at my arm, at the trembling keys. The brief alarm on their faces told me what I suspected—that any kind of rent was out of their reach. I didn't care. It's not like the fucking landlord was checking in on us, anyway.

"We can discuss the details later," I said, aware of the sudden hush that had settled on the roof. Something like the hush after I had told my Priya story and Maine her Elijah one. Something like phantom pain. After all the confessions and pain and hope we'd heard these past two weeks, I doubted anyone would complain about my offering this family the apartment.

There were soon faint murmurs of approval, even an "Amen."

"It has some abandoned furniture," I said, loud enough for any dissenters to hear. "Pretty shabby, but at least you'll have some chairs and a bed. Follow me." I walked to the roof door. "I'll take you down there."

The family all staggered to their feet and followed me, lugging their overstuffed suitcases back down five flights of stairs. My arms ached to help them but if I ever hoped to see my dad again, risking those outside germs was a barrier I wasn't willing to cross. At 2A, I unlocked the door and pushed it open. I went to turn on the light and then remembered there was no electricity.

The father walked in, dragging the suitcases, and the mother followed. He put everything down while the old lady, holding the child's hand, came in. They paused in the middle of the living room. Faint light filtered in through the broken blinds facing the Bowery.

"Sorry about the electricity," I said. "You'll have to use candles for now. I've got some in my apartment I can bring up." And then I pictured the piles of Wilbur's old junk, some of which might be useful, at least the stuff he hadn't stolen from my compatriots on the roof. "And some other things. I'll leave the keys here in the door."

I went back to my apartment and filled a cardboard box with candles, some cookware, glasses, silverware, a few china plates and cups. As I was packing up the box, I heard their footsteps above me and felt a sudden rush of relief, grateful they weren't ghost steps any longer. Finally, I thought—I hoped—I'd be able to sleep.

I carried up the box and put it on the floor just inside the door. The mother thanked me. I could see the father behind her, holding his mother's arm, studying the room around them. I gave them the biggest smile I could behind my mask, and then hurried off back up the staircase. As the door swung to, I thought I heard the old woman murmuring, "Isn't this how we came in?"

I was surprised to realize how eager I was to get back to my scratchy red sofa seat on the roof, back to our random, damaged, peculiar little community. I didn't want to miss any stories.

But when I opened the creaky roof door, my couch was no longer empty. Instead, a man was seated there, his back to me, already telling a story to the group. I couldn't believe I'd been so easily displaced. My anger started to flare when the sound of the voice stopped me. I froze. This wasn't possible.

"This was when my wife was sick. She'd struggled with depression most of her life—a horrendous childhood in Romania, her parents executed by Ceaușescu's Securitate. But here in the States, I couldn't get her help. The medical system just couldn't do anything. I'd take her to the emergency room, and we'd sit there for a dozen hours and they'd give her a sedative and send her away. Again and again.

"I was so glad when my daughter came home with that baby bird cupped in her hand. It distracted her from having a mother who couldn't get out of bed. The bird had been thrown out of the nest because it had a crippled leg, its claws bunched up like a fist. It was a tiny pink hairless thing with goggle eyes. I had a pet starling as a child, and so I was particularly happy to see her having the same experience.

"She put it in a shoebox lined with a towel. She ran around our apartment in Queens swatting flies and smacking cockroaches and dropping the mangled bugs into its mouth. It was always hungry and would peep madly whenever it saw her. When she'd finished killing all the bugs in the apartment she raided the fridge for raw hamburger and rolled it into pellets and dropped those in. My daughter fed that bird day and night. I could hear it peeping and she'd get up out of bed and I could hear her rustling about and feeding it, and the peeping would stop for an hour or two and then start again.

"She named him Skyling, because she said he belonged to the sky, even though he couldn't fly. She was Earthling, he was Skyling—that's what she told me. He grew fast. Pretty soon he'd sprouted black feathers that shimmered dark blue in the sunlight. He had beady yellow eyes that peered at you while he cocked his head. She went to the library and got out a bird book and found out he was a grackle. According to the book, grackles would eat everything, including garbage. She fed it sunflower seeds, boiled eggs, Pop-Tarts, and Ding Dongs. But what Skyling loved most of all were Fig Newtons.

"He was not a songbird. He did not make pretty sounds. He croaked and made a noise like nails scritching on a blackboard. When she stroked his head he closed his eyes and craned his neck out to get scratched like a dog.

"My daughter figured he wasn't going to fly unless his crippled foot could be made to grip a branch, so every day she pried his claws open and fastened them around her finger. One day when he was on her finger, she gave him a little toss, and he fell to the floor with a thump and set up a furious racket. He didn't like being tossed like that. Ha! But she did it again and again, and he finally got with the program and learned how to fly. Pretty soon he was flying around the apartment. I bought a bird cage and hung it on a hook in her bedroom. We put his food in the cage, and he would fly inside there to spend the night.

"When summertime came, my daughter begged to take Skyling outside. I was worried that the bird would fly off, but she insisted he would never leave her. This was when my wife's depression was getting worse. She was entering her final downward spiral. Of course I didn't know that at the time, but I was desperate to keep our kiddo out of the house and away from her mother as much as possible. She knew her mom was sick and had to stay in bed, but exactly what was going on, of course she didn't know. She carried that bird in his cage to a little park on Whitney Avenue called Veterans Grove. And then she opened the door and he flew out and up into a tree. But when she banged on the cage and put a Fig Newton inside, he came right back in. My girl would go to that park as often as she could. She'd open the cage door and he'd fly around in the treetops, sometimes for hours, but as soon as she rapped on the cage he'd fly back in and start croaking and fretting for his Fig Newton.

"My wife killed herself in the fall. Pills. Thank God Yessie was at school. I told her her mother had gone back to Romania. How could I tell her the truth? Maybe I did the wrong thing, because my baby was so angry that her mom had left us. The truth is, my wife, in her own crazy way, believed she *had* to end her life *because* she loved Yessie. She was terrified she would destroy our daughter's life with her mental illness.

"He won't leave me, she'd always insisted about Skyling. She was so sure. But a week later she took him out to Veterans Grove and there was a flock of grackles in the treetops. When she opened the cage door, Skyling flew up there and joined them. No matter how much Yessie whistled and banged his cage and tried to tempt him down with Fig Newtons, he wouldn't come. She stayed there, calling to him up in the tree until sunset, when the flock took off and disappeared southward over the rooftops.

"For weeks after, she went to Veterans Grove with a pack of Fig Newtons and the cage, banging on it and calling to him. But he never came back.

"So, like I said at the beginning of my story—that's when I decided that, no matter what, I would stay by her side forever. For however long she needed me."

He stopped; the story was over. I was afraid to move, to speak, to do anything that might break the spell.

But, then—I couldn't help it. The half sob, half gasp that escaped my throat echoed across the rooftop. All heads turned toward me.

Skyling. I remembered him so well. For years, I would listen for him in the New York parks. I think, if I'm being honest, that part of the reason I moved to the woods in Vermont for those years after college wasn't just for Lynn, but because I had this harebrained idea that it would somehow be easier for Skyling to find me out there.

"Dad?" I managed to croak, my limbs still numb with shock. "What . . . are you doing here?" I took in his broad face, his thick white hair, brushed back, his twinkling green eyes wide with surprise and delight.

"Yessie! My girl! What are *you* doing here?"

"I'm . . . the super."

"You are? How grand! You were always so clever with your hands. Oh, I was so worried about you after you got that bout of asthma," he said. "And then you just disappeared. Why didn't you call?"

"But . . ." I still couldn't process what was happening. "Are you okay?"

"Never better."

"How did you get here?"

"It's a bit of a blur." He rubbed his forehead.

My mind was reeling. Had Maine brought him? Impossible. Here was my dad, but not as I saw him last, lying in bed in New Rochelle at the manor, a wreck of himself, flesh sagging off his bones, eyes the color of dust, skeletal hand clutching and unclutching the blanket. I was dizzy with some combination of terror and joy.

"I remember," he said slowly, his brow creased in the effort to recall, "going to sleep in my bed in our apartment on Poyer. And then I had a dream. I dreamt that I woke up in the strangest place. A woman in white came into the room, and when she spoke, it was in a language I couldn't understand. I tried to remember how I got there, but I couldn't remember anything about my life or who I was or what had happened. As I searched my mind in a panic, desperately trying to remember, one thing did come back to me: that I had a daughter. *You.* But here's the horrifying thing: I could remember your face but not your name. Beyond that, my life was blank."

As I listened to this, a most peculiar icy feeling crept its way down from the nape of my neck.

"In that terrible dream, I was frightened of losing that one memory I had, so I drew your face on a piece of paper. Then I hid it."

He took another long, deep breath.

"And then I don't remember all the details, but . . . Here I am."

"But Dad, what about the nursing home? The pandemic? We're in a lockdown!"

He waved his hand as if dismissing the entire thing, not even listening. "Yessie, my little one. You look so healthy! Is your asthma better?" He got up from the couch, rising from the red velvet with no problem— when he couldn't even sit up in bed a month ago. As he stood up, a piece of paper fluttered from his lap and landed on the asphalt of the roof, near Vinegar's foot.

We all stared at that piece of paper. It had a delicate sketch of a girl on it.

He chuckled self-consciously. "My little Earthling. I didn't want to forget."

At that, I couldn't stand it anymore. That paper broke the spell. *Screw Covid*, I thought, as I rushed toward him and buried my face in his chest, felt his arms wrap around me. I didn't even care if this hug doomed us both. The first human touch I'd known in weeks—it felt like years, whole lifetimes even, that this lockdown had stolen from us. I could feel my tears soaking his shirt.

The Lady with the Rings cleared her throat, then did it again more loudly. "Honey, don't forget about distancing. You wouldn't want to give your dad, well, you know . . ."

There was a pause, and then the Therapist, who had been staring down at the well-worn drawing, raised her eyes and spoke quietly: "I don't think that matters anymore."

"What?" Eurovision was annoyed. "Of course it matters. We've got to flatten this damn curve."

"I don't think so."

"Oh, for goodness' sake," started Darrow, then he stopped.

Nobody moved.

"How ridiculous," Eurovision said. "What in the world are you talking about?"

"She's talking about us," said Amnesia. "All of us. I mean, it's all a blur, like he said. I've been wondering myself—how did I get here?"

"We live here!" said Eurovision. "We're quarantined in this dump because of a deadly pandemic!"

Ramboz asked, "Is anyone else a little confused?"

"Well," said Darrow, "before Covid, I had a very nice apartment in Chelsea."

Looking almost mischievous, the Lady with the Rings raised her hand and pulled down her mask, rings clinking. She took a deep breath and smiled.

"What are you doing?" Eurovision said.

"I think . . ." she said, slowly, "that we don't need to worry anymore about masks and social distancing. That we might be beyond all that now."

Hello Kitty said loudly, "Beyond all what? What are you saying?"

My dad looked to me for help. Thinking back to that terrible bout of asthma I got in March, I realized I understood. "What she means is, she can't get Covid anymore," I said. "None of us can."

Eurovision, gripping the sides of his throne with white knuckles, as if clinging to the world itself, cried out, "Why's everyone staring round at each other like that? What's happening?" He sprang from his chair, knocking over his kerosene lantern.

"*Dios mío!*" yelled Florida, leaping away from the pile of leaves that ignited at her feet.

"Jesus Christ! Fire is what's happening!" screamed Vinegar, as the flaming kerosene spread over the asphalt membrane of the roof.

With a shriek, Eurovision tried to douse the flames with a fresh-poured martini. Bad idea. Roaring, the flames burst up, and he stumbled back.

Vinegar grabbed her bottle of wine, stepped over to the fire and shook the wine out over the flames. I dumped my thermos of Pastis on the fire and others sacrificed their drinks, with varying degrees of success, until Hello Kitty tossed a whole bucket of ice on the puddle and in a moment the flames were out, leaving a smoking, stinking, bubbling, alcoholic mess of asphalt.

As we stood there, shocked, panting, surprised, safe, staring around the circle at one another . . . somehow, I began to laugh. I grasped my father's hand. I could *feel* him. Proof that we were made of the same stuff. If he was dead—and I knew he must be—then he was a ghost and all the rest of us were, what? Spirits as well?

My confused memory of being in the hospital, the haziness about how I got the super's job, the mysterious noises and footsteps above me, the haunted feeling of the building—it all suddenly made sense. We were the haunts.

Covid had taken us all.

The lightness and even relief that had taken hold in me was spreading to the others. We didn't need to be afraid of each other anymore, terrified of the danger of human contact, worried about breathing or touching or sharing.

Eurovision, the last to understand, slowly sank down in his chair and covered his face with his hands. Vinegar walked over to him and put her arm across his shoulders. We were quiet for the longest time, slowly removing our masks one by one, while the clouds cleared and the stars came out in the great dome of night above us. I squeezed my father's hand. I was looking forward to hearing so much more about my mother.

Eventually, Eurovision raised his head. "Well," he said, peering around at us. "Here we are, I guess. I'm still the emcee of this rooftop gathering."

We smiled back at him, unsure what to do now.

He stood up and looked around, clasping and unclasping his hands. "It seems to me, there are more stories left to tell. Who has one?"

Leaning against my father's chest, feeling his strong, familiar arms around me, I gazed at the city beyond our rooftop. I imagined the ghosts of Covid all around us, everywhere, and I knew: There were so many, many more stories.

NYC FIRE INCIDENT DISPATCH DATA
Starfire Computer Aided Dispatch System

Incident_Datetime: 2020 April 13 11:59 PM
Address: 2 Rivington St NY NY 10002
Responded: FDNY Engine Co. 145, Ladder Co. 117

Notes: Report of possible fire on rooftop of abandoned building at 2 Rivington St. On investigation a quantity of burned candles were observed and evidence of a small fire, extinguished. Recent squatter presence noted: chairs, graffiti, blankets, miscellaneous abandoned property. No identification recovered except for one (1) large, bound, handwritten manuscript, name and address on inside cover: Yessenia Grigorescu, 48–27 Poyer Street, Queens, NY 11373. Further investigation revealed Grigorescu was deceased of Covid-19 on 03-20-20, at New York-Presbyterian; no next of kin located. Manuscript archived at Property Clerk Division, NYPD, Front St.; awaiting claimant; no further action taken; incident closed.

About the Contributors

Charlie Jane Anders (Day 8: Amnesia, "The Soft Shoulder") is the author of a forthcoming novel called *The Prodigal Mother*, plus the novels *All the Birds in the Sky* and *The City in the Middle of the Night*. She also wrote a book about saving yourself with creative writing called *Never Say You Can't Survive: How to Get Through Hard Times by Making Up Stories*, plus a story collection called *Even Greater Mistakes*. She cohosts the podcast *Our Opinions Are Correct*.

Margaret Atwood (Day 10: The Spider, "The Exterminator") is the author of more than fifty books of fiction, poetry, critical essays, and graphic novels. Her latest novel was 2019's *The Testaments*, a cowinner of that year's Booker Prize and a sequel to *The Hand-maid's Tale*.

Jennine Capo Crucet (Day 5: La Reina, "Langosta") is a novelist, essayist, and screenwriter. She's the author of three books, including *Make Your Home Among Strangers*, which won the International Latino Book Award, was named a *New York Times Book Review* Editor's Choice book, and was cited as a best book of the year by NBC Latino, the *Guardian*, and the *Miami Herald*, among others.

Joseph Cassara (Day 6: Eurovision, "Rabbit Trauma") is the author of the critically acclaimed novel *The House of Impossible Beauties*, which won the Edmund White Award for Debut Fiction, two International Latino Book Awards, and the National Arts & Entertainment Journalism Award for Best Fiction Book, and was a finalist for the Lambda Literary Award for Gay Fiction. His short fiction, essays, and criticism have been featured in the *New York Times Style Magazine*, the *Boston Review, Asymptote*, and *The Queer Bible*. He is currently a professor in the MFA program at San Francisco State University.

Angie Cruz (Day 3: Florida, "Apt. 3C") is a novelist and editor. Her most recent novel is 2022's *How Not to Drown in a Glass of Water*. Her previous novel *Dominicana* was the inaugural book pick for GMA Book Club and shortlisted for The Women's Prize, longlisted for the Andrew Carnegie Medals for Excellence in Fiction and the Aspen Words Literary Prize, a RUSA Notable Book, and the winner of the ALY/YALSA Alex Award in fiction.

Pat Cummings (Day 11: The Lady with the Rings, "Playhouse") is the author and/or illustrator of more than forty children's books. She received the Coretta Scott King Illustration Award for *My Mama Needs Me*, written by Mildred Pitts Walter. Her books, both fiction and nonfiction, include *Trace*, *C.L.O.U.D.S.*, *Talking with Artists*, and more. She teaches children's book illustration and writing at Parsons School, The New School for Design, and Pratt Institute.

Sylvia Day (Day 10: Tango, "On Carnegie Lane") is the author of *The Crossfire Saga* and over twenty other award-winning novels, including ten *New York Times* and thirteen *USA Today* bestsellers. Her work has been translated into forty-one languages and adapted for film. She is a number one bestselling author in twenty-nine countries with over twenty million copies of her books in print.

Emma Donoghue (Day 4: Eurovision, "The Party") is an award-winning author, screenwriter, and playwright. She wrote the screenplay for the 2015 film of her international bestseller *Room* (nominated for four Academy Awards), and cowrote the 2022 Netflix adaptation of her 2016 novel *The Wonder*. Her most recent novel, *Learned by Heart*, was released in 2023.

Dave Eggers (Day 12: the Super, "Storyteller") is the author of *The Every*, *The Circle*, *The Monk of Mokha*, *A Hologram for the King*, and many more books. He is the founder of McSweeney's, an independent publishing company in San Francisco that publishes books, a humor website, and a journal of new writing.

Diana Gabaldon (Day 2: Whitney, "The Ghost in the Alamo" / Day 4: Lala, "A Stillness at the Heart") is the author of the Outlander series of novels, most recently 2021's *Go Tell the Bees That I Am Gone*, a *New York Times* bestseller. She also started and ran a scholarly journal, the *Science Software Quarterly.*

Tess Gerritsen (Day 4: Maine, "The Doctor") is an international bestselling author. Her books include 2023's *The Spy Coast* and 2022's *Listen to Me.* Her series of novels featuring homicide detective Jane Rizzoli and medical examiner Maura Isles inspired the TNT television series *Rizzoli & Isles.* She is also a filmmaker.

John Grisham (Day 4: Darrow, "Another Brother for Christmas") is the author of forty-seven consecutive number one bestsellers. His recent books include *The Judge's List, Sooley,* and *A Time for Mercy.* He is a two-time winner of the Harper Lee Prize for Legal Fiction and received the Library of Congress Creative Achievement Award for Fiction.

Maria Hinojosa (Day 1: Merenguero's Daughter, "The Double Tragedy as Told by the Gossip from 3B") is an anchor and executive producer of *Latino USA* on NPR, and the founder, president, and CEO of Futuro Media Group. She has authored four books including *The Latino List* and *Raising Raul: Adventures Raising Myself and My Son.* She won the Pulitzer Prize in audio reporting for her seven-part podcast series, *Suave*.

Mira Jacob (Day 4: Amnesia, "The Woman in the Window") is a novelist, memoirist, illustrator, and cultural critic. Her graphic memoir *Good Talk: A Memoir in Conversations* was shortlisted for the National Book Critics Circle Award, longlisted for the PEN Open Book Award, nominated for three Eisner Awards, named a *New York Times* Notable Book, and was named a best book of the year by *Time, Esquire, Publishers Weekly,* and *Library Journal.* It is currently in development as a television series. She is an assistant professor at the MFA Creative Writing Program at The New School and a founding faculty member of the MFA Program at Randolph College.

Erica Jong (Day 11: Amnesia, "The Vagina Monologues") is the author of over twenty-five books in forty-five languages, including *Fear of Flying, What Do Women Want?, Seducing the Demon: Writing for My Life,* and *A Letter to the President.* She has won many awards for her poetry and fiction all over the world, including the Fernanda Pivano and Sigmund Freud Awards in Italy, the Deauville Award in France, and the United Nations Award for Excellence in Literature.

CJ Lyons (Day 3: Hello Kitty, "Iron Lung") is a *New York Times* and *USA Today* bestselling author of over forty novels and a former pediatric ER doctor. Her novels have twice won the International Thriller Writers' Thriller Award as well as the RT Reviewers' Choice Award, Readers' Choice Award, the RT Seal of Excellence, and the Daphne du Maurier Award for Excellence in Mystery and Suspense.

Celeste Ng (Day 1: Therapist, "The Curses") is the author of three novels, most recently *Our Missing Hearts*. A three-time *New York Times* bestseller, Celeste's essays and short stories have appeared in the *New York Times* and the *Guardian* among other publications. She is a recipient of the Pushcart Prize, a fellowship from the National Endowment for the Arts, and a Guggenheim Fellowship.

Tommy Orange (Day 13: Darrow, "The Tweaker") is the author of 2018's *There There*, a finalist for the 2019 Pulitzer Prize and recipient of the 2019 American Book Award. He currently teaches at the Institute of American Indian Arts.

Mary Pope Osborne (Day 9: Whitney, "A Journey to the East, 1972") is the award-winning author of more than 100 books for children and young adults. She is best known for the Magic Tree House series. Her personal contributions through her Gift of Books Program have provided over 1.5 million books for underserved children.

Douglas Preston (Days 1–14 frame narrative: Yessie / Day 6: Ramboz, "The Red Sox Impossible Dream" / Day 14: Yessie's Father, "Yessie's Bird" / Day 14: Ramboz, "The Tapes of Charlotte P.") is an author of thirty-nine books of both nonfiction and fiction, of which thirty-two have been *New York Times* bestsellers. He is the coauthor, with Lincoln Child, of the Pendergast series of thrillers. He worked as an editor at the American Museum of Natural History in New York and taught nonfiction writing at Princeton University.

Alice Randall (Day 5: Pardi, "Lafayette" / Day 8: Pardi, "Jericho") is a *New York Times* bestselling novelist, award-winning songwriter, educator, and food activist. She is the winner of the NAACP Image Award, the Pat Conroy Cookbook Prize, and the Phillis Wheatley Book Award, among other honors. She holds an honorary doctorate from Fisk University and is on the faculty at Vanderbilt University.

Ishmael Reed (Day 12: The Poet, "The Experimental Poet") is the author of over thirty books of poetry, prose, essays, and plays. His books of poetry include 1972's *Conjure*, a finalist for the Pulitzer Prize and nominated for the National Book Award. His most recent poetry collection is *Why the Black Hole Sings the Blues, Poems 2007–2020*. He is also the author of many critically acclaimed novels, including 1972's *Mumbo Jumbo*, 2011's *Juice!*, and 2021's *The Terrible Fours*.

Roxana Robinson (Day 12: Whitney, "Appraisal") is the author of eleven books—seven novels, three story collections, and the biography of Georgia O'Keeffe. Four were *New York Times* Notable Books. She has twice received the Maine Writers and Publishers Fiction Award as well as the James Webb Award; her novel *Cost* was shortlisted for the Dublin Impac Award. She has received fellowships from the National Endowment for the Arts and the Guggenheim Foundation. She received the Barnes and Noble Writers for Writers Award from Poets &

Writers and the Preston Award for Distinguished Service to the Literary Community from the Authors Guild. She teaches in the MFA Program at Hunter College.

Nelly Rosario (Day 14: Family of Strangers, "Rivington Rosary") is the author of *Song of the Water Saints: A Novel*, winner of a PEN Open Book Award. She holds an MFA from Columbia University, and her fiction and creative nonfiction appear in various anthologies and journals. She is the recipient of the Sherwood Anderson Award in Fiction and a Creative Capital Artist Award in Literature. Rosario is assistant director of writing for the MIT Black History Project and associate professor in the Latina/o Studies Program at Williams College.

James Shapiro (Day 7: Prospero, "Shakespeare in Plague Times") is the author of *1599: A Year in the Life of William Shakespeare*, which was awarded the Baillie Gifford "Winner of Winners" nonfiction prize, and *The Year of Lear: Shakespeare in 1606*, which won the James Tait Black Prize. His latest book, *Shakespeare in a Divided America*, was a *New York Times* Ten Best Books of 2020. He teaches at Columbia University and serves as Shakespeare Scholar in Residence at the Public Theater in New York City.

Hampton Sides (Day 10: Maine, "Elijah Vick") is the author of the bestselling histories *Ghost Soldiers, Blood and Thunder, Hellhound on His Trail, In the Kingdom of Ice,* and *On Desperate Ground.* He is an editor-at-large for *Outside* and frequent contributor to *National Geographic* and other magazines. His journalistic work has been twice nominated for National Magazine Awards for feature writing.

R. L. Stine (Day 11: Comedian, "The Interloper") is the author of Fear Street, the bestselling teen horror series of all time, and the children's horror series Goosebumps. Guinness World Records cites him as the most prolific author of children's horror fiction novels.

Nafissa Thompson-Spires (Day 2: Vinegar, "My Name Is Jennifer") is the author of *Heads of the Colored People: Stories,* which won the PEN Open Book Award and the *LA Times* Art Seidenbaum Award for First Fiction, and was longlisted for the 2018 National Book Award, among other honors. Her work has appeared in various publications including *The White*

Review, the *Los Angeles Review of Books Quarterly*, *StoryQuarterly*, *Lunch Ticket*, and *The Feminist Wire*.

Monique Truong (Day 9: Hello Kitty, "Buster Style") is a novelist, essayist, and librettist. Her novels are 2003's *The Book of Salt*, 2010's *Bitter in the Mouth*, and 2019's *The Sweetest Fruits*. She is the recipient of a Guggenheim Fellowship, New York Public Library Young Lions Fiction Award, Bard Fiction Prize, American Academy of Arts and Letters' Rosenthal Family Foundation Award, John Gardner Fiction Book Award, and John Dos Passos Prize for Literature, among others.

Scott Turow (Day 6: Blackbeard, "Iraq") is the author of many bestselling works of fiction, including *The Last Trial*, *Testimony*, *Identical*, and *Innocent*. His books have sold more than thirty million copies worldwide and have been adapted into movies and television projects. He has frequently contributed essays and op-ed pieces to publications such as the *New York Times*, *Washington Post*, *Vanity Fair*, *The New Yorker*, and the *Atlantic*.

Luis Alberto Urrea (Day 8: La Cocinera, "Alicia and the Angel of Hunger") is the critically acclaimed and bestselling author of seventeen books. He is a 2005 Pulitzer Prize finalist for nonfiction and member of the Latino Literature Hall of Fame. His newest books include *Good Night, Irene* and *The House of Broken Angels.*

Rachel Vail (Day 7: the Super, "A Gift for Your Wedding to Which I Was Not Invited") is the award-winning author of more than forty books. Her newest work includes the picture books *Sometimes I Grumblesquinch* and *Sometimes I Kaploom*; the middle-school novels *Well, That Was Awkward* and *Bad Best Friend*; and the play *Anna Karenina* adapted from Leo Tolstoy's novel.

Weike Wang (Day 9: NYU, "The Chinese Exchange Student") is the author of 2017's *Chemistry* and 2022's *Joan Is Okay*. She's won the 2018 PEN Hemingway and a Whiting Award, and was named a National Book Foundation 5 under 35. She teaches at the University of Pennsylvania, Columbia University, and Barnard College.

Caroline Randall Williams (Day 12: Pardner, "Ghost Cracker and Rosie") is an award-winning poet, young adult novelist, and cookbook author.

She joined the faculty of Vanderbilt University in the fall of 2019 as a Writer-in-Residence in Medicine, Health, and Society. Her works include *Lucy Negro Redux* and *Soul Food Love*.

De'Shawn Charles Winslow (Day 5: Wurly, "Remembering Bertha") is the author of *In West Mills*, a Center for Fiction First Novel Prize winner, an American Book Award recipient, a Willie Morris Award for Southern Fiction winner, and a *Los Angeles Times* Book Award, Lambda Literary Award, and Publishing Triangle Award finalist. He is also the author of 2023's *Decent People*.

Meg Wolitzer (Day 7: Tango, "The Apron") is the *New York Times* bestselling author of *The Interestings*, *The Female Persuasion*, *The Position*, and *The Wife*, among other novels. She is also the host of the literary radio show and podcast *Selected Shorts*.